T0156557

The Janitor Solves a Murder

iUniverse books may be ordered through booksellers or by contacting:

iUniverse
1663 Liberty Drive
Bloomington, IN 47403
www.iuniverse.com
1-800-Authors (1-800-288-4677)

Because of the dynamic nature of the Internet, any Web addresses or links contained in this book may have changed since publication and may no longer be valid. The views expressed in this work are solely those of the author and do not necessarily reflect the views of the publisher, and the publisher hereby disclaims any responsibility for them.

ISBN: 978-1-4401-3273-5 (sc)
ISBN: 978-1-4401-3275-9 (dj)
ISBN: 978-1-4401-3274-2 (ebook)

Printed in the United States of America

iUniverse rev. date: 4/2/2009

The Janitor Solves A Murder

A Novel by

Paul Daffinrud

iUniverse, Inc.
New York   Bloomington

This book is dedicated to my wife Judy whose suggestions and ideas helped contribute to the successful completion of this work.

CHAPTER 1

October 6

Jerry Ringgold passionately inhaled a deep breath of the crisp, fresh clean air of an early October Minnesota morning. He held the air in his lungs for as long as he could to allow the natural elixir its time to work. He exhaled the air completely, took another deep breath and continued this regimen until he began to experience a feeling of euphoria and energy. It was time to mount his Cannondale Cyclocross bicycle and begin the day's training. He put on his ochre colored Bell Ghisallo helmet, tied the strap firmly under his chin, geared the bike and coasted down the parking lot driveway of Ramsey House; the college dormitory that was to be his residence for the next year.

It was early morning and the sun was barely awake. The traffic was non-existent and the city lights had been extinguished. His ride would take him around the outskirts of Milrose. He would begin his journey on County Road 7 and peddle north for two miles until he reached the first gravel township road that turned west. Most of the farm land on both sides of this stretch of the county road was owned or leased by Angus Sullivan who was in the fields steering his large green John Deere combine down the orderly rows of corn. The fall harvest was over for most crop farmers and the fields were plowed under, exposing a rich black loam that would remain barren until spring. A few farmers still lingered in their fields anxious to pick their remaining crop before the weather turned ugly. Angus was one of them because of his many acres of corn that were not done yet. August and September had been unseasonably dry and the corn thrived as it fully matured; warm days and cooling temperatures at night made it ideal for picking corn. The farmers would have a good year and the town would prosper because of it.

The path along the township road was rough and unsteady. The road hadn't been regraded for a while and a washboard effect developed over the summer months forcing the bicyclist to slow down or face losing control of his bike. This two-mile stretch of road was home to several farmsteads. The white two story farm houses were well built and sizeable, emerging from a previous era when large families were the norm. A red barn, a machine shed, and a blue metal silo complemented each house and were visible from the road. The lone exception to the bucolic existence on this stretch of road was the Taylor place with its weather beaten barn, ramshackle house and a machine shed that leaned so far to one side that it was bound to topple over any day. The lawn, having never been mowed, covered everything in the yard. Andy had a wife that no one remembered seeing since the two children were young. The youngest daughter, Faith, quit school when she turned sixteen and was living at home and not doing much of anything. Sam, who also quit school at sixteen, was now nineteen and employed at the Shell gas station in Milrose. People didn't think much of Andy Taylor and for good reason. He was unsociable, unkempt, vulgar, lazy and mean. He kept to himself and made no attempt to socialize with anyone in town. This was fine with the citizens of Milrose and life went on in the little town with ne'er a thought of Andrew P. Taylor.

Finishing the two miles of gravel road Jerry turned south on another county road that was blacktopped and travelled two more miles. This stretch of road appeared desolate to the bicyclist because no farm buildings were visible and the crops had been plowed under. He began accelerating to reach his maximum speed before beginning the last two miles of the county road that took him east. When the eight-mile loop was complete he would repeat it five more times before quitting. He was training for his first bicycle race, the St. Paul 100. When he was at the peak of his endurance he would be circling the perimeter of the town fifteen times. As he was finishing his fifth trip and on the eastbound county road, he felt the urge to take a leak and exited the road, making a right turn onto College Street. Two blocks later he veered onto Academy Street which took him to Cedar Park. His final destination was a small wooden pavilion with bathrooms and a seating area with two picnic tables. The small structure was at the southern end of the park, hidden away from the other park areas. As he approached the vicinity, he quickly noticed no one was around. The area was his and he opted to take advantage of the solitude. He dismounted the bike, leaned it against a tree, unhooked a water bottle from his saddle bag and took a large gulp before replacing it. Several metal garbage cans surrounded the pavilion and overflowed with beer cans, beer bottles, wine bottles and McDonald's wrappers. Several empty pizza boxes lay open on the picnic tables and cigarette butts littered the area underneath. The pavilion was a favorite hangout for the students at Milrose State. Many of the student musicians from the college congregated in the evenings with their guitars, violins, banjos and drums and entertained each other. If an audience showed up, all the better; the more the merrier. On weekends, local bands gathered at the pavilion for a jam session. It was a way for them to practice their music and perform in front of a live audience. The students listened with enthusiasm as they drank a little beer or wine, smoked some dope and enjoyed the music. The genre of the music was different every weekend. One week it would be jazz, blues or country and the next week could be completely different - maybe hip-hop or oldies. The students never knew what to expect when they came to the pavilion. They were being entertained; they loved it, and that's all they cared about.

The young bicyclist, his prematurely thinning black curly hair soaked in perspiration, sat at one of the wooden picnic tables that faced the pavilion. He could get a scenic view of the entire park from where he was sitting. Idyllic to thinkers, a playground for the sportsmen and party central to the college crowd, Cedar Park was aptly named for the thousands of cedar trees that adorned the park, many of them over a hundred years old. The forty-acre park had numerous walking paths that had been created by the county engineering department and covered with wood cinders. The wide paths were well maintained and enjoyed by the local retirees who were seen every morning walking the cinder laden trail. On the north side of the park was a children's playground, a picnic area, four horseshoe pits, two softball diamonds and Cedar Pond. This was the popular section of Cedar Park and was used everyday throughout the summer. Family picnics and softball games ruled the activities on this side of the park except for Wednesday nights when the horseshoe league showed up and no ball games were scheduled. As the weather turned warmer the park became more popular and remained so until the end of September, but, as the leaves began their change of color and the temperature became cooler the enthusiasm for outdoor life began to wane. Only the die hard walkers, a few fisherman and the college students were left to enjoy what the park had to offer. A half dozen fishermen in their 14' aluminum boats could be seen trolling or still fishing at Cedar Pond until the weather would not cooperate any longer and they had to give up their sport until spring. Bass, bluegills and crappies were the main inhabitants of Cedar Pond and a good fisherman caught his limit in a day if he had the time and the patience.

Invigorated, Jerry felt his endorphin level rise. The peacefulness of the place, the freshness of the air and being close to nature elated him. The air was cool and a light breeze blew the fallen leaves in a circulating manner that made Jerry think that they were dancing to the rhythms of nature and its wonders. He had become transfixed to his surroundings when he realized that he hadn't gone to the bathroom yet. He walked to the bathroom door and yanked on it - it was locked. A wooden sign was attached to the door stating that the bathroom was open from 8 am to 10 pm daily. It was a half an hour before the doors would be unlocked so he walked to the rear of the pavilion to perform his needed duty. He faced the rear of the building, began relieving himself and unconsciously gazed at the wooden wall in front of him. His mind was wandering and he was thinking about what he would do with the rest of the day. He slowly raised his eyes upward along the graffiti filled wall when he suddenly found himself staring into another pair of eyes. They were dark, hollow and ominous and returned his stare. Startled, he backed away from the wall, fell to his knees and gasped for air. He had never seen anything like that in his life.

CHAPTER 2

A couple of minutes quickly passed before Jerry Ringgold regained enough composure to comprehend what had happened. He needed to remain calm, stay at the scene, wait for the police and avoid the rear of the building. He ran the short distance to his bicycle and opened a small black leather bag under the seat and fumbled for his cell phone. He flipped it open, dialed 9-1-1, gave the dispatcher the information she needed and hung up. He paced back and forth in front of the pavilion waiting for the police to arrive. He didn't smoke but he thought that if he did this would be one of those perfect times to light up.

Detective Sergeant Sally Fairfield rolled onto her stomach and removed the pillow from under her head. She placed it tightly over her ears so she couldn't hear the cell phone ringing in the kitchen. She gave no thought to who might be calling and she didn't particularly care; it was Saturday morning and it was her day off and she didn't want to be disturbed. She had a splitting headache; she was tired and she was hung over. The land line next to her bed started ringing and she pulled the pillow closer to her ears. The phone rang four times and the answering machine kicked in.

"Hello Sally, I know you're there. Pick up the phone Sally. We had a homicide last night and we need to go and investigate. I'll pick you up in fifteen minutes."

She blindly grabbed the phone and managed to get it to her ear. *"Yea, it's me here."* She dropped the phone on the bed, picked it up and put it to her ear upside down. She knew her response was garbled and unintelligible; she tried to speak again but thought better of it. The voice on the other end sounded familiar - vaguely. *"Hi Sal.*

You sound terrible or else not awake. You coming down with something? I hope not cuz I really need you today. Hello, you still there? Like I said, we've got a homicide on our hands. I'll will pick you up in fifteen minutes and fill you in on the details when I get there." He hung up before she could say anything. She briefly stared at the phone wondering if she was dreaming or not. She decided she was dreaming and dropped the receiver next to her pillow and fell back to sleep.

She was snoring loudly when she was awakened by a loud banging on the front door. She vaguely remembered the telephone conversation a few minutes earlier. She thought it was a dream but she was beginning to think that her judgment may be a little frayed this morning. *Of all mornings, God, why this one? We've never had a homicide in Milrose. Why now, you know I don't feel well. I know it's my fault and I shouldn't have had so much to drink and I know I shouldn't have stayed out so late but I figured I could sleep late. Make this go away God!*

She painstakingly got out of bed, careful not to move her head. The throbbing pain above her eyes was unbearable and the ringing in her ears confused her thinking. She walked to the door and peeked out the small square window that allowed her to see who was at the door. She cautiously opened the door and knocked herself in the head; forgetting to back away from the large metal door as it swung open. "Come in Bob. I need a couple of minutes; I am not feeling very well this morning. Say, maybe you could do this yourself and I could come in later and help."

"Not a chance, the Chief would be really pissed if he found out you didn't help because you were hung over."

She looked at him, curious how he knew she was hung over. "I went out for a few drinks with the girls after bowling, okay?" She scratched her head trying to remember what she had just said. "We were having so much fun I completely lost track of time. I didn't think I would be working today or I wouldn't have even gone out."

He leaned against the kitchen entrance and listened to her story. When she looked at him he pointed to his watch. "C'mon Sal, hurry up and get ready, we gotta' get going."

She walked to the bathroom and looked at herself in the mirror. She looked a fright and didn't know where to even start putting the pieces together. She needed a shower but knew she didn't have time. She paused for a second before grabbing a hair bush and forcing it through her gnarled hair. Next, she grabbed her toothbrush from the medicine cabinet, applied a dab of toothpaste and did a quick brush job. She put on a pair of worn jeans and slipped into a clean black tee shirt. "Where we goin'?" she asked as she attached her badge and handcuffs to her belt, threw on her shoulder holster and inserted her Luger 9mm into it, and put on her brown nylon windbreaker. She decided to put on her Milrose Police Department baseball cap to cover her dishevelled hair.

"Cedar Park - somebody found a girl murdered there," her partner Bob Carpenter patiently answered. "The call came in about a half an hour ago so we better get going." He walked to the front door and opened it for his partner.

****

Jerry Ringgold was pacing back and forth when he heard the familiar sounds of police sirens. He knew they were coming his way. The approaching sirens were irritating to his ears and when they stopped abruptly he was thankful. He stood near his bike and waited. He heard the crumpling of leaves and the snapping of twigs as the hurried footsteps approached. Within what seemed like a nanosecond two uniformed officers arrived, noticeably out of breath. He pointed to the rear of the pavilion and without stopping they ran to the back of the building. He overheard one of the officers talking on his police radio before they reappeared from behind the building. One of the officers was holding a roll of yellow plastic tape while waiting for the other officer to get off the phone. The officer with the tape in his hand began unrolling it while the other officer closed his cell phone and placed it in his shirt pocket. He grabbed one end of the tape and attached it to three large cedar trees surrounding the building. The tape was yellow with large black letters and it came with a warning - POLICE CRIME SCENE DO NOT CROSS. He watched the officers do their work and about twenty minutes later he heard more footsteps coming in his direction. Three more people suddenly appeared; one of them wore a police uniform and two of them, a man and a woman, wore regular street clothes. The uniformed policeman carried a shiny aluminum briefcase in each hand and closely followed the two plainclothes officers.

Jerry watched as the three newcomers went directly to the rear of the pavilion. They noticed him standing by his bicycle but did not acknowledge him, their minds focused on other things. He lingered under a mature cedar tree near the pavilion and watched and listened as the officers performed their tasks. The large tree had lost most of its yellow, brown and red leaves. They had fallen to the ground and were haphazardly arranged in a large pile under Jerry's feet. He resolved to sit down on the pile of soft leaves and wait for one of the officers to come and talk to him.

Detective Sally Fairfield paced back and forth in front of the pavilion taking digital photographs of the empty bandstand pavilion and the area around it. She was looking for evidence at the same time she was pacing but was having no luck in finding any. Engrossed in her work she had forgotten about the young man and his bicycle. She suddenly remembered him and abruptly looked up, hoping that he was still there. She remembered he was tall with curly black hair and very thin. She hoped she would be able to identify him if his impatience got the best of him and he left the scene. She was angry at herself, normally she would have talked to him before she began the investigation of the crime scene but she wasn't thinking straight and she still had a bad headache. She guessed he was the one who called this in. She was relieved to see him sitting under a tree waiting patiently waiting for someone to talk to him. She recognized his curly hair and the full moustache. He seemed nervous as if he wasn't quite sure what to do with himself while he waited. When she approached him she noticed that his eyes were reddened either from rubbing them too hard or from crying - or maybe he was hung over from last night's partying. She knew what that was like; she was experiencing it right now. She walked over and introduced herself.

"Hi, I'm Detective Fairfield of the Milrose Police Department. Are you the one who called this in?"

He looked at her, relieved that someone had finally noticed him. He nodded in the affirmative, looked at her and offered his hand to shake.

"What's your name?" she asked, shaking his hand. She pulled out a small note pad from the side pocket of her windbreaker, adjusted her baseball cap and looked at the troubled young man in front of her and waited for an answer.

"Jerry Ringgold."

"What were you doing here Jerry?"

"I was taking my morning bicycle ride and I had to take a whiz so I rode into the park to find a bathroom. They were locked so I went to the back of the building and that is when I seen it - I mean her."

"Did you see anyone else in the area?"

"No, just some older people walking on the other side of the park but no one around this area."

She studied him carefully before asking him for his full name, address and telephone number. He was visibly shaken from what he had witnessed that she dismissed him as a possible suspect but hoped he would be helpful to the investigation once he calmed down. She knew the victim had been killed recently, the body was still warm and she guessed that death had occurred less than four hours ago. Jerry Ringgold had to have been the first person at the crime scene since the killer. He handed her his driver's license and told her his cell phone number and she wrote it down in her notebook.

"You a student at Milrose State?"

"Yes," he answered hoping that she was through with him for now. He wanted to get back to the dorm as soon as possible and try to put this out of his mind.

"Did you recognize the young woman that you saw back there?" She pointed to the rear of the pavilion and watched his eyes follow her direction.

"No, officer, I didn't look at it long enough to recognize it. I remember hair covering her face and she had on this ugly purple bathrobe and it was dirty. And her eyes, they were open and staring at me and it gave me the chills. I turned my head away as fast as I could; I don't remember much of anything else."

She looked at him; his mind seemed focused on other things as he turned away from her and stared at his racing bike. She could tell he was anxious to leave so she pulled a business card out the side pocket of her windbreaker and handed it to him. "If you think of anything more, please give me a call right away. Also, I would like you to come to the morgue when the body gets cleaned up and take another look. You might recognize her and it would be a big help to us."

He took her card and shoved it in his pants pocket. "I'll help anyway I can."

Sally watched as he mounted his bike and rode off. She hoped he would be able to identify the body.

****

Detective Fairfield stared at the woman impaled against the wall. Whoever did this was trying to make a point or send a message. The young woman hanging on the wall was crucified like Jesus Christ had been over two thousand years ago. The victim was young, maybe eighteen or nineteen. Her full-length black hair was in such disarray that it hung unevenly over each shoulder with several strands of hair covering a portion of her face. Her eyes were dark brown - transfixed and lifeless, staring into an unknown. Her head was bowed down, the mouth wide open, white froth trickling from its corners. On her head was a hastily placed rose bush twig with several thorns partially embedded in her flesh. She was wearing a faded purple full-length gown that was several sizes too big. All that was visible on the body were her small hands, her feet and part of her face that wasn't covered with her hair. Her legs were crossed and her feet were resting on a makeshift wooden support. Each arm was extended as far as it would go and a square and rusted nail was embedded in each hand. A sword was thrust into her side piercing the body and exiting out the other side of the rib cage. Sally grabbed the victim's ankle and squeezed it gently, the body was still warm and the stiffness that comes with rigor mortis had not set in yet. The body could not have been dead for more than a couple of hours.

It was her first murder investigation and the newly appointed detective wondered if she was up to the task. The department had sent her to a two week crash course on investigative techniques shortly after her promotion but she wondered if that was enough. She was toughened from her four years in the squad car and the figure of the murdered young woman nailed onto the pavilion wall didn't bother her. She had seen a lot of death since she first joined the police force, most of those being from traffic accidents or suicides. She felt sorry for the parents and the siblings and the friends and the grandparents that would be affected by the death of this young woman. Sally knew the victim's death wasn't easy and when the family found out how she suffered before she died it would be even harder on them. This tragedy would have an effect on them for the rest of their lives. Sally wondered if the victim was a student at Milrose State. She didn't recognize her and presumed she wasn't local. She may have drifted into town and happened to be in the wrong place at the wrong time. A lot of questions needed answering. She walked to the rear of the pavilion, stared at the dead woman and wondered what monster could have done this. She thought about the satisfaction she would get when the scumbag was caught.

"We need to take the body down. The lab boys from the State won't be here for another five hours and we can't leave the body hanging for that long. It needs to get to the hospital lab and put on ice." Her partner informed her and directed the three officers at the scene how he wanted the removal done. "Besides, we have all the pictures we need and we'll leave these guys to protect the scene until the lab boys come," he told Sally as he watched the body lowered and carried to the front of the pavilion. A black heavy plastic body bag was lying open on the ground. The body was gently placed inside and the vinyl bag and zipped shut. An ambulance and two EMT's arrived minutes earlier and were standing next to the body bag ready to load it and transfer it to the hospital.

Detective Carpenter walked up to the EMT's and told them what he wanted done with the body once it got to the hospital. "E.R. has already been contacted and they will be waiting for you. They are going to want the body in pathology and on ice right away. Tell them we'll be in after we're through here."

Sally was moving slowly, careful not to move her head too much. The three aspirin she had taken had not helped and she wanted this day to be over. Her partner noticed her sluggish movements and her pallid appearance; she still looked terrible. "Do you want to get some lunch?" he asked, knowing she needed to get something into her stomach soon. "We can eat and be back before the lab guys get here."

Detective Fairfield looked at her watch, it was quarter to twelve; they had been at the crime scene almost four hours. She was getting hungry; she needed food in her stomach, something to absorb the liquid that was sloshing around in her intestines. Maybe she would feel better with some greasy deep fried food in her stomach after she ate. "I'm ready if you are," she told her partner. It was going to be a long day in more ways than one.

13

CHAPTER 3

The employees and the inmates at the cop shop referred to it as a plain wrapper; John Q. Public considered it no more than an unmarked squad car but to the two detectives it was a simple means of transportation allowing them to do their work unnoticed. The squad car was four years old and next year they would be getting a new one. The speedometer was pushing a hundred thousand miles and the cobalt gray paint job was showing signs of fatigue. Detective Carpenter maneuvered the car into one of the few available parking stalls at the restaurant. The lunch crowd filled the small diner but he knew the service was fast and they wouldn't have to wait too long for their meal to come. They needed to get to the hospital and back to the crime scene. The Horn Inn was the only mom and pop restaurant left in Milrose and it was the local favorite for law enforcement, fireman and other government workers. The food was good, the service remarkable and the price affordable on a city employee's salary. The chain outfits had assailed Milrose over the years and even though the food at the Horn Inn was the best in town and the prices were reasonable, people needed to dine out at name brand places like Appleby's or Perkin's or TGIFridays. It was a vanity thing, like being able to say that *I stopped at Starbucks this morning for a latte.* The restaurant was still popular but that popularity was waning. The competition for the food dollar was increasing each year and the cash register at the Horn Inn was showing it; each year it was ringing up less and less sales. Detective Carpenter was sure that in a couple of years the Horn Inn would go under as all the other mom and pop operations had done in the past.

A hostess was not available to seat them; she was busy waiting on customers. They noticed an open booth next to a window, walked over, slid in and waited for a waitress to show up. Bob Carpenter ordered a glass of ice water and a salad and watched his new partner order a cup of coffee, a hamburger and a large order of french fries. When she finished ordering she reached into the side pocket of her windbreaker and pulled out a pack of cigarettes and moved the ashtray that was sitting on the table top closer to her. She took out a cigarette from the pack, tapped the filter end on the table a couple of times and lit it. She inhaled deeply and held the smoke in her lungs as long as she could before slowly exhaling. Detective Carpenter looked at his partner disapprovingly but said nothing to her. He knew it would do no good; when it was time for her to quit, she would. Sally relished each drag of the cigarette and was grateful that this restaurant didn't care if you smoked or not and neither did the customers because most of them smoked. She finished her cigarette as their food was coming and snuffed it out in the glass ashtray. She glanced at her partner while she was pouring catsup on her hamburger and her french fries. He had bowed his head and quietly uttered a short prayer before he took his first bite of the salad.

Bob Carpenter had been on the force for twenty years and had gone through the ranks as she was now doing. He was a uniformed patrolman for four years before making detective lieutenant. Serious crime was unheard of in Milrose and that was the main reason he had been the only detective on the department for the last three years and used to working alone. He was a man of impeccable character, deep religious faith and a devotion to a healthy lifestyle. The two detectives were different in many ways, Sally had a few unhealthy vices, like smoking, drinking, poor eating habits and not getting enough sleep but she knew she was a good person and was well liked by her fellow workers and friends. Now her faith, that was a different question altogether. She wished she had the faith of her partner but she didn't and that's the way it was. She knew her lifestyle was anything but healthy as evidenced by this morning's hangover. She would someday get her act together; but she was having too much fun for now. She looked at him and smiled. She knew what he was thinking about her cigarette habit. She liked the man sitting across from her and the more she worked with him the more she enjoyed his company. If the truth be known she was slightly attracted to him, he was ten years older but didn't look it. No visible signs of gray or silver were in his hair and Sally wondered if it was because he had good genes or if his hair was dyed. He was as physically fit as anyone she knew, the result of working out in the local gym everyday except Sundays. They were different in many ways but what was it about opposites attracting…..He was widowed and she was single, both eligible for marriage if the right person came along. She looked at his light brown wavy hair and thought that he was an exceptional human being for a man of thirty eight years old. She admired his square, solid cheekbones; it gave him a look of strength and solidness. His nose was short and wide and blended well with his deep set blue eyes. Let's face it; she thought to herself, he was handsome. He took care of himself, more than she could say for herself. He jogged every morning, didn't smoke, didn't drink and ate sensibly. She was his opposite, but not his nemesis, and they worked well together. She hoped he liked working with her. She was the first partner he had. The position of detective sergeant was newly created and she had beaten out three male officers for the job. There had been some animosity toward her at first and it was rumored that she got the job because she was a woman. The rumors died down as time went on. She had proven herself to be good at her new job and was quickly accepted by the other officers. She had wondered why the Chief decided to add another detective to the department. Crime was almost non-existent in Milrose and she hoped she would have enough work to do to keep busy. "The Twin Cities got growing pains and getting to close to Milrose, it won't be long and the crime and the weirdo's will find their way to our quiet little town." The chief prophetically told her when she arrived for work her first day as a detective. This morning's discovery of the body in Cedar Park may have proved his prophecy right and assured her that there would be plenty of work for both of them for the next few months. Of course they hadn't tackled anything of this magnitude before but they had solved a few burglaries and an armed robbery in the short time they were together. She looked at her partner and tried to smile. She liked him, he was a happy person and she admired that. He was the man she would have liked to have found for herself.

She took a sip of her coffee and looked at her partner. "Is this your first murder case?"

"Yep, and it's a gruesome one. I thought maybe my first one would be death by shooting. You know a .22 caliber into the head and no bleeding or something clean like that. This one is ugly."

"Where do we start?" she asked, fingering the handle of her coffee cup.

He looked at her and smiled. She was enthusiastic and he liked that. She would someday take his place and he felt comfortable with her doing so. "First we do the autopsy - that's going to give us a lot of information. We also need to ID the body, find the next of kin and then we need to do our real work. We need to find out all about her. Where she lived, who her friends were, what her hobbies were and did she have a boyfriend. I think we also need to call in the Bureau, see if Josh Trimble will be able to help us on this one. He's good and he has the resources of the Bureau to back him up. I will give him a call when we get back to the station."

Sally knew all about the Minnesota Bureau of Criminal Apprehension and hoped that one day she would be lucky enough to work for them. This case would give her some valuable experience when it came time to apply for a position there. It would be a long shot because rarely a position at the Bureau opened up. "When do we start?"

"As soon as we're done here," her partner answered.

The rest of their lunch was eaten in silence; their thoughts focused on the case and wondering who the sicko was that could have done this. They hoped he was not local and this was not the beginning of a serial killer on a rampage or a satanic cult on the loose.

CHAPTER 4

Jethro Hadley stormed out of the Human Relations department, purposely slamming the door behind him. He had been fired and he was furious. He was 'unreliable' they said and that was about it. They took his company keys and had security escort him to his car. He left without saying a word to anyone but he had his own thoughts, *three years with this company and this is the thanks I get. No one was going to treat him this way and get away with it, he would show them. He would get the head of human resources or maybe he would get Mr. Peters, the President.* Of course, these were idle thoughts which would never come to fruition because Jethro Hadley was a coward among men and had very few, if any, redeeming traits. He got into his car, slammed the door shut, rolled the window down and cursed at the guard that was waiting for him to leave. The guard stood near the entrance to the personnel department and watched Jethro Hadley's car screech out of the parking lot.

His first stop after squealing out of the driveway in front of the security guard was his favorite bar, *The Couplings*, a small tavern on the outskirts of Milrose. It was his favorite hangout and he could be found there almost every night. He would get drunk tonight, he was sure of that, and tomorrow he would look for another job. He walked into the bar, said hello to the bartender and walked to his favorite bar stool where a cold beer was already awaiting him. He poured the beer into a glass and gulped it down and set the empty bottle in front of him for the bartender to see. The bartender quickly noticed that his first beer was gone and pulled another one from the beer cooler, uncapped it, brought it over and set it in front of him. "Having a bad day there Jethro?" The bartender asked sarcastically. He didn't like Jethro much, but he was a good customer. "Yea, got fired from my job today, can you imagine that? Three years of my life I gave to that company and they fire me. They're nothing but a bunch of assholes anyway."

Another full beer was in front of him as soon as he finished his second. The beer tasted good tonight he thought to himself as he looked around the bar. He was lighting another cigarette when a woman he had never seen before took a seat on the barstool next to him. She was cute; he wondered who she was but didn't have the courage to ask, at least not yet. She was wearing a white cotton dress with large yellow polka dots. She crossed her legs while getting comfortable on the bar stool and Jethro clearly noticed her exposed knees. She put her shabby brown purse on the bar and fumbled for some money. As she did, her cigarettes fell out and onto the bar. She took one from the pack and placed it in her mouth; looking at the man next to her she asked him if he had a light. Jethro reached into his shirt pocket and pulled out a yellow Bic lighter and held it toward her. After her cigarette was lit she took a second look at the man next to her. "Name's Florence, what's yours?"

"Jethro."

"Like in Jethro Tull?"

"Yea, I guess," he answered; he wanted to start a conversation with her but he didn't really know how to go about it. "What's your name?"

"Florence, I already told you that, Florence Johnson."

With a little awkwardness between them at first a conversation did begin and Jethro and Florence sat at the bar together the rest of the evening and at closing time they were the last customers remaining and had to be asked to leave the bar.

"Do you mind of I stay at your place tonight, I got no place to stay and it's too late to get a motel room." She asked, her winsome voice pleading for him to invite her to his house. He looked at her and smiled; what a nice ending to a lousy day.

Jethro and Florence were together every night after that and spent their free time at *The Couplings*. After two months of courtship they decided to get married. They got a church lined up and rented the Knights of Columbus hall for the wedding dance and planned their honeymoon. Most of the regular crowd from *The Couplings* attended the wedding because Jethro had promised free drinks and a band at the wedding dance. Everyone got drunk, especially the newlyweds. They were both out of it by the time that the evening was over. They decided to skip the honeymoon and go directly home.

Nine months from the day of the wedding Hezekiah was born and the relationship drastically changed. They couldn't afford a babysitter and Jethro would go to *The Couplings* every night without Florence, leaving her home to tend to their son. She had grown to hate the man she naively married a year ago and the quarrelling began. The marriage was crumbling and the arguments escalating and becoming more violent. Once a week the Milrose Police were called to a domestic disturbance at the house. The two officers would get them quieted down and leave, knowing they would be back again next week for more of the same. Money was tight; Jethro still hadn't found a job and Florence refused to work. The weekly unemployment checks were scarcely enough for the family to survive on and Jethro continued spending his nights at *The Couplings*. He had become oblivious to his wife and his son and to finding work. One day Jethro got tired of it all and went to the bar and got drunk. He never went home that night or ever again. It was rumored that he went to Texas but no one knew for sure. Florence never heard from him again.

Child Protection Services desperately wanted to take Hezekiah from his mother and place him in a foster home. The outcome of their investigation sent up warning signals of all kinds but it was all predicated on hearsay evidence. The mother-son relationship wasn't normal; they knew it and there wasn't much they could do about it. It had been hard to prove that Florence Johnson was an unfit mother. It was hard to take a child from a parent, especially a mother, and Florence Hadley appeared to fit all the criteria of being a responsible and good mother. The social services workers knew they had to get proof of Florence's instability before any judge would issue an order to take the child. They checked on Hezekiah every week, never on the same day and never at the same time, but Florence knew the Child Protection Services game well and was always prepared for them. She needed to have Hezekiah near her; she needed somebody to help pass the time of day. She cared very little for her son but she needed him. She couldn't bear to have social services take the child and put him in a foster home. The house would be spotless and Hezzy would be eating at a clean kitchen table when they visited. She had fooled them once again. They would go away in disgust hoping that next time they would get the proof they needed. The social workers knew what she was doing and hoped that one day she would trip up and they would find the house in total disarray, Hezekiah dirty, no food on the table and Florence drunk. It was going to happen; it was only a matter of time. As soon as the two social service workers walked out the door she immediately went to the kitchen, opened a top cupboard door and brought down a full bottle of Jack Daniels. She would start drinking until she passed out.

The welfare checks were more than enough for her and Hezekiah and by the time that her son was twelve years old the social service people stopped coming around as often. Once in a while a social worker would appear at the front door and ask to see Hezekiah but he was never home. He was spending most of his time around downtown Milrose with his new friends, getting into trouble of some kind or another. By the time Hezekiah had turned thirteen the social services workers stopped coming altogether, they had finally given up. When Florence was certain that she was safe from the welfare people she started drinking earlier in the day and Hezekiah was left to fend for himself day and night.

When Hezekiah was young he had a great fear of his mother so when she told him that he couldn't miss any days of school because if he did the cops would throw him in jail, he believed her. He went to school every day but wasn't mentally equipped to retain what he had learned. After school he hung around downtown Milrose and soon joined a peer group that thought and acted like he did. They were all from broken homes and as angry as Hezekiah. The small gang was always in trouble with the police and most of the time it was because of their loitering in Cedar Park or downtown Milrose. Once in a while though, when they felt the urge, they would beat up some innocent kid for the fun of it and would find themselves in court once again. Hezekiah was a quick learner when it came to living on the streets. It was his real home and he had adapted to it well.

Hezekiah Hadley sat on his bed with his legs crossed; each of his long arms resting on a bed railing. His eyes were fixed on the small television sitting on his dresser. The six o'clock news was on and he giggled lasciviously at the top story of the day. *The body of a young woman was found in Cedar Park. She had been brutally murdered and the police were actively working on the case. No clues had surfaced yet and the police were waiting for an autopsy to be completed in hopes of determining the identity of the young woman. Several clues were left at the scene and the police are working diligently to solve this case.*

He flipped the channel to another news station hoping to hear another story on the murder. He was bouncing up and down on the bed as if he were on a trampoline. The news coverage of the murder had him excited and he forgot what he was doing and forgot that his mother was downstairs and could hear him and the noise he was making. The bed itself jumped off the floor and soon he heard his mother yell up to him. "Knock off that noise or I'll come up and beat you senseless, so help me, I will." His attention was still focused on the television and he ignored the words of his crazy mother. As he was bouncing up and down on the bed, oblivious to what was going on around him, he noticed the figure of his mother standing in his bedroom doorway. Her arms were crossed and she was sternly watching him. She stared at her son; she hated him and was sickened by him. His long greasy hair was flowing up and down with the motions of his body. His mop, as she referred to it, was now dyed a lime green and uncombed. His long earrings were jangling to the rhythm of his body. The earring on his left ear dangled a couple of inches from his ear lobe; a small silver cross attached to it. The other earring did the same but a small black key had replaced the silver cross.

Florence walked over to her son and slapped him on the face several times. He cowered in the bed and reclined into a fetal position covering his face. She began hitting him in the buttocks as hard as she could, but she was frail and weak and her strikes were harmless. Hezzy waited for the beating to end and when his mother finally left the room he reached under the bed and pulled out a small wooden box. He took the small key from his earring and opened it. He hurriedly but gently took the object out of the box and slid the black cotton bag off of the human skull. It was time to polish his dearest possession.

CHAPTER 5

Special Agent Josh Trimble, Detective Sally Fairfield and Lieutenant Bob Carpenter were sitting on a brown leather lounge sofa in the waiting room of the morgue at Milrose Memorial Hospital waiting for the pathologist. The two Milrose detectives were briefing Special Agent Trimble on the details of the murder and the crime scene. They were thankful he had agreed to come and offer some assistance in the case. His experience and the resources of his department could only help in solving the case. The agent was neatly dressed; his light gray polyester slacks were recently pressed and the matching blazer looked as if it had just come from the dry cleaners. He had on a yellow dress shirt and aloha tie with a gold tie pin with the initials BCA emblazoned on the front. His well tanned face and hands hinted that he had spent some time in a tanning booth but the tie indicated that he may have just gotten back from a trip to Hawaii. His muscular and trim body suggested that he was a man who took care of himself. His short blond hair was neatly combed; the same military style he had worn since leaving the Marines. His pale blue eyes, rounded chin, the unnoticeable cheek bones and the slight Scandinavian accent confirmed that he was a native Minnesotan.

Josh Trimble was sitting comfortably on the thick cushioned sofa reviewing the detective's reports when the pathologist entered the sitting area. He immediately stood up as the young black man introduced himself. "I'm Doctor Goodland," the doctor extended his arm and all three of the officers shook his firm hand and introduced themselves. "Are all three of you going to join me?"

The three officers nodded their heads, confirming that they would all be witnessing the autopsy. They followed the doctor into his laboratory with Sally being the last one in line.

The laboratory was cold and sterile and the two detectives wished they hadn't left their jackets in the lobby. Agent Trimble took off his blazer and slid into the hospital gown that was issued to him by Doctor Goodland; he put on plastic shoe covers and gloves and motioned for the two detectives to do the same. They both got their gear from the same closet that Agent Trimble retrieved his from and carefully put on their hospital garb. Satisfied that the officers were clothed properly, the pathologist excused himself and said he would be back shortly.

This was the first time that Detective Fairfield had been in the laboratory of a pathologist. She looked around and studied the surroundings. At the far end of the lab was a large refrigerator with four doors, each large enough to put a body into. In the middle of the lab stood two waist high stainless steel tables three feet apart, both empty and each having a small drain toward the front. Several spigots, faucets and pipes circled the drain. A two inch raised metal edge surrounded the table to prevent spillage. On the shelves around the lab were specimen jars filled with different body organs. The smell of formaldehyde was overpowering to the new detective but she figured she would get used to it in time. The shiny tile walls and the dull floor surface were spotless. "Now this was a sterile environment," Sally thought to herself as she awaited the return of Dr. Goodland.

The doctor returned to the lab in a full set of scrubs and carrying a tape recorder. Shortly after Dr. Goodland's appearance a young man entered the lab in similar scrubs as the doctor. Doctor Goodland introduced him as Nathan Brown and informed the officers that he would be assisting in the post mortem examination. The young man's eyes startled Sally Fairfield at first. She could tell a lot about a person by his eyes and these radiated evil. She had never seen him before but she had a premonition that she would run into this man sometime in her career and it would be because he had done something horrific. The doctor turned on his tape recorder and proceeded to announce the time, the date and who was in attendance at the post mortem examination. Satisfied that he had included what was needed he laid the small tape recorder on a small stainless steel stool next to him. The assistant proceeded to the large refrigerator and opened one of the bottom doors and pulled out a steel gurney with the body of Jane Doe on it. He rolled the gurney next to the table where the autopsy was to be performed and he and Dr. Goodland lifted the body onto the work table. The doctor examined the tag on the toe of the deceased and verified that it was the same body that was requested for an autopsy by the Milrose Police Department. Doctor Goodland proceeded to describe the body. He measured it, weighed it, and examined the eyes and the body for scars. "The body is that of a Caucasian female, name unknown and age approximately eighteen or nineteen years old. Her height is five-foot-three inches and she weighs one hundred and three pounds. She has dark brown eyes, black hair and a birthmark on her left elbow about the size of a quarter. Her teeth are in exceptionally good condition and the external body is free from scarring but there is multiple bruising on the body consistent with someone hitting or punching her with a fist or other blunt object. There is a 1/4" puncture wound in each hand and several small puncture wounds around the top of the skull. On the left side of the victim is a larger puncture wound exactly 1" by 3/8". The wound severed the lung and pierced through two rib bones." The doctor placed four tools on the table that he identified as a scalpel, a scissors, a bread knife and a rib cutter. The autopsy was beginning and Detective Sally Fairfield suddenly wondered why she had picked this profession as her career.

Doctor Goodland picked up a large scalpel and made an incision in the trunk of the body. It was in the shape of a Y starting from each shoulder, meeting at the sternum and proceeded down to the pelvic area. Next, the skin, muscle and other tissue were peeled off of the chest wall.

Sally was beginning to feel ill. She felt herself turning white and her stomach was starting to make funny gurgling noises loud enough for those in the room to hear them. She felt nauseous and faint. She couldn't watch any more of this. "I have to leave, I don't feel very good." The doctor looked up at her; his eyes gave her an understanding smile, and he motioned with his hand that it was okay to leave and that he understood. She went outside of the hospital, walked to her car, unlocked the front driver's side door, took a cigarette from the open pack that was lying on the front seat, lit it and leaned against the squad car. She felt stupid and was unsure how her teammates viewed this new-found weakness of hers. She also wondered why she had not been prepared for this at the police academy.

She was smoking her third cigarette when an ambulance arrived and drove up the concrete ramp that led to the emergency room. The red and white vehicle stopped to the side of a large sliding glass door as Agent Trimble and Lieutenant Carpenter were walking out. They were laughing as they approached the squad car. Aware that Sally was leaning against the car and smoking a cigarette they stopped laughing; knowing how she must feel they took on a more somber demeanor but would still tease her about her actions in the morgue. "Hi Sal, we missed you," Agent Trimble joked as he approached her.

"Let's go to the station and we'll fill you in," her partner suggested as she opened the driver's door and slid in behind the wheel. Agent Trimble opened the rear door and slid into the back seat, her partner got in the passenger side. She shifted the car into gear and drove the short distance to the station.

CHAPTER 6

The Sioux County Sheriff's Department and the Milrose Police Department worked together in the same building. The Law Enforcement Center was built close to the courthouse and the public defender's office mainly to ease the transportation of prisoners to and from court. The all brick structure was erected ten years ago and two years ago it began experiencing growing pains as the town began to expand. Both departments had doubled in size over the last few years and plans were in the works for a new Judicial Center. The jail occupied a part of the building and had twenty-six cells which were composed of two cell blocks. Twenty cells for male prisoners and six cells for female prisoners. The male cell block was always full and it seemed as if the female cell block was starting to head in that direction also. The communications center was housed in the building and took up one fourth of the first floor. The basement of the Law Enforcement Center was a large open area that was used for meetings and training sessions. A gun range with a poor ventilation system, a small work out area with a sauna, a few free weights and a multi-purpose exercise machine occupied most of the bottom floor. Two bathrooms, both with showers and a scale, were located next to the workout area. Neither of the scales worked properly and maliciously added ten pounds to your true weight. It wasn't long before the use of the scales diminished. To the rear of the building were three garages, two for the Sheriff's squads and one for a police squad. A sally port was separate from the other three garage stalls and was directly connected to the booking room of the jail. All prisoners were brought in through the sally port for precautionary measures.

The three investigators entered the building and buzzed the dispatch room by pushing a small button on the wall. Once the button was pushed a buzzing sound alerted the dispatcher that someone was waiting at the door to enter. The dispatcher eyed camera two and flipped the toggle switch that electronically unlocked the door. The whole process took less than a second. They opened the door and walked down the hallway with Detective Carpenter leading the way. He walked into his office and was followed by his partner and Josh Trimble. He took a seat behind his desk as Sally and Josh sat on folding chairs facing him. It was quiet in the office until Detective Carpenter broke the silence. "Well that was interesting."

Josh fidgeted in his chair to get more comfortable. "I think what we need to do now is divide up some of the work. The autopsy provided us with a lot of information and we need to follow up on the leads as soon as possible. It surprised me that the post-mortem showed that our victim was drowned before she was hung up on the wall. That seems a little odd to me. I'll follow up on that and get the water sample to the lab so they can analyze the contents of the water. That may tell us where she was drowned. Bob, I'd like you to follow up on the sword. What kind of sword was it, where was it bought and if possible by who and find out what's it used for. Is it a ceremonial sword or is it used in some sort of ritual or is it a self defense thing. Also, those burglaries you've been having around town, go over your reports and see if any antique square nails were stolen from any of the businesses." Josh paused a second. "Oh yea, there were no fingerprints at the scene except for the few on the sword. The lab already has the prints and is working on identifying them. Because of the lack of prints I think our killer was either wearing latex gloves or regular gloves. Check on the pharmacy burglary you had a couple of months ago and see if the inventory of stolen items shows that latex gloves were stolen. I don't know if there is a connection between the murder and the burglaries but those square peg nails have me puzzled and I thought I remember seeing those nails at Bensons Hardware store at one time. We need to find out where the killer got those nails."

Josh got up from his chair and walked to the window and stared outside. He was quiet and somber and deep in thought. He turned to Sally and thoughtfully described what he wanted her to do. "Sally, if this girl was not from Milrose she might have driven a vehicle here. Check with the traffic guys and see if any cars have been sitting unattended around town for more than twenty four hours. Especially, check all the college parking lots. Now for the rose thorns. I need you to find a horticulturist at the college and have him look at the thorns. Maybe he can determine what brand they are and what variety. When you get that information find out if any business in town sells that particular rose. If you get lucky and find a store that sells those roses, talk to the clerks and see if they remember anybody who purchased those particular roses. It's unlikely that they will remember, but it's worth a try. Or, the roses could have been stolen from somebody's garden so check around town and find out who grows roses and talk to them. See what kind they grow. Maybe these roses were stolen from somebody's garden. Who knows, the murderer may live in close proximity to those roses. I'll follow up on the bathrobe she was wearing. It was old and worn, maybe it was bought at the Salvation Army or some other second hand store. I'll also check up on people who had rummage sales in the last six months and find out if any of them sold this robe. It's all a long shot but we gotta' start somewhere. And Sally we need to find out the name of the victim. You're going to have to go to the college and go through the photos of their students. I think they all have college ID's with pictures on them so those pictures must be stored somewhere. I'm sure the school won't mind you taking a look at their computer. You need to go back at least three years so you have your work cut out for you. Maybe she was a student there, maybe not, but right now it's the best shot we have. We need to find out who our victim is." He was looking at Sally and noticed that something was bothering her. She had heard what he had said but her mind appeared to be drifting in a different direction. "What's a matter Sally? Your mind seems to be wandering someplace else."

"I was looking at the report and it says she was a virgin. At first I thought that was a little unusual but then I realized that she could be a practicing Christian, or Jew or Muslim or maybe she just didn't like men. These facts alone could help us nab our killer. Maybe it was some guy who was frustrated by her because he wanted to have sex with her and she wouldn't put out or maybe there was a girlfriend involved. Could be a love triangle thing between three women; I mean, just the fact that she was a virgin could give us some clues as to who the murderer was."

29

"That's why it's so important to find out who she is," Detective Carpenter added.

Agent Trimble had one more comment and then he was ready to go to the squad room for a smoke. "We know she wasn't raped which actually hurts our case a little bit because we could have got gotten a DNA sample from the semen. Now we have no DNA evidence whatsoever. The viciousness of the crime tends to tell me there was a lot of hate involved in her murder. I think this is an isolated case and I don't think we have a serial killer on the loose but I really want to find this jerk and find him fast."

Josh pulled out a cigarette from his shirt pocket and motioned to Sally if she wanted to join him for a smoke and a cup of coffee.

"I'd love to," she answered and led the way out of the office and to the squad room.

CHAPTER 7

"MILROSE PRIDE," the official college newspaper, ran a small story about the murder on the front page of its Monday morning edition.

This last Saturday morning a local bicyclist, a student at Milrose State, found the dead body of an unidentified young woman in Cedar Park. We have been notified by the Milrose Police Department that the identity of the victim has not been discovered and they have asked our help in this matter. If anyone knows of someone missing over the weekend please get in touch with this paper. The particulars of the case have not been released yet and we were told that a news conference will be held tomorrow morning at the Law Enforcement Center at 10:00 a.m. The case is being investigated by the Milrose Police Department and the Minnesota State Bureau of Criminal Apprehension. This paper will report the news of this case to our readers as soon as we get it.

Sally took a sip of her extra strong coffee without the benefit of cream or sugar to diffuse the strength. She glanced up from the two page college newspaper and stared out the triple-paned bullet-proof window of her office. The window faced the street and she noticed there wasn't much traffic. A couple of hours earlier the rush hour had been in full swing and the street was bustling with cars, but only a few of them roamed the streets this time of day, mostly senior citizens getting out of their house and doing some shopping. On a good day the small window allowed a little sunlight into her dimly lit office but today's overcast sky made the crowded office appear morose. Her thoughts wandered on this gloomy day as she watched the snow flurries slowly descend upon Main Street. Four inches were forecast with a possible three more inches tomorrow. Two days ago it was beautiful outside. Minnesota weather sucked sometimes. She read the story again, folded the paper and set it on the corner of her desk. She would cut out the headline and the story and paste them in her scrapbook. The story brought back thoughts of the young girl, dead and lying in the morgue as a Jane Doe; she would be there until she was identified and somebody claimed the body. Today she would go to the college and start the search. Trimble was right; she needed to go back three years in her pursuit for the identification of Jane Doe. The victim was college age and there was a fifty-fifty chance that she could have been or is a student there.

She heard a small tap on her door and looked up from her desk and noticed that her boss, Chief Rowlands, had a dour look on his face.

"Come in Chief," she said and motioned for him to take a chair.

The Chief sat down in one of two uncomfortable chairs that were in her office, leftovers from the old police station that had been torn down years ago. She studied him briefly trying to get a fix on his mood. If anyone resembled a member of a barbershop quartet, it was him. His thick red hair was greased and combed back; his waxed and neatly trimmed handle bar mustache matched the color of his hair. He was wearing a red pin stripe shirt with a red bow tie and red suspenders. She was sure that in his past life he sang bass for a barbershop quartet in the late 1890's. She liked him, he was a good chief and his little eccentricities didn't bother her at all.

"What have you got so far Sal?" he asked.

She filled him in on where they were in the investigation. He asked a few questions about the case and she was able to answer them all. She wished she would have been able to tell him that they knew who the murdered girl was and that they had a suspect in custody but that was not to be for now.

"What's the next step?"

"We've notified all law enforcement agencies in the surrounding states and asked that if they have any missing persons matching the victim's description to let us know. NCIC has also been notified. We've heard nothing back as of yet. The weekend is coming up and I am hoping something comes through today. For now I am going to take a drive out to the college and see if the victim may have been a student. I'll be going through their database for the last three years so I am going to be tied up for a couple of days."

The Chief appeared satisfied with the progress that had been made and got up from his chair to leave the office. "Good luck Sally. I mean it. I think this is the first murder we have had in this town, isn't it?" Chief Rowlands turned to go but hesitated as if suddenly remembering something. He turned to face Sally. "I've arranged a news conference for tomorrow morning at ten. The newspapers from all over the state are interested in the case and will have reporters here to ask questions about the victim and our progress on the case. I'll need both of you here for it and if you can get Josh to come all the better."

"Okay and I hope it's our last," she answered as her boss walked down the hall to his office. She got up from her desk, snuggled into her winter police jacket and dislodged the squad car keys from her leather belt. Holding the keys firmly in her hand she left the office and walked outside to her squad. She got into the car, started it and lit up a cigarette. The college was hidden from view by the two hundred acres of woods that surrounded it. It was a short drive from town and Sally was walking in the door of the admissions building ten minutes after she left the station.

The front desk clerk looked up as Sally walked into the corridor of the college. She recognized her friend immediately. "Hi Sal, how's it goin'? Whatcha doin' here?"

"Hi Lois, how's that bowling arm doing? Heard you had a one seventy game last week."

"Yep, we celebrated a little too much afterwards though. When you gonna' join us again, we need a substitute."

"Haven't got time now, maybe in a month or so. Besides that I'm still recuperating from the other night when we took all four and celebrated too much. Can't do that much anymore."

"That's cuz you're out of shape," her friend replied.

Lois and Sally had been friends since she joined the police force. They had a lot in common. They were both single, liked to have a good time and were both looking for Mr. Right. "Lois, I need your help."

"Anything."

"You heard about the murder, yea?"

"Terrible thing, what's this world coming to?"

"I don't know. The world seems to be going crazy," Sally answered wondering if the world really was going nuts. "This girl that was killed, well, we don't know who she was. She was college age and I thought maybe she might be a student here. How do I go about checking your data base? Your students have picture ID's, right? I was wondering if you kept copies of the pictures in a file or something."

"Yea we do. The pictures are taken with a digital camera and stored on the computer. Let me call Mrs. Blomberg and see if she is available to help you. She takes the pictures but I don't know who she gives them to after that."

Lois punched a number on her phone and talked to someone on the other end. Sally hoped it was Mrs. Blomberg and that she would have time to see her.

Edith Blomberg was a short, plump and jovial woman. Her hair was graying and she looked as if she might be ready for retirement in a couple of years. Sally introduced herself and explained why she was here. Mrs. Blomberg directed her to a computer, helped her punch in a few keys and showed her how to use the program.

"There are twenty five hundred students here, this might take some time."

"I've got the time Mrs. Blomberg; this is very very important and thanks for being so helpful." Detective Fairfield situated herself in front of the computer and began the task of studying each female face that popped on the screen. She guessed there were at least thirteen hundred or more pictures to look at for the current school year and who knows how many for the past three years.

She glanced at her watch, it was four o'clock and her back was beginning to show signs of fatigue. She had been at the computer for close to five straight hours and her eyes were going bonkers. She decided to call it a day; she would come back Monday and look at the remaining photos. She didn't know how many pictures she studied but none of them matched the victim. A lot more were left to look at and she hoped that the next time she came it would be more rewarding.

The weather cleared up and the sun was shining, its warmth had melted the morning's snowfall. All that remained on the road surface was slush that would leave her newly washed car encrusted in mud. She had spent the entire day on the same computer looking at the pictures. She had come up empty handed. She had another thought, maybe a long shot but certainly worth a try. Was it possible that she wasn't a student at the college but was friends with one of the students? She was in Milrose for a reason and Sally knew that the young unidentified victim was killed somewhere else before she was taken to the crime scene. The body was still warm when it was found and rigor mortis hadn't set in. She had to have been murdered shortly before she was brought to the park. Was her murderer someone she knew, someone she drove down to visit. It was possible. She had to have known her killer.

CHAPTER 8

It was four thirty in the morning and Sally was out of bed, awake and cognizant. She was not an early morning person, never had been and probably never would be. This was a rare occasion in her life. She had made a pot of brew with her Mr. Coffee and sat down at the kitchen table and drank it. Next to her cup of coffee was a glass ashtray that contained three new cigarette butts. An open newspaper lay in front of her. She had read it cover to cover and had even read the obituaries. She had not slept well since the murder and that was the main reason she was up early. It was stupid laying in bed, wide awake, thinking about the crime, when she could be in the kitchen having her coffee, smoking her cigarettes and mulling over the crime in a way more to her liking. It bothered her that the killer was still out there somewhere. She wanted him caught but without the victim's name and no suspects the likelihood of catching the killer any time soon was a long shot. She couldn't erase Dr. Goodland's assistant out of her mind. Although nothing indicated that Nathan Brown was involved in the murder, she could not dismiss him as a suspect. She didn't tell anyone of her suspicions but she knew something was seriously wrong with the man. Her female intuition was usually right and it told her that Nathan Brown was capable of just about anything, including murder.

The brightness of the morning told her it was time to get ready for work. She looked at the small clock on her kitchen stove and seeing that it was seven thirty she got up from the table, walked into her bathroom and began her morning routine. The hot water felt good on her back, and she was surprised at how awake she was after having gotten so little sleep. By nine o'clock she was backing her squad car out of the driveway and heading to work.

She arrived at the Law Enforcement Center at nine twelve and parked the squad in her assigned parking space. She would have enough time to grab a cup of coffee before the meeting with the Chief and her partner. With coffee cup in hand she walked toward the Chief's office. He was standing in the doorway leaning against the door frame and watching her walk down the hall. He was pointing to his wristwatch which suggested to her that she was late for the meeting. Now that she thought of it the meeting was at nine o'clock and not nine thirty. Oops!!

The Chief motioned for her to come into his office. Her partner was already sitting down and she guessed that he had been in the Chief's office for a while; he was drinking a bottle of orange juice and studying his notes. She walked in the office and offered the cordial "good mornings" and took a seat next to her partner. The Chief closed the door and sat at his desk facing them, not mentioning that his newest detective was late.

"You two guys ready for this?"

The two detectives gazed at each other before looking at their boss. "Not really, just let them know what we've got, be honest with 'em."

"Well not completely honest. We're gonna' fill them in on most of it but I think we will leave a few details out like the rose thorns and the square nails. We'll leave that information for just the perp and us. The news media doesn't have to know everything. We don't want somebody confessing to this that really didn't do it, I mean it happens a lot and we want to keep secret details that only the killer would know about. A little assurance that we got the right guy."

Detective Carpenter looked up from his notes. "I take it you are going to do most of the talking Chief?"

"Yes, the news media expects it. They want to talk to the guy where the buck stops. So that would be either me or the Sheriff."

"What about Josh Trimble?" Sally asked.

"We get a lot of help from the BCA and Agent Trimble but the Sheriffs and the Chiefs of Police in the state have an unwritten agreement with the BCA. The bureau offers all the assistance they can and we take the credit when a case is solved. It's a political thing; it's always been that way and probably always will be. Makes for a lot of good will between agencies. What do you think would happen if they took all the credit? No one would use them and that wouldn't be good for anybody."

The Chief looked at his watch, it was time to go downstairs and meet with the media. He was followed downstairs by his two detectives and he entered the meeting room first. The cameras were running and the Chief was the center of attention as he approached the podium and introduced himself and his two detectives working on the case. Sally Fairfield and Bob Carpenter each took a seat on a folding chair on opposite sides of the podium.

The Saint Paul Pioneer Press people were the first ones to ask a question. "Have you identified the victim yet?"

The Chief had anticipated this to be one of the first questions. "No, we haven't but we are focusing our efforts at the college right now. We think that at one time she was a student there or that she was familiar with someone who was a student there."

The questions continued and were easily answered by the Chief. He was well prepared and the press seemed satisfied with the information they were getting. The news conference lasted fifty minutes. Everyone hoped that the next time a news conference was called it would be because the killer had been caught.

After the conference Detective Fairfield went into her office and dialed Jerry Ringgold. On her desk were several photos of the dead girl. These pictures were taken at the autopsy before the examination. Jane Doe had been thoroughly scrubbed, wiped and groomed for the pictures at Dr. Goodland's laboratory. Detective Carpenter had taken forty four pictures of the girl; most of them for forensic purposes but some with a sheet covering her body with only her face uncovered for identification purposes. Jerry Ringgold answered the phone on the second ring and told Detective Fairfield that he had nothing going on and that he could be at the station shortly.

She had the photographs sorted and numbered and neatly arranged on her desk. She was studying them herself when the intercom in her office buzzed. She pressed the button that opened the communications and the dispatcher informed her that Jerry Ringgold was here to see her.

"Good morning Miss Fairfield."

"How are you doing?" she asked, looking at him and noticing that he still appeared shaken up over the whole incident.

He looked at her, trying feebly to hide his emotions but couldn't. "Not well, I have been real lethargic since that morning. I can't comprehend a world where that kind of evil exists. If I don't get better I am going to visit with the school counselor."

"Sorry to hear that, I hope things work out for you," she replied and smiled sympathetically as she pointed to the pictures on her desk. "These are the photographs of the dead girl. I would like you to examine them carefully and try to remember if you have ever seen this girl."

He gently picked up each picture and studied it carefully before setting it back on the desk. When he was finished studying the photographs he thoughtfully looked at her. "She was a beautiful girl. So beautiful." He paused. "So beautiful in fact that I do remember seeing her. It was a couple of weeks back, and I was taking a jog in the park and I noticed her with this other guy, a nerdy looking fella'. I only remember because she was so gorgeous and he was so weird. I remember he had green hair and long earrings and walked stupidly. I had never seen her before and I have never seen her since."

"Do you remember which day that was, it could be important."

He thought about it for a while and looked at the calendar on the wall. "Could you flip the page back to September?"

She got up and took the calendar off of the wall, turned the page to September and handed the calendar to him.

"It had to been on the afternoon of the fourteenth, that's a Sunday and that is the only day of the week I jog. I usually bike."

"Do you remember about what time of the day it was?"

"Yea, it was around four in the afternoon."

"You don't happen to know her name or anything else about her. Like what was she wearing, was she happy or sad; what was her emotional status when you saw her."

"She was wearing a sweatshirt, a gray one but I didn't notice any writing on it, it was blank. She had on black slacks and white tennis shoes. She didn't look happy or sad and it looked like she was talking to this guy not as a friend but as a counselor or something. Like she was trying to give him some advice about something. They weren't holding hands or anything like that and they really weren't affectionate at all. It didn't look like that kind of relationship at all, you know. I just couldn't figure why she would even be with this guy. Sorry, Miss Fairfield, that's all I can remember for now."

"It's Detective Fairfield, Jerry. Are you sure you can't remember anything else about her. It is really important. Could you have seen her at the college at any time? Try to think, could you have seen her in class or at the student union or in between classes?"

"I really don't think I had ever seen her before. I would have noticed, she was that kind of girl."

"Will you do me a favor, Jerry? Will you grab picture number twenty three off of my desk and show it around the campus and see if anybody recognizes her. I really need to find out who she is Jerry. If you could help me out I would be forever grateful."

The young bicyclist took the picture and stuffed it into his shirt pocket. "I would be glad to help any way I can Miss Fairfield. Everybody on campus wants this guy caught. We're all a little bit afraid and worried that he might be searching for another victim." He thanked the detective for the work she was doing and knew how hard it must be and again wished her luck in catching the killer. He turned and walked out of her office. She watched him go and hoped that she would be able to call him one day and tell him that they had found the killer.

Sally was picking the photos up from her desk and putting them back in the case file when she noticed the Chief standing in the hallway looking at her. His arms were crossed and he was smiling. The same cocky smile he donned when he was about to deliver good news.

"Hi Chief, what's happenin'?"

"When you're through here, come down to my office and bring Bob too. I've got something I want to show you guys." He turned and was gone as quickly as he had appeared. Sally was curious what the Chief was up to. She hoped he had good news about the case. When she had finished putting the pictures back in the case file she gave Bob a call on the interdepartmental phone sitting on her desk and told him about the chief and what he said.

When she walked into the Chief's office she noticed his once clean desk littered with everything from chewing gum wrappers to a golf ball. Next to all the hodgepodge of items was a small gray backpack, old and weather beaten. "Angus Sullivan brought this in a few minutes ago. Says his dog brought it home. I took the liberty of opening it up taking out the contents. The purse was the last thing to fall out and when it did I picked it up and opened it up. Inside the billfold was the driver's license. The picture on the license matches perfectly with our Jane Doe. Her name is Harmony Ann Day."

Sally stood in front of the Chief's desk looking at the items strewn all over when her partner walked into the office. She was delighted as she turned toward him. "We got the purse of our murder victim, name's Harmony Ann Day." She picked up the drivers license, studied it and handed it to her partner.

The senior detective studied the license and set it back down on the Chief's desk. "Who found it?"

"Angus Sullivan's dog brought it home. We'll have to buy that dog the biggest steak he's ever had," the Chief answered, pleased that he would finally have something to report to the news media. A week had already gone by and the press was calling every day to see if they had discovered the identity of the girl. Now he would be able to tell them some news and they would be pleased. They would finally have some information to give to the anxious public. He would ask them to wait until they had notified the family and he knew they would honor his request.

"Well, Chief, looks like we need to inventory everything and then head out to the Sullivan place and see if we can locate where the dog found the purse. We can use my office to tag the contents of the purse before we lock it up in storage. Sally we'll need your camera to get a picture of every item in the purse." Bob picked up the purse and its contents and put them in an evidence bag. He was careful not to touch any of the evidence.

****

Angus Sullivan was working in his machine shed when the squad pulled into his yard. Noticing them he grabbed a rag and wiped his hands and walked out to greet the two detectives. He knew what they had come for. "Hi Sally, Hi Bob, s'pose you're here to figure out where my dog Willie found that purse."

"Yea we are" Bob answered as they each got out of the squad car. "We hope we can find where he picked up the purse. Could be few more clues for us there."

Angus pointed to an area between the barn and a smaller out building. "Right there is where old Willie came back carrying that purse in his mouth. He was cocky as hell thinking he had really made a find. He walked right toward me, looked up and expected to be praised for his new discovery. He was a little disappointed when I took the purse away from him but he got over it real fast when I offered him a milk bone."

"The Chief figures we should give him the biggest steak he has ever had as a reward," Sally said as she bent down and petted Willie.

"Fine with both me and Willie. I think his footprints will lead you directly to the place he found the purse. Kind of lucky, though, that a little snow is left on the ground so you can track Willie."

"I'll follow Willie's paw prints and Sally's gonna' drive around the section. Between the two of us we should be able to find the place where the purse was dropped."

Sally found the area first. She was driving slowly down the township road that abutted the Sullivan acreage when she noticed a fresh mound of dirt next to a telephone pole on the road right of way. She was getting out of her car when her partner arrived. She yelled at him to get his attention and pointed to the fresh mound of dirt. "Looks like Willie smelled something in that purse and dug it up. Doesn't look like it was buried deep either. Luckily the ground isn't frozen yet."

Detective Carpenter got the digital camera out of the front seat of the squad and began taking photographs. Several boot prints surrounded the small grave where the purse was buried. The same boot prints lead to and from the road. He took a photograph of each print and placed a small ruler along the side of a few prints to verify the shoe size and confirm that all the prints were made by the same shoe. He would have liked to have gotten plaster casts of the prints but that would have been impossible. The light covering of snow on the ground was too fresh and too fluffy. He pointed to the farmland adjoining the area where the purse was found. "That's Andy Taylor's land. He hasn't even got his crop out yet."

Sally looked at the standing corn and shook her head. "Well, I ain't wasting my time going up to his place and talking to him. It would do no good."

CHAPTER 9

Nathan Brown fumbled for his apartment keys. They were in his right hand pants pocket intermingled with gum wrappers, a Bic lighter and a few small coins. Once they were located he pulled them out and unlocked the heavy oak door that opened into his apartment. The smell of marijuana, cigarette smoke and alcohol filled the stale air of his apartment. He was ignorant of the musty odor and had never thought to open a window to air the place out. He quickly shed his scrubs and put on a dirty pair of blue jeans and a wrinkled black t-shirt. The small one bedroom apartment was in disarray; dirty dishes filled the two sinks and countertops. Dried and burnt food bonded to each of the four burners of the stove and a few cockroaches scuttled near the base boards looking for food droppings. McDonald's wrappers were strewn throughout the apartment, dirty clothes lay in scattered piles and cobwebs were in each corner of the house. There were six apartments in his building and four similar buildings in the complex. His apartment was on the ground floor with his entry door facing the parking lot and garages. Each unit had its own garage; he did not yet own a car and he used the extra space to store miscellaneous junk. He had hoped to buy a car soon. He was trying to save money for a down payment and had managed to save a portion of each check. It wouldn't be long and he would be able to own his first automobile. He had in mind the type of vehicle he wanted and hoped he would be able to find it. If any section of the town was considered downtrodden, it was his neighborhood; he was forced to live in it because the rent was cheap and he was able to walk to work.

He had made no friends since moving to Milrose and that's the way he preferred it. The few people that knew him never asked him about his personal life or past. He liked to wear goth and he was a loner and neither of these traits set well with the people of the town. Gothic inferred to them weirdness, anger, Columbine and Dracula and they stayed away from Nathan Brown. The women of the town would often cross to the other side of the street if they saw him walking toward them; they were afraid to make eye contact with him. The women talked amongst themselves about the young pathologist assistant and they all agreed something was definitely wrong with that young man. He appeared anemic and malnourished, pale on the outside and dark on the inside. He was of average height, five feet ten inches tall but he only weighed one hundred and thirty five pounds. He had a resemblance to Ichabod Crane with his thin frame and tousled hair. His features were well observed by the townsfolk and they avoided him. They envisioned him with a cascade of weapons at his disposal; *that kind always did.* Did he have a gun or a knife or maybe even a bomb? Heaven only knew if he was armed but some people were sure that the newest resident to the town was someone to watch out for. His thick glasses with dark plastic rims fit his persona and he knew people were afraid of him. They had good reason to be for he had killed before and he would do it again in a heartbeat. He loved killing and the power it gave him over another human being as they pled for their life. It was not a sexual thing with him at all but if the opportunity presented itself to him all the better.

He remembered the first day he arrived in town. He bought a copy of the local newspaper and searched the help wanted ads. The one ad that interested him was placed by Dr. Goodland seeking an assistant in the morgue. He found a pay phone, dialed the office number and was told that the job was still open and that he could stop by and pick up an application. He arrived at the doctor's office a short time after he had phoned, walked directly to the desk clerk and asked for an application form. She gave him a clip board and an application and he sat in one of the soft green vinyl chairs in the waiting room and hurriedly filled it out and handed it back to her. Before the first day of his arrival in town was over he had found an apartment, picked up some groceries, hooked up his phone line, paid for his utility hook-ups and set up his computer. The next day he called Dr. Goodland's office to leave his phone number with the desk clerk. He was told that an interview had been set up for this afternoon if he could make it. He assured her that he could and before the afternoon was over he was

Dr. Goodland's denier. Jobs were plentiful in Milrose and no one was interested in working in a morgue. Nathan Brown had been the lone applicant for the job that had been open for over two months. He had become more excited about his new job after he found out what it entailed. He would tell people that he was a pathologist's assistant instead of a denier. That was two years ago and Nathan Brown was content with his life.

It was two years and one month ago that he had been released from the juvenile correction center in Topeka, Kansas. When he turned eighteen they had to let him go. He had spent five hellish years at that place. He promised himself that he would never spend another night in jail. He would kill again but he would never get caught again. He had learned from his mistakes and had become street wise while in the detention center. His years at the juvenile center were tough on him and played a big part in the development of his character; he entered the facility a young boy, nervous, afraid and insecure. He left the facility an angry man, needing power to satisfy his insecurity. He had always been a loner; he didn't want to be around people and they didn't want to be around him. Because of his looks and his personality he had been beaten up so many times by the other residents of the center that the warden felt he had to lock him in solitary confinement for his own protection. That is where he spent his years at the center. It was what Nathan wanted anyway and he was happy in solitude, planning what he would do with his future. He did a lot of thinking and planning; thinking about whether he would kill again, planning the perfect crime and thinking about where he would live and what he would do. There was a lot to think about in solitary confinement and it kept him busy.

When Nathan Brown was twelve and a half years old he had brutally murdered the eight year old daughter of his neighbor. To this day he did not know why he killed her. She was always happy, had a lot of friends and left him alone. He was sitting on his back porch one Saturday morning and she was sitting on her swing set facing away from him. She was singing "Jesus Loves Me" when he got up from the porch and walked up behind her and choked her until she turned white and then blue and he let her go and she fell off of the swing. He knew she was dead and that he had to hide the body. He went to his garage, got a shovel and carried it to the unused sandbox in the rear of his yard. It took him over an hour to dig a hole that he thought would be big enough for the body. He went over to his victim and began dragging her to the sandbox. When he had the body close to the shallow grave, the lady on the other side of his house came out to see what was going on. She knew something wasn't quite right as she watched out her kitchen window and saw him drag the little girl from the swing to the sandbox. Sensing that something was terribly wrong she ran outside and up to the boy. She looked at him in disgust as she bent down to examine the girl. Realizing that she was dead, she grabbed the boy around his waist, hoisted him up and carried him to her house where she called the police. She was a large woman and strong and was able to hold onto the boy until the police and ambulance arrived. Nathan was handcuffed and the girl was loaded into the ambulance. Nathan's attorney was able to get him sentenced as a juvenile and he was sent to a juvenile correctional facility until he was eighteen.

Nathan sat in front of his computer as he brought up the pictures of the latest autopsy. On the screen appeared dozens of pictures of the Jane Doe that had been murdered in Cedar Park. He carefully studied each one and smiled.

CHAPTER 10

Chief Rowlands insisted that his two detectives drive to Minneapolis immediately and find out what they could about Harmony Ann Day. He was anxious to report something positive to the press and he wanted them to know his department was working hard on the case. He wouldn't release the name of the victim until the detectives finished their work in the Twin Cities and the next of kin had been notified.

Sally had expressed her disdain for driving in the metro area on many occasions; because of that her partner offered to drive. He stopped at his house first and packed a small overnight bag and then drove Sally to her house where she did the same. Once she was in the car and had fastened her seat belt she called Agent Trimble and informed him that an identity had been made on the body; her name was Harmony Ann Day and she was from the Twin Cities area. Agent Trimble suggested that they meet in an hour and a half at the Copper Kettle restaurant off of I-35 north of Burnsville. The two detectives agreed and after stopping at the Law Enforcement to speak with Chief Rowlands they made the one-hour drive to the Burnsville restaurant.

Josh Trimble's dark green four-door unmarked Chevrolet had not arrived yet. The two detectives opted to go inside, grab a booth, order some coffee and wait for him. There were half a dozen uniformed officers seated throughout the restaurant, including four Highway Patrolmen huddled together in one booth and deep in conversation. Two deputy sheriffs were sitting on the opposite side of the restaurant each eating a large breakfast. Sally knew that if law enforcement frequented a restaurant the chow had to be good and the price reasonable.

Sally ordered a cup of coffee and Detective Carpenter ordered a large glass of juice and told the waitress that they were waiting for another person and when he showed up they would order some breakfast.

When her coffee arrived she realized that it was stronger than she liked so she grabbed the cream and poured a small amount into her coffee, stirred it and looked at her partner. "Do you know anyone in Milrose with green hair?"

He thought about the odd question for a minute and remembering, he answered "Yea, I do. Crazy Hezekiah."

"I thought his hair was black."

"It was until about a month ago when he dyed it this putrid green. It fits him though, as weird as he is. Why?"

Sally took a gulp of her coffee and carefully set the cup back down on its saucer. "Jerry Ringgold came to see me this morning and I showed him the pictures of our victim and he said he recognized her. He said this guy with green hair was walking with her in Cedar Park a couple of weeks ago."

"What would she be doing with a creep like Hezekiah Hadley?" Detective Carpenter asked.

She was about to answer his question when she noticed the agent Trimble's car pull into the restaurant parking lot. "Josh is here," she said as she observed him park his squad car and walk toward the restaurant. She waved as she watched him enter the restaurant. He did a quick glance around and noticed Sally waving her arm. When he spotted her and Bob, he walked over, removed his winter coat and tossed it in the empty booth next to theirs.

"Hello" he said as he slid into the booth next to Sally and rubbed his hands together to warm them up. "Little nippy out there today. You guys order yet?" He picked up one of the menus lying on the table, looked at it briefly, made his decision and laid the menu back down. When the waitress appeared he ordered a cup of coffee and a hamburger. The other detectives gave the waitress their order and handed her their menus.

"So, tell me about this Harmony Ann Day," Josh asked fidgeting with his coffee cup handle.

Sally told him about the information on the driver's license. "We ran a forty-five and everything matched so we figure the license is current. We're going to the address on the driver's license and check it out. We may be staying overnight in the Cities. The Chief wants us to stay until we have obtained all the information on her that we can. Do you know a reasonable hotel in the downtown area?"

"The Radisson's probably your best bet. If you stay over give me a call. I'll meet you in the bar for a couple of beers when you're through."

"Okay, a beer might taste kinda' good. How about you Bob, wanna' have a beer later?" she teasingly asked.

Bob Carpenter ignored Sally's comments; he wasn't comfortable in bars but to be polite he would join them. He liked them both and enjoyed their company. "Anything new on your end Josh?" he asked, hoping for an answer.

"The water in her lungs and stomach was definitely not tap water. It wasn't lake water or river water; it resembled water that would be used for irrigation or farm work. The lab called it unrefined water. I don't know if that helps much. I think we will have to file that information away for now because I wouldn't know where to start on that. Haven't done much else on the case, how about you guys?"

Sally looked at both her partner and Josh. "Haven't had much time either. We had the press conference and then we got the purse that ID's our victim and then we found the spot where the purse had been buried then we slept and now we are here. Not enough hours in a day but we feel we really made some headway the last twenty four hours."

"It seems like we're overwhelmed with evidence. We gotta' remain patient; it's all going to fit together sooner or later," Bob added as the food was brought to the table. They ate in silence, enjoying their meal.

Sally was the first to break the quiet. "We'd like you to come with us when we go to her address. We don't even know if there will be anybody there. We hope so."

"I'll come along. I've got nothing that urgent for today and this is a big break in the case, who knows what we may find out," Trimble answered as he took one last swallow of coffee and got up from the booth. "I'll follow you."

****

The two detectives and Agent Trimble had no trouble in finding the address. The street numbers on the duplex were large; painted a dark brown against a bright yellow façade which made them easily readable from the street. "That's it," Sally said as she pointed to the address they were looking for. Her partner stopped the squad car and glanced at the house before parking across the street. Agent Trimble pulled behind and all three detectives got out of their car at the same time. The three officers walked to the front door of 15116 Lyndale Avenue South and knocked on it, hoping that someone would answer it. They heard footsteps inside of the house and soon the front door opened and an attractive young woman about the age of Harmony Ann Day stood at the door facing them. She had Scandinavian hair and eyes, a thin figure and a pleasant smile. She was wearing a white t-shirt and gray flannel warm-up pants. Detective Fairfield introduced her two partners and was about to state their purpose for being there when the young woman matter-of-factly asked if this was about Harmony.

"Yes it is, does she live here?" Sally replied and noticed that tears were beginning to form in the young woman's eyes.

"She's dead, isn't she?"

Sally looked at her, surprised by the question and asked if they could come in.

"Yes" the young woman replied and opened the door motioning for them to enter. "I'm Pamela Rosewood, I live with Harmony."

The three investigators took a seat on the couch and Pamela sat in an old weathered recliner facing them. She was fidgeting with the string that kept her warm-up suit from falling down. She was silent and waited for one of the three people in front of her to begin the conversation.

Agent Trimble removed a notebook from his shirt pocket, opened it and looked at the visibly shaken girl in front of him. "Yes, Pamela. She's dead, she was murdered and we are here to investigate her death."

"I knew it, I just knew it. When I read about that murder down in Milrose and Harmony not showing up I figured it had to be her. I knew she was in Milrose that day, she was planning on attending college there, you know. We weren't just roommates, we were friends. We grew up friends in Bemidji, went to high school together, we were in the same grade. We moved here together. Thought we would be adventuresome, move to the big city and all that."

"Pamela. Why didn't you call us?" Fairfield asked.

"I was going to, I picked up my cell phone many times but I was afraid. Afraid that I would be told that the murdered woman was Harmony. I am not a strong person and I didn't know how I would handle the news. Once I even got in my car to drive to Milrose but when I got to the edge of Minneapolis I chickened out. I guess that I thought as long as I didn't know, she would still be alive and would walk in the door at any time. I'm sorry I should have, I know."

"We understand. Especially if you two were that close. And we feel bad that it was your friend. What can you tell us about Harmony? We need to know as much about her as we can. There might be something in her life that is connected to her unfortunate death." Sally reassuredly asked.

Pamela got up from her recliner and walked into another room. When she returned she handed a framed photograph to Agent Trimble. "This is Harmony with her parents on her graduation day. Her parents are wonderful people, they don't know yet. Harmony called them a couple of times a month but it hasn't been all that long since she last called them."

She paused not knowing what to say next. "Someone's going to have to tell them. I know I can't. Can you have someone do it?"

"We'll take care of that," Sally Fairfield whispered. "But please go on and tell us about Harmony."

"Not much to really tell. We grew up together in Bemidji, went to the same school and the same church and had the same friends. Harmony was a good student, B average. She was on the volleyball team, sang in her church choir. Oh yeah, she was a devout Christian, very religious, her whole family was. We both did not know what we wanted to do after high school. We had thoughts of going to college, or a vocational school. We even talked about joining the Marines or Navy or one of the branches of service. We didn't think about that long. Seemed too dangerous for us, especially with the world the way it is now days. We dropped that idea and the college idea too. We decided to work for at least a year and maybe we would know then what we should do with our lives. Well, we decided to rent a place in Minneapolis and experience the big city. We both got jobs at Honeywell with the same hours so we thought that was great. We would only need one car. We could drive to and from work together. We didn't go out much during the week but on Friday nights a few people from Honeywell went to this small bar called Izzy's for happy hour. It was there that we got to meet a lot of our co-workers. Saturday nights we usually went out for a pizza and were home fairly early because Harmony had church the next day. She never missed church. That is all I can think of right now."

When she finished she began to cry and Detective Carpenter retrieved a handkerchief from his pocket and handed it to her. She grabbed it and dabbed her eyes and desperately tried to regain her composure. When Bob Carpenter felt the time was appropriate he asked her about Milrose College and Harmony.

"About six months ago Harmony decided to go to college. She said she had an epiphany and that she now knew what she wanted to do with her life. She wanted to be a social worker. She checked out several colleges, even the University of Minnesota but decided that Milrose offered just what she needed. She applied and was accepted and when she got the acceptance letter we went out and celebrated. We drank champagne that night and neither one of us felt good the next day. I haven't drunk champagne since. She'd been down to Milrose a couple of times, registering for classes, buying books and getting familiar with the campus. She was going to start the second semester which was sometime after the first of the year. She had hoped she could find a dorm room because the rules at Milrose College were that you had to live your freshman year in the dorm. She even suggested that I could move to Milrose after her first year and we could get an apartment together. But I got this good job with a good company and there really wasn't much for good paying jobs there so I told her I'd think about it but I really didn't think I would leave Honeywell. Anyway the last time she went there was last week and that's the last time I seen her." She brought the moist handkerchief to her nose and gently wiped it. She paused a second, excused herself, got up and went into the bathroom. Ten minutes later she returned and looked fresher.

"How you feeling?" Agent Trimble asked.

"Sad."

"Would you like a few minutes?"

"I'll make us some coffee." Pamela Rosewood said and got up from her chair and walked into the kitchen without asking the investigators whether they wanted coffee or not. When she returned she had four cups of coffee, a small bowl of sugar with a spoon in it and a pitcher of cream all on a silver serving tray. She set the tray down on the coffee table in front of the sofa and handed a cup to each of the investigators. Bob Carpenter took his coffee to be polite but didn't drink it.

"Pamela," Detective Fairfield asked while she was mixing cream and sugar into her coffee and stirring it. "Did Harmony have a boyfriend?"

"Yes, but I didn't really like him and I don't think Harmony was that crazy about him either and I think she was about ready to dump him. His name's Pete Krueger, works at Honeywell too. Shipping and receiving. They met at Izzy's one Friday night and became more friends than anything else, but Krueger - he wanted more than a friendship. I didn't see what Harmony seen in the jerk. He was a short little shit and I think he weighed less than me. He had these piercing black eyes that could see you right through you; there was evil in those eyes. He had tattoos on both arms and what I really don't understand is that Harmony hated tattoos so I can't figure out that relationship. Oh yeah, another thing. He practiced martial arts; he was heavy into kung fu and stuff like that. That's about all I can tell you about him but if you need a suspect, I would sure start with him."

Agent Trimble quickly but carefully scribbled the information about Peter Krueger in his notebook. "Do you know if her boyfriend ever used weapons in his martial arts?"

"I'm not sure, but I think so. He never talked much about it but he had this magazine with him one day that showed these two guys on the front page. They were holding swords and were about ready to fight or something. I mean, he's the kind of guy that would be into that."

"Where can we find this Pete Krueger?" Detective Carpenter asked.

"I don't know where he lives, someplace in North Minneapolis. Check at Human Resources at Honeywell, they can tell you."

Agent Trimble stood up and the other two detectives did the same. "We have to go now Pamela, we hope you can get through this okay. If you think of anything more, here is my card and please call me."

Pamela reached out her hand to accept the card and with her other hand gave Detective Fairfield the picture of Harmony with her parents. "On the back of this picture are the names of her parents,

Harold and Gladys, and their address and phone number. I would appreciate it if you would get in contact with them and let them know what happened to Harmony. I just couldn't do it, I know I couldn't."

Detective Fairfield took the picture, looked at the backside of the photograph and looked back at Pamela. "There's something I forgot to ask you and it's important. What kind of car did Harmony own? Maybe if we knew the make and the color of the car we could have our guys be on the look out for it."

"It was an older pickup, at least ten years old and it was a foreign job. Datsun or Nissan maybe and it was yellow and the right fender was painted blue."

They all said their good-byes to Pamela Rosewood and Sally assured her that she would make sure that Harmony's parents would be notified.

The three investigators stood in front of their squad cars discussing the conversation that had taken place with Pamela Rosewood. Peter Krueger had become the prime suspect in their investigation and he needed to be talked to but that would have to wait until tomorrow. It was getting dark and they needed to get to their hotel, get cleaned up and have supper. They would also need a good night's sleep to be refreshed for tomorrow when they talked with Pete Krueger. Sally mentioned to Josh that they were going to go to the hotel and that he should come and join them for supper. He agreed and they both got into their squad cars and drove away. Sally enjoyed and appreciated that her partner was doing all the driving. She would make it up to him some day. She took her cell phone from her purse and set it on her lap, reached over and picked up the police radio and called the dispatch office and asked for the number of the Bemidji Police Department. After a few minutes waiting she got the number from dispatch and as she was writing the number down she was told that two rooms, each with a king size bed, had been confirmed for them at the Radisson Hotel for that night. She acknowledged the information with the familiar ten-four, replaced the microphone in its cradle and dialed the Bemidji Police Department. The man that answered the phone identified himself as a police officer. She identified herself and asked to speak to the Chief of Police. She explained to him about Harmony Ann Day and asked him if he could send someone to the house and break the news to her parents. The Bemidji Police Chief told her that he personally knew Harmony's parents and that he would do the unpleasant task himself. Delivering bad news was the hardest part of her job; she was not good at it and she hated having to do it. She was glad someone else would be doing it this time. She informed her partner that rooms had been reserved for them at the Radisson Hotel for one night. She was hungry and she wanted to freshen up. She was excited about staying in a fancy hotel and she wanted to get there as soon as she could. "Put the pedal to the metal Bob, let's get there and have some fun, we deserve it. It's been a good day."

The Radisson Hotel was one of the oldest and popular hotels in the area. Constant renovations and a good location kept the hotel in favor with business travelers and tourists alike. When Sally walked into the front lobby she was overwhelmed. The only hotel she had ever stayed in was a Budget 8 and that was nothing like this. The floors were marble with gold and white squares alternating throughout the main floor. The paneling around the lobby was dark cherry and imitation palm trees were carefully situated along the walls. Scattered throughout the large lobby were seating areas with two comfortable looking cloth chairs and a small round table between them. There was a table for four that had place settings on it and four empty coffee cups. This looked inviting and Sally thought this would be where she had her coffee in the morning, read the paper and review with her partner the information that Pamela Rosewood had given them.

They checked in separately and each was given a room with a king size bed. When Sally got to her room she excitedly opened the door to see what kind of luxury was in store for her. She wasn't disappointed. The carpet looked new and the gold and red design blended well with the beige colored walls and the thick drapes. The armoire was large enough to hold her entire wardrobe, both here and at home, and there was a mini-bar sitting next to it that would certainly whet her appetite. Every type of junk food along with her favorite beer were crammed inside waiting for her to consume. There was a dark cherry writing desk next to the armoire and by the window there was a small seating area with a yellow cloth chair and a small table similar to the ones she had seen in the lobby. This was heaven, or the next thing to it, and she was going to enjoy the precious few hours she had here.

Bob Carpenter had called Josh and told him that they had checked into the Radisson and asked if he still wanted to get together.

They decided to meet in the bar for a couple of drinks and later have supper at the hotel. Bob advised that if it was okay with Sally it was a date.

Sally was about to get into the shower when the phone rang. It was Bob and he advised her of the plans. She thought that it sounded great and told him that after she showered and dried her hair she would meet up with them in the bar.

Sally had missed the first round of drinks. She walked into the bar and spotted her partner and Josh Trimble sitting at a table. She ordered a draught beer from the bartender, carried it over to their table and sat down. They were quiet when she joined them; she needed to get a conversation going. "You know Josh, it is good to see you again. I don't think Bob or I have seen much of you since the murders over in Bishop. It is good to have you on this case. I still can't get that Bishop case out of my mind though, that was some good police work." Sally remembered the case well. It had been covered by every newspaper in the state. The Pioneer-Dispatch had the best coverage and wouldn't let the story go until the killer had been found. There were seven murders in all. The first was the most gruesome. Mary Helms and her two daughters were found dead in their farmhouse. The son who was eight years old heard what was going on and hid under his bed. Somehow the killer missed him and left the farmhouse without harming him. After that the kid had a lot of emotional problems and became catatonic. The police never did get much information out of him. That was on Halloween night and was followed by the killing of a couple of young girls in a gravel pit and a few months later an elderly lady was murdered and after that a middle-aged woman was killed in her home. The local priest was the prime suspect but he had escaped in a single engine Cessna and crashed up in the Superior National Forest. It was never known if he survived the crash or not. The plane was found a couple of days after the crash but his body was never found."

Josh was in a talkative mood; he was in his environment and savored every moment of it. "Well Sally, since then I had been working on a murder up in Wheat County but I got a suspect. He's in jail and there's enough evidence for trial which will probably be starting the first of next year."

"Do you think the pastor did it?" Bob asked, rehashing the case in his head, trying to remember the details of the whole thing.

"That's a question I have been wrestling with every day. At first I was sure he was the killer cause he was a little weird and there was certainly enough evidence for an arrest warrant but the more I got into the case the less sure I am. I am not convinced he had a motive; I just wish he had been found and was alive. I would like to interview him again with different questions this time. The Helms dog was the best witness we had. Remember Bob. I'm sure you read about it. When they televised the funeral, the family dog was at Mary's parents' house and how he went crazy when the pastor started giving his eulogy. I think there is more to the case and if something comes up, which I think it will, I'll get back to work on it."

"I read the book about the case; in fact I even bought it. It was good; I have it in my library. How'd it sell?" Sally asked.

"*Alter Ego,* not that great, but it did okay." Josh answered.

"I wonder if it will ever be made into a movie. I wonder who would play you." Sally needled him because she knew he had been the brunt of few jokes at the agency because of the book.

"Probably that famous actor Bud Weiser and speaking of that I think it's time for another one. Sally, you ready?"

"Sure, why not, but at three dollars a beer a person can't drink too much."

The waitress sat two beers on the table, one in front of Sally and the other in front of Josh. Bob did not order anything; he was still nursing his orange juice.

Josh poured his beer into the frosted mug that accompanied it and took a large gulp. "So what did you think of Pamela Rosewood?"

Detective Carpenter's smile quickly faded as he answered. "I feel sorry for her. I mean, she and Harmony come to the big city for some excitement and a new life. They both get good jobs and things seem to be working out for them and this happens. Now she is in the big city all alone and hardly knows anybody. I don't know what she is going to do because now she has to pay rent for both of them and I am sure she can't afford that but it sounds like she really enjoys her job and doesn't want to leave that."

"You're right Bob, but you take things too seriously, things will work out for her. She seems to be a bright girl, attractive too. She'll work through this. I do think though that we have a prime suspect in this Pete Krueger. Sounds to me he was a little domineering and he was into martial arts. Remember the sword used in shaolin. He might be into that and if he is he might be our man. Those kind of swords aren't plentiful you know. We got to talk to him tomorrow. That's the first thing we gotta' do." Sally answered and lit her third cigarette since ordering her first beer.

"I'll go with you. This case is now my top priority and anyway if I can help, I will." Josh offered. "When we are through with these beers, let's go eat."

They all agreed and after supper Bob and Sally went to their rooms and Josh went back to the bar for a night-cap.

CHAPTER 11

The Honeywell Corporation, one of the largest employers in Minnesota, has one of its plants in Minneapolis. Bob Carpenter drove into the parking lot and followed the signs to the visitor parking area. "This parking lot is bigger than our whole town," he quipped as he pulled into one of the few remaining parking spots for visitors. They arrived later than he wanted but his partner was slow in getting ready for the day and then she needed her coffee in the surroundings of the lobby and then she needed to read the paper and then she was finally ready. It was as if she wanted to squeeze every minute out of the 'hotel experience' as she called it. He couldn't blame her; she had probably never experienced luxury of this kind before. He remembered his frustration level when he called her room at seven-thirty and no one answered. He tried again at eight and again at eight-fifteen and at eight-thirty he took the elevator down to the lobby and searched for her. He found her sitting at a small table near a large window with french panes enjoying a morning cup of coffee and reading the Minneapolis Tribune. She seemed oblivious to the world around her and he knew she was savoring every moment of the 'hotel experience'. He walked up to the dark mahogany table she was sitting at and stood in front of her, hoping to get some reaction. She ignored him and kept on reading. "Sal, we got to get going, its eight-thirty; we got work to do."

Detective Fairfield was not about to be rushed this morning. They would be putting in a long day and she was going to begin it the way she imagined that she would. "I'm hungry, let's get some breakfast first." Her partner reluctantly agreed and resigned himself to following her game plan for today. He would never understand his partner; they were about as different as two people could be but he liked her and enjoyed working with her. She was a good person and he liked good people.

Upon entering the immense Honeywell building, they walked to a small reception and information area and identified themselves to a young woman sitting in front of her computer and asked where they could find the Human Resources Department. She exuberated home town friendliness as she looked up at them and smiled. "Welcome to Honeywell, is this your first time here?" They answered yes and she directed them down a hallway stating that it was the fifth door on the right hand side. A security guard was seated at a small desk next to the receptionist; overhearing the conversation he arose and escorted them to the right door.

Upon entering the Human Resources Department they realized they were in an office that was bigger than the entire Law Enforcement Center. A large number of square cubicles lined the four walls and another twenty or more were connected in a grid pattern in the middle of the room and all were occupied with smartly dressed employees looking very busy. No one was sitting at the front desk when they entered. They stood for a minute hoping to get noticed; when no one showed up after a few minutes they turned and noticed a small waiting area with several comfortable looking chairs. They each grabbed a chair and sat down staring at the empty desk in front of them. Tired of sitting and doing nothing they each got up and took a magazine from a small wooden rack hanging on the wall. They sat back down, leafed through their magazines and waited. Bob skimmed through his magazine quickly and was about to replace it and get another when a woman entered from a side door and took a seat at the front desk. She was a young woman, large in stature and wore a brilliant colored blouse tucked into white slacks; she noticed them almost immediately and asked if she could be of assistance. They introduced themselves and asked to see someone who might help them locate one of their employees.

"Just a moment," she said and made a phone call. When the short conversation was over she directed them to a small office cubicle where a young man sat looking very intently at his computer. Detective Carpenter stood at the opening to his office and tapped on the makeshift wall. The intent man looked up from his computer and invited the two detectives in.

"Peter Krueger, let's see here, something should come up soon." He was more muttering to himself than talking to the two detectives seated in front of him. The young man working the computer was in his early twenties and neatly dressed. He had short blond hair and wore dark plastic rimmed glasses. Detective Carpenter noticed a college diploma hanging from the wall; he had graduated less than five months ago from the University of Minnesota. This was his first real job. "Here it is - Peter Krueger. Works in shipping and receiving and has been with us about a year and a half. High school degree, single, no complaints, works the day shift. Is that helpful?"

"Is it possible that we could talk to him? It's kind of important." Sally pleasantly asked.

"You'd have to talk to his supervisor and that is," he pressed a key on the computer and studied the screen, "Don Wilson, but shipping and receiving is in another building." He pulled out an eight by eleven piece of paper with a detailed map of the complex. He showed the detectives where they were and how to get to Don Wilson's department. They thanked the young man for his time and left, eager to meet Pete Krueger.

"Krueger's not here," his supervisor answered. "Took three weeks off. Left about a week ago."

"Could we have the exact day he left and when he will be back to work?" Sally asked.

"Let's see," the supervisor answered as he opened a screen on his computer. "Left last Monday and will be back to work the Monday after next."

"Do you know where he is spending his vacation?" Detective Carpenter asked.

"Yea, as a matter of fact I do. He said he was going out to Montana and do some fishing with friends he had out there. Even knew the area, said it was by Wolf Point."

"Do you have Krueger's address?" Detective Fairfield asked. It would be the last question for the supervisor and they hoped he would provide it without much trouble. He was cooperative and wrote down the address and the phone number on a slip of paper and handed it to Detective Fairfield. Sally placed the piece of paper in her notebook and the detectives thanked Don Wilson for his time and they left.

****

Pete Krueger's apartment was situated on the east end of downtown Minneapolis and was one of the oldest buildings in that area. It had been a warehouse for plumbing supplies for many years and ten years ago had been renovated to an apartment complex. The building was old but it had been constructed with Chicago common bricks and was sturdy. The inside had been gutted and remodeled and new windows added. A fresh coat of brown paint shined up the exterior. But that was ten years ago and now days the paint was peeling and the weathered brick faded to a rusty orange. The inside of the building wasn't much better. Coffee stains, alcohol stains and cigarette burns enveloped the original hue of the worn and ripped carpeting that covered the concrete floor. The wooden staircase that led up to the narrow hall containing the first floor row of apartment doors had the same worn carpet. The detectives checked the mailboxes at the entrance of the apartment and located Peter Krueger's apartment. It was on the fifth floor and they weren't sure if they should take the elevator or walk. They took a chance and entered the elevator and pushed the fifth floor button. The elevator jerked and swayed as it made its way to the fifth floor. They found the apartment and knocked on the door, not anticipating an answer but they had been surprised before.

A middle-aged Chinese woman answered the door. Her eyes were dull yellow and shallow signifying a bad case of hepatitis or heavy pot use or both. Sally guessed it was the former. She was wearing a multi-colored bathrobe; its once bright colors were diminished from time and wear. Her short black hair was disheveled and oily and looked as if it hadn't been washed for some time.

"Yes?" she sarcastically asked; an unfiltered half smoked cigarette dangling from the corner of her mouth. She was having a hard time focusing on the two people standing at the door.

"We're looking for Pete Krueger, is he here?" Sally politely asked.

"Nope."

"Do you know when to expect him?"

"What do you want him for?" she mumbled, ashes falling from her cigarette.

"We just want to talk to him ma'am."

"You're cops ain't ya?"

"I'm Detective Carpenter and this is Detective Fairfield. We are from the Milrose Police Department."

"Long ways from home ain't ya'?"

"It's about his girlfriend Harmony Day, it's kind of important." Sally stated matter-of-factly.

"He don't have no girlfriend. I'm his girl and I take real good care of him."

"You into martial arts too, Miss - sorry I didn't get your name." Detective Carpenter asked.

"Didn't give you my name and I'm not going to and no I am not into martial arts. Tried it a few years ago, too much dedication."

"How about shaolin, you know anything about that?" Sally asked.

"Pete's into it but wait a minute, that's enough," she said and slammed the door shut.

The detectives walked to their car and Sally called Josh Trimble on her cell phone. The BCA agent was going over the information he had gotten from Sally Fairfield on Hezekiah Hadley when he answered Sally's call. Sally was sure he was the one seen walking with Harmony in the park two weeks before her death and she wanted Agent Trimble to use the resources of the Bureau to get more information on him.

"I've got a lot of information on this Hadley character, he's a real nut case, and a burglar and he also does a little exposing on the side. I'll fax a copy to your office," the Agent replied.

Sally knew about the burglaries but she didn't know about the exposing. How could that little bit of information have slipped by her. Either he wasn't charged with the indecent exposure or he was found not guilty by a jury or a judge or he was a juvenile when he committed the acts. It also might have happened in another county because she had never heard of this side of Hezekiah Hadley. He was beginning to look more and more like a serious suspect. "I didn't know all that Josh, thanks. I think we're going to have to bring him in for questioning." Sally filled the Agent in on what details she had and the eye witness who had seen Hadley and Harmony Day in the park on the afternoon of September 14th. "I need to know why he was in the park with her and how he knows her. Anyway the reason I called was that we talked to Krueger's live in. She's a real winner but she confirmed that he was into martial arts and she knew what a shaolin sword was. Looks like we got ourselves two good suspects, Hadley and Krueger. We'll talk more when we get back. Just wanted to check in and see how you're doing on your end."

They each said their good-byes and hung up. Sally turned to her partner and advised him that she was dying of starvation and suggested that they pull into the next restaurant they saw.

CHAPTER 12

The movements of Hezekiah Hadley were slow and furtive as he crept from one cedar tree to another. He was methodical and quiet, slowly moving his way toward the pavilion. He figured no one was in the park but he had to be cautious; he couldn't afford to be seen. It would ruin everything if he was noticed by anyone - it would screw up all his plans. It was four o'clock in the morning and the park was invisible to the eye. The moon was new, the stars had disappeared under the cloudy sky and there was no breeze. He was silent as he carried the U.S. Army knapsack that held the booty from his latest victory, Benson's hardware store. The burglary had been easy, the easiest of them all. The cheapskate Benson didn't even have the place alarmed. He maneuvered to the next tree, his movements replicated from video games he played. His wardrobe was from Rainbow Six, a video game he had played maybe ten thousand times. His camouflaged boonie hat was nestled firmly on his head, its draw-string pulled tightly against his adam's apple. His jacket and trousers too were camouflaged, a gray and white tiger stripe design that allowed him to blend in unseen amongst the trees and shrubbery of Cedar Park. His face and hands were blackened thanks to some charcoal briquettes that had been stored in his garage for the last few years. He wore no boots or shoes. His black socks were the only covering he had to protect his feet but he knew they would leave no prints. His entire military wardrobe was obtained from the army surplus store in downtown Milrose. It was of course taken in the middle of the night and not paid for. He wore the prized outfit on the nights he pulled his burglaries. He would lie low for a while after tonight; the loot he was about to bury should finish his collection - he had all he needed for now. He felt good wearing his army clothing, it made him feel important. He had wanted to join the army and even tried to enlist. He didn't care about serving his country; he only wanted to kill people and do it legally. He was rejected by the Army; *Mentally Unfit for Duty* they called it. He was angry at their decision and burglarized eight businesses the following week and set fire to a vacant house. He watched it burn to the ground as the firemen worked hard to put out the fire and save the house next door.

The pavilion was in his sight, no one was around. You had to be careful at the pavilion because sometimes, even at this hour of the morning there could be a couple of lovers lounging around the area. He walked to the rear of the pavilion and deeply breathed in the air. He was sure he could smell the scent of dried blood even though it had been washed off the day after the murder. He found the tree he was looking for and set his knapsack down. He took a penlight from his pocket, turned it on and placed it in his mouth holding it with his teeth. He was careful not to point the light in any direction but down. He carefully opened the sack and laid the contents beside him. A utility knife, a length of three-eighths inch nylon cord, a hammer, a box of sixteen penny nails, duct tape and a scissors lay on the ground in front of him. He unfolded his entrenching tool, a combination fold-up shovel and pick and dug up the green metal box that was buried under the tree. He caressed each item as he placed it in the box. When that was done, he closed the box and covered it up. He knew that he was now ready to kill but the timing had to be right.

CHAPTER 13

Detective Carpenter stuck his head into his partner's undersized office. He was wearing his parka and a fur lined cap. The temperature had dropped to five above zero overnight and he was about to leave the office to investigate another burglary. "Benson's Hardware was hit last night, you want to come along?"

Sally looked up from her paper-strewn desk and glanced at the clock on the wall. "I better not; if I don't get caught up on this paperwork I'll never see the light of day. Can you handle it alone?"

"Yea, no problem, see you when I get back."

A string of burglaries had kept the two detectives busy over the last six months. They had their suspicions of course. A half a dozen burglars lived in or around Milrose and at any given time three or four of them were in jail which allowed the other two or three to continue their craft. It was a revolving door for these burglars. One would be released and one would be sentenced. Two of the known thieves had been out of jail the entire time that the burglaries were happening. Hezekiah Hadley and William Markham - both were unemployed but always had plenty of money for beer, cigarettes and pot. Unless someone new had joined their ranks they were the two main suspects of Detective Carpenter and Detective Fairfield. The local burglars were getting better at their chosen profession and were careful not to leave any evidence at the scene except for the pry marks and that couldn't be helped. They had learned well from the lessons of the past and jail time had given them the opportunity to mingle with other burglars and learn their secrets. The usual motive was money - money to buy drugs, money to by booze, money to buy gas. Burglars weren't into working for a living and always searched for the easy way out. The thieves had their fences that bought the stolen goods for pennies on the dollar and then sold the items for a hefty profit. Once the fences were caught and some of the stolen goods recovered the entire operation would tumble down like falling dominos. There is no honor among thieves it is said and one thief will rat on another one to save his own neck. But when money was stolen, that was different. It was nearly impossible to trace and that is what had made it so hard for Detective Carpenter to get a handle on the last nine or ten burglaries. The only thing that appeared to be missing was cash.

Benson's Hardware was the oldest hardware store in town. Located in the middle of the business district it was sandwiched between a dry cleaning business and a clothing store. An alley ran behind the businesses and was mostly used for loading and unloading by the store's suppliers and its customers. The alley was dark at night. The few lights that illuminated the alley were those that lit the rear doors of the business. Benson's Hardware had a small light bulb above the rear door that once worked but had burned out several years ago. Mr. Benson, who was a trusting sort, never got around to replacing it.

Detective Carpenter was taking pictures of the rear door and the marks made by an unknown tool to pry the door open. This was the last of the pictures that needed to be taken. "Mr. Benson, you need to get an alarm system put in, that could deter a burglar and give us a better chance of catching him." He pointed to the light above the rear door. "That light has to be fixed Mr. Benson. That is an open invitation to a burglar."

"I know, I know, my insurance company tells me that when I install one, my rates will even go down. Just haven't gotten around to it yet. Guess I'll have to hire someone to do it."

"You're sure that all that was taken was petty cash. Ninety-eight dollars and twelve cents."

Sam Benson studied the detective as he scanned the store with his eyes. "I think that's it. I don't keep the best inventory records but if I find something missing I'll call you."

The detective closed his notebook and told the owner of the store that if anything comes up he will call him. He left the store, got into his squad car and radioed dispatch center that he was ten-eight. More reports he thought; soon his desk was going to look like Detective

Fairfield's. The murder case was going to take up a lot of their time and these burglaries would have to be put on the back burner he thought to himself as he pulled his squad car into his assigned stall in front of the Law Enforcement Center. He entered the Center and walked to Sally's office.

"What do think of these burglaries Sally? It's got to be the same person. M.O.'s the same on each one. No prints on anything, no shoe prints, no finger prints, nothing. The pry marks on the door all indicate the same tool was used in each burglary. Not much was taken in the burglaries, a few odds and ends and petty cash. Why wouldn't they go after the valuable stuff? Hardware stores carry plenty of expensive things but all that was taken was a hundred bucks from petty cash. Do you think he needs the money for drugs?"

"Don't know, we're just going to have to catch him in the act. They always screw up, some night they are going to trip an alarm and then we got them. I have a hunch that our green haired monster may be involved. I think we'll have to tell the guys to keep a closer eye on him at night and make a note if they see him any where around town after dark," Sally answered. She was trying to clean and organize her desk and she had a piece of paper in her hand when she stopped, trying to think of something she wanted to tell her partner. "Oh, I almost forgot Bob, the funeral for Harmony Ann Day is this afternoon at three. I think we should go. See if we can find a little more out about our victim."

Bob looked at his watch. "We can make it if we leave soon. We got nothing to lose by going. Let's do it. Can your paperwork last one more day?"

"Yea, one more day ain't going to hurt. Besides that I'm going to put in some overtime to get it all cleaned up. Chief won't mind."

"It's a two and a half hour drive, Sal. Want to take your car or mine?"

Bob offered to drive his squad car and as they travelled further and further north on Highway 169 Sally observed a dynamic scenery change. Once they were north of Minneapolis the rich fertile prairie land of southern Minnesota was replaced by sandier soil with Scotch, Birch and Norway pines trees as tall as fifty feet and visible as far as the eye could see. This was northern Minnesota and many of the lakes had Indian names, like Mille Lacs and Winnibigoshish.

Bemidji is an Ojibwe name that means 'lake that traverses another body of water'. It is the home of Paul Bunyan and his faithful companion Babe the Blue Ox. The Mississippi River and Lake Bemidji border the town. The town and the surrounding area is a paradise for fishermen and hunters alike. Many of the lake homes and lake cabins in the area are owned by young, affluent techies who flock to the nearby lakes every weekend. From Memorial Day through Labor Day the population of Bemidji and the surrounding area doubles. The winter months are quiet except for the first two weeks in November when deer hunters descend upon the town like migrating geese.

"Did you run a check on our Peter Krueger through NCIC?" Bob Carpenter asked as he looked at a map of Bemidji, trying to figure out how to get to the church.

"I did that while you were at Benson's Hardware, should have an answer any time now," she answered as she pulled a cigarette out of her shirt pocket, lit it and rolled down the passenger's window and waited for her partner to complain as he always did.

"Do you have to smoke that thing in the car?"

"You can't smell it, the window's down."

"Yea but the smell is still going to be on my clothes."

"Live with it, okay."

The police radio beckoned to be answered and Sally grabbed for the microphone and acknowledged the call. "Your NCIC check came back a hit," the dispatcher informed her. "Your subject has eleven priors, all in the last three years, all for assault. Looks like he has quite a temper. The report will be waiting for you in dispatch."

She answered the call with ten-four and turned to her partner. "Looks like one of our prime suspects just became more of a prime suspect. I'll check up on those assaults when I get back. See where they happened and how bad they were. Looks like Mr. Krueger has a short fuse."

They arrived at the church in plenty of time. The funeral wasn't going to start for another half of an hour. They entered the large stone church and were ushered to a pew near the middle of the nave. Friends, mourners, well-wishers and relatives began taking their seats within a few minutes after the two detectives sat down. By the time the funeral started the church was full. A lunch was served after the burial and when word got out who the two strangers were at the funeral several of the friends and relatives came over to them and introduced themselves and began talking about Harmony. How she was a devout Christian, wanted to be a social worker, the nicest girl you'd ever want to meet and what a tragedy this whole thing was. Sally frantically wrote down the names of everyone they talked to for future follow-up.

CHAPTER 14

It was the third year in a row he had driven to Montana to do some fishing. He liked to fish in the fall of the year because they were easier to catch and they tasted better. Each evening he fried his catch in a cast iron skillet over an open fire and couldn't imagine eating fish any other way or in any other circumstance. There were fewer fishermen to contend with as the cool weather of autumn set in. The cold weather didn't bother him, he actually preferred it. He was lucky to have found this spot on the Missouri river; it was uninhabited, serene and scenic. He didn't know if he was on state land, private land or the Fort Peck Indian Reservation. No one ever questioned him so he continued fishing and camping on the small patch of land outside Wolf Point every year for the past three years. He had a small one man tent, a sleeping bag and a few cooking utensils which he used to make breakfast and supper. On weekends he drove the short distance into Wolf Point to drink beer with the intention of getting drunk. He had stocked up with plenty of beer at his campsite but still liked the tavern environment. Bars had always fascinated him. He loved the sounds of a tavern, the sharp thud of pool balls banging each other, the clanging of the pin ball machines and the televisions which were always on and tuned to some sporting event. He liked the smell of a tavern, distinct over any other smell in the world. He also liked watching people but didn't want any part of them or their lives. It was in these bars that he got in the most trouble; the alcohol changed him and enhanced his anti-social behavior and one wrong word could set him off and a fight would ensue. He had never lost a fight; he was good with his hands and an expert in martial arts. A fight with Peter Krueger didn't last long.

His opponent would soon be unconscious and lying on the floor or ground in a pool of blood and he would be handcuffed and off to jail.

It was Saturday night and he was driving into Wolf Point and his favorite bar - Mully's. There were several bars in Wolf Point but Mully's was his favorite. The fishing had been good that day and he had caught well over his limit, throwing them in his ice cooler with plans to clean them the next morning. For now, all that was on his mind was a night of fun at Mully's. When he entered the bar it was empty except for the bartender who was standing behind the wooden horseshoe shaped bar trying to look busy. He walked to a stool at the far edge of the bar, ordered a beer and sat down. The bartender brought him his beer and placed it in front of him. He didn't talk to his customer; he knew that the man ordering the beer was not there for conversation so he kept quiet and picked up the five dollar bill that lie wrinkled on the bar. He brought back the change and left his only patron alone by himself.

This was his second Saturday night in Montana and he was sitting on his favorite stool at Mully's. He had ordered his eleventh beer or was it his tenth or maybe his twelfth; he had lost track after finishing his sixth but he was having a good time. He was thinking of Harmony. *Who did she think she was trying to be all uppity and Christian-like with me? Lin Su, now that was a woman. Do anything I asked and didn't ask why. Not Harmony, oh no, she had to know why I believed the way I did and why I did the things I did, she was a pain in the ass.* His thoughts were interrupted - by someone trying to get his attention.

"Hey buddy, where'd you get all those tattoos?"

CHAPTER 15

It was mid-autumn and that meant that the days were getting shorter, the nights longer and the weather cooler. They attended the burial at The Good Shepard cemetery and drove back to the church. The ladies guild had prepared a warm meal for all those in attendance; the lure of homemade food attracted both detectives. They had been invited to stay for lunch at the fellowship hall of the church by Harmony's parents. They made a decision to stay and would make the return trip to Milrose in the dark. They were both a little embarrassed by the amount of food they ate but there was plenty to go around and they didn't want any of it to go to waste. It was their reasoning and it excused their gluttony but they hadn't eaten a meal that good in years. Friends and relatives of the Day family had contributed most of the food and even with the help of Detective Fairfield and Detective Carpenter there was more food on the tables than could ever be eaten. It always happened this way but leftovers somehow found their way to somebody's home or to the nearby homeless shelter or to a family in need. After eating the last forkful of apple pie Bob Carpenter looked at his watch - it was time to go. The sky had already darkened and they wouldn't be back in Milrose for another couple of hours. He motioned to Sally that it was time and she nodded her head in agreement. They said their good-byes to the people they had met and were gone. They were a mile from the station when the radio dispatcher called their unit. Sally instinctively grabbed the mike and answered "go ahead".

"We got an update on your NCIC check. Your person is in jail in Wolf Point, Montana, charged with attempted murder."

Sally acknowledged and put the microphone back in its cradle. "Looks like we're going to Montana, Bob."

Wolf Point was in the northwestern part of Montana and was the county seat of Roosevelt County. It was a small town, population 3,000, and bordered the Missouri River Valley; and this was where Pete Krueger went fishing each year. He was one of the two prime suspects in the murder of Harmony Ann Day and now a more permanent resident of Montana than he wanted to be.

"I don't have the budget to send you two to Montana. We've used up all our over-time allotment as it is with all this extra patrol at night trying to catch these burglars and your overtime on this murder case. Our budget ain't real big the way it is. I don't have any special contingency fund for this sort of thing."

"We need to interview him Chief; we think he's our killer. Can't you explain to the city fathers about this? They want this thing solved as bad as we do. They are getting calls from nervous women wondering if there is a serial killer on the loose and why hasn't anybody been caught yet. They don't like complaints from their constituents. I would think they would be more than happy to cooperate. You'd look pretty good in their eyes and the eyes of the public if an arrest was made," Detective Carpenter argued passionately. He didn't want this case lost because of a few dollars that were needed.

The Chief thought about this and looked at his newest detective. "Sally, I think I can talk the council into letting one person go but I don't think they'll agree on sending two of you. Can you handle the job?"

"Of course I can," she answered, firm in her belief that she was up to the challenge. "What about the BCA, do you think Agent Trimble could go? He has been a big help so far, knows the case well and he has had more experience interviewing murder suspects."

"Give him a call; the State always seems to have enough money for this sort of thing," the Chief answered thinking that it might be a good idea to have Trimble along. "While you're gone I hope our lieutenant here can solve these burglaries. We can't have the public lose confidence in our department and if we don't solve something soon my head is going to be on the chopping block and I am not going to be happy."

For economic reasons it was decided by the chief and the council that Detective Sally Fairfield and Special Agent Trimble would take the Amtrak to Wolf Point. The State of Minnesota would pick up the tab for Agent Trimble. The thirteen hour trip from St. Paul would be an overnighter but was the cheapest and best way to travel.

Detective Carpenter pulled his squad into the unloading zone in front of the St. Paul Amtrak terminal and stopped. Agent Trimble opened the back door, slid out and walked to the rear of the car. The trunk popped open as he neared it; he reached inside the trunk compartment and lifted two small pieces of luggage out and placed them on the sidewalk. Sally reached for her pancake shaped brown suitcase that was frayed on all sides and picked it up. She noticed that Agent Trimble's suitcase had a handle that he had extended so he could pull it on its built in wheels. It was a sparkling new burgundy piece of luggage with chrome wheels and a special side compartment for his slacks and sport coat so they wouldn't get wrinkled on the trip. Once the extension handle was pulled out he left the suitcase on the curb and walked over to the car and thanked Detective Carpenter for the ride. Sally Fairfield looked at her threadbare suitcase comparing it to the new one that Agent Trimble had set in front of her; she looked at her watch, it was almost ten-thirty. The train was scheduled for departure at eleven-fifteen p.m. They had forty-five minutes to check in. The train station wasn't busy and Sally guessed that check in would be no problem. She walked toward the front door, suitcase in her hand with Agent Trimble following close behind. Sally approached the ticket counter and handed both sets of tickets to the counter person and was given a boarding pass and directions to their gate. The train was beginning to board when they arrived. Detective Fairfield looked at her ticket and then at the numbered cars. They both walked to their car where she handed the tickets to the conductor and walked up the steps and onto the train. They had adjoining seats in coach class and were excited for the trip. Neither one had ridden on the Amtrak before but had anticipated a pleasant trip. They both would have liked separate sleeping compartments but knew with budget constraints that was out of the question. The seats were wide and comfortable, almost as good as first class in a plane. A reading light was above each passenger seat. The seats tilted back like a recliner with an extended leg rest, all designed to make the passenger as relaxed as possible. After getting comfortable Agent Trimble pulled a paperback novel from his carry-on and began to read. He noticed that his partner had fallen asleep. He hoped they would both be rested for the next day's interrogation.

The Amtrak Empire Builder chugged into Wolf Point at eleven forty-one the next morning. They ate a huge breakfast in the dining car, had their fair share of coffee and seemed alert enough for today's meeting with Peter Krueger. A uniformed deputy sheriff was waiting for them when they disembarked the train. "I'm Deputy Johnson, Sheriff Moore sent me to pick you guys up and bring you to the station."

Agent Fairfield watched the young deputy as he began loading their luggage in the trunk of the squad. After rearranging some wooden boxes he managed to find a place to set the luggage. He closed the trunk and opened the front passenger door and motioned for Sally to take a seat in the front with him. Agent Trimble opened the rear door and slid into the seat behind Detective Fairfield. The deputy took his seat behind the wheel, took off his Stetson hat, placed it on the seat next to him and began talking about Wolf Point, the Sheriff and law enforcement in general. He seemed eager to talk to someone in the same profession but from a different part of the country.

Sally eyed her host as he was talking and noticed his dark shiny hair and how it was combed back almost into a duck–tail, like something out of the fifties. She thought Brylcreem had gone out style a while ago but his hair looked kind of sexy with that little extra oil added to it. "Get much excitement out here?" she asked to make small conversation.

He turned to her and smiled. "Not like the big city with its murders and rapes and armed robbers. There's not much to do out here in the middle of nowhere although I think people drink a little more than they should so we have more bar fights and domestics than anything else. Fact is, this Krueger guy, that's the closest we've come to real serious felony out here for years."

"Beat him up bad huh?"

"Yep, the guys gonna' be in the intensive care unit for a while."

"Did you make the arrest, deputy?" Josh asked.

"Nope, Sheriff and two of his night deputies got him out at his camping site. He was passed out when they got there so they cuffed and dragged him into the squad and brought him right here to jail. Speaking of jail, folks, here we are."

The sheriff was sitting at his desk waiting for his two visitors. When they entered his office he got up from his seat, introduced himself and motioned for them to sit down. Sally took a seat in a large overstuffed green leather chair and Agent Trimble seated himself in a similar one next to hers. A small metal table sat between the chairs, a glass ashtray was sitting in the center of the round table.

Sally noticed the empty ashtray. "Can we smoke in here Sheriff?"

"Absolutely, we don't go by all them rules that the government seems to be throwing at us. We're a little more independent out here. Anyway smokin's not illegal."

Sally knew she was going to like the Sheriff right away. He was in his mid-fifties and his head was completely bald except for a small dark patch of hair that covered the side of his head. He had a gray mustache that seemed in contrast with the remaining dark hair on his head. There was a little pudginess to him but not much and he looked like he was an outdoorsman. His skin was tan and weathered. She could tell he was proud of his uniform and his job. The dark cherry desk in front of him was without clutter; the sign of an organized man and his uniform was pressed and fit as if it was tailored specifically for him.

"What can you tell me about Krueger?" Sally asked.

Sheriff Obed Moore folded his hands and looked at both of them. "Well he's one angry little shit and he's tougher than nails. Kicked the crap out of Joe Verchay and Joe's one big fella', over six foot three and about two hundred forty pounds. The whole thing happened in front of Mully's - that's a local bar - and it didn't take long either. The bartender says this Krueger guy has been coming in regular the last couple a weeks. Keeps to himself and don't talk much but drinks a lot of beer. Anyway this night he's had several beers already when this Joe Verchay comes in. Now Joe likes to cause a little trouble himself and he sees this little fella' sitting at the bar and he starts picking on him about his tattoos and before the bartender knew what happened the two of them are outside. When he gets outside he sees Joe lying on the ground and there's blood everywhere and this other guy, he's gone. The bartender knows where he's staying 'cause Krueger had told him earlier. Anyway we call for an ambulance and when they haul Joe away we head for his camp. We find him sleeping so we cuffed him and brought him in and threw him in jail and charged him with attempted murder. I haven't talked to him since I arrested him and he hasn't called anyone.

He's still in isolation and all he does all day long is pace back and forth in his cell. The guy's kind of creepy."

"Does he know we're coming, Sheriff?" Agent Trimble asked.

"Haven't told him. Thought the element of surprise might be a better thing with this one."

"Thanks Sheriff." Sally offered, anxious to see her suspect. "When can we talk to him?"

"I'll have my deputy take you to the interrogation room now and I'll have him brought to you."

The interrogation room was part of the cell block. The small room was 8 foot by 10 foot with block walls painted lime green. A gray metal table was in the middle of the room and bolted to the floor; on each end of the table was a gray metal chair also bolted to the floor. An overhead camera moved slowly to the right and then to the left, viewing the entire room. It was in a shell of bullet proof glass and everything that went on the room was recorded and filed.

The prisoner stood in front of them. He was dressed in an orange jumpsuit that was at least two sizes too big for him. Handcuffs and leg cuffs constricted his movements. He glared at the man and the woman who were seated at the table waiting for him. He did not talk; he would wait for them to start first. He knew enough about cops by now that the less you said, the better off you were. He was as Sally had pictured him to be – short, wiry and tattooed, with a small earring in left ear. She guessed his height to be not more than five foot six and his weight at one hundred and thirty five pounds. His brown hair was cut short, almost to the skin. A small goatee protruded from his lower chin. His eyes were as dark as a moonless night but they were also clear and as piercing as the shaolin sword that was thrust into Harmony Ann Day. Evil and hate emanated from his eyes as he tried to stare her down. He didn't acknowledge that there was anyone else in the room; he never once looked at Agent Trimble. His intent was to frighten the female cop, an easier prey than the man. His attention was on her and he smiled at her as he mentally undressed her.

Sally knew what was going through his mind as she got up from the table and asked him to take the seat that she had been occupying.

"Got a cigarette?" he coldly asked.

"Sit down and I'll give you one." Remembering the words of the Sheriff about smoking in the building she looked for an ashtray.

Not seeing one she thought they would use the tile floor as an ashtray and she would clean up afterwards. He sat down and she pulled two cigarettes from her pack and offered him one and took one for herself and put it in her mouth and lit it. She leaned over the table, extended her hand and offered him a light. He put the cigarette in his mouth, bent over the metal table and met Sally's extended hand and lit his cigarette from her lighter.

"This is Special Agent Josh Trimble from the Minnesota Bureau of Criminal Apprehension and I'm Detective Sally Fairfield from the Milrose Police Department. We are going to read you your rights now and would like to ask you a few questions." She waited for a hint of emotion and not detecting any she read him his rights. He nodded his head that he understood his rights and Sally wondered why she had to keep reading these rights to scumbags like him who knew the Miranda warning backwards and forwards. She knew that if she didn't read him his rights the case would more than likely be thrown out of court. She would always be perplexed as to why the criminal was always treated more like a victim than the criminal that he was. Peter Krueger couldn't deny that his rights were read to him as the camera had recorded the whole thing. Even his nodding was acceptable to the courts that he understood his rights. "Do you know why we are here?"

"No" he calmly answered and took a deep drag from his cigarette.

"It's about Harmony Ann Day."

He looked at the detective, remained silent and circled the room with his eyes. He wanted her to know that he was bored with this line of questioning.

"She's dead."

Still nothing. She thought she detected a slight smile from one corner of his mouth but wasn't sure. One thing she knew was that she did not much care for the man sitting across from her.

"She was murdered, impaled on a wall resembling the crucifixion of Christ."

He was emotionless and extended his middle finger to the camera that was watching him.

"After her murder, you skipped town and came here. That looks a little suspicious to us and we think you might have had something to do with it."

He took another cigarette from the pack that the detective had left on the table. "Got a light?" he leaned into the lighter that Sally Fairfield hesitantly offered him and after having lit his cigarette settled back into this chair. "You ain't got nothin' on me; if you did you would have arrested me. Me and her, we were like oil and water. I don't know what I seen in her except for she was a good looking chick and that was all. No personality, all she talked about was religion and that drove me nuts. When I got back to Minnesota I was gonna' look her up and dump her. I sure as hell didn't kill her. I mean, what for - why would I kill her?"

"Tell me about your shaolin sword."

Peter Krueger stared at her; his cold eyes piercing and evil. "What do you mean?"

"We know you're into it. Have been for quite some time. Martial arts, shaolin, self defense and all that stuff. Where's your shaolin sword? S'pose somebody stole it huh?" Sally arose from her chair and walked over to him, staring at him intently. She leaned down and in a soft voice whispered. "Tell me about it you little piece of crap." She crossed her arms and continued staring at him.

"Somebody did steal it. Honest," he answered defensively.

"And how did that happen, Mr. Krueger?"

"I was in Milrose, took Harmony down to the college 'cause she had some things she had to do there. I dropped her off at the college and then I went to a bar and had a few beers. I had this sword in my car but I didn't notice it missing until the next day. The sword was gone but the sheath was still there."

"Where was this sword?"

"Lying in the back seat, I mean anyone could have taken it; the car was unlocked."

"So why would they take the sword out and leave the sheath?"

Pete Krueger dropped his cigarette on the tile floor and smashed it out with his prison slippers. "This interview's over. I think I want an attorney."

The two detectives glanced at each other. They knew that they would have to end the interview. They did not want to take any chances screwing up their case, especially with the prime suspect. As the detectives were about to leave the deputy sheriff entered the interrogation and informed their suspect there was a phone call for him. He walked into the next room with the deputy sheriff and picked up the receiver.

"Hey Hezekiah, how did you know I was here?"

CHAPTER 16

The Clinton boarding house was a clapboard affair that easily distinguished itself from the other structures nearby because of its fresh paint job and immaculately manicured lawn. It was one of the tallest and largest buildings in town with three floors and covering a full quarter acre of land. Occupying the first floor was a small restaurant that served three meals a day and was open from six in the morning until eight at night. Next to it was a lounge that specialized in beer, wine and other spirits to whet the palate. This was the social gathering place of those that had reached middle age and was busy most evenings. It was closed on the Sabbath and would remain that way as long as Mrs. Clinton owned the building. A large red woolen rug with a gold border covered the wood floor in the waiting room which was next to the cocktail lounge. Red leather chairs and a red leather couch were available for patrons, whether they were waiting to check in or perusing the day's paper. An enormous brick fireplace faced the red leather furniture and a pleasant warmth radiated from the dry wood that had recently been placed in it. A lone elevator awaited any new guest that checked in and was located between the lounge and the red leather couch. The elevator was an addition brought on by the Americans with Disabilities act. Of course you could take the stairs to your second floor room or your third floor room if you were so inclined but most people took the elevator.

A snowstorm was in the making when Detective Fairfield and Agent Trimble arrived back at the Clinton Bed and Breakfast. Visibility had been reduced to a quarter mile as the snow thickened and the wind picked up. The ground was covered with white and the austere trees began to collect snow on their branches. They exited the Sheriff's vehicle and thanked the deputy for the ride. The house looked inviting and cozy to Agent Trimble as he noticed the fresh coat of yellow paint on the building and the white picket fence that surrounded the entire house. They huddled hurriedly to the front door, one hand carrying their luggage, the other free to hold the lapels of their jackets tight around their necks. They opened the enormous front oak door and immediately felt the warmth that generated from the fireplace.

They walked up to the small check-in area and registered and received two adjoining rooms on the third floor. "Just a moment," the clerk said as she turned and picked up an envelope from her desk and handed it to Sally. "This is from the Sheriff; he e-mailed it to me a couple of minutes ago."

Sally opened the letter and looked at Josh. "Krueger's been appointed an attorney and we can meet with them tomorrow morning at eleven o'clock."

"Well Detective Fairfield looks like you can sleep in tomorrow morning."

She looked at Josh and knew what he was thinking. *If we can sleep in tomorrow we can have some beer tonight and there is a bar right here so we don't even have to leave the building.* "Want to have a few beers tonight Josh and enjoy our last night in the wide open spaces before returning to the real world?"

"Splendid idea Fairfield, I wish I had thought of it myself."

****

The storm had intensified overnight. Three inches of snow had accumulated on the ground and the winds had fiercely attacked Wolf Point with gusts up to fifty miles an hour. It was seven o'clock in the morning and Special Agent Josh Trimble had finished breakfast and was downing his last cup of coffee. He stared out the restaurant window and seeing nothing but white he returned to his newspaper hoping that Detective Fairfield would come to the restaurant and join him although he guessed that she would not show up until nine. He finished the newspaper and his coffee, paid the bill, left a generous tip and returned to his room. At eight-thirty his phone rang; it was Sally wondering if he would care to join her for breakfast at nine-fifteen. He told her that he'd already eaten but would meet her at the restaurant and join her for a cup of coffee.

He had beaten Sally to the restaurant and was smoking a Camel cigarette, enjoying another coffee and staring out the window when Detective Fairfield arrived. She spotted him immediately and walked over to his table pulled out a chair and sat down. "You can smoke here?" she asked, still astounded that there were places left where one could enjoy a cigarette with her coffee.

"Yes" he answered and pointed to the sign above the cash register. In bold italic print it advised that this was a smoker friendly restaurant.

She reached in her purse, pulled out a pack of cigarettes, laid them on the table, took one out and lit it. She inhaled deeply and enjoyed the feeling it gave her. "How should we approach Krueger today?" she asked.

"That's up to you; you did a great job yesterday so I think I will let you take the lead again today."

She looked at Agent Trimble, digesting what he had said. Coming from him that was a compliment. She knew he meant it and she felt confident that she was handling the investigation well. He was dressed immaculately as always and wondered how he had found an entire new wardrobe in the small suitcase he had brought along. His tanned skin seemed out of place in Wolf Point but it made him even more attractive than he was. "Well, he's got his attorney with him today so I don't know what direction that's going to take us. I think I'll talk as if we are accusing him, let him wonder what we really have on him. Let him know we think we know he is the killer and give him just enough facts in the case that Krueger and his attorney will think we have enough for an indictment. We don't of course, but they don't know that."

"Sounds like a good approach to me, as soon as you finish your breakfast we should get over to the Sheriff's office and meet with him before we start talking to Krueger."

The meeting with Krueger was held in a different room than the one they had used yesterday. The gray berber carpeting smelled new and there was a fresh coat of dull algae green paint on the walls. A five foot wooden kitchen table with six wooden chairs surrounding it sat in the middle of the room. A coffee pot was sitting on a small push cart near the table and a fresh brewed pot of coffee awaited them. A camera hung from the upper corner above a kitchen cabinet and monitored whatever happened in the room. The small lunch room was separated from the cell blocks and was used mostly by jail personnel for their breaks. The space doubled as an interrogation room and Agent Trimble, Detective Fairfield and Krueger's court appointed attorney were seated at the table making small talk when the prisoner entered the room escorted by a jailer. He stopped suddenly and fixed his eyes on Detective Fairfield while he waited for the shackles to be removed from his wrists and his ankles. When his hands ands his legs were free he took a seat next to his attorney.

Sally looked at the young attorney wondering how good he was. She had been up against dozens of them in court. Some were excellent, most were average and a few were just plain incapable of putting together any kind of defense and sometimes she felt herself feeling sorry for the poor defendant. Her first impressions of people were usually right on. *He's just a snot nose kid, this is probably his first case and he wants to make an impression on the court. He's going to act the hotshot and bring up his client's constitutional rights over and over again. He's going to be a pain in the butt just like his client.*

The attorney returned the smile to Detective Fairfield. After his client was seated he addressed the two law enforcement officers. "I'm John Bauer and I will be representing Mr. Krueger on the charges facing him from the State of Montana. He has asked me to attend this interview and he states that you are trying to implicate him in a murder in Minnesota. Is that so?"

"We're in the investigative stage only Mr. Bauer. The reason why we are here talking to your client is that he was the boyfriend of the victim Harmony Day. We only want to ask him some questions that may help our investigation and also clear Mr. Krueger if he wasn't involved. Would you like us to read him his rights again? He was read them yesterday and acknowledged that he understood them." Sally queried.

"We can dispense of the rights, my client advised me that he was read his rights yesterday and that will suffice. Mr. Krueger seems to think that after talking to you yesterday that you were accusing him and that is why he has asked for an attorney."

"Your client wasn't very cooperative yesterday which immediately makes us suspicious. His actions were those of a guilty person," Sally answered

The young attorney ignored the comment. "You may begin your questioning but be aware that I may direct my client to not answer your questions or I may end this interview any time I want."

"We understand your concerns counselor but we hope to get this matter cleared up before we return to Minnesota."

"Please proceed," the attorney replied as he pulled out a yellow legal pad from his shiny new briefcase.

Sally took control of the interview like her partner had suggested and was confident that she would be able to extract enough information from Peter Krueger to keep the investigation alive. With him as the prime suspect she didn't want to screw up the investigation by making a blunder in her interrogation of him. She noticed his demeanor had changed from yesterday. He was calmer, surer of himself and more polite than he had been the previous day. "Mr. Krueger, Harmony Day was killed on the Saturday night before you went to Montana. Can you tell us where you were that night?"

"I was with my real girlfriend."

"Does she have a name?"

"Yea."

"What is it?" Sally asked, matter-of-factly. Her eye contact was steady and fixed as she stared down the prisoner. He needed to know that she was in control of the interview and not him.

"Lin Su."

"Tell me a little about Lin Su." Sally remembered the brief encounter she and Detective Carpenter had with his girlfriend. She had been very uncooperative at the time and Sally wanted to learn as much about Krueger's other girlfriend as she could.

"Nothin' to tell."

Sally stared at her suspect and he glared back at her defiantly. "Listen you little shit, we're trying to get some answers here that could maybe help you. We've got enough evidence right now to get a murder indictment. Make it easy on yourself or hard on yourself, your choice, but I am not going to put up with your bullshit."

"Ahem," the young attorney interrupted. "I will not allow you to talk to my client that way. If you continue with your character assassinations I will end this interview right away."

"Your client is not being cooperative and you know it. Either you convince him to cooperate with us or we walk and proceed with getting an indictment."

The attorney backed off and nodded to his client that he should answer the question.

"Lin Su lives with me in Minneapolis. We have been together for over a year. She's twice my age but we hit it off pretty good. Better than I did with Harmony. She'll back up my story that I was with her."

"Did anyone else see you two together that night?"

"No, but we had a pizza delivered that night and I paid the delivery boy for the pizza. There is got to be some record of that you can check on."

"What time was that?"

"About nine o'clock."

"That's all fine and dandy but Harmony was killed about four in the morning which would give you plenty of time to have your pizza, drive to Milrose and kill Harmony and then return to your apartment and get ready for your trip here."

For the first time during the interview Peter Krueger got nervous, a drop of perspiration trickled down his forehead and onto his nose. Sally noticed the tiny droplet and felt more confident that they were interviewing the right guy. She brought out a photo from her briefcase and placed it on the table in front of the prisoner.

"Does this look familiar?"

"Why should it?" he answered.

Sally felt he was now on the defensive and wanted to keep it that way. "Because it's yours. Harmony Day was stabbed with this and it's got your fingerprints on it. So we know that you knew Harmony Day and you hadn't got along with her very well in the last week or so and that she didn't want to see you anymore. And now we got the murder weapon that belongs to you with your prints on it. So I figure that I ain't going to have no trouble getting an arrest warrant."

Peter Krueger, nervous and agitated leaned over to his attorney and whispered into his ear. The attorney looked at the two interrogators. He was surprised at the evidence that was presented to his client and he wondered what more there was that he did not know about. "I'd like to speak to my client alone. If you two could leave the room for a few minutes, I will call you when we are done."

Sally and Josh agreed to the request and left the room. They went to the squad room and each lit up a cigarette, put a quarter in the coffee machine and watched the thick black coffee drip into their respective cups. "We should have grabbed some coffee in the interrogation room, it smelled fresher than this stuff," Sally commented as she pulled her full cup from the machine.

"That was pretty gutsy telling him that we knew the sword was his and that his fingerprints were on the weapon," Josh said as he sat down in one of the orange plastic ergonomically designed molded chairs and placed his coffee cup on the table in front of him.

"Nothing in the law says you can't tell a little lie to get the information you need."

"What if it wasn't his sword? He would know we were only bluffing and that you had nothing on him."

"I know it was a hell of a gamble but I felt it was worth taking. If it doesn't work we'll just have to try harder to get the evidence we need."

Josh was contemplating the interview that had taken place. If Sally was right it would be a big break in the case. He liked her approach to Krueger and was impressed with her abilities. A deputy sheriff appeared in the coffee room and advised them that the attorney and his client were now ready to see them.

They entered the room, took a seat and waited for the attorney to make the first move. "My client admits that the sword in the picture is his but like he said yesterday the sword was stolen from his car. He knows who took it though."

Pete Krueger interrupted his attorney, looked at Detective Fairfield. His cold assessing eyes made her uneasy. "I know who your killer is."

"Who is it?" she asked, staring back at him.

"Not so fast missy. I'm in a bargaining position here. If I give you the name then I want some assurances for me. First, I want the charges dropped against me in Montana. I want to get the hell out of this town as fast as I can. And second, I don't want to testify against this person. He's bad news; he'd kill me if he knew."

"How do we know you're telling us the truth?"

"I'll give you the evidence you need. Enough to prove it."

Sally was not expecting to hear this when she walked into the room. She wasn't sure if he was lying or if he really did know who the killer was. She didn't want to jeopardize the case by being too anxious to accept the offer. He could still be the killer and probably was. It had become apparent to both of them that the prisoner did not have a lot of experience dealing with law enforcement and they would try and use that to their advantage. He knew he was in trouble in Montana and Minnesota and he needed an out any way he could get one. "I'll talk to the Sheriff about what you just told us, but to be honest, I doubt if he is going to go for it unless your information proves right."

He was confident, feeling that he had gained the upper hand. Knowing that at least one of his demands might be met; he quickly developed a feeling of authority and power. "Go talk to the Sheriff now. The sooner I can get out of this hell hole the better I'll feel."

Sally stayed with the attorney and his client while Agent Trimble left the room to talk to the Sheriff. He returned in a half an hour and advised Peter Krueger that the Sheriff would agree to his terms if he could prove beyond a doubt who the real killer was.

"I need that in writing," the young attorney answered without hesitation. "It's not that I don't trust the Sheriff but we would both feel better if it was documented."

"The Sheriff is putting it in writing as we speak, but let me stress that this information must be correct and that it's enough information for us to get an arrest warrant."

The attorney was about to answer Special Agent Trimble when a deputy brought in a piece of legal paper and handed it to the attorney. He read it and nodded to his client.

Peter Krueger was wringing his hands in anticipation that he would get out of this situation and be headed for Minnesota in a very short time. "Hezekiah Hadley's your killer."

"Tell us all about it Mr. Krueger" Sally was excited but cautious with what she had just heard. Hezekiah Hadley was the other suspect in Harmony's murder and she was curious what Mr. Krueger had to say about it.

"Hadley's been nuts over this girl. She didn't care about him one hoot but she thought she could get him straightened out, you know, get him headed in the right direction. She didn't know Hadley like I did. He's crazy and there ain't nobody gonna' change him. Anyway, she spent a lot of time with him, working with him, trying to convert him. He played along with her 'cause he liked her and he wanted her. He tried to make advances on her but she always pushed him off. He was getting frustrated by her and told me that if she didn't come around he was going to kill her. I think he's killed before but I'm not sure. Anyway I know he is capable of it. Every time he was with her he was more crazy for her and also more angry 'cuz she wanted nothing to do with him and for sure didn't want any kind of romantic relationship with him. He knew I had this sword and he was google-eyed over it, he wanted one just like it, said he needed it for something. I always had it in my car and one day when I was down in Milrose with Harmony I had the sword in the back seat of my car and after I left Harmony I got in my car and noticed that the sword was missing. I knew it had to be Hadley that took it. I never seen it since."

"That's it, that's all you've got, that's not enough for an arrest warrant. That's hearsay; no county attorney is going to get an arrest warrant with that information." Sally looked at the defendant and closed her notebook. "You're wasting our time Krueger, we're going to go now."

The suspect wanted the get out of jail free card that was lying in front of his attorney and he felt it slipping away. "Wait there is more. Hezekiah's the one that has been committing all those burglaries around Milrose. He was stealing only items for a murder, items that he needed to kill her. That's all he would take, he would leave everything else and that's why a lot of those places that got burglarized couldn't account for anything being taken. If there was some petty cash around he would take that but nothing more than he needed for this murder he was planning."

"How do you know all this?"

"Cuz me and Hezzy are buds, we hung out together when I came to Milrose. He told me about the burglaries and told me that he planned to kill somebody. Now I know he meant Harmony."

"But he didn't say he wanted to kill Harmony, right?"

"No, but who else could he mean?"

"That is not enough Mr. Krueger, I need him to tell you he killed Harmony, can you get him to say that?"

"I ain't gonna' do that, I ain't no stool pigeon. I told you what you wanted now I want out of here now or we'll sue, that's right we'll sue. We got a piece of paper promising to let me go. We'll sue won't we Mr. Bauer."

His attorney did not answer him; the room was silent waiting for his next move. He took his time and stared at each person in the room before he pushed the chair away from the table and got up; he kicked the chair over and walked to the door. "Get me out of here; you're all a bunch of dinks."

"Mr. Bauer, you got yourself one hell of a client. Now we got this shaolin sword with Krueger's fingerprints on it. The sword was rammed through the body of Harmony Ann Day. We know when the murder happened and your client can't really account for his whereabouts at the time of the murder except to say he was with his girlfriend Lin Su, whose reputation may be somewhat dubious. He was Ms. Day's boyfriend at the time of the murder and they weren't getting along well. They were arguing a lot and he's got quite a temper, eleven priors in fact. Now Mr. Bauer, don't you think that a judge might issue a warrant on that evidence?"

The young attorney looked at his client standing at the door and turned to Detective Fairfield. "I don't think I have enough experience to handle this kind of case yet. I am going to recommend that the courts find someone more suitable for Mr. Krueger." The young attorney said and opened his briefcase, placed the papers that he had laying on the table into it, closed it and asked Detective Fairfield to call the Sheriff and tell him that Mr. Krueger is ready to go back to his cell and that our interview is over for now.

Sally reached toward the wall and pressed the intercom button and announced that they were through for now. Two deputies promptly arrived and placed handcuffs and leg shackles on the prisoner and led him away. "We are going to tell the Sheriff that his offer to Krueger is void, all his information is hearsay and wouldn't even be allowed in court much less at an evidentiary hearing," Sally told the attorney as she followed him out of the room.

He stopped and looked at Detective Fairfield, "I know, he's going to face charges here and I am guessing he will be resting comfortably in his jail cell for quite some time. One good thing, you'll know where to find him if you need to."

CHAPTER 17

They both agreed there wasn't much more that they could accomplish in Wolf Point. Sally called the Amtrak station and booked the return trip to Minnesota. Their suspect wasn't going anyplace soon. They informed the Sheriff they would be leaving, and thanked him for his help. A deputy gave them a ride to the Clinton Boarding house where they checked out and prepared for the long ride back to St. Paul. They called Chief Rowlands and informed him of their arrival time and waited for the Empire Builder to arrive in Wolf Point. They had two hours to kill before the train arrived and both decided that a beer would taste good while they waited. They found a cocktail lounge in the terminal entered, took a seat at the bar and each ordered a beer.

The return trip was uneventful. Agent Trimble and Detective Fairfield had both decided, unbeknownst to each other that they would forget about the case on the train ride and enjoy the scenery, catch some shut-eye, read their books and engage in some small talk. They would clear their minds for the time being and arrive in St. Paul refreshed. Sally was seated near the window and she was half dozing and half looking at the scenery as it passed at sixty miles per hour. She liked Agent Trimble; she thought she might have a slight crush on him she thought to herself. She turned sideways and looked at him; he was reading and paying no attention to her or the scenery as it whizzed by. The same thoughts came back to her, *what was wrong with her, why couldn't she find a man like Trimble or for that matter Bob Carpenter. The good ones seem to have been all taken, or were they? Carpenter was widowed with no children and Trimble wasn't married. Was Josh divorced, did he have a girlfriend? She would have to find out, maybe let him know that she might be interested in him.* Those thoughts vanished as fast as they came as the porter came by to ask if they wanted anything to drink. She ordered a Coke and Agent Trimble declined; he was too engrossed in the book he was reading. The porter returned and handed her the soda she had ordered, she thanked him, took a small sip, set it on the tray in front of her and looked at Agent Trimble. "Josh."

"Yes" he answered, closing his book and looking at her.

"Got a girlfriend?" she asked, her hands clammy and warm. She was uneasy asking the question and hoped that Josh wouldn't think she was getting too personal.

"Yea, been seeing a young lady named Marcie. I met her when I was working on the murders in Bishop. She's a nice lady and we get along well. She understands my job and the hours involved and she accepts it."

"Ever been married?"

"Oh yeah, but that didn't work out well. Everything was fine in our marriage until I joined the Milrose Police Department and that's when all hell broke loose. She was working days and as a rookie cop I was working a lot of three to elevens, we never saw each other and she did not like that. She wanted a little excitement in her life, you know, going out to nice restaurants, see some plays, take in a couple of movies a week, stuff like that. She gave me an ultimatum, quit the police force or get a divorce. I chose the divorce and we actually split up on amicable terms. She moved to Las Vegas a couple of years ago and I hear she is doing well for herself. Luckily, there were no children. I would have probably quit the force to save the marriage if there were kids involved."

Sally took another sip of her Coke. *Well there goes another one. One of these days I will find a guy, I know it. I'm 28 years old, I don't want to end up an old maid but I don't want to get desperate either.*

"How about you Sally, got a boyfriend?"

She looked at him and didn't know how to answer that question. She had not expected it and was caught off guard as she blurted out "NO."

"Really, you're a good looking woman, nice features, and great personality. You'd be a real find for the right guy."

"Thanks, but I haven't had much luck finding the right guy."

"You know what the problem is don't you?"

"Not really," she said, thinking that finally she would find out what was wrong with her. *All of her girlfriends were married; she was the only woman in her entire high school class that wasn't married yet. It had to be her and now she would find out.*

"You're a cop. Most guys are afraid of cops whether they admit it or not. The hours are horrendous for raising children and being a wife and what husband wants his wife going to work wearing a nine millimeter and a bullet proof vest. And then factor in your husband doesn't know if you will be coming home from work at the end of the day because you have been killed in the line of duty."

"I never thought of that. Just a job to me. I wouldn't quit though, I found something I love to do and I wouldn't give that up." *So that's it. Makes sense to me.*

CHAPTER 18

Bob Carpenter and Chief Rowlands were parked curb side in the loading and unloading zone of the Amtrak terminal waiting for Sally and Josh to show up. Bob had checked with one of the front desk personnel - the train was on time and had pulled into the station a few minutes ago. Agent Trimble and Detective Fairfield walked outside into the brisk twenty degree weather and noticed Bob Carpenter's squad. The coolness felt good. The air in the train had become stuffy and the terminal wasn't much better. They noticed Chief Rowlands sitting on the passenger side and the trunk open. They put their luggage in the trunk and each of them slid into the back seat from opposite sides.

"How was the trip?" Chief Rowlands asked, turning around to face his passengers in the back seat.

"Very interesting sir," Sally answered. "I think Krueger's our guy. We may have to go back to Wolf Point some time in the future when we get more evidence against him. I think we should take what we have to the judge and get a search warrant for his apartment. I think we have enough probable cause for that and I am hoping that we find enough there to make an arrest."

"Sounds good to me," the Chief answered, satisfied that some progress was being made in the case. "You know Sally, we are getting a lot of flack from the news media and the people in Milrose. They're getting a little nervous about the rash of burglaries and then this murder. We've got to come up with something soon. Bob's had no luck with the burglaries; he can't seem to find anything to connect either Markham or Hadley to the burglaries and he's beginning to think there is a new burglar working the area."

Sally reached out and tapped her partner on the shoulder. "Bob, I may have a lead on our burglar. Krueger says it's Hezekiah Hadley. Says he is stealing items from the stores that he needs to do a killing he has planned. Krueger says he is planning on murdering somebody soon but he doesn't know who it is. Krueger seems afraid of him."

"He said that?" Bob asked, jerking his head to the right to eye Sally.

"Yeah. He was trying for a get out of jail free card by giving us that information. It didn't work, we don't even know if it is true."

"We've been keeping a close eye on Hadley. I've had the guys on patrol write in their reports whenever they see Hadley and where. Nothing that he does would indicate that he's our guy. Of course they could have missed him somehow. All the burglaries are occurring between two-thirty and four in the morning and there is nothing in the reports of any of our boys seeing him around those hours. Either he is getting better at what he does or our guys are going blind."

The squad car pulled in front of Sally's two bedroom home and she got out, grabbed her weathered suitcase from the trunk and said her goodbyes. She was refreshed from her train trip and the short drive from St. Paul to Milrose brought her thoughts back to reality. She unlocked the front door, turned on the living room lights and checked the house. Satisfied that everything was as it should be she changed into her pajamas, sat on her couch and turned on the television. She hadn't seen any television since she left on her trip and thought she would catch up on some news.

At three o'clock in the morning she woke up from the couch wide awake. She walked to the kitchen and started a pot of coffee and when it was brewed she poured herself a cup, sat down at the kitchen table and mulled over the case once again. *Could Hezekiah Hadley be the murderer? Maybe Krueger was telling the truth. She would have to check the burglary reports and see if any square peg nails had been stolen from any business. And the latex gloves, what about them? There was the burglary at Milrose Drug, they would certainly carry latex gloves. She would go over the reports with Bob tomorrow. Could Hadley have stolen the items he needed to commit this murder? If Krueger didn't kill her, was his sword stolen like everything else used in the murder? Two suspects? Well, better than none.*

While Sally was at her kitchen table contemplating the murder of Harmony Ann Day, Nathan Brown was at his kitchen table stoned on marijuana and beer. Today was his day off and he was going to have some fun this morning. When he got in this mood he thought of the years he spent at the juvenile detention center. He hated being there and he hated the other boys even more. His beatings were severe and several times he had been taken to the infirmary for treatment. He got up and went to the refrigerator and pulled out another beer. He knew he liked to murder, it gave him a feeling of power over people that he otherwise would never have. *He knew that he had enjoyed killing the little girl but the last one, that was his best. He had planned it for weeks and when it was over he felt good. He would never be caught again, he was too smart for that. He had learned a lot at the detention center. But who would be his next victim he wondered?* He finished half his beer and passed out on the kitchen table. A couple of hours later he woke up, stumbled onto his bed and slept for several more hours. He woke up groggy and with a hangover but the thoughts of the night before both haunted and excited him. He was going to start plans for his next adventure and with his knowledge of pathology instruments it would be a good adventure.

CHAPTER 19

Bob Carpenter loved basketball. He was the center for his high school basketball team and because of his extraordinary talent he led his team to the divisional championship as a senior but the team lost their first game in the state tournament and his high school basketball career was over. When he was in the middle of his senior year he was offered a full scholarship to play basketball at Brigham Young University. He'd had several offers but BYU was his first choice and he gladly accepted their offer. He never excelled on the court like he would have liked and never made it off the second team. The competition for first string at BYU was tough and he was not as good as first stringers. He couldn't complain though, his tuition had been paid for and he was at Brigham Young. Bob Carpenter was a good Mormon. Prior to his sophomore year he served a two year mission in Brazil and when he was finished he returned to his education at BYU. After graduation he joined the Marine Corps and was assigned to the military police. After his stint was over, he applied for a job at the Milrose Police Department. He was the first applicant they had with both a college degree and a military background. He was twenty-eight years old and ready to start a career. He had wanted to continue in law enforcement and use the skills he had learned in the Corps. Law enforcement offered job security, a decent salary and good retirement. After his rookie year he met and married a Mormon girl and bought a house. They had both wanted children, lots of them, but it wasn't to be. A year into their marriage his wife was killed in a car accident. She was visiting some friends from church in the county outside of Milrose. As she was driving down the country road that would take her to her destination a semi blew a stop sign and sideswiped the car killing his wife instantly. It was a difficult time for Bob Carpenter and his mother and father-in-law and everyone in Milrose. The Carpenters were well liked in town and everyone showed up for the funeral and to pay their respects. Bob's devout faith carried him through the tragedy as he entered the world of being single once again.

It was ten-thirty in the morning. Detective Carpenter looked at his watch and gazed at the entrance to the Horn Inn. He was sitting in one of the five booths along the wall of the restaurant waiting for his partner. Only two other customers were in the restaurant beside him. He had offered to buy her breakfast this morning to thank her for the tip on the burglaries and he hoped her information would help clear them up and put Hezekiah back behind bars. Sally walked into the restaurant at ten thirty-five, spotted her partner, walked to his booth and slid in the opposite side. Without saying a word she picked up the menu in front of her and opened it. She knew it by heart but still scrutinized it thinking that there might be something that would appeal to her hunger besides the number four - two eggs, hash browns, meat, toast and coffee. Nothing caught her fancy so she decided to have the number four once again. "Are you a Christian?" she asked, putting down her menu and looking at him.

"Wow, no good morning, just, are you a Christian. I was expecting a little more than that considering I am buying your breakfast."

"Sorry, good morning Detective Carpenter. I am a little off this morning, I have decided to quit smoking and I am a little bit on edge right now."

He smiled thinking that it was about time. "I'm glad to hear that Sally. What brought this change of heart on? I figured you for a die hard smoker, that you'd never quit."

The waitress came to the booth and both detectives ordered their usual. Sally was quiet until her cup of coffee arrived and took her first taste of the caffeine she so dearly needed. "When I was in Wolf Point I smoked a lot. When I got back my lungs hurt bad and I decided that maybe I better try and quit. This is the first time I have tried so I don't know what to expect. I do feel kind of edgy and my temper is a little short but I hope that passes. You are lucky you never started. I wish I hadn't; I started when I was sixteen. My girlfriends all smoked and I wanted to fit in. I smoked before school, during lunch break and after school. It didn't take long and I was hooked. I think the hardest times for me will be when I drink coffee or alcohol. I can do it. If I set my mind to do something I do it, but it is going to be a battle."

The food had arrived and Bob Carpenter poured syrup on his breakfast and took a bite of his French toast, savoring it for the moment. "Thanks for the tip on Hezekiah. It all makes sense. I don't know how our guys missed him. I checked their logs and compared them to the nights of the burglaries and there is no mention of Hezekiah Hadley being seen. You would have thought that at least once in the span of four months when the burglaries were being committed that he would have been seen. I think if we can get him this time that the judge will be finally be fed up with him and his burglaries and send him to prison. He needs prison and the town needs for him to be in prison."

"I think the information is good, I think Krueger knows him very well and was willing to fink on him to get out of jail. Hadley is sure capable of burglarizing. He ain't the brightest guy in the world but if it is him, he is a good burglar."

"Why did you want to know if I was a Christian? Where did that come from?"

"Well you know that our murder victim was killed to resemble the crucifixion of Christ and we know that there is something significant in the way she was killed. I just thought that being a Christian you might be able to shed some light on that."

"I've thought about it and there are a few possibilities but the one that keeps sticking in my mind is that our killer did not like Christians. He was mocking the religion and in his mind making some kind of a point and at the same time purging the world of one more Christian. That is only a guess but it deserves some consideration. It wouldn't hurt to do a background check on both Krueger and Hadley and see what their religious backgrounds are and how they were brought up. I don't know but I doubt if either one of them has ever set foot inside of a church but one of them knows a little bit about Christianity because they knew how to stage the murder scene."

"I'll do that, I'll find out if they were religious," Sally answered while finishing the last of her meal, "and thanks for the breakfast."

CHAPTER 20

Sally was in her office sitting at her desk and staring at the lime green, glossy concrete block wall in front of her. She hated lime green and the fact that it was high gloss didn't help. It was depressing and she had once thought of coming into her office some night and repainting the whole thing a more earth tone and soothing color. Whoever picked this color scheme should be shot or at least punished in some severe manner, she thought. She was on her second day of not smoking and she was in the midst of the full effects of nicotine withdrawal. Her lungs hurt, her psychological dependence was in full bloom and her physical dependence was even worse. *Why the hell did I decide to quit now; we're right in the middle of a murder case and I should really wait until it is over before I quit. That's it, I'll quit when it's over. But no, I have already gone one day and that is more than I have ever done since I started smoking. NO, I am going to get through this day first and maybe tomorrow I'll smoke but not today.* The wall stared back at her and they watched each other for what seemed a long time. Sally had become lethargic and wondered how long it would take before the symptoms started to abate. She worried that her resolve would weaken and that she would give into her cravings. She wondered how long the nicotine addiction would have a strangle hold on her. She would have to take it one hour at a time, not one day at a time. Whatever she had to do to make it work, she would do. She hadn't even looked at her desk and hadn't noticed the manila envelope sitting on the right corner addressed to her and her partner. It was from the Bureau of Criminal Apprehension and was unopened. She noticed it when she took her eyes off of the wall. She slowly opened it, not knowing what its contents were but hoping it had something to do with the Harmony Day case. She pulled five letter size pages out and read the heading on the first page. It was the toxicology reports and the lab reports on the Day case. The reports agreed with the autopsy reports. The victim was severely beaten before she was drowned. The water in her lungs was determined to be unrefined water. The chemical analysis and the list of foreign objects in the water indicated that the water was similar to that found in an animal trough. *So where was she killed? And, how was she taken to Cedar Park and why did the perp hang her up on the pavilion? What was the motive for her murder? All were questions that needed answering.* The information from the BCA was helpful, and answered some questions but also opened the door for many more questions. She would talk to her partner and Agent Trimble as soon as possible. She was sure that Agent Trimble had a copy of the report and had studied it thoroughly. She wondered when the three of them would get together when the overhead intercom crackled and the dispatcher informed her that Clayton Barnes was here to see her. *Oh great, she thought, what does Barnes want, doesn't he know I am busy. Didn't anybody know that she wasn't herself today so why was all this happening, couldn't she just have one peaceful day, no wonder she smoked. Anybody in this job would smoke. I suppose he wants to know how I am coming on the Harmony Day murder.* "Send him in," she replied to the speaker in the wall.

Clayton Barnes was the mayor of Milrose. He was well into his third term and was a very popular mayor. His genuine concern for the people of Milrose was evident and they felt good knowing he cared for them and their concerns. Clayton Barnes also owned the only real grocery store in the town. Milrose was growing and someday would be big enough to support a major supermarket or a super Wal-Mart. Clayton Barnes knew that when that day came, his retail days would be over. For now he would enjoy his status as the only grocery store in town. He walked into her office and sat down in one of the two folding chairs in front of her desk, "Good morning Detective, how are you today?"

"Okay, I guess, and how are you?"

"Just fine Sally, just fine. You look like you're tired. Are you getting enough sleep? I know this murder case is taking up a lot of time but you need your rest. By the way, how are you coming on the case?"

"Mayor, we're gathering new evidence everyday. We've got a couple of good suspects but just not enough to bring either of them in yet. The toxicology reports just came in so that's going to help us determine where she was killed. We know how she was killed but we don't know why."

"Well good luck and get some sleep, you look terrible."

"Mayor, to be frank with you I have been getting enough sleep, it's just that I am on my second day of not smoking and I am having a difficult time."

"I understand, went through it myself about twenty years ago. I still crave a cigarette every now and then. But listen, I didn't really come here to discuss the Day case; I wanted to talk about Mrs. Hadley. I think something is wrong. She usually comes in a couple of times a week and picks up a half gallon of milk and other small grocery items along with her cigarettes and vodka. I haven't seen her in over a week but her son Hezekiah has been in a couple of times for food. He doesn't say much, just charges it to his mother and leaves. Anyway, she's got these habits, she needs her cigarettes and her alcohol; for her to go this long without them makes me a little suspicious if she is okay or not. I was wondering if you could have someone check up on her and see if she is all right. I'd really appreciate it."

Sally informed the mayor that she would send a squad to the house and check on her and she would let him know what's going on. The mayor thanked her and left. She pushed the intercom button on her phone and asked the dispatcher to send a car out to the Hadley place and check on the welfare of Mrs. Hadley. She picked up her phone and dialed her partner's phone extension number. She wanted to tell him that she was sending a squad car out to check on Florence Hadley. She thought he might like to ride along. He might get lucky and spot something from the burglaries at the Hadley place. He wasn't in his office so she left a voice message for him.

It wasn't long after the call to her partner that her desk phone rang and it was her partner thanking her for the information and that he would be riding out to see Florence Hadley with Officer Thurgood. She relayed to her partner what the mayor had said and that he was worried about Mrs. Hadley. She told her partner that something seemed fishy out at the Hadley place and to please be careful. He said he would and that he would get back to her when they cleared from the Hadley place.

"Okay," she answered and slowly hung up the phone. She was wondering about what her partner might come up with at the Hadley place. She still considered Hezekiah Hadley a good suspect along with Peter Krueger in the murder of Harmony Day. Is it also possible that they were both involved in her murder?

****

Detective Carpenter and Officer Thurgood walked up the steps of the Hadley home, stood on the small front porch and knocked on the door. They knocked several times before it opened. Hezekiah recognized the two men in front of him and wished he had not opened the door. He thought about slamming the door in their faces but decided against it. He stood in the doorway looking at the officers and did not say a word.

"Is your mother home Hezekiah?" Officer Thurgood asked.

"Nope." He kept his response short and began closing the door when Detective Carpenter placed his foot in the doorway to prevent him from doing so. "Where is she Hezekiah? She hasn't been seen for a while and some people are worried that she might be sick or something. Just let us know where she is and we'll see for ourselves how she is and then we'll leave."

"She's fine, I'll tell her you stopped by and were concerned for her."

"Where is she? You can at least tell us that much."

"I don't know, she said she was going out. She didn't say where."

"No one has seen her for a while Hezekiah and that concerns us. When was the last time you saw her?"

"I don't know, maybe a week, maybe a little longer."

"And you weren't concerned that she has been gone that long?" Officer Thurgood asked.

"No."

The uniformed officer looked around the cluttered and unmowed yard and then at Hezekiah. "What kind of car does your mother drive?"

"An Oldsmobile, but I don't know what year. I gotta' go now." He looked at the foot that was still blocking the doorway preventing him from closing the door. "I said I got to go. Can you move your foot so I can close the door?"

Detective Carpenter did not move his foot and studied the young man with green hair standing on the other side of the door. *Hezekiah knew where his mother was. If something happened to her, he was going to find out before he left.* "Where's the car?"

"I think it's in the garage, I don't know, maybe she took it, I don't know."

"Can I go look in the garage?" the uniformed officer asked.

Hezekiah looked at him expressionless; the officer took a step back waiting for an answer. "What's it going to matter if we look in the garage?"

"Not without a warrant."

Detective Carpenter hadn't paid much attention to the young officers' reaction to Hezekiah. He was trying to sneak a look into the house. He hoped to see an item from one of the burglaries and he needed to see it in plain sight. They had more than one reason for being here and if he could just see something, anything, he would have enough for a search warrant. And there it was, on top of a small table next to the couch. An opened gray metal cash box was facing him, inside the box written on masking tape were the words PROPERTY OF SHEAR WORKS BEAUTY SALON. He remembered that box was part of the inventory of stolen items from the Shear Works burglary four months ago. He now had what he needed for a search warrant. And the next step was to see Judge Armstrong. Knowing that they were not going to get any cooperation out of Hezekiah the officers stated that they were leaving for now but they would continue looking for his mother. Detective Carpenter removed his foot and Hezekiah slammed the door.

CHAPTER 21

Judge Armstrong lived a bucolic existence. When not working at his office in the County Courthouse or presiding at the bench, he could be found on his forty acre farm tending to his vegetable garden, playing with his three black labs, working in the field or riding his horse, Simpson. He preferred being on the farm and away from civilization but he knew it was necessary for him to work so that he could enjoy the rural lifestyle while providing for his family. It hadn't always been like that; when he was still single he spent a lot of time in the bars and on the golf course. He liked the urban life style and never thought of any other way of life. The excitement and the fast paced lifestyle intrigued him and he loved it and wanted more of it until he met his future wife. She had introduced him to the pastoral lifestyle years ago when they were both freshmen in college and he had accepted it with some reluctance but he was crazy in love with her and he wanted to please her so he went along with her crazy ideas of a simpler life style. The more he experienced this new way of life the more he was beginning to enjoy it and wondered how he ever lived in his other world. They had met in college as freshmen, she wanted a career in earth sciences and he was planning for a career in law. They got married when they were juniors and after college she worked for the Minnesota Department of Conservation and provided for their personal and financial needs while he got his degree at the William Mitchell School of Law. After graduating he took a job with the county attorney's office and worked as a prosecuting attorney for several years. When Judge Abrams died, the Governor appointed him to fill the vacancy. He had been a District Court Judge for the last sixteen years.

He sat at his large and congested oak desk leaning back on his wooden swivel rocker that had been given to him by his father as a present when he graduated from law school. His shoeless feet were propped on the corner of the desk and in front of him were the two detectives that had requested to see him and who wanted a search warrant.

Judge Armstrong and Bob Carpenter had been friends for many years and it was Detective Carpenter that had requested the meeting. "Judge, as you know, we have had a string of burglaries in the last six months. We are sure we know who was pulling them off and we would like a search warrant to serve on him at his house. The information we have is that Hezekiah Hadley is our burglar. I and Officer Thurgood were at his house on another matter and I noticed that on a piece of furniture in the living room was the cash box that was taken from the Shear Works Beauty Shop burglary a couple of months back. The metal box was open and the inside of the box had a calling card attached to it that had the name of the beauty shop and the name of the owner on it. This was in plain sight to both me and Officer Thurgood. Also, we were interviewing a guy by the name of Peter Krueger in Montana who is a suspect in the Harmony Day case and also a friend of Hezekiah Hadley. He's in jail out there on an attempted murder charge and I think he was hoping that if he gave up some information we could help him get out of his predicament in Montana. He told us that Hezekiah Hadley was the guy who has been burglarizing the businesses in Milrose and that he was collecting his loot to use in a murder he has planned out. We're not sure if Krueger is telling the truth or not but there is no reason to doubt him at this point. We would like to get Hadley locked up before he does another burglary or kills someone."

The Judge rubbed his chin as was his habit when he was pondering a decision. "Bob, I need you to put in writing what you have just told me and I will issue a search warrant. Krueger's implication of Hadley is hearsay and we can't use that as probable cause but seeing the cash box with the name of the business is so we'll go with that. In fact I'll have it ready for you when you get me your affidavit."

Three hours after leaving Judge Armstrong's chambers with the search warrant in hand Lieutenant Carpenter, Detective Fairfield and three uniformed police officers arrived at the Hadley residence. Bob Carpenter knocked on the door several times and when there was no answer he motioned for the three officers to check out the house and garage to look for Hezekiah. Sally waited at the doorsteps with her partner anxious for Hezekiah Hadley to answer the door. They did not have a no-knock search warrant so if he didn't show up they would have to come back another time. The officers made their rounds of the house and the garage and returned to the front steps and shook their heads meaning they had no luck and that no one appeared to be home. The patrol car left first and was followed by the two detectives. They would come back and keep coming back until they found Hezekiah at home.

CHAPTER 22

Wolf Point was the county seat of Roosevelt County. The courthouse, the Sheriff's office and the jail were all located in the small town and in close proximity to each other. It was Sunday morning and Peter Krueger was the only prisoner in the cell block. He had been put in a large cell that contained four bunks, two lower and two upper. They were made of heavy gauge steel, bolted and welded to the wall. One of the walls held two of the bunks and on the opposite wall were the other two bunks. A metal table was in the middle and it was able to seat four people. The square table was bolted to the floor in a similar fashion as the bunks along with the four chairs that surrounded it. The prisoner had been given a plastic coated mattress pad and a plastic coated pillow along with one sheet, one pillow case and one thin gray wool blanket. He had his choice of bunks and he picked the lower one on the wall farthest from the door. There was no radio and no television in his cell which didn't bother him. He didn't need the noise right now, he needed to think. He relaxed on his bunk, lying on his back, crossing his legs and staring at the bottom of the bunk above him. His thoughts were on escape; he needed to get out of Montana and he needed to get to Lin Su and get out of Minnesota too. He wanted to be as far from Hezzy as he could get. It wasn't that he was afraid of Hezekiah. He could kick his butt in a fight any day of the week but he didn't trust him to fight like a man. He was capable of anything, shooting at you from a distance, walking up behind you with an axe and whapping you over the head or stabbing you when you were sleeping. If Hezzy ever found out he squealed on him, it would only be a matter of time before the green haired monster would try to kill him.

"Hey Petey, how's it going?"

Pete looked up from his bunk, directing his attention to the small window in the cell door and said nothing. Staring at him through the small cubicle in the door was the one guard in the jail that he detested. He was well aware of the guard that was talking to him; he hated being called 'Petey' and the guard knew it. The guard was the only person that dared call him that name because he knew that his prisoner couldn't fight back. He didn't much care for this guard and had thought that when he made his escape it would be when this guard was on duty. It would be his last day on this earth because he would kill him and enjoy doing it. He didn't bother to answer the guard and watched the glass window in the steel door. The small window was covered by a sliding metal door and was slid open when the guard made his rounds, it allowed the guard to make note of what the prisoner was doing at the time he peeked in. It all went into the jailor's log. The guard was looking into the cell to see if the prisoner was all right and to take his order for breakfast. He had a choice of cereal and a roll or oatmeal and a roll. He always ordered the oatmeal because it was harder for the guard to make than the cereal. He got a glass of orange juice and cup of coffee with his breakfast. The other guards would give him another cup of coffee if he requested but this particular guard never gave him a second cup, even if he asked nicely. He would remember and he would get even.

Today would be a long day. He had no one to talk to but he didn't mind. He didn't much like people anyway. The day was spent pacing the floor and smoking cigarettes. Luckily he had a carton with him at the campsite and they were included in his belongings when he was brought it. After eating his breakfast he started feeling ill and dizzy so he lay down on his bunk. He instantly fell asleep and slept all day. In the middle of the night he developed a fever and chills. The thin wool blanket he had wrapped up in didn't come close to keeping him warm as his fever and his chills got worse. The flu like symptoms remained with him throughout the night and all the next day. The guards that checked on him periodically noted that he hadn't gotten out of bed since last night. As his sickness continued into the second day the guards were starting to worry that something might be seriously wrong with their prisoner. At four o'clock in the afternoon two guards opened the jail cell door and walked over to him and asked him how he was feeling. He was sick enough by now that he knew he needed to see a doctor and told the two guards that were in his cell that he was really really sick. They told him that they would try to get him in to see a doctor tomorrow morning. He fell asleep and slept well the rest of the afternoon and throughout the night. In the morning he woke early and felt good for the first time in two days. The fever was gone, the chills had vanished and he felt better than he had for a long time.

One of the guards stopped at his cell and informed him that his doctor's appointment was at ten and that he should be dressed by nine-thirty and that two of the deputies would take him to a doctor in Wolf Point.

He didn't tell the guard that he was feeling much better; he was sure this was the opportunity he had been waiting for. This would be the day he would escape and never come back to Montana again. He decided to clean himself up after two days of being bed ridden and stepped into the shower letting the hot water pound on his refreshed body. He offered several poses to the female dispatchers in case they were watching. He lingered in the shower and when he was through he dried himself off on a small hand towel provided by the jailors. He slipped back into his skivvies, brushed his teeth, and combed his hair. The two deputies were at his cell door at exactly nine thirty and he was ready to go with him. He faked his illness by walking slow and coughing a little with a few groans thrown in for good measure. When he left his cell he was escorted to the booking room where he was handcuffed behind his back and led to a squad car. They arrived at the doctor's office at nine forty-five.

The waiting room was small with eight or ten chairs. There were a few patients waiting to see the doctor and the two deputies and their prisoner sat together waiting for the nurse to come out and get them.

It wasn't long and he was inside a small examination room waiting for the doctor. The two deputies waited outside the room which gave him some time to check out the surroundings. There was no chance of escape from this room so he had to work fast. This was his only chance and he wasn't going to screw it up. He knocked on the examination room door from the inside. "Deputies, I need to go to the bathroom real bad."

One of the deputies opened the door and motioned with his finger to follow him.

"Can you take these cuffs off, I ain't going anywhere, I'm too sick."

The deputy thought about it for a minute and moved the cuffed wrists from his back to his front. He double locked the handcuffs for extra precaution and opened the bathroom door for the prisoner. Once inside he knew he had found the escape route he needed. The bathroom was old, a crank out window faced the alley with a lever on it that opened and closed the window at will. Another door led somewhere but he didn't know where. He couldn't believe his luck as he tried the lever and sure enough it opened the window. There was plenty of room for him to fit through the window frame and as he was about the climb up to the window and make his exit the deputy knocked on the door and said that he would be coming in. He closed the window and walked to the door and opened it. "Thanks, I needed that."

He was back in the examination room waiting for the doctor when an old man with white hair and a white moustache entered the room. He was wearing a white gown and introduced himself as Doctor Maxwell. The doctor asked him to tell him about his symptoms, which he did, and continued to fake his illness. The doctor did a brief examination before escorting him to a larger room for a more thorough exam. He asked the doctor if it would be possible to have his handcuffs taken off. He wasn't going to run, you could be sure of that, as sick as he was. The doctor got up from the chair he was sitting on and asked the deputy if he would please uncuff his patient because he may have to have a chest x-ray done. The deputy was reluctant but the doctor assured him that his patient was in no condition to run. "You're going to be standing right here anyway, so what's the harm?" The middle-aged deputy walked over to his prisoner and reluctantly removed the handcuffs for the doctor. Why was it, he thought, that doctors were so trusting of their patients?

"The examination is going to take about an hour. Why don't you go grab yourself a cup of coffee and have a seat in the reception area. I'll call when you we're done."

"I would prefer to stay in the room doc. This guy's a felon, he's dangerous, and I wouldn't feel right about leaving him alone with you."

"I'll be fine deputy, I promise you. Now please leave so I can finish examining this young man," the doctor demanded.

The deputy was hesitant about leaving but he didn't want to get into an argument with the doctor so he quietly left the examination room and hoped that nothing went wrong. He informed the deputy standing outside the door that he was going to get a cup of coffee and that the doctor wanted to be alone with Krueger.

Pete Krueger eyed the other door in the room and guessed it was the same door he had seen when he was in the bathroom. "I gotta' go to the bathroom real bad doc. Is there one nearby?"

Without hesitation and without looking or talking the doctor innocently pointed to the door that was going to lead Peter Krueger to freedom. The half dressed prisoner got up from the examination table and walked to the door, opened it and disappeared. Dr. Maxwell was writing some items on his chart when he started feeling uneasy about how long the prisoner was taking to use the bathroom. He laid the chart on the examination table and walked over and opened the bathroom door. The prisoner was gone and the small window above the sink was open. The doctor hollered for a deputy.

When the deputies entered the small room the doctor pointed to the open door that led to the small adjoining bathroom. "He said he had to use the bathroom, I didn't think anything of it until he didn't come back. I'm terribly sorry. I should have listened to you."

The two deputies walked into the empty bathroom and noticed the open window and knew exactly what had just happened. They had lost a prisoner.

****

He knew he would have to move fast. The deputy sheriff would return soon. He opened the bathroom window and had plenty of room to squeeze out. He was gone from the building in less than a minute but he didn't have much time and he needed to get out of Wolf Point without being seen. It was daylight, it was a small town and all movements by any stranger would be noticed and mentally recorded. The first order of business was to steal a car. The best place to do that in a small town was at the local Wal-Mart. There would be plenty of cars in the parking lot and his chances of being detected were less here than anywhere else in town. He had several choices of cars to choose from. He needed one that did not stand out. A four door sedan would work fine. The second car he came to was a newer model Toyota and the door had been left unlocked. He looked around to see if anybody was walking in his direction and satisfied that he had at least a couple of minutes to work on the ignition he hopped inside and had the car running in under a minute. He drove out of the parking lot and headed toward Williston, North Dakota. He would go back to the Twin Cities and get Lin Su and they would drive down to Mexico. He had heard that once you crossed the border into Mexico you were safe from law enforcement in the States. As he was leaving Wolf Point he heard sirens wailing from all directions of the town. He knew what that meant and who they were after. He would be long gone before they got themselves organized. It would be another half hour before they found out about the stolen car and by that time he would be in North Dakota, past Williston and on the way to Minnesota. He was lucky to have picked a car with a full tank of gas. That would get him past Williston by several hours and it wouldn't be until dark that he would need gas. He would find a gas station that wasn't very busy, get his gas, pick up some food and rob the place and kill the attendant if he had too. This was survival and he would do anything to stay out of jail.

After he passed Williston he was forced to take two lane highways until he got to Minot where he picked up Highway 2 which would take him to Grand Forks and into Minnesota. When he neared Rugby it was well into sunset and he noticed that his gas gauge showed a quarter of a tank. The time was right for what he needed to do; he pulled off the highway and into a small convenience store-gas station. He got out of his car and lifted the pump handle and inserted it into his tank. He pushed the desired grade of gasoline he needed and filled his tank. When that was done he went inside and picked up some candy, chips, cookies and sodas. He walked up to the counter and informed the clerk that he had a gun and that she was to give him all her money and she wouldn't get hurt. It was easy; she nervously opened the cash register and handed him seventy eight dollars. He took the money along with the groceries and got into his car and took off. He headed west on the freeway and when he was a couple of miles down the road he turned around and headed east once again. If she was watching which way he went, she would tell the cops he went west and that is where they would concentrate their efforts.

Pete Krueger had wished he had a gun and he would have taken care of the clerk. Dead people don't talk. He would get a gun the first chance he got. He stayed on Highway 2; there was very little traffic and he had the urge to see how much guts this little car had but he didn't want to take any chances of getting stopped. He was too smart for that; years of staying one step ahead of the police had given him the experience he needed to elude the law and avoid jail. He was getting tired and when he got to Devil's Lake he pulled into a rest area, found a secluded spot and parked his vehicle. He left the car running with the heater on and slept. When he awoke the sun was coming up. He backed out of his parking spot, exited the rest area and headed east on Highway 2, still groggy from his sleep. The next rest area would allow him to clean up; he hadn't washed or brushed his teeth since leaving the jail in Wolf Point. He was a stickler for personal hygiene, the one good thing his mother ever left him.

A small green sign with white letters appeared on the side of the road telling him that Grand Forks was five miles away. Below that sign was a blue and white sign that said 'rest area ahead'. He exited the highway and pulled up in front of the bathrooms, it was going to feel good to wash up and brush his teeth. He needed to call Lin Su and let her know what was going on. She could be trusted and she needed to know where to meet him. The apartment needed to be cleaned out and all their possessions packed into the trunk of her car. Marijuana, cigarettes, credit cards and money were on top of the list but clothes and toiletries were important also. A pay phone stood at the front of the information kiosk, he searched his pocket for change and found enough to make the call to Lin Su. He had woken up hungry and was in need of some breakfast. After arrangements were made for Lin Su to meet him, he was off to Grand Forks and then to Minneapolis.

CHAPTER 23

The senior deputy was embarrassed that he had to make the dreaded phone call to the station and inform the dispatcher that his prisoner had escaped. With over eighteen years on the department he knew better than to leave a prisoner alone whether it be with a doctor or anyone else. It was an obvious faux pas and now he would be the brunt of jokes for the next few weeks. Not only that - the adjoining counties would hear the radio transmission and they too would join in the unmerciful barrage of jokes. He called in with the information and before he was off the radio he heard the shriek of sirens coming in his direction. The Sheriff notified him that a chopper would be going up soon and a full scale manhunt would be in progress within the hour. He stood outside the doctor's office and waited. When the Sheriff arrived he sheepishly explained to him what had happened and how the prisoner managed his escape. Obed Moore remained silent as he listened to his deputy apologize. He advised him that the Chief Deputy would be coordinating the search and that he was to report to him for instructions. Two deputies were doing a thorough search of a three block area surrounding the doctor's office when Sheriff Moore radioed and advised them that a car had just been stolen from the Wal-Mart parking lot. He wanted them to stop what they were doing and head for Wal-Mart and talk to the victim. Upon arrival at the parking lot the two deputies realized that the victim was the wife of one of the police officers in Wolf Point. She said that when she came out of the store she couldn't find her car. She thought she remembered where she had parked but when her car wasn't where it was supposed to be she had some doubt and searched up and down each row. When she still couldn't find it she was sure that it had been stolen. She called her husband on his cell phone and he immediately contacted the police department who contacted the Sheriff's office. The description of the car and its license number was given out to the surrounding counties and the Montana Highway Patrol. It was obvious to everyone that Peter Krueger had now added auto theft to the list of charges against him. The Sheriff knew the prisoner better than anyone else and was sure that he would be heading for Minnesota. He had the Highway Patrol contact the North Dakota Highway Patrol and the Minnesota Highway Patrol. Maybe someone would get lucky and spot the car before Mr. Krueger committed another crime.

The search was called off at dusk. Nothing had been found and it was presumed that the prisoner, Peter Krueger, was long gone. At seven fifteen a report came into the Sheriff's office that a small gas station and convenience store off of Highway 2 in Rugby had been robbed and the robber fit the description of the escaped prisoner. The clerk did not get a good description of the car because it was too dark. All she could tell the police that it was a newer model four-door and that it got on Highway 2 and went west. The North Dakota State Patrol had two cars on the road between Montana and Rugby and one car between Rugby and the Minnesota border. They would do their best to find the car but with the shortage of manpower they couldn't promise any miracles.

CHAPTER 24

Nathan Brown had enough money saved that he could think about buying a car. He didn't have all the money he needed but he had enough for a good down payment and insurance. Tomorrow he would car shop and he felt good knowing that he would finally be getting a car. He had never owned a car and had few driving skills but he would learn. It was Friday night and he didn't have to be back at the morgue until Tuesday morning. He decided to walk downtown and have a few beers and celebrate his latest decision. He was getting tired and bored being confined to the apartment every night; he needed some adventure in his life. His life was going to change now that he was getting a car and he might as well start with those changes tonight. He put on the cleanest of his dirty clothes and walked the mile and a half to his favorite bar, *The Couplings*. He hadn't been there for a while because he was saving all his money to get wheels. He was anxious to get there and he was beer thirsty so he walked faster. He neared the tavern as the pink neon lights atop the brick building lit up and were flashing on and off when he arrived. Large double red wooden doors marked the entrance of *The Couplings*. Nathan stood in front of the doors for a second before opening one of them and walking in. He walked to the end of the bar, grabbed a stool, sat down on it, and ordered a glass of beer. The bartender brought it over and set it in front of him. Nathan grabbed an ashtray, lit a cigarette and took a sip of the beer. It was going to be a good night he thought to himself.

Customers came and went and later in the evening a few women entered the bar, some stayed for the evening and some left after a couple of drinks. One of them he recognized, she worked at the Horn Inn as a waitress; he thought her name was Helen but he wasn't sure.

He had decided to get drunk tonight; he was excited about getting a new vehicle. He was giddy and euphoric about the car but afraid and nervous at the same time because he was going to kill again. He didn't know who it would be and didn't know how he was going to do it but he was going to do it and it was going to give him power and control. Nathan Brown was torn. He still had a little bit of conscience left and it told him that killing was wrong. But he felt good after he killed. It was like the devil was talking in his left ear and an angel was talking in his right ear, both trying to guide his decision. The devil, of course, would win out as it always did with Nathan and he would begin searching for a victim after he got his car. At closing time he stumbled the mile and a half distance to his house. He fumbled for his house keys and finally opened the door. He stumbled to his bedroom, fell into bed and slept until mid-morning the next day. After a half-hearted attempt to clean up his apartment he left and walked to the nearest car dealership. After a couple of hours of looking and some decision making he ended up buying a ten year old black mini-van. He paid the minimum down knowing that he could afford the cheap monthly payments. Buying insurance was his next errand, all he needed was minimum coverage and he would be ready to go. After purchasing insurance he took his new possession for a spin. He drove around Milrose several times and after tiring of that he drove into the countryside. The crops had been harvested and the plowed up fields were black with a sprinkling of snow lying on top of the half-frozen ground. He had spent a couple of hours driving around and enjoying his new van but he was getting hungry and decided to go to the Horn Inn for a late lunch. On his way to the restaurant he stopped at the local gas station and filled up. "This was a full service gas station and always would be" the owner always said. Samuel Taylor wiped his hands on his coveralls and walked over to his customer. He filled the tank, collected the money and went back to his oil change. He had seen his new customer around town a couple of times but never paid much attention to him. This was the first time that Samuel Taylor had seen his customer driving a vehicle, usually he was walking.

Helen DuPont was on duty when Nathan Brown walked into the restaurant and sat down at the counter. He ordered a hamburger, french fries and a coke. Helen had taken his order and took it back to the chef. The man whose order she had just taken made her nervous.

She could feel him staring at her and whenever she looked toward him he would avert his eyes elsewhere. She knew he was ogling and who knows what thoughts were going through his mind. She couldn't wait for him to finish his hamburger and leave.

Nathan remembered the waitress from last night. She was in *The Couplings* with another girl. They didn't stay long and after a couple of drinks they left. Twice in less than twenty four hours he had seen this girl. Was it an omen? Maybe she would be next.

Helen DuPont was going to be his next victim, he was sure of that now. The killing would not be sexual; he was not perverted like that. No, the killing was to give him a feeling of godlike power. To control the destiny of another person's life, now that was real power and would satisfy his hunger for quite some time. Now that he knew who he was going to kill, he had to figure out how he was going to do it. He had several scenarios worked out; it all depended on where he did it. It was to be a ritual killing though, one that would satisfy his cravings; he needed for her to beg for her life before he ended it.

Every night that Nathan came home from work his routine was the same. Make a sandwich, toss it on a plate with a few chips and open a beer. After his meal he would light up a joint and relax; the rest of the evening would be wasted. He would sit at the kitchen table thinking and planning his next victim's demise. The design of his plan had to be flawless because no clues could be left at the scene; he couldn't afford to get caught and he swore silently to himself that he would never go to jail again - he would die first. He was ready.

The cloudless sky was a bright azure, the air was frigid and he could see his breath as he walked toward his mini-van. Today he would go to the Horn Inn and visit Helen. The planning stage had begun and he needed to know a lot more about her lifestyle and her habits before he would be able to put his plans into action. He drove to the Horn Inn on a late Saturday morning, parked his vehicle near the employee parking area, locked it and walked into the restaurant. A large breakfast crowd had gathered and all the booths were taken. He sat down at the counter and waited for a waitress. He knew he stood out like a sore thumb in the small cafe with his black clothes but he had no other clothes to wear; he was total Gothic. It was at times like this that he wished he had owned some different clothes, ones that wouldn't stand out in a conservative God-fearing town. He didn't want anyone remembering that he was in the restaurant before Helen DuPont died. He was in luck, Helen was working. An older woman took his order while his next victim was working on the other side of the restaurant. He wanted to know when she got off work but he couldn't ask. He couldn't bring any suspicion upon himself, especially today.

He knew what kind of car she drove; he had followed her enough times. He would take his time eating and when he was through with his meal he would wait in his van until she came out. He guessed she would get off work after the lunch crowd left. At two minutes after two Helen DuPont walked out of the rear door of the restaurant. She searched for her keys in her purse as she walked toward her car. Once she neared her car she pushed the automatic lock release in her hand and opened the driver's door and got into her car. She slowly drove out of the employee's parking lot not noticing the black mini-van leaving the parking lot behind her.

She drove to Barnes Grocery Store, parked her car in the large lot and walked inside. When she came out she was pushing a grocery cart to her car. She unloaded the plastic bags of groceries in her front seat and then she walked to the trunk, opened it and lifted two cases of soda into it. She slammed the trunk and walked to the driver's side, got in and drove to her apartment with Nathan Brown following. She took the groceries out of her car and carried them into her apartment. She then returned to her car and carried the two cases of soda up the one flight of stairs and disappeared through her front door. Her stalker had noticed her every move.

CHAPTER 25

Bob Carpenter walked in to Sally's office and stared out her small window without saying a word. After a few minutes of silence he turned to her and spoke. "Krueger's escaped."

"What? How did that happen?" She asked.

"A couple of deputies took him to the doctor and he climbed through a bathroom window. Stole a car from the Wal-Mart parking lot and also robbed a convenience store in Rugby, North Dakota. Looks like he's heading our way. Probably going to his apartment to get his girlfriend. I contacted the Minneapolis PD and filled them in on Krueger. They said they will keep an eye on the place for us and if they see Krueger they will arrest him but they need a copy of the warrant. I contacted Wolf Point and they are going to fax the stuff to the Minneapolis PD, Hennepin County Sheriff's Department and the Highway Patrol."

"Sounds like you got things covered. Our friend Mr. Krueger's got himself in a whole shitpot full of trouble now. Let's see - there is attempted murder, escape and auto theft in Montana, armed robbery in North Dakota and suspicion of murder in Minnesota. This guy is going away for a long time."

"Gotta' catch him first." Detective Carpenter answered.

"You gotta' think positive Bob, we'll get him and when we do he'll confess to killing Harmony Day, case closed."

Detective Carpenter wished he could share his partner's enthusiasm but he was more pragmatic than he liked and he couldn't change that. Most of the time he saw the cup as half empty. He took a seat in her office and watched his partner peel an aluminum wrapper off a small piece of gum. "How's the not smoking coming along?"

"I've weakened, I haven't had a cigarette but I had to get the nicotine gum. It helps me get through the day and I am not a pain in the ass when I'm chewing it."

"Good girl, I'm proud of you."

She accepted his praise and was even surprised at herself for going this long without a cigarette. She wasn't over it by a long shot but she had never gone this long without a cigarette and she was hopeful. "Bob, I got a call on my cell last night from Pamela Rosewood."

"The victim's roommate, I remember her, nice gal."

"I thought so too. She told me that she remembered another person that Harmony talked about in Milrose. Guy by the name of Sam Taylor. She thought he worked at a gas station somewhere in town. Anyway she says that Harmony was working with him to overcome some of his problems. She said he was from a dysfunctional family and he was confused and having a hard time coping. He told her he hated going home because of his father and that his father was mean and would beat him and his sister a lot."

Her partner got up from his chair and walked to the window again. "That's Andrew Taylor's kid she's talking about. He's one mean son of a gun and his son is a little on the strange side too. Quit school when he was sixteen, same as his sister; he's been working at the Shell station ever since. He keeps to himself though and doesn't cause any trouble. Our victim sure knew how to pick 'em."

"Remember, macho man, that she wanted to be a social worker and she was on the religious side. Bad combination, she sees the world differently than we do and unfortunately it cost Harmony her life. Let's go have a talk with Mr. Taylor."

The Milrose Shell station had been on the corner of Main and Oak streets for as many years as Sally was old. It had gone through several renovations in the past few years to keep up with the times. The station had expanded - a two stall garage had been added for oil changes, lube jobs and other small automobile repairs. This is where Sam Taylor spent eight hours a day. He was standing under a newer model SUV draining its oil into a large red oil drum when the two detectives entered the garage. Sally could not see the face of the man standing next to the oil drum but she guessed it was Sam Taylor. "Sam Taylor?" she asked speaking in a loud tone.

"Yo, you got him," he answered from under the hoisted vehicle.

"We're from the Milrose Police Department, I'm Detective Fairfield and my partner is Detective Carpenter. We need to ask you a few questions."

"About what? I didn't do nothin' wrong."

"We didn't say you did Sam," Sally answered.

"Then what do you want?"

"We need to talk to you about Harmony Day."

"Don't know no Harmony Day."

Detective Carpenter looked under the automobile directly at Sam Taylor. "We know differently. We can talk about it here or we can go down to the station and talk, your choice."

Sam Taylor looked at the tall man who was speaking to him. He shrugged his shoulders, wiped the oil from his hands and walked out from under the vehicle. "I met her about a month ago. She had stopped in for some gas. I was working the pumps and we got to talking and she seemed interested in me so we talked until her tank was full and she took off. A couple of days later she shows up in the garage, says she just wanted to stop by and see how I was doin'. We talked some more and soon she was coming in a couple of times a week. We got to be friends but there was nothing more to it. I got a few problems of my own and she suggested that maybe she could come out to the house and we could talk about them. I think she was out there at least twice, maybe three times. We never went in the house because my old man is kind of ornery. He sits in front of the TV with his smokes and his Jim Crow. He gets mean when he drinks so I just stay away from him when he is like that, which is most of the time. My sister don't go near him either. I have this little corner of the barn that I fixed up as kind of an office so I would take her in there when she came out to visit me. She never did see my old man. She knew I was from a screwed up family and I think she wanted to see me make something out of my life. She was working on me to get my GED. She almost had me convinced too when she got murdered."

"Did Harmony ever talk to your mother or your sister?" Sally asked.

"Once Faith joined us in my office and we three talked for a couple of hours. Me and Faith get along real well and we talk together a lot but it was nice to have someone else to unload on. Faith really liked Harmony and so did I."

"Did she mention anyone else she was befriending other than you and Faith?"

"No, detective, but I think she was being friends with some other losers too. It seems like she liked being around us. I don't know why."

"We don't think you are a loser, Sam. You've had a few bad breaks but you can turn your life around. You're still young and you seem like you've got a good head on your shoulders. You know, in honor of Harmony, you should get your GED; you don't want to spend the rest of your life here do you?"

"It's not all that bad, and thanks for the confidence. Maybe I will get my GED, I mean what would it hurt."

Sally handed him her card. "If you can think of anything please call us. We want to catch her killer as soon as possible before he does this again. I don't care how insignificant you may think it is please call us. Okay?"

He accepted the card, looked at it briefly and put the business card in his wallet.

"Will do."

CHAPTER 26

Lin Su spent the morning clearing out the apartment. She emptied the closet first, carrying their clothes to the car, carelessly throwing them into the trunk. Small personal items came next, landing on the scattered clothes. The worn and torn brown leather couch, the broken recliner and the nineteen inch color TV remained in the apartment for the next resident or the apartment manager to worry about. She had followed Peter's directions and hoped that he would be pleased with her. She owned two medium sized suitcases and in them she packed a full carton of cigarettes, two ounces of marijuana, Pete's gun and his toiletries including washcloths and towels in one suitcase. She hastily packed her toiletries a bathrobe and underclothes in the other suitcase. A full case of beer was the last thing loaded into the car. She set it on the backseat and walked back to the apartment to see if she had missed anything. She had thought about taking the food out of the refrigerator and throwing it in the back seat with the beer but she abandoned the idea and left the food in the cupboards and the refrigerator. She drove off smiling, hoping never to see the apartment again.

The brown four door rusted 1982 Chevrolet pulled into the parking garage next to the Radisson hotel and after receiving her ticket from the automatic machine she found a parking place on the fifth floor. She looked at her watch; she was right on time. He would be here soon so she got out of the car, leaned against the trunk, lit a cigarette and waited. As she was stomping her cigarette out on the concrete floor, she noticed him walking toward her.

He looked anxious as he hurried toward her. "You got the gun?"

"It's in the car, love, but first let me hold you." She wrapped her arms around him and held him close. Lin Su had missed her boyfriend and was glad to see him. She had thought that she may never see him again and this moment made her realize how much she really cared about her man.

He grabbed the thin arms that were fastened tightly around his neck, loosened them and pushed her away. "We got time for that later, we gotta' get out of here. You got everything I told you to bring - clothes, money, credit cards, weed?"

"They're all in the suitcases along with the gun. The trunk's full of our clothes cuz I didn't have enough suitcases to put 'em in," she answered, excited to get going.

"We'll get new duds on the road if we have to, leave 'em," he answered, then turned and walked away.

Some of her favorite clothes were in the trunk, she didn't want to leave them but she didn't want to argue with her boyfriend and she didn't want him mad at her so she shrugged and obeyed his orders. If Peter wanted to stop and get new duds, that was all right with her. She defiantly grabbed the two suit cases and followed him as he walked up one floor of the parking ramp. When they got to the stolen Toyota he opened the trunk and grabbed the two suitcases that Lin Su had been carrying. He said nothing about them as he lifted them into the trunk. They got into the car and drove out of the parking lot onto Fifth Street. When things had settled she turned to her boyfriend and placed her hand on the back of his neck and caressed it. "I missed you." She snuggled up next to him, glad to feel the warmth of his body once again. "Where are we going?"

He put his arm around her and told her that they were going shopping. It took him twenty minutes to get to Cedar Avenue and then to Harmon Killebrew Drive and then into the Mall of America. He parked the Toyota in the east parking lot and told Lin Su to wait at the car and that he would be back with a new one. He wanted something bigger. The Toyota didn't fit his needs; he wanted an SUV. He wasn't worried about being spotted in the new car. With all the traffic in the Twin Cities he wouldn't even be noticed and by the time he was out of Minnesota nobody would be looking for him. He would be safe as long as he obeyed the traffic laws. He entered the Mall through the Sears store which faced the east lot. He walked through the Mall and exited

Nordstrom's and found himself in the large west lot. The lot was large and three quarters full. He would have his pickings of any vehicle he wanted. He found a dark green Lincoln Navigator in the center of the parking lot. It was what he was looking for and within two minutes he was driving the Lincoln to the east lot to pick up Lin Su. They quickly transferred the luggage and slowly drove out of the large lot, careful not to draw attention to themselves. They got back on Cedar Avenue and drove to the entrance of I-35 and turned south. If they wanted, they could stay on I-35 all the way to Texas.

"Where we going love?" Lin Su asked.

"I gotta' stop at Milrose and see Hezekiah and then we're going south to someplace warm for the winter." He didn't know where yet, it could be Texas or Florida or Arizona. He would decide that after he left Hezekiah's.

The Hadleys lived on the edge of town in a small dilapidated farmhouse on an acre of land. A miniature barn stood adjacent to the house; it had once been home to a few cows and a horse but was now empty and weather beaten. Between the house and the barn was a two car garage that housed Mrs. Hadley's Oldsmobile and an empty freezer. A narrow pathway ran between the buildings, hardly visible because of the tall grass, dandelions and thistles. When the Lincoln Navigator pulled into the farmyard Hezekiah was cleaning out the trunk of his mother's car. When he noticed the strange vehicle come onto the property he thought about running, but didn't. He was sure it was the cops coming to snoop around again but quickly realized that they wouldn't be driving a vehicle this fancy. As the Navigator got closer he saw that the driver was his friend Pete Krueger and he had Lin Su with him. He lowered the trunk of the Oldsmobile to prevent his friend from seeing inside and walked over to the SUV as his friend was stepping off the running board and onto the ground. "Hey Pete, I thought you were in jail somewhere in Montana."

Lin Su exited from the passenger side as Hezekiah was talking to her boyfriend. She heard what Hezekiah said and she answered before Pete had the chance to reply. "He broke out; no jail is gonna' to hold my love."

"Zat true?" Hezekiah wanted to know.

Peter looked at Lin Su and sneered at her. He wanted her to know that she was supposed to keep her mouth shut. He looked back at Hezekiah, "Yea, got tired of the place."

His friend was impressed. "Let me get you a beer, bet you're thirsty, huh?"

Peter Krueger turned down Hezekiah's offer. He didn't feel like a beer and if he didn't want one then his girlfriend didn't want one either. He was anxious to get back on the road. He didn't want to be anywhere near Milrose if he didn't have to. Those two detectives he talked to in Montana would sure like to get a hold of him right now. No, he wanted to get going but he had some business with Hezekiah. "What was you doing when we pulled in?" He pointed at the Oldsmobile and Hezekiah turned to look at it.

"Nothing," Hezekiah sheepishly answered. He was sore at his friend for asking. It was nobody's business what he was doing in the trunk of his mother's car.

Peter dropped the question and got to the matter at hand. "I need the hundred bucks you owe me. Me and Lin Su are going down south for the winter and I'm a little short of cash right now."

"Ain't got no money," Hezekiah answered.

Pete Krueger studied his friend for a moment. He was sure he was lying to him. "All them jobs you did at those business places, I know you got money from them, all I wants' my hundred. You couldn't have spent all that already."

Hezekiah was getting angry. His friend was asking too many questions and demanding money besides. He grabbed Peter Krueger and started shaking him. He didn't say a word but Krueger could see he was going crazy. It didn't take much to set Hezekiah off. Even though Hezekiah outweighed Krueger by over a hundred pounds he was no match for him. A couple of martial arts moves had Hezekiah lying on the ground moaning. Pete looked at the overweight body sprawled on the ground and waited for him to get up. Hezekiah didn't make an attempt to lift himself off the ground and remained motionless, staring at his friend. Pete backed away from him. "I'm going into your house and I am going to find the hundred bucks and then I am going to take it and then I am going to kick your ass so you better be gone when I get back." Pete turned toward the house and began walking. Hezekiah got up and grabbed an old rusted shovel that had been lying on the ground near him and quietly walked toward Krueger.

Lin Su watched the crazy man get up and grab the shovel. She knew that her boyfriend might be in trouble. She reached into the vehicle and found the 9mm Luger stashed in the console between the two front seats. She pulled it out and chambered a shell. She feared that Hezekiah heard the sound of the gun being chambered but he didn't; his mind was focused on Pete Krueger. When he was near enough behind her boyfriend he raised the shovel ready to strike. Lin Su fired and Hezekiah fell to the ground screaming, blood was gushing out of his right ankle and when he saw the pool of blood forming by his leg he started cursing at Lin Su and Peter Krueger. Lin Su aimed the gun toward his head and ordered him to shut up. After hearing the gun shot Krueger stopped, turned around and looked at Hezekiah, sneered and walked into the house. Hezekiah held his leg and watched him disappear through the front door. Hezekiah remained quiet; holding his bleeding ankle. The gun was still aimed at his head and he feared that she was going to kill him. When Peter Krueger came out of the house he was holding money in each hand and counting it as he walked. He didn't know how much he had; he knew it was over a hundred dollars but he didn't care - he was taking all of it. He stopped in front of Hezekiah who was still on the ground whimpering. He kneeled down and whispered. "If you tell anyone I was here, I'll come back and I'll kill you. Understand."

Hezekiah attempted to wrap a handkerchief around his wounded ankle; he looked at them both but didn't say a word. They were both laughing at him when they got into the Navigator and left.

"Nice shooting Lin Su. Where'd you learn how to shoot like that?"

She was happy she had impressed him. He didn't impress easily and having him notice her made her feel good. It reassured her that her boyfriend was in love with her and that he would not leave her. She had overlooked Harmony Day. She knew what was going on and she knew he had probably killed her but it would be only a matter of time before he came back to her. No woman could treat a man like she did. "Thanks, my dad taught me how to shoot. He had all kinds of guns, revolvers, rifles, automatics, you name it and I've shot it."

They crossed the Minnesota border before he realized they were low on gas. He pulled into the first truck plaza he saw and filled the Navigator. He was surprised at what it cost him. He was able to fill the Toyota's gas tank for one half of what it cost him to fill the Lincoln and the Toyota got much better mileage. He didn't know how long his cash would hold out but he knew where he would be able to always get some more. He went into the truck plaza to pay for the gas, pick up some soda, some junk food and ten lottery tickets. He might get lucky. He got back into the SUV, handed the lottery tickets to Lin Su and got back on I-35. Next stop, Kansas City, if the gas held out.

Lin Su spotted a Holiday Inn as they approached north Kansas City. The familiar green lettering was lit up and the vacancy sign was on. Peter Krueger exited the freeway and was soon parked under a canopy in front of the hotel office. They checked in at the front desk where a young lady dressed in a dark suit registered them into a room with two double beds. Lin Su handed over her credit card while Peter Krueger picked up the two suitcases and ambled to the elevator door and waited. The elevator carried them to the fourth floor where they got off and looked for their room. They were in such a hurry to find their room that they didn't notice the directions to their room number were stenciled on the wall outside the elevator. It took them two trips around the hotel floor to locate their room. When they did they unloaded the two suitcases on the one of the beds, left the room and took the elevator down to the first floor and went to the small hotel restaurant to eat. The junk food they had been eating on the road hadn't filled them up but the Twinkies, chips and sodas had worked to quench their appetites until they could eat a good meal. A small blackboard rested on an easel at the entrance of the restaurant and on it was written the special for the evening - prime rib, mashed potatoes and a vegetable. After being seated Krueger ordered the special and a beer for each of them. Neither one could remember the last time they had eaten this well. When they were finished with their meal they sauntered to an elaborately furnished bar next to the restaurant and ordered another beer. When closing time came they were still there and quite drunk. They quickly finished their beer and Peter ordered two more, signed the tab and carried the beers to the room with Lin Su staggering behind him.

They slept well that night and it was the first time that he had slept in a real bed since leaving for his fishing trip in Montana. They got up late, took a shower and went to the same restaurant for a late morning breakfast. They were both hungry and gulped down the large portions in front of them. When they were done they went back to their room and grabbed the two suitcases and took the elevator down to the first floor lobby. They walked up to the check-out desk and advised the clerk that they would be leaving and handed Lin Su's credit card to him. An older man with coarse white hair combed into a pony tail was at the desk this morning. He was dressed in the same brown suit as the girl that had checked them in the night before. He took the credit card and ran it through the machine. He came back to Lin Su and informed her that the credit card she had given them did not cover all the expenses and that it was maxed out. He advised them that they owed the hotel another $15.48 to take care of the bill.

"Did you win anything on those lottery tickets I gave you?" he asked Lin Su. She shook her head no so he reached into his pocket and pulled out a twenty dollar bill and handed it to the desk clerk.

After they had loaded the luggage in the back of the SUV they got into the vehicle and started it. Before putting it into gear he turned to Lin Su, "We need some money, Lin Su. I thought you had more money on your card. I don't have much left with filling up the gas guzzler and we're getting low on gas again. We're going to stop at a bank here in K.C. and make a withdrawal. I am going to have you drive the car and I am going to go into the bank and get the money. So, here's the plan. I-35 goes right through K.C. so we're gonna' find a mall and most likely there will be a bank in the mall or one nearby. That's where we'll hit. I am going to go in first and check the place out and we'll figure out where I need to have you park. We also got to cover our license plates 'cause there will probably be security cameras in the parking lot and we don't want those plate numbers broadcast to all the cops in the state."

They were almost through Kansas City before they found the Oak Park Mall. Peter Krueger pulled the Navigator off the freeway and drove into a huge parking lot that abutted the mall. He parked the Lincoln and he and Lin Su got out of the vehicle and walked toward the mall and entered. They searched the entire mall and did not see a bank. They walked outside and looked around, trying to see a bank somewhere, anywhere. They noticed some brick buildings about two blocks away. The area appeared to be a small business district so they got back into the vehicle and drove to it. They found two banks in the midst of the buildings. Peter decided that the Wells Fargo bank would be the easiest of the targets. No cameras were evident anywhere in the area so Peter left the license plates uncovered. Pete Krueger walked into the bank, looked around briefly before walking up to one of the tellers and asked if she would be able to change a twenty. "Two tens would be fine," he answered before the teller had a chance to ask. The twenty dollar bill got changed and he walked outside and met Lin Su. He advised her where to park and grabbed the 9 mm from the console and walked back into the bank. He walked up to a different teller and informed her that he had a gun and that she should quietly give him all the money in her till and that she needed to put it in a sack. She nervously did so and handed it to him. He took the sack and walked out of the bank into the waiting vehicle and Lin Su drove off. As she was approaching I-35 he opened the sack and took out the money and counted it. He had gotten over thirty five hundred dollars for two minutes work. Not bad, he thought to himself.

The thick stack of twenty dollar bills fascinated him, never in his life had he held so much money in his hand. After counting and recounting the money he put it back in Lin Su's purse and looked up to see where they were. "There's a small town up ahead, pull off at the next exit and let's find a Wal-Mart or Home Depot. We need to change cars again. We gotta stay one step ahead of the cops."

Lin Su did as she was told and pulled off into a small town south of Kansas City off I-35. It didn't take long to spot a Wal-Mart and Lin Su obediently pulled into a parking stall and waited. Her boyfriend exited the car and she knew he would be back in a few minutes with a new car. She hoped it would be as nice as the Navigator. A white Escalade pulled up next to her, the driver leaned over and opened the door and motioned for Lin Su to do her thing. She unloaded the two suitcases and the beer from the Navigator and put them into the rear of the SUV. She got in the front seat with the sack of money and her purse. Pete Krueger drove off, careful not to draw attention. "Next stop Oklahoma."

"Where we goin' love?"

"Nogales, Arizona, the town's right on the Mexican border. If it looks like things are getting hot there for us we'll just cross over in another country the cops can't do a thing about it."

Lin Su liked the plan. She had never been outside of Minnesota and she was surprised that Kansas didn't look much different than Minnesota. The farmland was flat, no hills or mountains loomed in the background and the land was plowed up like it had been around Milrose. She was excited to see the west and had no idea what to expect. "How we getting there?"

"Oklahoma first, then down to Texas then west to New Mexico and Arizona."

They were both quiet, watching the prairie land pass and thinking about their new future together. They didn't speak to each other until they entered Oklahoma City, found Highway 40 and finally turned west. From here on in the scenery would change to rocks, boulders, sand, cacti and some lava rock. Feeling safe from the cops they stopped a few miles outside of Oklahoma and ate at a Denny's. It was the second good meal they'd eaten in one day. It had been a wild twenty-four hours and they both wanted to talk about it and relish it but the restaurant was full and they were afraid someone might overhear them. They enjoyed their meal, carried on with some small talk and left without being noticed. Krueger left a twenty dollar bill from the bank robbery on the table to cover the food and the tip. They got in their new Cadillac Escalade, found the ramp to I-40 and began their westward trek.

"Oh, I forgot to tell you, love, some cops came by the apartment looking for you while you was in Montana."

He turned to look at her. His expression told her that she shouldn't have said anything, she had angered him now. "Why didn't you tell me sooner, why did you decide to tell me now? You dumb bitch."

"I didn't think it mattered." She was starting to get mad; she didn't like being called a bitch.

"Didn't matter! If I had known they had been there I would have had you totally clean out the apartment. There are things there that could implicate me in other crimes."

"Like Harmony Day?"

"Don't ever mention her name to me again or you'll get what she got."

"You killed her didn't you? That's why the cops were there? I told them I was your girl and not Harmony Day but I was wrong. You were using both of us weren't you?" She screamed.

"I told you to shut up!"

"What did she have that I don't have, huh? Wasn't I good enough for you, didn't I satisfy your needs. I know you killed her, that's why the cops was there, wasn't it?"

He was sick of her yelling at him. It was time to shut her up, he reached over and punched her on the side of the head. Her head snapped back and she went limp. She slid down in the seat, her eyes fell shut and a small trickle of blood ran down her cheek from the corner of her lip. He hoped she would stay this way until they reached Nogales. He knew who the cops were that had come to see Lin Su. It was that female cop from Milrose and that State Agent, what's his name, Trimble or something like that. He wanted as far away from them as he could get.

CHAPTER 27

He had never experienced the kind of pain that he was now. His ankle was on fire and he couldn't move his leg. The blood was oozing out like a miniature oil well; the bullet had severed a main artery. He ripped off his shirt and tied it around the wound preventing the loss of even more blood. He crawled to the Oldsmobile opened the door and pulled himself into the front seat. He started the car and drove to Milrose. As he was turning into the Milrose Memorial Hospital he passed out and the next thing he remembered was a doctor and several nurses standing around him. He leg was bandaged and he was on pain medication and he felt good, real good.

At the same time that Hezekiah Hadley was enjoying his pain killers the two detectives were on their way to the hospital to interrogate him about how he happened to get shot and to serve him with the search warrant they had been holding the last couple of days.

The white privacy cloak was pulled back and the two detectives entered the small enclosed area encircling his emergency room bed. Sally handed him a folded piece of paper. "Here Hezekiah, here's a search warrant for your house. You're officially served so you can enjoy your hospital stay and we'll be back to talk to you when we are through with the search." She had turned to go when she stopped, hesitated and turned toward the patient. "Oh by the way, we'll be back. We're going to want to talk to you about how you happened to get shot - so give that some thought too." Sally was looking for some hint of expression from Hezekiah but the pain killers disguised whatever he was thinking.

When Detective Fairfield and Detective Carpenter left the hospital they met up with three Milrose uniformed police officers at the Hadley residence. Their assistance was needed for the search. A thorough search of the house, the garage and the small barn would take up most of the day even with five officers taking part. Detective Carpenter couldn't think how lucky they had been in getting the warrant served; they had been unable to find Hezekiah for the last few days and anxiously wanted to search the house before he was able to destroy any evidence. They were both curious how Hezekiah happened to get shot in the ankle, but that would be left for another time.

Detective Carpenter began his search in the living room where he had seen the Shear Works metal cash box sitting on a small table. It was sitting in the same place he had seen it before. He took several photographs of the box and its contents. Inside were five uncashed checks made out to Shear Works Beauty Salon so he carefully laid them on the small table and with his digital camera photographed each check. The box was empty except for the checks. He placed each check in a small plastic evidence bag and tagged the box as evidence. It was enough evidence to solve one of the burglaries. He hoped that more evidence would be recovered in the house and the garage that would link Hezekiah to the other unsolved burglaries. He called the Chief on his cell phone and told him what he had found so far and would he please station a man at the ER to watch Hezekiah to make sure he didn't leave the hospital. Whoever was stationed at the ER could arrest him for burglary if the need be but otherwise he would make the arrest when they were done with the warrant.

By the time they were through with the house and the small barn they had labeled and secured twenty seven items that were connected in one way or another with the string of burglaries. It looked like Peter Krueger was right; Hezekiah Hadley was the burglar.

All that remained was the garage and it was here that Detective Carpenter hoped the pry bar would be found. This was the piece of evidence he wanted the most; it would link all the burglaries to the same person which he knew was Hezekiah Hadley. Sally began her search at the rear of the garage. She opted to start with a small stand alone freezer that was partially covered up with an old blanket. It was plugged in and still working which surprised her. She removed the blanket and opened it anticipating a few frozen food items scattered here and there. Instead she came face to face with Florence Hadley; her eyes open and staring into space. Her mouth was open, her eyelids iced over and her hair tangled and frozen. Ice had formed on her face and ears and Sally had what appeared to be her second murder victim in less than four months. The body was stiff - frozen solid and looked as if it had been lying in the freezer for at least a week. "Bob come over here, you gotta see this. We got another murder on our hands."

Bob Carpenter didn't have the honor of arresting Hezekiah Hadley. That went to the officer guarding him. When the emergency room was quiet and the nurses and doctors were tending to other patients Hezekiah slowly and carefully slid off of his gurney and quietly snuck up behind the guard. The police officer thought he heard something behind him and as he was turning around he received a blow to the face by Hezekiah's crutch which knocked him to the floor. Hezekiah jumped over the officer and tried to run for the exit door but the pain killers were wearing off and the throbbing pain in his ankle was exploding as he fell to the floor screaming in agony and holding his wounded leg. Two nurses and a doctor heard the commotion and showed up immediately. The doctor held Hezekiah on the tile floor until the police officer recovered, came over and handcuffed the prisoner. The officer lifted up his prisoner and carried him back to his room and tossed him onto the bed. He checked with the doctor as to the condition of the patient and if the prisoner was well enough to check out of the hospital. The doctor said that he was healthy enough to go to jail. That was all the officer needed to know, he took him off the gurney, pulled him to the squad car and threw him in the back seat and called the station telling them he was coming in with a prisoner. He next called Detective Carpenter and explained the situation to him and that the patient was now a prisoner and he could visit him in jail.

After completing the booking process the jailers escorted him to cell number 8. This was a holding cell which was also used as an isolation cell and where Hezekiah would remain until tomorrow morning. The two detectives wanted him isolated from the rest of the cell block until they had a chance to talk to him.

It was after ten o'clock at night when the two detectives finished their work for the day. They had written their reports, bagged and classified all evidence, printed out pictures of the house, the garage and the small barn. There were photographs of every room of the house, pictures of all the evidence and pictures of the freezer and the murder victim which had been identified as Florence Hadley, the mother of Hezekiah. How she was killed was still not known. The autopsy would tell them that. They were sure they had the killer in jail. Florence Hadley must have been the person Hezekiah had talked about killing to Peter Krueger.

It was mid morning when the two detectives arrived at the Law Enforcement Center. They were met with congratulations from the Chief, the Sheriff, the Chief Deputy and other personnel at the law enforcement center. They went to their offices and shed their winter gear. Sally grabbed a cup of coffee while her partner sat at his desk studying the photographs from the search warrant. He thought he might get lucky on the warrant but he had no idea that it would be as successful as it was.

Hezekiah was shuffled into the interrogation room. He was in handcuffs and leg shackles and told to sit down. He did as he was told without a word. A deputy sheriff entered the room to guard the prisoner until the two detectives arrived. Hezekiah sat on a folding metal chair with his head bowed as he waited over an hour for the Milrose detectives to show up. He was anxious to know what they had found. He figured they had found his mother in the freezer and some of the items from the burglaries. There were some other things he had hoped they hadn't found.

The two detectives dismissed the deputy and entered the small room. Sally sat in a chair facing Hezekiah while Detective Carpenter stood and leaned against a wall. He was the first to speak. "Well, well, Hezekiah. Looks like you got yourself in a lot of trouble this time. It was interesting searching your house. We found lots of things. Want to hear about them?"

The prisoner kept his head lowered, not wanting to make eye contact with either of the two cops talking to him. It was silent in the room and they waited for an answer from Hezekiah. The silence bothered the prisoner and Hezekiah couldn't stand it any longer. He raised his head and looked at the young female cop seated across from him. "Like what?"

Sally let her partner do the talking and she took notes. "Like a pry bar." He handed several pictures of the pry bar to Hezekiah. He picked the pictures up, looked at them and flung them back at the detective. "Never seen that before in my life." He wondered why they didn't talk about his mother. *They had to have found her in the freezer. What if they didn't? What if they never looked in the freezer? It was possible. If they had found mother they would have said something. They wouldn't be talking about some stupid burglary when they had a real murder on their hands.*

The interview was going nowhere. Hezekiah was not talking. He hung his head again, fiddled with his hands and whistled softly to himself, ignoring his interviewers. At eleven thirty a deputy knocked on the door and advised the two detectives that it was lunch time for the prisoner and would they like his food delivered to the interrogation room or to his cell.

"Put him in his cell," Sally answered the deputy. She looked at her partner and whispered that they should go get something to eat. Bob Carpenter agreed. The deputy escorted the prisoner back to his cell and the two detectives left after the deputy was gone. The interview was far from over.

They were having lunch at the Horn Inn and working on a strategy to get their burglar and murderer to talk. "I don't want him to know yet that we've found his mother. That's what's on his mind and he may be anxious to tell about the burglaries if he thinks he can get out of jail on his own recognizance. He's going to want to hightail it out to his house and get rid of that body. I don't know where else to start, do you Sally?"

"Not really, but I think if we don't get anywhere with Hadley we should call in Josh. We could use his interviewing expertise." She answered as she was debating whether to have some pie and ice cream when it hit her. She wasn't craving a cigarette after this meal. She felt good about that and ordered desert. She knew the worst was over and that she had kicked the habit. It was the hardest thing she had ever done and she was proud of herself. "I think I'm over the cigarettes, Bob."

He was finishing his piece of homemade lemon pie when she gave him the good news. "I'm proud of you, Sally. Don't ever start again, okay?"

She nodded as she slid out of the booth. They would go back to the station and spend the afternoon in the same little room with Hezekiah Hadley.

They began the questioning by asking the prisoner why he stole the sword from Peter Krueger. "Krueger says it was laying in the backseat of his car when you took it. He says you always liked that sword and wanted it real bad. He says you wanted it to kill somebody, he says you wanted all those things that you got in those burglaries to use to kill somebody. He told us lot of things." Detective Carpenter looked at the prisoner and waited for a reaction. Hadley wouldn't like being ratted on.

"Krueger said that?"

"That and a lot more. He'll even testify in court that you told him about the burglaries. What if I told you that I found your prints on the sword? We got you, Hadley. We found a lot of the items from the burglary in your house. That's what's called prima facie evidence. Means we got you and with the testimony of your friend, Mr. Krueger, you're going away for a long time. So, you want to talk to us or do you want to do this the hard way. You know that if you cooperate with us the judge is usually more lenient but, if you don't, then you could be going to the big house this time and you know what they do to people like you there."

For the first time during the interview Hezekiah looked up at the two detectives in the room with him. "Give me a cigarette and I'll tell you what you want to know."

"We don't smoke," Sally answered thinking how nice it was to be able to say that. "Anyway, we don't allow smoking in this building."

"Then take me back to my cell and the next time you want to talk to me make sure I have a lawyer, okay - and cigarettes. No cigarettes, no talkie, talkie."

Sally knew they were lucky that Hezekiah had refused to have an attorney present. He had done so because he did not plan to talk to them; he didn't think he needed one. She made a quick decision and summoned for the deputy. She asked him to take the prisoner to his locker and let him get his cigarettes.

"Sally, you know the rules," the deputy questioned. He did not want to get into trouble for allowing a prisoner to smoke. The jail was his charge and the Sheriff would have his hide if he found out someone was smoking back there. All he needed was for the other prisoners to smell the smoke and all hell would break loose.

"I'll take all responsibility and we'll keep the door closed at all times."

The deputy took the prisoner back to his locker and waited while Hezekiah looked through his belongings until he found his cigarettes. He eventually found them inside his shoe and the jailor brought him back to the interrogation room. In the prisoner's hand was a full pack of cigarettes, a lighter and a plastic ashtray. He set the items in front of him and lit his first cigarette. "If I tell you about these burglaries I want you to wrap them all up into only one offense, okay? You know, like we did last time."

"I don't know Hezekiah, that's up to the County Attorney and he may not have a lot of patience with you considering this is the third time you have been picked up for this sort of thing. I can talk to him but I can't make any promises. Let's see what you've got to say first."

The investigators were aware that the prisoner was proud of his exploits but were surprised that he remembered them in such detail. He didn't know the exact dates of the burglaries but he was close enough. He confessed to nine burglaries that spanned a period of four months. He committed the burglaries around three-thirty. He had watched the night cops and knew that they stopped for their coffee breaks at one of the restaurants on the freeway around three-thirty. They were the only cops on duty so he knew he had at least a half an hour to steal what he wanted. "Pete would do the watching and I would go inside. It was easy; no one in this town had alarms. I had all the time in the world. Me and Pete would split the money fifty-fifty."

"So Peter was involved too?" Detective Carpenter asked.

The prisoner was chain smoking and the room was filling up with second hand smoke. Sally realized she had probably made a mistake by letting Hezekiah smoke but he was talking and if that is all it took to engage his mouth she would explain to the Sheriff and hoped he would understand. Her partner gave her a dirty look as he fanned the smoke from his face.

Hezekiah hadn't told them everything. He didn't tell them about the stash he planted under a tree in Cedar Park. The items he was going to use on his mother. He didn't tell them about all the burglaries, the ones where he got into the business without a pry bar, the ones that had certain items he needed that would never be missed. He didn't tell them why he had taken what he had. He needed to get out of jail and get to his house; he had to move that body.

It was four thirty and both detectives were ready to call it a day. They ended the interview and called the deputy and had him take the prisoner back to his cell. They would be back for more interviews in a couple of days.

CHAPTER 28

Moses Taft hired a professional hit man to murder his wife. He had planned on killing her himself or hiring someone to do it. He knew he didn't have the stomach for it so option number two was the only available choice. He had planned on getting rid of her over a year ago but could never muster up enough courage to do so but when he took out a million dollar life insurance policy on her four months ago he got braver and more confident. Moses Taft was anxious to begin a new life, one of leisure, pleasure and women. He wouldn't miss the old bitch nagging at him every day of his life. *Do this, don't do that, pick up your clothes, clean the car, go to the grocery store and on and on and on.* He couldn't stand it any more and he wanted his wife out of his life as soon as possible. Because of his eagerness and impatience to begin his new life he didn't plan the murder as well as he should have. He was careless in hiring the hit man - he had asked too many people if they knew of someone that would *take care of his wife.* One day on his way to work he received a phone call from a stranger who said he had heard that he was looking for someone to do a special job for him and that he would be able to do it for a thousand bucks. Moses was excited, he had finally connected. He arranged a rendezvous for that evening and when the meeting was over plans had been formulated and a deposit of five hundred dollars made and his wife was as good as dead. He would never know the man's name or anything about him. The hit man wanted it that way and Moses saw no reason to question him, after all he was the professional and not Moses. A month after the meeting with the unknown man, Moses told his wife that he needed to fly to Chicago for the weekend on some business. She knew he was lying to her but she didn't care, he would be gone for a few days which would leave her alone without 'him' around to annoy her. She was tired of her husband and relished a quiet weekend alone. She briefly questioned him about the trip but he was tight lipped and she let the matter drop. He had been acting strange lately, he seemed nervous and excited and she thought he may have found a girlfriend and that he was cheating on her. She couldn't imagine who would want him but there was always some fool out there who wanted a man. If she ever found out that he was unfaithful to her it would be her excuse to leave him – everybody would understand that kind of reasoning. He was away from his wife and his home for two nights and three days and returned late Sunday night. Entering the house, it seemed quieter than usual. He knew and hoped something was wrong. He quietly walked through the house; it appeared it had been burglarized. It was part of the plan. He inspected each room and left the kitchen for last. It was there he would find the body. It was part of the plan. He called 911. He would tell the police he looked in the kitchen last and that is where he found her. She was slumped on the tile floor, nude, her throat slit and blood everywhere. The BCA's forensic unit was called to investigate the crime scene and they found several fingerprints that matched those of an ex-con by the name of Roger Borman. Borman was arrested and confessed to the crime. He implicated Moses Taft who he claimed had hired him for a thousand bucks to kill his wife. In exchange for his testimony against Taft he would receive a reduced sentence.

Taft was immediately arrested and it was discovered that he hadn't gone to Chicago on a business trip like he had told his wife but had spent the three days in a Minneapolis hotel room in the company of two hookers who verified that he was with them the whole three days. Josh Trimble was the lead investigator in the case and quickly discovered that Moses Taft had taken out a one million dollar life insurance policy on his wife within the last couple of months - motive. He located two other ex-cons who admitted that Taft had approached them about killing his wife. He had more than enough evidence to present to the grand jury. The grand jury returned an indictment of first degree murder. Moses Taft plea bargained the charges down to second degree murder and would spend the next twenty years of his life at Stillwater Prison.

To Josh Trimble the wearisome part of his job was the time spent in the courtroom. Today was no exception. The judge had requested him to be in court for the sentencing hearing. The prosecution may have some questions for the Agent and the judge wanted him in the courtroom for that reason. Everything was expected to go smoothly but it didn't always go that way. Taft had been cooperative during the whole ordeal and accepted his fate. He was to stand in front of the judge, admit his guilt and describe to the judge in detail the series of events that led up to his having his wife killed. He needed to admit that he hired Roger Borman and why.

The hearing was supposed to begin at ten a.m. but Josh knew that never happened and it wasn't until eleven-thirty that he found out the judge was ready to begin. Josh had been sitting and waiting in the first row behind the attorney's tables since nine-forty-five. The whole time he was waiting he was thinking about Marcie and he wondered what had gone wrong with their relationship. He thought they were getting along great and all of a sudden she decides that she wants to call it quits. She sprung it on him last night and she wouldn't tell him why. All Marcie said was that if he didn't know why she was calling it quits then it was pointless to continue the way they were. He had thought long and hard about what she had said and still could not figure out what went wrong. The only thing that he could think of was that he hadn't been home much lately. The Taft murder case and the Milrose case had kept him from being home with Marcie for the last few months. He guessed that was the reason but he couldn't be sure. He was glad to see the prisoner brought in; he stopped thinking about Marcie. Two deputies brought the shackled prisoner into the courtroom through a side door and sat down at one of the attorney's tables and waited for the judge to enter. By twelve-thirty the prisoner had been sentenced to twenty years at Stillwater prison and was escorted from the courtroom in his handcuffs and leg irons while members of the press waited outside the courthouse to get pictures of the prisoner as he was led to the waiting patrol car.

Josh Trimble's day was over, it was Friday and he was calling it a week. He would now concentrate all his efforts on the Harmony Ann Day case. He had to drive through Milrose on his way home so he decided to stop and check with Sally Fairfield and Bob Carpenter and see how their murder case was developing. It was an hour and a half drive to Milrose and when he arrived in town he realized he was hungry. He hadn't eaten breakfast or lunch that day so he pulled into the Horn Inn, grabbed a booth and ordered a sandwich and a cup of coffee. When he was through eating he looked at his watch and realized that it was almost three-thirty. He paid for his meal and drove to the Law Enforcement Center.

Sally had gone for the day and Detective Carpenter was about to leave when Josh arrived. The detective lieutenant filled him in on what had been happening on the case and Josh was amazed at how much he had missed by being gone for a week and being tied up with the Taft case. Detective Carpenter excused himself saying that he had an appointment he had to keep and that he needed to go. "Oh, by the way Josh, if you got time you should stop out to the bowling alley tonight, Sally's subbing for another girl. I think they bowl at six-thirty and I'm sure she'd like to see you. Maybe she can fill you in a little bit more than I have."

Josh stopped at the offices of Chief Rowlands and the Sheriff and spent an hour with each of them. It was all small talk but Josh wanted to kill some time before he went to the bowling alley. He couldn't start drinking yet, he still had another hour to drive home.

Sally was putting on her bowling shoes when he arrived at the bowling alley. She was busy with her friends and he didn't want to bother her so he took a seat at the small bar next to the bowling lanes and watched her and the team work their magic. Sally had finished picking off a spare and walking back to her group when she noticed Josh at the bar. He was having a beer and when he noticed that she was looking at him he waved to her. She waved back and then sat down with her team and cheered on the next bowler. After the first game she walked over and sat next to him. He told her that he would buy her a beer when she was through bowling and she was happy to accept the invitation.

An hour and a half later the game was over. "We took all four games - time to celebrate." Sally said as she sat down on the stool next to him. "I'm buying, big boy, what ya' havin'?"

After a couple of beers and some small talk Sally filled Josh in on Hezekiah and Pete Krueger and finding Florence Hadley in the freezer and their interrogation of Hezekiah and his admission to the burglaries. Josh filled Sally in on his break up with Marcie. The three other girls on the bowling team invited Sally and Josh to join them at a table and they graciously accepted the invitation. Before the evening was over Josh had asked Sally for a real date. She looked at him and seemed confused but accepted his offer.

CHAPTER 29

The complainant was patiently waiting in front of his garage when Sally pulled into his driveway. As one of the two detectives on the department it was her responsibility to investigate any thefts that occurred in the town. Her hands were full with the two murders and Hezekiah Hadley but the petty crimes also needed her attention; the Chief insisted on it and the taxpayers deserved it. It looked as if she was going to be getting in a lot of overtime in the next few months. When it was all over she will have accumulated over five weeks of vacation and she was going to use every last day of it.

She got out of the car and walked up to the man waiting for her. He was older, maybe fifty or sixty and dressed Minnesotan with blue jeans, flannel shirt, work boots and a Minnesota Twins baseball cap. He held out his hand as she approached. She walked up to him, shook his hand and looked in the open garage.

"This is where it was parked," he said, pointing to an empty space in the rear of his garage. "I've had that tractor for five or six years. Noticed it gone this morning. Funny how things work. I always padlock the side door but last night I got to doing something else and I completely forgot to put the lock on the door. After I got into bed last night I remembered the door but I thought it wouldn't matter if I didn't lock it just one night. Can you believe it? The one night I don't lock it is the night that someone walks in and steals my garden tractor. What are the odds of that?"

Sally took notes of the theft and after she had all the information she needed she assured the complainant that she would work hard to find his tractor. She got into her car and looked at her watch; it was ten minutes after nine. She decided to treat herself to a cup of coffee at the Horn Inn before going back to the office. She pulled in the lot and found a parking space near the front door. She got out of the car, and walked to the Minneapolis Tribune newspaper dispenser, put in her two quarters, opened the door and took a copy out.

She found a booth in Helen's section, laid her newspaper down, took off her jacket and tossed it in the booth next to her and sat down. She knew Helen would be at her booth in a short time with a glass of water and a cup of coffee.

Helen promptly appeared at her booth and after she placed Sally's coffee and water in front of her she took a seat across from her. Sally looked at her questioningly, wondering what Helen might want. "I don't know how to say this or what to do about it but I need your advice."

"Go ahead, I'm all ears," she answered and took a sip of her coffee.

"There's this guy in town. He works for Dr. Goodland."

Helen had Sally's attention. "Nathan Brown."

"Yea, how do you know him?" Helen asked.

"I worked with him at an autopsy."

"What do you think of him?" Helen was nervous asking the detective these questions. She thought she was making too much out of what could be just her imagination but she wanted to know about Nathan Brown. She had bad feelings about him and they wouldn't go away.

"Helen, to be real honest with you, I'm not too crazy about the guy myself. What's the concern with him?"

Helen put her elbows on the table and folded her arms. She looked around the restaurant and noticing that they weren't busy she told Detective Fairfield about her problems with Nathan Brown. "It started a little over a week ago. I was with a girlfriend at *The Couplings* and Brown was there. He was sitting at the bar by himself and we were in a booth on the other side of the room. I noticed him staring at me and it made me a little nervous so I turned my head away from him and my girlfriend glanced his way once in while. She told me that he was watching me a lot and I was getting the creeps so we had two drinks and left. The next day he comes into the restaurant and has a late breakfast and is watching me again. At two o'clock I got off work. My car was parked in the back of the building where the employees' park and I was walking to my car and I noticed this black van sitting in the employees parking section. No one that works at the Horn Inn drives a black van so I looked at it and there was someone behind the wheel. You guessed it, it was Nathan Brown. He was pretending he was reading a book but I could tell he was staring at me. Since then I see him all the time. He has been coming into the restaurant every day for lunch. He never did that before. I've seen him drive by my apartment and then pull into our lot and stop his van and stare at my apartment. He scares me anyway and with him kind of stalking me I am worried. What can I do?"

While she was waiting for an answer she noticed that Detective Fairfield's coffee cup was empty. She got up from the booth and walked behind the counter and grabbed two pots of coffee and walked around the restaurant refilling the customer's cups. When she was done she walked over to Sally's booth and sat down again, placing the two partially empty coffee pots on the table in front of her and looked pleadingly at Sally.

"I'm afraid I can't be much help. He isn't doing anything illegal and I would have to have a legal reason to talk to him about this. I mean, he may not be even stalking you. Maybe he's just trying to work up enough nerve to ask you for a date. I'll tell you what I'll do, I stop in at noon once in a while for lunch and I'll sit next to him, let him know I'm around so if he has any crazy notions he'll remember me before he tries anything. I'd like your work schedule and once in a while I'll park in the employees' parking lot when you get off. If he's there I'll have a talk with him as to why he is parked where he is. Once again, letting him know I'm around. I'll also drive by your apartment once in a while and check on you. That's all I can do for now, sorry."

Helen smiled and thanked her. She slid out of the booth and picked up the guest check next to the coffee. "Coffee's on me. Thanks, I feel better now."

Sally left the restaurant with Helen's work schedule in her hand and walked to her car and couldn't get Nathan Brown out of her mind.

CHAPTER 30

Lin Su had no idea where she was when she woke up. She was in a car, she knew that much and the car was moving but her memory wouldn't connect as she tried to remember what happened to her and why she felt dizzy and weak. She tried to open her eyes and had difficulty with the left one. It felt heavy, she reached to touch it, and the eye was swollen and sore. She remembered now, she was having an argument with Pete and he hit her. The blow came fast, she never saw the clenched fist nor felt it connect with her face. The last thing she remembered was arguing with Pete about Harmony Day. She sat up and bent over to look at her face in the rear view mirror. The area around her eye was purple and red and green and swollen; the left eye was cemented shut and she was unable to open it. A small trickle of crusted blood emanated from her lip and stopped half way down her chin. She wanted to get the blood wiped off of her face; she grabbed a small white handkerchief from her purse and whetted it with her spit. She wiped her chin and looked into the rear view mirror again. She had washed most of it off and was content with her looks for now. She would wait until they stopped for gas and she would go into a bathroom and clean herself up good. She sat back in the seat and stared out the side window. The scenery had changed while she was unconscious. The landscape was brown and the trees had disappeared. They were in the desert and she had no idea where they were but she wasn't going to ask Pete. She was not going to talk to him for now. She remained quiet and watched the roadside go by speedily by.

"We'll stay overnight in Albuquerque," he told her. He didn't look at her; he kept his eyes glued on the road. They continued their silence and Lin Su reached over and turned on the radio, she needed some noise. When she found the station she wanted she resumed her position leaning against the passenger door and watching the dry, arid land as it zoomed by. After they were almost through Albuquerque Krueger spotted a motel, pulled off the freeway and on to the service road that led to a Budget Six. He pulled in, got out and walked into the office and registered. He intentionally got a room with two single beds and they each slept on one and didn't talk until breakfast the next morning.

She broke the silence after she ordered breakfast. "We gonna' be in Nogales today?" It was time to talk to each other and she had forgiven him. It would happen again and again and she knew it. She loved him and would have to put up with his bursts of anger. She didn't want to take a chance on losing him.

"Yea, I figure we should be there tonight sometime. We'll get a hotel room and tomorrow we'll start checking the place out for apartments to rent. I may try to get a job cuz we're gonna' run out of money eventually." He was glad they were talking again but he would never admit it.

They finished their breakfast and with their plans laid out they started their journey to Nogales, Arizona and a new beginning. They arrived in the town at eight o'clock that night and found a cheap hotel with a king size bed. The next day was successful; they found an apartment to rent and Lin Su had applied for two waitress jobs. The rent was affordable and it looked as if Lin Su would get one of the two jobs she had applied for. Peter knew he would have to find employment if his plans were to be successful. He knew he would never find the kind of job he had at Honeywell but he would settle for anything right now. He wanted to make this work and he would do what was needed to achieve that goal. The bank robbery was easy and the payout was more than he had ever dreamed of but the risks were too great and he didn't want to go back to jail. The time he spent in jail in Montana still lingered on his mind and he didn't want to spend another night, ever, behind bars. He would think about finding work later, for now it was time to explore the town and check out the local bars.

Peter Krueger wasn't one to sit around and do nothing. He needed to find work or something else to do to occupy his mind. He was sitting at the kitchen table nursing his headache from last night's bar hopping. The pile of money from the bank robbery was neatly stacked in piles of twenties, tens and fives. The pile of twenties being the tallest. He was counting and recounting the money and remembering the thrill he had gotten when the teller handed him the bag of money. Next to him was a Smith and Wesson .357 he had bought off of an illegal alien at a rest area outside of Phoenix. He had eighteen hundred dollars left, but he figured he would have a job before they ran through the rest of it. Lin Su had made the suggestion first and he hadn't thought much about it but as he was thinking about the money in front him and whether to get a job or not he realized that the idea she had brought up earlier may prove profitable. She wanted to drive to Laughlin and check it out, maybe win some money, enough to hold them for a while. The more he thought about it the more he liked it. He was a good craps player and if he could double their money or maybe quadruple it at the crap table it would hold them for a long time. They had paid the deposit and the first months rent which took up most of their cash but now all they had left to pay was the utilities and food and that shouldn't cost much; they would have at least fifteen hundred dollars to gamble with. He looked at his girlfriend who was lying on the couch smoking a joint. "Let's go to Laughlin and win some money. We'll leave tomorrow morning."

The drive took all day and they pulled into the Colorado Belle Resort and Casino at seven p.m. They booked a room for two nights and if their luck held out they might stay longer. The crap table should be easy pickings. He would shoot craps and would give Lin Su a hundred bucks to play the slots, between the two of them they might get lucky.

They were both tired when they arrived in Laughlin; it had been a long day of driving. They had stopped once for gas and picked up some sodas, chips and two cups of coffee and that is all they'd eaten since leaving Nogales. After checking in at the front desk they went to their room on the fifth floor. Once inside their room Lin Su unpacked their suitcase while Pete took a shower. She took her shower after him and they were ready to go down and get some food; they were both hungry. The gambling would have to wait until tomorrow. He was tired, Lin Su was tired and they both wanted a good night's sleep. He wanted to be rested for tomorrow when he took the casino's money.

At five o'clock a.m. he was up, wide awake and ready to gamble. He left Lin Su in bed asleep and took the elevator down to the casino.

It was early in the morning and one crap table was open with a few people shooting dice. He threw down twenty five bills on the table and the croupier picked them up, counted them and handed Krueger five hundred dollars in chips. He placed a fifty dollar bet on the come line and won. He let the fifty ride and waited for the next roll of the dice. He had a good feeling; he was on his way to riches, like taking candy from a baby. He lost the next bet and the table turned cold on him. In less than an hour his money was gone, disappearing like a popsicle on a hot summer day. He couldn't believe the bad luck he was having. He knew that in time and with enough money he would eventually win but he didn't have more money and didn't have time so he left the table and looked for Lin Su. He found her at one of the dollar slots; she had doubled the money he had given her. When he found her, he told her that they had to leave Laughlin. He didn't explain why. With Lin Su's winnings he was able to pay for their room with enough left over for gas and a few meals. Something needed to be done.

He checked his watch and it was eight fifteen in the morning. By the time they got to Kingman the banks would open and he would get his money back. The plan was the same as the one in Kansas City. Lin Su would wait in the car while he went in the bank and relieved it of its money. He would get more this time because he would empty two cages instead of one. That would double the take and this time they would be more careful with the money. He tucked the 9 mm in his belt and left the .357 with Lin Su. He wouldn't have to use the gun but he wanted the teller to see it. It would help convince her that he meant business.

The banks in the town were beginning to open when they pulled into Kingman. Krueger drove around the town three times before he decided on the bank he wanted to hit. It was a small bank on a corner with a small parking lot adjoining it. There were two exits leaving the parking lot and each one led to a street that led to the freeway. The location was perfect and the parking lot was an extra advantage. Several open parking spaces were available, Lin Su parked the Escalade in one that was close to the bank and allowed her easy maneuverability to take either exit.

Peter stepped out of the SUV and walked to the bank. He was confident and couldn't wait to get back into the vehicle and count his money. He walked up to the teller and told her he had a gun and that he wanted all her money. The first teller was a young Filipino woman who calmly took all the bills from her till and placed them in a white cloth bag and handed it to Krueger. He guessed she had been trained what to do in case this kind of thing ever happened. She remained calm and after handing him the money she turned her head away from him to avoid eye contact. When he was finished with the first teller he walked over to the teller's cage next to the Filipino girl and as if scripted he told her the same thing. This woman was older. She wore thick plastic framed glasses and was chewing gum loudly. She was surprised at first when he made his threat but she calmly did the same thing as the first girl did as if rehearsed. When he had both bags of money he turned from the tellers and walked out the front door of the bank - at the same time that two squad cars pulled up to the front door with their red lights flashing. One of the tellers must have pushed an alarm, something he hadn't counted on. He panicked and pulled out his 9mm and started firing. He felt his right leg heat up and he went down. From across the street the police were being fired upon by an oriental lady. They turned their attention to her. As she was about to fire another round at them they returned fire. Lin Su was struck six times in the heart and abdomen with 9mm shells from three different guns. She died instantly.

CHAPTER 31

Helen DuPont would have to step on it if she was going to make it to work on time. She shouldn't have stayed up as late as she did but mid-terms were next week and she wanted to be ready for them. She punched in at nine o'clock on the nose. She had made it with no time to spare. She liked to be on time for work, in fact it was almost an obsession with her not to be late. She put her time card back into its slot and grabbed her apron and put it on. She quickly checked the specials of the day, put her guest check book in her apron pocket, and looked in the mirror to see if she was presentable. She didn't have time for a cup of coffee today, the restaurant was full and they needed her on the floor right away. She grabbed two coffee pots, one regular and one decaf and walked around the restaurant refilling cups and saying her good mornings to the customers. She was familiar with all of them, knew them by their first names and what they ate for breakfast and what their choices of coffee were. This helped when it came time for the customers to leave their tips. Walking around with the coffee pots allowed her to get a feel for the mood of the customers at the Horn Inn and notice if anyone had not been waited on.

Helen had been looking forward to her sophomore year all summer and it had finally arrived. She would no longer have to share a dormitory room with someone else. She had moved into a small one bedroom apartment near the campus immediately after spring semester. It was mandatory at Milrose State that all students reside on campus their first year. It wouldn't have been bad if she had gotten a roommate that she could get along with but the one she had was a party girl. She drank and caroused every night of the week coming in at all hours of the morning, always waking Helen out of a sound sleep.

Once, in the early morning hours she stumbled into the room after a night of debauchery, sashayed over to the closet, pulled down her pants and urinated all over Helen's shoes. That was the last straw, a heated argument ensued the next morning over the incident and the two roommates didn't talk to each other for the rest of the school year. As far as Helen was concerned her roommate had no redeeming qualities and on top of everything else she was a slob. Her personal hygiene was egregious and her consideration for the cleanliness of the dorm room was worse. Helen kept the bathroom spotless, the floors mopped and the small room free of litter. The odd couple combination didn't work for either one of them. Helen had tried to get moved into another dorm room but there were no openings and she had to spend the year in roommate misery.

Three waitresses covered the floor at the Horn Inn and each had their own section. Josh Trimble and Sally Fairfield walked in and sat at a booth in Helen's section. They noticed Helen heading in their direction as they were getting comfortable. She was average height, maybe five-six or five-seven and thin, not underweight but pleasant to look at and admire. A long braided pony tail hung halfway down her back and bounced up and down as she approached booth three where Sally and Josh sat. She was wearing wire rimmed glasses and had a short pencil stuffed behind her left ear. She had two cups of coffee and two glasses of water on her tray and set them down in front of two of her favorite customers. Josh and Sally preferred sitting in Helen's section if possible; both were convinced she was the best waitress in town and enjoyed her friendliness and positive attitude. She never screwed up their orders and was always there with coffee. Helen noticed something different this morning as she pulled her pencil from behind her ear and took the guest check book from her apron pocket and waited for their order. Instead of sitting across from each other they were sitting on the same side of the booth. Something must have happened between these two she thought to herself. Since first meeting them she thought they were made for each other. She had a slight crush on Agent Trimble but she knew he was too old for her and Detective Fairfield seemed like a person she would have liked to have had for a friend - she liked them both. They were always in a good mood and joked with her and when they left the restaurant there was always a nice tip lying on the table. She knew what they were going to order before they told her and she had it half written down while carrying on a brief conversation with them. They were both smiling and seemed to be in a jovial mood this morning.

CHAPTER 32

Parker Hill didn't like change, never had and never would. His thinking was that everything should have stayed the way it was as of November 21st 1963. "The next day the country lost its innocence with the assassination of the young and vibrant President." He would preach his theory to anybody who would listen to him. "People had felt good about America back then. There were hopes and dreams and a can do attitude. Those feelings resurged again when Ronald Reagan was elected President but quickly vanished when he left office." He also didn't have much going for the baby boomer generation of which he was a member. "They brought drugs to America, free love, deviant behavior, religious mockery, rampant divorce and sexual diseases - but more than that they brought an 'it's all about me' attitude." He disliked most things that his generation stood for which in his mind was nothing at all. The thing he could never and would never forgive or forget was what some of those of his generation did to the returning soldiers who served their country in Viet Nam. It was members of his generation that spit on those soldiers returning from the war. No sir, he would never, could never forgive them. Parker Hill was a dime store philosopher who never had the opportunity to go to college and attained all his knowledge from books. Parker Hill loved to read.

When he graduated from Milrose High School he didn't have enough money to go to college and his parents could not afford to send him so he took a job with the Milrose School District as a janitor. Thirty years later he still worked at the same place but was now the lead janitor. He enjoyed his work and enjoyed the students. He did notice a difference with each passing year. The attitude of the students was changing, discipline in the school was weakening and the drop out rate was increasing. He couldn't explain what was happening but thought that much of the blame should be put on the lawyers. Any disciplinary action in the school usually resulted in a law suit and the teachers were afraid to discipline a student. When he was a student at Milrose if he screwed up he got disciplined by his teacher and if his father found out there would be hell to pay when he got home. That was all before November 21st, 1963 and what was happening in the schools was indirectly related to the baby boomers who had become overly protective of their children. He and his wife had six children and they weren't afraid to discipline any of them if the need should ever arise and it did every now and then. With six children it was bound to. He had put all of his children through college and the youngest had graduated only last year from Princeton. He was proud of his children but was looking forward to being able to put a few dollars away for retirement.

Those in town that knew Parker Hill respected him and his family. "He was a man you could trust, his handshake was his bond and you don't find many people like that any more," the townsfolk would often say when Parker Hill's name was brought up in conversation. He had missed only four days work in the last thirty years and that was because he was so terribly sick that he couldn't get out of bed and his wife insisted that he stay home until he felt better. She could wield a lot of influence in the family if she had to.

He was leaning on his broom talking to the vice-principal, telling him about the notice he had received in the mail. The letter informed him that he was being placed on a jury roster for the coming year and that he could be called at any time and should be prepared to serve. "Not much to worry about, there isn't much action here in Milrose," the vice-principal assured him.

"You're probably right but we've had this murder and all those burglaries and I am guessing that somebody is going to be caught sometime soon," Parker answered back.

When the vice-principal left to go to his office Parker went back to his work but was thinking about what it would be like to serve on a jury. Parker Hill liked the vice-principal and as a matter of fact he liked most of the people in Milrose. There were exceptions of course and the one that stood out in his mind the most was Andy Taylor. He had seen Andy Taylor in school several times, having been called to the school many times because of discipline problems with either his son or his daughter. He would yell at the teachers or the principal or anybody that was in ear shot of his voice, always taking the side of the children and screaming that he had more important things to do than spend his time here. Parker was usually in earshot of these tirades and there were times he would have liked to gone over to Andrew Taylor and socked him in the nose. He never did of course, his character as a man wouldn't allow it. He didn't know that one day soon their paths would cross again. This time in a different manner altogether.

The local women of the town liked Mrs. Taylor. There was something about her, something nice and good and sweet. They could never figure why she got herself hooked up with such a worthless man as Andrew Taylor – 'that good for nothing'. After their marriage she could be seen in town every Wednesday morning picking up a few items at Barnes Grocery. She never bought much and people knew the reason; Andy Taylor never gave his wife enough money to do some real shopping. After Faith and Sam were born she was seen less and less on Wednesdays and as time went on she wasn't seen at all. People began to get worried about her and were convinced that her husband had killed her or had her locked up in the barn or something. She was eventually forgotten about and once in a while someone would see Faith or Sam picking up a few groceries and they would think about Mrs. Taylor.

Those that had been invited to the wedding remembered the wedding ceremony and the dance that followed. The new Mrs. Taylor appeared happy enough that evening and danced with most of the men, conversed with the wives and danced several times with her new husband who had become quite drunk by evening's end.

Some of the husbands, having been coaxed by their wives, considered going to Andy Taylor and talking to him about what had happened to his wife. They would tell him that they were curious why no one had seen her in town for the longest time. They didn't though; they were unsure what he would do to trespassers - probably shoot them were their thoughts which were enough to keep them away. The Sheriff's Department was asked to get involved in finding out about Mrs. Taylor and they had gone to the farm on a couple of occasions. Andy greeted them at his front steps before they were able to get out of the squad car. He would not let them look around and they had no probable cause to get a search warrant from Judge Armstrong and the matter was dropped and Mrs. Taylor drifted into oblivion. Andy Taylor was not bothered again and everybody was left to wonder what happened to Mrs. Andrew P. Taylor.

Andy Taylor grew up on a one hundred and sixty acre farm outside of Milrose and it was enough land to support the family, but not enough to allow them anything but the necessities of life. Andy grew up working on the farm and attending school occasionally until at sixteen he quit school to help out on the farm full time. His father was dying of cirrhosis of the liver and he was now the man that was responsible for keeping the farm running. He wasn't a good farmer, not like Angus Sullivan or his neighbor Joseph Brown, but the crops always got planted and harvested mostly on time and there was enough food for the family to exist on with a little left over for booze and cigarettes.

Once a week on Friday afternoons Andy Taylor would get in his 1949 Chevrolet and head for Milrose to pick up two quarts of Jack Daniels and a carton of Marlboro. His children were too young to get the items for him and he had to do it himself. Today he had to make two stops, one at the liquor store and one at the post office. He had received a notice in his mail box that there was a letter at the post office that he needed to sign for. He debated whether to pick up the letter or not but he was curious about the letter and drove across town to the small post office. After signing for the letter he began walking to his pick-up, opening it and reading it as he walked. He had been summoned for possible jury duty. He would be on the roster for the next year and that he was to notify the Clerk of Court if his serving on jury duty would be a hardship on him.

****

Angus Sullivan, along with Parker Hill and Andy Taylor, was a life long resident of the Milrose community. He graduated from Milrose High School twenty years before Parker Hill, went to the University of Minnesota where he got his bachelors degree in agricultural science, got married after graduation and moved home to the family farm. His father owned three hundred and forty acres and Angus knew from the time he was a boy sitting on his dad's Oliver tractor that he wanted to be a farmer like his father. A second house was built on the farm for Angus, his wife and the baby that was on its way. He was happy to work the farm with his father until he had enough money saved for some land of his own. One day his father told him that the neighbor was selling his one hundred and sixty acre farm and that he thought Angus should consider buying the farm and that he would help him with the down payment. Angus could pay him back by helping his dad work the home place. Angus was excited over the news. He would finally be able to have a farm of his own and he excitedly agreed to have his father help him out. Angus was a good farmer and a wise businessman and fifteen years after he bought his first farm he was running two thousand acres of farmland. Most of it was owned and some was rented. Angus was an only child and when his father died he inherited the family farm which put his total land holdings to around twenty five hundred acres. He was one of the richest men in the county with a net worth of several million dollars. He was a County Commissioner and had once been asked to run for a seat in the U.S. Congress. He declined that invitation but was a large contributor to the Democratic Party and followed politics closely.

It wouldn't be long now. A week after Christmas and he and his wife would be driving to Florida for the winter. The winters were difficult for his wife; she suffered from arthritis and their doctor suggested a warmer climate in the winter. They discovered Florida, fell in love with it and spent the last twenty winters there. They would be back in the spring, early enough to plant the corn and the soybeans. The farm kept him busy with planting, cultivating, fertilizing and repair of machinery. He enjoyed working and couldn't imagine any other life for him. Although he enjoyed the warm winters in Florida, there wasn't much for him to do except sit around the house and watch TV or read or put together jigsaw puzzles. He liked working with his hands and being active and he enjoyed the mild winters but he was bored. He didn't enjoy sitting around, he felt each moment of his life was precious and he didn't want to squander a minute of it. His wife enjoyed Florida and her arthritic pain all but disappeared each winter. By the time March rolled around Angus was ready to get back to the farm. He never told his wife that he was bored and restless and anxious for the return trip. He was quiet on the subject but his wife knew his feelings and felt blessed that she was married to such an understanding man. Her happiness and her temporary relief from pain pleased him as he tried to make the best of the situation. They would be off to Minnesota on Palm Sunday and he would be back to the life he loved. Mid April through the first part of October kept him busy with planting and cultivating and harvesting. He was always glad when the last of his acres were harvested and he could plow the ground under and let it lay dormant for next year's crop. He liked having things to do and knew that he would never be able to retire.

The morning had brought a light sprinkling of snow and, as he walked down the long driveway to get his mail, he could see where his feet had been. A fresh layer of snow had made everything look pure. He pulled the mail out of the black metal oblong box and walked back to the farmhouse. He sat at his desk opening the mail when he came upon a letter from the District Court. He may have to postpone his trip to Florida this year.

CHAPTER 33

Hezekiah studied the top page of the legal pad for the last time and pushed the handwritten confession over to Sally. She lifted it from the table and read it. She was satisfied that the confession was reasonably accurate except for Krueger's involvement. She believed that Hezekiah acted alone and that he was implicating Krueger because his friend had shot him in the ankle and robbed him and he wanted revenge. She knew that Krueger was in Montana when two of the burglaries happened and figured he'd have an alibi on the others also. Hadley had copped to nine burglaries and Sally was reasonably sure that the County Attorney would charge him on separate counts. No plea bargaining this time, Hezekiah had entered the 'big time'. With nine burglary charges staring him in the face Judge Armstrong wouldn't be quite so lenient. His priors would be taken into account and both detectives were sure that the Judge would impose a high bail which would keep Hezekiah in his jail cell until everything could be sorted out.

They wanted Hezekiah locked up while they continued their investigation into the death of his mother and the murder of Harmony Day. They were certain he killed his mother and was somehow involved in Harmony Ann Day's death. They needed to do a lot more questioning of Hezekiah and they wanted him in jail and accessible. The bail hearing was tomorrow and they were well prepared for it. The County Attorney and the Judge both knew of the other investigations being carried on with Hezekiah. The County Attorney seemed more than willing to ask for a high bail and Judge Armstrong seemed more than willing to impose it. Bob Carpenter was prepared for court; he had worked on the burglaries from the beginning and knew the details by heart and was sure he could discuss them in court without notes. Sally was going to accompany him to court and as they were going over the details of the case, the dispatcher buzzed them on the intercom and informed them that a man and his wife were here to see them. "Send them in," Sally replied to the dispatcher.

The middle aged couple peeked into the office and seemed unsure if they were in the right place. "Come in and have a seat." Bob Carpenter introduced himself first and then introduced his partner and asked what they could do for them.

The woman began to speak first. "It's about our daughter, she goes to Milrose State and we haven't seen or heard from her in almost a week and we are worried about her. Last Sunday was my birthday and she didn't call and wish me a happy birthday. That's not like her. She always calls on my birthday or she makes sure she comes home for my birthday. Birthdays were important to her. So when she didn't call I got worried. When she didn't call on Monday I tried calling her and no one answered, no one has answered all week. I called some of her friends and they said they hadn't seen her all week and the college told me she hadn't been in class all week. So you can see why I am worried sick."

The husband held his wife's hand and looked at the two detectives. "We drove all the way up from Kansas, that's how worried we are. Our daughter was always in contact with us and when no one else had seen her that really got us worried."

"What's your daughter's name?" Sally asked, curious if she knew her.

The man felt foolish when he thought about the question; he suddenly realized he had jumped into the story so fast they both had forgotten to introduce themselves or tell them who their daughter was. "Her name is Helen DuPont. I'm George DuPont, her father, and this is her mother, Ada. Helen is a student at Milrose State College. She's a sophomore there and is planning on becoming a teacher. She's a good girl; she doesn't do drugs or get drunk or anything like that. She's sensible, always has been. She was also choosy who her friends were. She wouldn't hang around with no losers, if you know what I mean."

"When was the last time you heard from your daughter?" Detective Fairfield asked remembering her conversation with Helen over a week ago.

Ada DuPont knew precisely when she heard from her daughter. "It was last Friday around four in the afternoon when she called. She had just gotten off work. Oh, I almost forgot, she works at the Horn Inn. She told me she was going to her apartment to get freshened up and after that she was going out for a couple of drinks with a girlfriend of hers."

The two detectives looked at each other and at the DuPonts. "I think we know your daughter. We go to the Horn Inn quite often and we usually sit in your daughter's section. We like her and enjoy having her wait on us. We knew her name was Helen but we never knew her last name." Sally was being truthful; they were both very fond of the young college girl.

The mother reached over the desk and handed a picture of her daughter to the two detectives.

"This was taken in August so it is the most recent. She hasn't changed much since the picture was taken."

The detectives glanced at the photo to satisfy themselves that they were talking about the same girl. Satisfied that Helen DuPont was one in the same person, they asked to keep the picture so they might pass it around, hoping to find somebody that may have seen her. "It may come in handy," Sally said.

"Is there anything else you can tell us about her, like did she have any boyfriends?" Sally asked.

Both parents considered the question and agreed that all of her time was spent between work, classes and homework. "She went to church on Sundays. She was catholic and attended St. Andrews. We're sure she didn't have any boyfriends or she would have told us. That's about all we can tell you for now."

"How do we get a hold of you if we need to?" Detective Carpenter asked.

"We're staying at some hotel on the outskirts of town; I forgot the name of it but its pretty good size."

"The Country Suites," Detective Fairfield offered.

George DuPont shook his head acknowledging that the detective was right. "We're in room 338 - call us anytime day or night if you hear anything."

Detective Carpenter got up from his chair and Detective Fairfield did the same. The DuPonts took the cue, arose, thanked the two officers, grabbed their hands and shook them.

Sally walked the DuPonts down the hallway and to the front door and assured them that they would do everything in their power to find their daughter. She didn't tell them about her conversation with Helen last week; they didn't need to know that yet. She didn't want to worry them more than they already were. When she returned to her partner's office she told him about her conversation with Helen at the restaurant. She was sure that Nathan Brown was responsible for the disappearance of Helen DuPont.

As steady customers of the Horn Inn Sally and Bob had both grown fond of Helen DuPont. She was always cheerful and upbeat when she waited on them; she warmed their hearts with her sharp wit. They hoped that this wasn't going to turn into another murder because it was well known in police circles that things always happened in threes. First Harmony Day, then Florence Hadley and now....... They had hoped the murder of Harmony Ann Day was an isolated incident. They wanted to locate Helen DuPont; they didn't care if she ran off with a circus performer or a carnie as long as she was alive. They did not want to find Helen DuPont dead.

"Let's start at the Horn Inn," she told her partner. "I'll buy you an orange juice."

It was a quiet part of the day at the restaurant. The lunch crowd had gone back to work and the afternoon coffee crowd had not yet arrived. They talked to the owner who told them that Helen had not shown up for work since Monday. "It's unlike her; she never missed a day of work. She didn't even call to say she was sick or wouldn't be coming in. I tried calling her but only got the answering machine. I left messages but she didn't return my calls. I even drove to her apartment to check on her because I was beginning to get worried. I knocked on her door a couple of times but there was no answer. Her car was parked in the lot so I figured she had to be home. It all seems a little strange to me now that I think about it."

"When was the last time you saw her?" Bob asked.

"She worked last Saturday morning and she had Sunday off."

"Did she seem okay, did she look like something was bothering her? Anything out of the ordinary?" Bob asked, jotting down notes on his small pocket notebook. "When did she get off work?"

"Two o'clock and that's the last time I saw her. She seemed fine."

"Was there anybody in the restaurant that morning that seemed out of place? You know a stranger or somebody that looked a little weird?" Bob asked, his notebook still open.

The owner thought about the question; he picked up a coffee pot and walked around the restaurant refilling coffee cups to the few customers still in the Horn Inn. He came back and set the pot down on a burner. "There was one guy, although he's local, Helen couldn't stand him. He made her nervous whenever he came in. He was sitting right where you are sitting, Sally, and he stayed for a long time."

Sally looked at Jake Horn and said. "Well, what's his name?"

"I'm thinking, I'm thinking," he said, his eyes closed as if he was deep in thought. "I got it," he said. "It's that guy that works for Dr. Goodland. The one that wears the black clothes all the time. He's real pale and real thin and he has these eyes that seem to look right into your soul. I can see why Helen didn't like him. That's the guy, I'm sure of it. I can still see him, he was wearing baggy black pants and a black nylon jacket and he had an earring in each ear and his hair was mussed up and dirty like he just got out of bed and hadn't taken the time to comb it."

"Nathan Brown," Sally whispered to herself but loud enough for her partner and Jake Horn to hear her. "I know the guy, he's creepy. In fact, Helen had talked to me about him. She was worried that he might try something and I feel guilty that I couldn't be much help."

For the rest of the afternoon the two detectives dedicated their time to finding out what happened to Helen DuPont and what she did after she got off work at two o'clock on Saturday afternoon. Mrs. DuPont called Sally to ask if they had found anything out yet. She had to tell them they had no information but that she would call them as soon as they found anything out. She felt sorry for the anxious parents and knew what must be going through their minds. They were concerned for their daughter and sensed that something was terribly wrong. They were holding up well under the circumstances and Sally wanted desperately to give them some good news. After talking to

Ada DuPont she replaced her cell phone in its holder and suggested to her partner that they start with the college. They drove the short distance to Milrose State and talked to her college professors. None of them had seen her since last Friday. The detectives knew each of Helen's instructors personally and dismissed them as suspects in her disappearance. The parish priest at St. Andrews was interviewed. He didn't remember seeing her in church last Sunday. The only reason he remembered it was that she attended mass every week without fail and always sat in the same pew; she wasn't there last Sunday. They interviewed her friends and got the same answers from them except for one girlfriend who told them that she and Helen had stopped out at *The Couplings* for a couple of drinks two Fridays ago. "We had two drinks and that was it and we left." She said they weren't there long and nothing seemed out of the ordinary with Helen. She had seemed happy and they talked mostly about college and work and had left sometime between seven-thirty and eight o'clock.

When the day was over and the detectives were finished talking to everyone, their concern for the safety of Helen DuPont increased. Tomorrow they would visit Helen's apartment. The parents had been there several times but were unable to enter. They didn't have a key and no one had answered the door when they knocked. The apartment manager was scheduled to meet with them at nine in the morning at Helen's apartment and the two detectives were hopeful that they could put this mystery behind them. They wanted to find Helen DuPont alive and healthy. They wanted to turn their concentration back to Hezekiah Hadley and his connection with the death of his mother, Florence Hadley, and the murder of Harmony Day.

George and Ada DuPont were waiting for the two detectives when they arrived with the manager. Sally was hesitant about going into the apartment with the parents. Her partner was also uncertain if this was a wise decision. They had explained to both of them that there might be something in the apartment that they should not see. The DuPonts insisted that they be allowed to enter the apartment and the detectives had to be forceful in telling them that they couldn't. If something was wrong inside the apartment it would immediately become a crime scene and they couldn't take any chances of corrupting it. Sally was the one who had to tell them they couldn't come in. She felt bad about it but it had to be done and the DuPonts needed to understand that.

Detective Carpenter entered first and Sally followed him in. They told the parents and the manager to stay on the second floor landing and they would come and get them if everything was okay. The nervous parents reluctantly agreed. The one bedroom apartment was small and most of it could be seen from inside the front door. The bathroom and bedroom were the only rooms not visible from the entrance. Immediately the two detectives knew they had a serious crime scene on their hands. There had been a struggle in the living room and a lounge chair was turned on its side, two purple vases knocked over, one was broken, one was not. A picture was hanging askew on the wall and the TV was on but muted. A struggle had taken place in the room and Sally's fear for Helen's safety intensified. She regretted that she hadn't done more to help the young waitress. She should have taken their talk the other day more seriously; she hoped that Helen was still alive. Sally couldn't let George and Ada in the apartment. First, they had another crime scene on their hands and second, she couldn't let them see what had taken place in the apartment. It would upset them more. She left the apartment and walked down a flight of steps where George and Ada were patiently waiting and told them what they had found. The apartment had been burglarized and there was no sign of Helen. She told them that she and her partner would be in touch with them when they were through. Ada started to cry and her husband put his arm around her and comforted her as he led her to their car. Sally watched them drive away and re-entered the apartment. Bob was waiting for her in the kitchen. He was wearing a pair or latex gloves and handed a pair to Sally. "I've called the Chief and filled him in on what we've got. He's going to contact the BCA and have the crime lab come down and do a crime scene analysis. He'll let us know when they leave St. Paul." He pointed to an open kitchen drawer. "This is where she kept her knives but I don't know if any of them are missing." He pointed to some small specks of blood in the kitchen floor. "There's not much blood, but somebody definitely got cut, let's hope it was the perp and not Helen. I think we should seal up the place and wait for the CSI team to show up. I haven't checked the apartment out that much and I don't want to contaminate anything. We'll let the CSI guys worry about that." He wanted to show his partner the bathroom and the bedroom before they locked up when his cell phone rang. He answered it, said a few words and hung up. "The BCA will be here in a couple of hours, the Chief wants us to hang tight right here until they show up." Sally leaned against the bedroom door jamb studying the crime scene. She thought the worst. When the crime lab was through she hoped that they would be able to provide her and her partner with some kind of evidence to go on. A fingerprint, semen or saliva that could be DNA tested - a shoe print - anything that would lead them to Helen. It wouldn't take long to conduct a search for a body in the small apartment so while the detectives waited for the BCA to show up they conducted a quick search of the small apartment. The living room, the small bedroom with a closet, the bathroom and the kitchen were thoroughly searched and no body was found. That was a good thing, Sally thought to herself. The assailant must have left the apartment with Helen. *But where did they go?* Carpenter had no idea of how Helen was taken from the apartment and if she was conscious or unconscious. Sally didn't know how the body was removed from the apartment either but she knew who did it, Nathan Brown, she was sure of it.

Sally watched the BCA van pull into the apartment complex. It looked like a UHAUL painted brown and if the color was a little darker it could be mistaken for a small UPS truck. Large yellow lettering on each side of the truck spelled out CRIME SCENE INVESTIGATION UNIT and below in smaller letters BUREAU OF CRIMINAL APPREHENSION. The two detectives had seen this particular van more in the last few months than they had in the last five years. They watched as it parked in an empty stall near Helen's unit. The driver opened his door, got out and put on a white lab coat. The passenger did the same. A third person exited the rear of the van dressed in the same attire as the two men in the front of the truck. The third man closed the rear doors and turned toward Sally, waved and smiled; it was Josh Trimble. He walked to the front of the van and joined up with the driver and the passenger as they began pulling testing equipment out of the side door. Josh looked up toward the apartment and noticed Bob standing on the landing. "Looks like we're going have to move our headquarters from St. Paul to Milrose, be a lot cheaper for the State." Josh yelled at the two detectives standing on the second floor landing watching him work. After the equipment was carried to the apartment Josh turned to Sally and asked. "What we got going on here?"

CHAPTER 34

Hezekiah Hadley stood in front of Judge Armstrong's bench and fidgeted with his manacled hands. A deputy sheriff stood motionless on his right while Detective Fairfield stood on his left side. He would plead guilty to nine counts of burglary and was certain he would get released on his own recognizance like he had in the past. *He couldn't wait to get out of jail. He needed to get to his house and remove his mother from the freezer and bury her somewhere fast. There was no time to waste, the cops could come out again and this time he might not be so lucky. He hadn't expected the search warrant. If he had, he would have disposed of the stuff he stole in the burglaries and he would have buried his mother sooner. His plans had gone awry with the search warrant. He hadn't expected that. He had gone to great lengths to prepare for her burial in Cedar Park but now that was not possible, thanks to the Milrose Police Department.*

"Hezekiah Hadley, is it your wish to plead guilty and waive your right to an attorney?" the Judge asked.

The defendant shook his head yes and focused his eyes on the floor.

"You need to answer so I can hear you, young man." Judge Armstrong ordered. The Judge was looking at the papers in front of him and he knew that the defendant hadn't requested an attorney. He was aware that the man standing in front of him was also a suspect in the death of his mother and a suspect in the murder of Harmony Ann Day.

"Yes Judge, I plead guilty and I would like to be released on my own recognizance until the sentencing."

The assistant county attorney was seated at a table near the defendant and stood up. "Your Honor, the State asks for bail of one hundred thousand dollars. We believe the defendant is a flight risk. He has no ties to the community and is not employed. He is also a suspect in a homicide investigation."

Hezekiah Hadley's head snapped in the direction of the assistant county attorney; he was expecting to be released on his own recognizance and the turn of events surprised him and scared him. He needed to get out of jail. He could still ask for his own attorney but that would take up more time. Time he didn't have. He decided to make a plea to the Judge. "Sir, I ain't goin' nowhere. I ain't got no money so I can't go nowhere even if I wanted to. I promise I'll stay around and do what you want me to do. Please, I don't want to go to jail no more." When he was through he looked at the judge and remained silent.

The Judge hadn't expected the plea from the defendant. Hezekiah seemed earnest enough in his request but the Judge knew he couldn't grant it. "Mr. Hadley," the Judge began, "you have been in front of this bench on several occasions. Each time you have been released on your own recognizance. The court did this in good faith that you would fulfill your obligations to the court at a future date. You have always been represented by counsel in the past and I think that it is imperative that you have counsel represent you now. If you don't, it will not go well with you this time around. Your past criminal history cannot be ignored anymore and if you are found guilty this time you will be looking at a fairly long jail time or prison time. Do you understand?"

Hezekiah shook his head that he understood what the Judge had said.

The Judge accepted his acknowledgment and informed the man in front of him with the green hair and earrings that he was going to refuse his guilty plea and he was going to appoint him an attorney from the prosecutor's office. The Judge dismissed the defendant. The deputy sheriff and Sally escorted the prisoner back to the jail.

When they returned to the Law Enforcement Center Sally and the deputy took the prisoner to interrogation room 'A' where they were joined by Detective Carpenter.

"I want a cigarette," Hezekiah demanded.

The detectives ignored the request and the prisoner did not push the matter.

"I didn't have nothin' to do with killin' Harmony and I don't know who did."

Carpenter looked at the prisoner and Hezekiah stared back and waited for an answer. "We know you knew her. We know you wanted to get intimate with her and she didn't want to. We know you burglarized those places because you wanted to get the tools you needed to kill somebody. Harmony Ann Day ends up murdered. All a coincidence? What would you think if you were us?"

"I didn't kill her." Hezekiah demanded.

Sally stood up and walked to the back of Hezekiah. "You know what I think. I think you and Krueger murdered her. He was her boyfriend, he had the sword but he says you stole it from him. I am not sure if I believe that. We have both your fingerprints and Krueger's on the sword and you both were mad enough at her to kill her. Neither one of you liked that she was a devout church going lady, in fact you both secretly hated her for it, didn't you?"

"Yea, we both hated that she was a goody two-shoes but she was nice enough you know. Why would we kill her?" The prisoner abruptly stopped talking; he folded his arms and stubbornly stared at the gray metal door that led into the interrogation room.

"What's the matter Hezekiah?"

"Take me back to my cell; I want to talk to my new attorney."

****

"What's going on?" Sally asked.

Detective Carpenter leaned back in his chair and folded his hands behind his head. He looked at this partner. "Don't know. I've been thinking about Helen DuPont. I hope we don't have another murder on our hands. Let's say hypothetically that we find her body someplace. Do you think we have one killer or two killers?"

"Think positive, we're going to find Helen alive. If something happened to her you can bet that Nathan Brown was involved and I don't think he had anything to do with Harmony Day. No, if you're speaking hypothetically I'd say we'd have two killers." Sally answered, "What brought this on?"

"Nothing. Just thinking out loud," her partner replied.

Sally looked at her partner; he looked comfortable sitting back in his chair with his feet on his desk. He appeared to not have a care in the world. "Well let me think out loud for once. You had everything under control until I got this promotion. Think back, there have been at least a dozen burglaries, the murder of Harmony Day, Florence Hadley is found dead in her freezer and now Helen DuPont has disappeared. All since I got promoted, I mean, I really didn't mind working traffic patrol. When my shift was over I went home and didn't think about work until I came in the next day. Now, I think about my job twenty four/seven. I'm not sure if it's worth the extra hundred bucks a month. I get so frustrated sometimes that I am getting the urge to light up again. Don't worry, I won't, but this job shouldn't have that kind of affect on a person. Is it me? What was life like before I became your partner? Nice I bet."

"It was boring - and Sally it's not you, honest. These crimes were all going to happen whether you were my partner or not. Maybe God had a hand in putting you in this position at this time in your life and my life for a reason. It's actually been kind of fun working with you."

Sally smiled; it was nice to hear her partner tell her this. In the time they had worked together they had never talked about much except police work. She had wanted to get to know more about her partner and maybe that would happen in time.

Bob removed his feet from the desk and sat erect as he faced his partner. "I'm still thinking about Helen DuPont. If Nathan Brown is somehow involved we've got to find him. The longer this goes on the greater the chance that we might find Helen dead. I think we should go to his apartment and talk to him. Let's see if we can get into his apartment, maybe get a quick look around. I think we should put a tail on him also. I know we can get one of the uniformed guys to volunteer. They're always looking for overtime. I'll feel better when we find her alive."

"I agree," she said as she stood up from her chair. "Let's go now."

Detective Carpenter looked at his watch. "I'm not sure if he is off work yet. Might be a wasted trip."

"He has Mondays off, I've already checked that out," Sally said.

"Let's do it," they said in unison as they grabbed their winter jackets and slid them on.

His black van wasn't in the apartment parking lot when they arrived. They parked their squad in an open space and walked to his apartment and knocked on the door. They tried several times with no answer so they left, determined that they would soon find Helen and that she was still alive.

****

The intercom buzzed. Detective Carpenter answered it and was informed that an attorney was here to see Hezekiah and he wanted to talk to both you and Sally first. "Send him in," he told the dispatcher and they waited to see who the court appointed attorney was.

Bill Pierce knocked on the outside of the open office door and then walked in.

"Not you," they both said teasingly. They liked joking with the young attorney. He was about as liberal as any human being could get. He openly promoted his far-left agenda and he actively pursued unpromising cases and hopeless causes. "Gaining a little weight there counselor. Capitalism has been good to you."

He ran his hand through his dark brown hair to smooth it out. It was an unconscious gesture he did when he was trying to come up with a good retort. He couldn't think of a comeback so he leaned against the office wall and smiled at the two of them. He was wearing an aged and soiled light brown suit. His shirt was green, red and yellow plaid with a daffodil yellow bow tie. The suit was one size too big for him and was the only one that either of the detectives ever remembered seeing him wear.

"The judge tells me there is more to this case than a few burglaries. You guys want to fill me in. I'm all ears."

Sally pointed to the empty chair next to her and asked him to sit down. She knew him to be an addicted coffee drinker and while he was digging for a legal pad from his leather briefcase and looking for a pen she got up and left to get him a cup of coffee from the squad room. She returned quickly and handed him the coffee and he gratefully accepted it. She sat down again and told him about his new client. "Here's the deal, Bill. Your client has admitted to nine burglaries. Right now we are charging him with all nine burglaries on an individual basis. The judge set the bail high enough so that he can't possibly get out of jail because we know he'll run. He's a suspect in the death of Harmony Day. We found his mother dead and stuffed in a freezer at his house and we have another possible homicide we are investigating. He could be involved in all these crimes and we need to sort it all out and keep him in jail while we are working on solving these crimes and building our case. That's the scoop for now; all we ask is that you don't talk about anything but the burglaries or Harmony Day. He doesn't know we found his mother. We want to spring that on him after he talks to you."

Bill Pierce carefully listened to Sally as he ferociously took down notes. "I hear my client was shot in the ankle. Want to tell me about that."

Detective Carpenter sat up from his relaxed position in his chair. "You're going to have to get that out of him yourself. He won't talk to us about it."

The young attorney had gathered all the information he needed from the two detectives and was ready to meet with his new client. A jailor appeared at the office door and escorted Bill Pierce to the jail block.

CHAPTER 35

The autopsy report was sitting on her desk in the middle of all the other clutter that had accumulated over the last few weeks. The bold letters on the manila folder read MEDICAL EXAMINERS REPORT/FLORENCE HADLEY. It had been put there by one of the new rookie police officers who had picked it up at the pathology lab for her. She opened it and read the contents slowly and carefully. Florence Hadley was a forty eight year old female who suffered from advance stages of emphysema, cirrhosis of the liver and malnutrition. She died from severe trauma caused by a blow to the back of the head with a blunt instrument. She died instantaneously. It was impossible to tell the time of death because of the victim's body temperature - a result of artificial freezing. There were no other signs of trauma on the body. Subject was in poor health and in a weakened condition.

Sally remembered the vacant eyes of Mrs. Hadley staring up at her from the freezer. They seemed to be pleading for help. The body was frozen solid and the two police officers that removed the body from the freezer had to be careful so a body part did not snap off.

She and her partner both knew that the son was responsible for her death. Krueger was right; his friend was planning to kill someone. Now that they knew he was capable of murder the focal point of the Day investigation would concentrate on Hezekiah and Pete Krueger.

Another search warrant was issued by Judge Armstrong for the Hadley house, garage and outbuildings. They needed to have this warrant to allow them to look for evidence that would link Hezekiah Hadley to the murder of Harmony Day and evidence that would link him to the murder of his mother. They hoped they would get lucky on both counts.

A team of officers including deputies from the Sheriff's Office, officers from the Milrose Police Department and two other agents from the Bureau of Criminal Apprehension scoured the area. A crime lab truck was available and was parked in the yard for quick analysis of certain types of evidence. In the kitchen a heavy skillet was found stuck in the rear of a cupboard. It appeared that there were small amounts of blood and a few strands of hair stuck to the bottom of it. The frying pan was given to the crime lab and they removed the samples from the bottom of the pan and prepared it for testing. A locked wooden box was found under Hezekiah's bed and it was brought out and tagged by Sally who took it to the lab to see if they could get it open. When the day was over they recovered a few more items from the burglaries, dusted for prints throughout the house, and discovered a human skull in the wooden box that had been found in Hezekiah's room. The metal skillet with the blood and hair samples had been removed from the cupboard and bagged for evidence. DNA testing would be done on the samples for comparison with Florence Hadley's DNA. If Hezekiah's fingerprints were on the skillet or anywhere on the freezer they would have enough probable cause to arrest Hezekiah Hadley for the murder of his mother.

CHAPTER 36

The BCA crime lab report was delivered in person to Sergeant Sally Fairfield by Agent Josh Trimble. The hair and the blood samples taken from the bottom of the frying pan belonged to Florence Hadley. A partial fingerprint of Hezekiah's left thumb was found on the smooth handle of the cast iron skillet and several of his prints were found on the freezer door and the freezer handle. The information on the report was presented to Judge Armstrong and he had no problem issuing a warrant for the arrest of Hezekiah Hadley. Hadley's attorney could argue in court later that his fingerprints were found on those items because he lived in the same house as his mother and it would not be unusual for his prints to be found anywhere in the house. They would worry about that defense when the time came. With arrest warrant in hand Detective Carpenter felt it was time to call Hezekiah's attorney and tell them that they would be serving the arrest warrant on his client for the murder of Florence Hadley and that they would be interviewing Hezekiah soon.

Hezekiah was visibly shaken when he walked into the interrogation room. Bill Pierce was seated across the table from Agent Trimble, Sergeant Fairfield and Lieutenant Carpenter. Hezekiah's attorney motioned for his client to have a seat next to him. Hezekiah walked over and sat down next to the young attorney, lowered his head and stared at the floor without uttering a word. He listened while Lieutenant Carpenter read him his Miranda warning and acknowledged that he understood his rights by nodding his head.

Lieutenant Carpenter looked at the prisoner hoping to get his attention. "Why'd you kill her Hezekiah? She was no match for you and according to the autopsy report she was very sick and was probably going to die within the next six months. You didn't know that, how could you, she didn't even know it. But I am curious why a young man of your size would walk up behind his mother like you did and crush her skull her in. What could possibly have been going through your mind?"

Hezekiah remained silent and continued to look at the floor. Agent Trimble waited for a few minutes and the room became silent. "We also want to know why you killed Harmony Ann Day."

Hezekiah lifted his head from the floor and studied Josh Trimble before answering him. "I told these two, these other two cops here, that I had nothing to do with her murder. Nothing."

Josh pulled a picture out of his jacket pocket and laid it on the table in front of Hezekiah. "Recognize this?"

Hezekiah looked at the picture and shook his head sideways indicating a no answer. He leaned back in his chair and looked at the tile floor again.

"This is a picture of a shaolin sword. It is owned by your friend Peter Krueger and he tells us that you stole it out of his car while it was parked downtown. This sword was used to kill Harmony and we found your fingerprints on it. Now how could you not know anything about this sword when Krueger says you knew all about it and admired it and wished it was yours? How can you not say it was your sword when your fingerprints are on it? How?"

Hezekiah sat straight up, folded his hands together and rested them on the table in front of him. "Yea, I guess I do remember Pete showing me the sword once, but I never stole it from his car, he's lying."

"Was he lying when he said that you admired the sword? Was he lying when he said you did those burglaries? Looks like he was right on there, wasn't he? Was he lying when he said you were planning to kill someone? I don't think so. I believe Pete. Seems kind of funny that two people you know well are both dead. How'd your fingerprints get on the sword?"

Hezekiah didn't care for the BCA agent that was interviewing him. He didn't like him at all. "I must have touched the sword when he was showing it to me."

Sally sensed Hezekiah's irritation with Agent Trimble and his anger toward his friend Peter Krueger. She had once heard the axiom that '*there was no honor among thieves*' and she was certain that the prisoner sitting at the table across from her was going to prove that adage correct. "Tell me Hezekiah, why are you protecting Pete? He ratted on you. We wouldn't have known about those burglaries if he hadn't told us and you wouldn't be here. We may never have found your mother either but thanks to Peter Krueger you are here being charged with her murder also. With friends like that........."

"He's the one that shot me. He and his chink girlfriend stopped by and wanted a hundred bucks. I told him I didn't have it and the chink shot me. While I was on the ground he goes into my house and takes all my money and walks out. He's counting it in front of me. There's a lot more than a hundred bucks there and he's smiling and so is Lin Su. They look at me bleeding to death and then they leave. I could've died, they didn't care. He's the one killed my mother, killed her when he was there. He was ransacking the house and my mother tried to stop him and he killed her. He's bad news and so is his chink girlfriend."

"What did they do after they shot you?" Agent Trimble asked.

"I told you they left. They got in this fancy dark green SUV and drove away. Lin Su looks at me as they are driving away and she laughs and then rolls down her window and aims her gun at me like she is going to shoot me again. I thought she was going to kill me. She's crazy."

Bob Carpenter checked his tape recorder before looking at the prisoner. "So, if Krueger killed your mother, did he leave her on the kitchen floor or what? How did she get in the freezer?"

"I put her in there so she wouldn't rot before the coroner came out."

"And you did this after you had been shot and were in a lot of pain," Lieutenant Carpenter continued.

"Yes," Hezekiah meekly answered.

"The problem with that scenario Hezekiah is that our lab boys found no fingerprints in the house that matched Krueger's," Agent Trimble replied.

"He was wearing gloves."

Trimble was losing patience with the prisoner, he reached over and retrieved the picture of the sword and put it back into this jacket pocket. "You're going away for a long time. Let's see, nine burglaries with a max of twenty years on each count that's one hundred eighty years. Now we might be able to work something out if you confess to killing your mother. I can't make any promises but I will talk to the County Attorney and maybe we can lump all these crimes into one. I know that if you are cooperative usually the County Attorney is willing to work with you. Otherwise, we could ask the court for one hundred eighty years on the burglaries and then another twenty or more years on the murder. Wouldn't it be better to just tell us what happened now and we can sort this out with the County Attorney?"

Hezekiah looked at his attorney. Bill Pierce, sensing that his client wanted to speak to him alone, asked that everyone please leave the room so he and Hezekiah could talk alone. Bob Carpenter, Sally Fairfield and Josh Trimble all got up and left the interrogation room. Sally showed Bill Pierce how to use the intercom and told him to buzz them when he and Hezekiah were through.

Sally was getting worried, two hours had gone by and no word from the attorney and client. She had decided that she was going to call the interrogation room and see if everything was all right when Bill Pierce called her. They were ready to talk to them about Hezekiah's involvements.

Bill Pierce did all the talking and Hezekiah remained motionless and once again kept his eyes on the floor. "We all know, you know, I know and Hezekiah knows that he committed the burglaries and he is willing to plead to them if some kind of deal can be made. What you don't know is who killed Florence Hadley and who killed Harmony Ann Day. Hezekiah can help you there. Let's say hypothetically that Hezekiah killed his mother and that he was involved in Harmony Day's death, what kind of deal could be made if all the charges got wrapped together into one. Say second degree murder."

Agent Trimble pushed his chair from the table, got up and stretched. "You know we can't make those kinds of deals, Bill, but we'll talk to the County Attorney, see what he says. We'll do it tomorrow. All we can do is put in a good word for Hezekiah; tell him that Mr. Hadley here was cooperative. You can talk to the County Attorney yourself if you like. For now we're charging your client with nine burglaries and the murder of Florence Hadley. We're also going to continue to work on solving the murder of Harmony Day and the evidence we've got so far points to your client as the killer. If he tells us what he knows about the murder, I'm sure the County Attorney will be more than willing to work with you in getting a fair deal for your client."

The young attorney looked at his client as he was combing his hands through his oily green hair. Hezekiah looked up the floor and glared at Agent Trimble. "Okay, okay I'll tell you what you want to know. I killed my ma. I couldn't take it no more. All she ever did her whole life was make fun of me. She never did nothin' for me. I hated her. Pete was right, I did those burglaries cuz I was going to use those things to murder my mother. I was going to hang her in the park just like Harmony Day. That's why I stole rope and nails and a hammer. I couldn't find a sword though. I liked the way Harmony died and I wanted to do that to my mother. I don't know; I must have lost it. I planned on killing her for a long time; I had it all planned out, I was going to kill her at home and take her body to the park and then hang it up. After I hit her on the head she fell to the floor, I knew she was dead. You can just tell those things. I wasn't going to kill her for a while but she made me so angry. She was yelling at me and she wouldn't stop yelling. I told her to shut up but she wouldn't. She was at the stove heating some water and she was yelling and yelling and there was this frying pan lying on the kitchen table and I picked it up and I swung it at her and she fell. I put her in the freezer until I could think of what to do next. I didn't feel bad she was dead. I wanted her out of the freezer though. I didn't like that she was in it. I wanted her out of the house forever. I wasn't counting on the cops getting a search warrant. I panicked when the two officers came out to the house looking for my mother. I should have known something was up. I should have moved her that night. So there, are you happy?"

It was late and everyone at the table was getting tired. It had been a long and fruitful interview. They had tried to get him to confess to the murder of Harmony Day but he wouldn't. As Hezekiah was being escorted back to his cell, he turned to Sally and mouthed something indistinguishable but she was certain that it had something to do with Harmony Day.

CHAPTER 37

When she returned to her office from the interview with Hezekiah, Sally noticed a message lying on her desk; she was to call Sheriff Moore in Wolf Point. She dialed the number for the Sheriff's department and when the dispatcher answered she identified herself. "He's off for the day, but he told me to tell you that your buddy Peter Krueger is in intensive care in Kingman, Arizona. He was shot in a bank robbery and will be going to jail as soon as he is released from the hospital. Sheriff says that if you want, you can call him tomorrow and he can tell you more about what is going on." Sally thanked the dispatcher and hung up the phone. Tomorrow was another day and she was going home. She was tired and her muscles were aching and she was hungry.

The next morning started with breakfast at the Horn Inn. She was joined by her partner and was surprised that he ordered the same breakfast she did. Normally he ate lighter and healthier. "I'm hungry this morning and the number four breakfast sounded good," he stated, noticing her surprised look when he ordered.

"Got a call from the Roosevelt County Sheriff's Department. Our friend Mr. Krueger got himself shot in a bank robbery attempt. He's in the hospital in Kingman, Arizona. I'm guessing the feds will want him when he is out of the hospital," Sally informed her partner as he was about to take his first bite of food.

"Is he ever going to get out of jail? That guy really flipped since he got in that bar fight in Wolf Point. I'd hate to be in his shoes."

"I know," Sally answered as she took a swig from her coffee, the fourth cup of the day. "Do you really think he had anything to do with murdering Harmony Ann Day? We've been working on this case for a while and I don't think I have ever asked you that question."

"I honestly don't know. I don't know if he killed her or if Hezekiah killed her or somebody else killed her. It's baffling to me. They both knew her but what was their motive? If I could figure out motive I would be a little more convinced. They are both crazy enough to do it. Krueger owns the sword, Hezekiah had the sword, both knew her and both wanted a more intimate relationship with her which didn't materialize. We know that Hadley is capable of just about anything and I think Krueger is too. It's also possible that they were in on it together. If that's the case, we could play them against each other - see what happens."

"I feel much the same as you, but I would really like to get this cleared up as soon as possible. Anything new on Helen DuPont that I should know about?" Sally asked.

"Nope. Nada," her partner answered, wishing he had good news for her.

When the two detectives arrived at the Law Enforcement Center after breakfast they went to Lieutenant Carpenter's office and called Sheriff Obed Moore. He was in his office and filled them in on the details of the bank robbery. He told them that Krueger's girlfriend, Lin Su, was killed at the scene when she fired at two officers as they arrived at the bank. The officers returned fire and took her down. She wrote down the details that she needed from the Sheriff and thanked him for his time and for returning her call. She hung up the phone and was about to fill her partner in on what the Sheriff said when there was another phone call for her. She picked up the phone and it was Peter Krueger. "Well Petey. Got yourself in a little more trouble, huh? When are you ever going to learn?" Sally offered to one her least favorite people.

"I didn't call to get a lecture from you. I called because I've heard about these jails down here in Arizona and I ain't gonna' be walking around in no pink underwear and workin' on no chain gangs. I want back in Minnesota. I'll do what I have to do. I heard that I can be extradited to the state that has the most serious charge against me, is that true?"

Sally wondered why he wanted to know that information but she informed him that he was right and that he would be extradited to the state with the most serious charge but that did not mean that the charges in the other states would be dropped. After he served his time here for whatever he would still have to go back to whatever state, and face charges there. "No matter what Petey, you are going to be in jail for a long time."

"I want to do my time in Minnesota first - that's why I called. I want to tell you now that me and Hezekiah killed Harmony Ann Day."

"Why are you really telling me this Mr. Krueger?"

"Because I am going to probably spend the rest of my life in jail anyway and I would prefer it be in Minnesota than Arizona or Montana. Can you come down and get me?"

Sally sensed that Mr. Krueger was pleading. He was trying to hide it, but she felt it. "I'll talk it over with the County Attorney and will get back to you."

****

Bob Carpenter and Sally met with the County Attorney the next morning and explained to him about the strange call they received from Peter Krueger yesterday and the interview that they had with Hezekiah Hadley the day before. They explained the facts of the case and emphasized that both were capable of murder. The sword that was used to pierce the victim's side was a shaolin sword that was owned by Peter Krueger and he admitted to owning it. The weapon also had Hezekiah's fingerprint on it. Sally explained the relationship that each of the men had with the deceased. Bob explained the frustrations that each had with Harmony Ann Day because she was unwilling to become intimate with either one of them.

"Krueger told us that Hezekiah was the one that has been committing all the burglaries around town and that he was also planning on killing someone using the items he obtained during the burglaries. His story checked out and Hadley confessed to the burglaries and is in jail as we speak. Yesterday we interviewed Hezekiah with his attorney present and he confessed to the murder of his mother and is expecting a plea bargain. He denies that he had anything to do with Harmony's death."

Mark Hutchinson was in his third term as County Attorney. When he was first elected to the job he had one other attorney working with him and they were able to keep up with the caseload. Ten years later there were five assistant county attorneys; they were all busy and there was still a backlog of cases. It seemed like child abuse, child neglect, spousal abuse, welfare fraud, criminal activities and sex abuse were running rampant in this once quiet little hamlet. The population of Milrose had expanded three fold in the last few years as people moved away from the Twin Cities area to smaller communities surrounding the metropolitan area. With the increase in population came more work for the County Attorney's office.

Only in his early fifties he'd had over twenty-five years experience in the legal profession. He knew his law and he was considered hardboiled by his opponents in court. It wasn't often that he would plea bargain down a case. If he did make an exception, it was because it was the defendant's first offense. You were dead meat in his eyes if you were in court for your second or third time. He sat back in his chair and twiddled a pencil. His tie was undone as it always was unless he was in court. "So if Krueger signs a confession that he murdered Harmony Day and he implicates Hadley, what are you going to do? Do you want us to charge them?"

Bob Carpenter shuffled in his chair and studied the man sitting across from him. "I don't know, that's why we're here. I think they were involved in Harmony's death but Sally here is not too sure. We're looking for more answers."

"I can understand your hesitation. Tell you what. Let's get Krueger back here. I'll contact the judge and get the ball rolling. You talk to Hadley again. If they both admit to killing her and they both have similar stories we should go with a murder indictment. The key to this whole thing is their confessions."

The agent in charge of the FBI office in Phoenix, Arizona was contacted by Sioux County Attorney Mark Hutchinson who explained the need to extradite Peter Krueger back to Minnesota. The agent in charge agreed to the county attorney's request and consented to let the suspect be transported to Minnesota for interrogation and possible arraignment on murder charges. They wanted him back in Arizona when Milrose was through with their investigation and Krueger was arraigned. The FBI had him on the bank robbery in Kingman but they were interested in talking to him about another bank robbery in Kansas City. An agreement was made between the County Attorney and the Federal Bureau of Investigation's office in Phoenix. Krueger had been released from the hospital and was being held as a prisoner in a county jail in Kingman. The bullet wound made by the .357 caliber Smith & Wesson was beginning to heal. He would require the use of a cane for the next couple of weeks and after that he would have full use of his leg once again. The next day Mark Hutchison was notified that Krueger waived extradition and that he could be picked up at the jail in Kingman. The County Attorney immediately called the Sheriff who assigned one of his deputies to accompany Lieutenant Carpenter on the overnight trip. Their plane landed in Laughlin, Nevada at three in the afternoon. Two rooms had been booked for one night at the Colorado Belle and a rental car was reserved for the short trip to Kingman to pick up Peter Krueger. They checked in, walked to their first floor room at the hotel and unloaded their luggage. The deputy sheriff headed for the craps table and Lieutenant Carpenter went to the restaurant for a sandwich and a glass of milk. When he was through with his sandwich he walked to the casino to check on his travelling partner. He came upon him as he was tossing two red dice onto the craps table. He raised his hands and yelled "YES"!! Bob figured he must have won something. He told the deputy sheriff that he was going back to the room and catch up on some reading.

"I'm up three hundred bucks. I'm buying breakfast," the deputy sheriff informed Lieutenant Carpenter the next morning. After they both ate a large breakfast they drove to Kingman and picked up their prisoner. Peter Krueger was quiet on the flight back, but Bob Carpenter sensed that Peter Krueger seemed relieved that he was leaving Arizona.

Josh Trimble wanted to be included in the interview with Peter Krueger. Sally had called him on his cell phone and informed him that Krueger had as much as admitted to the murder over the phone. He was at the main office of the Bureau in St. Paul when she called; she and Bob would be interviewing Krueger this afternoon at two p.m. Trimble had a light lunch at the Bureau cafeteria with two other agents before driving to Milrose. He was excited to see Sally again. Their first date had gone well and he hoped there would be another one in the near future. If things worked out like he imagined, the relationship might jump to the next level. She was different from Marcie - in a good way. She understood the life of a cop but she was as particular who she dated as he was. She wanted to find the right man and she wanted to get married but it all had to feel right. He had given marriage some thought but after one failed attempt he was going to be a little more finicky on his selection of a wife. He knew he had his faults and he would need to find someone that would overlook those faults and not try to change them or him. That is why he needed to know a lot about the woman he would marry. If a case could be made against Krueger and there was a trial, he would be seeing a lot more of Sally Fairfield.

Peter Krueger claimed indigence when he stood in front of the judge to answer the charges against him. Taking his testimony of indigency into consideration Judge Armstrong agreed with the defendant. Arrangements were made for a court appointed attorney. Bill Pierce's reliability in taking on indigent cases led Judge Armstrong to have his clerk call him and ask that someone from his office act as defense council for Peter Krueger. Through Bill Pierce's suggestion the court appointed one of his new partners. She was young, energetic and fresh out of law school and had the same liberal views that her boss did. Everyone in the office from the lawyers to the secretaries to the clerks were faithful in attending the County democratic conventions and caucuses and they were all willing and able to donate to any and all democratic candidates. The law firm was well known for enthusiastically defending indigents, criminals of any kind, work comp cases and discrimination cases, especially those that involved corporations. The firm was successful and had grown over the years and the partners were well liked and respected within the community. The firm's newest partner was Amy Brown and she was assigned the case and accepted the challenge gladly.

The young and vibrant attorney waited with Sally Fairfield and Bob Carpenter in the interrogation room for her new client to appear. Amy Brown's court appointed indigent defendant would be showing up any time and she was as prepared as she could be considering the short notice from the court. She had talked to her client at great length over the phone and felt comfortable with the information she had gathered from him.

Amy heard the key in the lock turn as the metal door opened and her client entered. He extended his arms to the jailor and his cuffs were removed and he took a seat next to his new attorney. Lieutenant

Carpenter asked Amy if she needed some time alone with her client before they got started.

She pushed up the wire framed glasses that were creeping down her nose, looked at her client, then at the lieutenant. "Maybe a few minutes."

Josh Trimble was sitting in the squad room when the two detectives entered. Sally poured a cup of coffee and sat next to Josh. "How's it goin'?"

"Fine. How's it going with Krueger?"

"His attorney is in with him now, shouldn't be more than a couple of minutes and we can go back and see him." Sally answered taking a sip of coffee.

After a few minutes the jailor entered the squad room and told the three investigators that Ms. Brown was ready for them. They all got up and followed the jailor back to the investigation room.

Amy Brown was the first to speak and did so matter-of-factly. "My client wants to confess to killing Harmony Ann Day and he wants you to know that he didn't do it alone. He and Hezekiah were in it together. He wants to know what'll happen to him if he confesses. He tells me that he never wants to go back to Arizona or Montana and he would like to do his time at Stillwater."

Josh looked at Sergeant Fairfield and at Lieutenant Carpenter. He noticed they were as surprised as he was with the news. Agent Trimble looked at Krueger trying to figure out his reason for what he was about to do. "Explain."

A yellow legal pad was lying on the table in front of the prisoner; he was holding a pencil in his hand and was doodling on the paper. He stopped scribbling and looked at the BCA agent. "I talked this over with my attorney here and she tells me that because I committed the more serious of the offenses here in Minnesota I would more than likely serve my time at Stillwater Prison first."

Agent Trimble was beginning to understand what Krueger was getting at. "I see what you want, you've done your research, haven't you, and your attorney has verified it. You know that murder takes precedent over bank robbery and criminal assault. You would probably do your time here but you will have to go back to Arizona and Montana sometime to face charges there. They may extradite you to their state after your sentence is completed here or they may just drop the charges, we don't know."

"How much time would I have to do here for murder?"

"It is up to the judge, could be life, but the average sentence for murder is seventeen and a half years. After that much time has gone by there is a good chance that the feds wouldn't pursue the matter. That's no guarantee though, but it is something to think about. Remember Mr. Krueger, the penalty for bank robbery is twenty five years and they are looking at two bank robberies. If convicted, you wouldn't be serving any time in Arizona. You would be in a federal penitentiary somewhere. The accommodations there don't include pink underwear. Personally I think you would be better off with the Feds than with us or the prisoners at Stillwater," Lieutenant Carpenter answered.

"The thing is, I know a lot of the guys serving time at Stillwater. If I copped out to bank robbery I would still be in an Arizona jail or prison while I waited to be transferred. My lawyer says I can always get transferred to a federal pen once I cop to the bank robberies. No, I am going to take my chances here. So what do you want to know?" Krueger confidently asked.

Agent Trimble stood up, leaned against the wall and folded his arms. It was his habit to stand when a suspect was giving a confession. "We want to be sure that you and Hezekiah are the ones who killed Harmony Ann Day and to do that I need you to tell me everything you remember about that night. I want you to think long and hard about that and I want you to tell us and then I want you to go to your cell and write it all down just as you told us. If you remember more later, please put it down."

Krueger was calm and articulate as he described that night. "It was a Friday evening. Harmony was going to stay over night and then drive back to the Twin Cities Saturday sometime. I had a date with her and we met at the college. I wanted to go out for a few beers but she wanted to go to a movie. We got into a little argument while we were driving in downtown Milrose and I seen Hezekiah walking so I stopped and asked him where he was going. He says 'no place' so I tell him to hop in. I could tell that this really got Harmony upset. She was a little afraid of Hezekiah. I know she was trying to work with him and get him straightened out but I kind of think she gave up on him because she was so scared of him. Anyway he gets in the car and says 'let's get some beer' and I agree. Harmony says to let her out of the car, that she wants nothing to do with us when we're drinking. We both start laughing and when I stop at the liquor store I hold her in the car so she can't get out. Hezekiah gets a case of beer and throws it in the back seat except for three bottles which he opens and hands one to me and one to Harmony and keeps one for himself. She takes her bottle and dumps it upside down on the carpet. I belt her one for wasting a beer. Hezekiah is laughing and she is screaming to let her out now. I drive out in the county and we park in a wooded area and start drinking more beer. Harmony is still screaming and fighting with me but finally stops and then doesn't talk, she won't say a word. After we've had six or seven beers Hezekiah decides he wants to take Harmony in the back seat. I tell him to go ahead and good luck. She starts screaming and hollering again and by this time I'm starting to get really pissed off so I smack her. This don't do much good and now Hezekiah is getting mad and he starts hitting her and soon we are both hitting her and after about ten minutes she goes kind of limp and it looks like she is dead. I didn't think we hit her that hard but we must have. We don't know what to do so we finally drive around the county trying to figure out where to put her and Hezekiah thinks of Cedar Park and we start talking about what a goody two-shoes she was and how she talked about Jesus so much that it drove us both nuts. Hezekiah says we should hang her on a cross like Jesus and I say where are we going to get a cross? So then, I come up with the idea of hanging her on the back of the toilets at Cedar Park and Hezekiah says that is a great idea cuz he has a bunch of things buried there that we could use to hang her with. He says he's got nails and rope and a hammer. We pull into the park around four o'clock in the morning, drag her out of the car and set her down on the ground in back of the toilets. Hezekiah digs for his things and finds them. He has a block of wood which we set on the ground and Hezekiah holds her up against the wall and I pound the nails into her hands. I remembered that I had some old, dead roses in the trunk of my car so I go and get them and take off the leaves and wrap the thorns around her head and then I take the sword and stick it in her. There was no one in the park so we took our time. It took us at least a half an hour to hang her up and then clean the area up so there were no clues. That's about it."

"When did you drown her?" Sally asked, not entirely convinced that the confession was truthful. She was sure that Peter Krueger was trying to get out of serving time in another prison.

"I don't remember that we drowned her. To be perfectly honest with you I don't remember a whole lot about that night. Hezekiah had brought some drugs, I don't know what they were but they made me feel real uptight and edgy. We popped a couple of the pills, I think they were yellow. After the fifth or sixth beer I don't remember much but I don't remember drowning her but we could have."

Josh wasn't totally convinced either. "Where did you say you picked her up?"

"At the college."

"You know, Peter, we checked all the parking lots at the college and we never did find her car. If she met you there, she had to have driven her car there. Can you explain that?"

"No, man. Except that someone could have dropped her off. I mean she could have borrowed her car to someone else for that night. She knew she wasn't going to need it and we were going to give her a ride anyway and she knew that."

It had been an enigma for the three detectives that her vehicle had never been found. The town of Milrose and the county had been searched thoroughly. Every alley, side street and abandoned country road had been explored with no luck. They had once thought that they might find her pick-up in the Hadley garage and when that didn't turn out they had given up the search and only hoped that through luck it would somehow show up.

Bob Carpenter got up from his chair and stretched. "That's it for today, Mr. Krueger. It's lunch time. We'll talk to Hezekiah this afternoon and then we will take the information to the County Attorney. Like we said before, if you remember anything else be sure to put it down in writing."

Josh offered to drive his state issued vehicle to the Horn Inn. All three were hungry and decided to have lunch before they talked with Hezekiah. They sat in the section that would have been Helen DuPont's, but a new girl came to their table and took their order. It didn't seem right that Helen wasn't there with their drinks, ready to take their order. They gave the new waitress their order and Josh lit up a cigarette. Sally looked at the cigarette and could almost feel the smoke swirling around in her lungs. She missed smoking but remembered how scared she got when her lungs hurt her while they were in Montana. She thought she would feel better when she quit but she didn't notice any difference. She had gained two pounds but that was nothing. She would work that off at the bowling alley.

Josh took a puff of his cigarette and carefully put into the ashtray. "I don't know about you guys but I am not sure about the confession. It seems plausible enough but he would have remembered if they drowned Harmony. I think what we need to do is send a couple of guys from our crime scene unit out to Montana and have them go over Krueger's car. If we find any evidence whatsoever to link Harmony with being in that car we should charge them both. From the story that Krueger tells us, they beat her up bad. There should be evidence of that in the car."

The conversation turned to small talk and when the detectives returned to the Law Enforcement Center they phoned Hadley's attorney and advised him about Krueger's confession and that they would be talking to Hezekiah in a few minutes. Bill Pierce arrived at the Law Enforcement Center ten minutes from the time he got the call.

Agent Trimble started the interview. "Hezekiah, the last time we talked - you said you had nothing to do with the death of Harmony Day. Your friend Peter Krueger tells us differently. In fact he gave a confession linking you and him together in her murder. We now have enough evidence to charge both of you. Do you want to make it easy on yourself or not. Give us your side of the story and we'll compare the stories and try to determine what happened that night."

"If that is why you brought me in here, you are wasting your breath. I had nothing to do with killing Harmony. Pete's lying. Bring him in here now and I'll prove it."

The interview didn't last long. Hezekiah denied everything that Peter Krueger said. On the way back to Bob's office Josh asked Sally what she was doing tonight.

"Bowling, want to come and watch?"

"I'll think about it," he answered.

Sheriff Moore had Krueger's vehicle in his impound lot. The lab boys wasted no time in flying to Wolf Point. They spent a full day collecting evidence and the next morning flew back to St. Paul. They had found hair samples and blood samples in Krueger's car and would run DNA samples on the evidence. By the end of the next day the results proved conclusively that both the blood samples and the hair samples were those of Harmony Ann Day.

CHAPTER 38

Nathan Brown couldn't be happier; he was in a state of euphoria, he was ecstatic - flying on cloud nine, but at the same time he was exhausted. He was mentally drained and tired because of what he had done. He had returned to his apartment ready to collapse but was too excited. He realized that it had been a while since he had taken a shower. He walked into the small bathroom, turned on the water and stripped out of his dirty clothes. The shower would feel good and wake him up. The hot water soaked and penetrated his body and it felt good. Too bad Helen DuPont couldn't be with him. He had her tied up in an abandoned house in the country three miles south of Milrose.

He had come across the house one day while he was cruising the county roads with his new van. He had driven by and noticed that the windows in the house had been smashed out and there were no cars in the driveway. The place looked abandoned. He had to get another look at it so he pulled a U turn in a field drive next to the abandoned building and drove back, turned into the driveway and parked. He studied the house for a long time and after he was certain that no one lived there he drove up the long dirt driveway and into the yard. He stepped out of the van and walked to the front of the house and glanced inside. Seeing nothing he walked around the house peeking in each broken window until he found himself once again at the front door. He confidently entered, knowing no one was in the house. Once inside he observed broken glass, smashed beer bottles, McDonald's wrappers and cigarettes butts strewn throughout. The thought had come to him that this might be a good place to bring Helen DuPont. He excitedly walked out of the house, got into his van and began formulating plans.

He knew her schedule well enough. She would be working Saturday night and she would be getting off at nine o'clock. He would wait at her apartment and when she got out of her car he would grab her and knock her out with chloroform. He would make sure that nobody was around first. He waited near her parking stall, it was dark and there was a banana moon dimly shining in the sky. It was perfect, there was no one around and when she came home he had her. Shortly after nine o'clock he watched her pull into the parking lot and drive to her stall. A half hour later she was tied up in one of the bedrooms of the abandoned house. She was still unconscious when he stretched duct tape across her mouth, tied her hands behind her back, with a short piece of clothesline rope, bound her ankles. It was cold in the house and he wanted to keep his victim healthy as long as he could. He covered her unconscious body with a thick bedspread he used to transport her body. He checked the duct tape on her mouth and the rope around her wrists and ankles and was satisfied that she was bound tightly. It wasn't enough; he wasn't going to let this one get away. He went to his van and brought the new three eighth inch chain he had just bought that morning at Benson's hardware into the house. He chained her ankles and attached the other end of the chain to an eye bolt he had screwed into a rafter in the ceiling. She was going nowhere and she wouldn't be making any sounds. She was his prisoner and would do whatever he wished. He would kill her when he was tired of her. He left, satisfied with what he had accomplished. He would return tomorrow with some food and water and they would talk. It had gone well and he was proud of himself for what he had accomplished.

He stepped out of the shower having used all the hot water. He dried himself and put on a pair of dirty underwear. He walked to the kitchen, opened the refrigerator and took out a beer. He lit a joint and thought about what he would do to Helen DuPont now that he had her under his control.

CHAPTER 39

Two criminal complaints were issued by the District Court of Sioux County. One was served on Hezekiah Hadley who now had two of them in his collection along with nine charges of burglary. The other was served on Peter Krueger. Both men were easy to find. They were in adjoining cells in the Sioux County Jail. The serving of the two complaints would be followed by a Grand Jury Investigation to determine if there were enough facts in the case to issue a first degree murder indictment. The indictment would give the County Attorney Mark Hutchinson the opportunity to plea bargain the charges down to second degree murder and avoid a costly trial. The County Attorney preferred a plea bargain and was sure that one defendant, Peter Krueger, would agree; it was the second defendant, Hezekiah Hadley, that he was worried about. He was certain that Bill Pierce would not accept any type of plea agreement. He would let a jury decide. His office was understaffed and a trial would put a severe drain on the resources of his office but if he had to go to trial, so be it. He would be ready.

A Grand Jury was convened a week after the complaints were served. The jury roster had been selected for one year, twenty three people would serve on this particular grand jury. No judge, defense attorney or prosecuting attorney would be allowed in the proceedings. Josh Trimble, Detective Sergeant Sally Fairfield and Detective Lieutenant Bob Carpenter would testify. The bicyclist, Jerry Ringgold, would also testify along with a dozen other people connected to the case. After hearing the facts in the case, the Grand Jury would decide to either issue either one or two first degree murder indictments or find that there was not enough evidence in the case and not issue any indictments and the defendants would then be charged with second degree murder.

For eight days the twenty-three person panel listened attentively to the testimony of the witnesses. Three days after the testimony ended they issued indictments for first degree murder on both Hezekiah and Peter Krueger. Hezekiah received the news from his attorney, as did Peter Krueger.

Amy Brown was uncomfortable with her client, Peter Krueger, pleading guilty to murder. Even though she knew that he was capable of murder she was not convinced he killed Harmony Day. Hezekiah, on the other hand, was crazy and capable of just about anything, and she thought that if he killed Harmony Day, he acted alone. She couldn't understand why her client was so insistent upon pleading guilty to something he didn't do. Why was he so adamant that he serve his time in Minnesota? She figured he would be found guilty of the bank robberies and maybe spend five to seven years in a federal pen. Everyone knew that doing time at the federal level was a cake walk. It was your own little private country club. She was also sure she would be able to get the charges dropped in Montana. It would take some doing but she thought that she could convince the authorities in Montana that her client was in so much trouble he would never see the light of day. They could drop the charges, clear out the case and they would never hear from Peter Krueger again. In fact, she could guarantee the authorities that if her client ever did get out of jail he would never show his face in Montana again. If she could clear him of the murder of Harmony Day, he would be looking at a few years in federal prison instead of twenty plus in Stillwater. She had tried to convince him to plead not guilty to the murder charges. Amy Brown felt she would be able to get a not guilty plea, she was sure of it. He listened to her and again refused her counsel and advice on everything she said. She did not understand his thinking and wondered what was going through his mind. What she didn't know was that he had a fool proof plan of escape that would take place before he even got to the state penitentiary.

The detectives wanted another stab at interviewing their suspect Hezekiah Hadley. Arrangements were made through his attorney and a meeting was set up in hopes of getting a statement. They would all sleep better if Hezekiah would admit to being with Krueger that night. It was the last meeting they would have with Hezekiah and he still claimed he had nothing to do with the murder of Harmony Day and said that he didn't know why Krueger was setting him up like this. His attorney insisted that his client was innocent and told the three detectives that he would prove it at trial.

"Mr. Hadley has informed me that he is going to plead not guilty to these charges. I don't believe that my client had anything to do with the murder and we'll prove it in a court of law. If that's it, my client would like to go back to his cell and I have a trial to prepare for. Good day gentlemen." Bill Pierce stood up and waited for a jailer to come and let him out of the interrogation room and the cell block.

Peter Krueger wanted the whole ordeal done with as soon as possible. He told his attorney to get a plea bargain hearing in front of the judge as soon as possible because he wanted to get this over with. The attorney agreed to his wishes and ten days after he signed his confession he was standing in front of Judge Armstrong.

Before Judge Armstrong would accept his plea he had the prisoner repeat to the court the events of the night leading up to the murder of Harmony Ann Day. He wanted to know how they killed her and why they killed her. He also wanted to know what their actions were after they knew she was dead.

"Your Honor, it's all in my confession. I can't remember word for word what I wrote. Read the confession, I wrote it and I stand by it."

"It doesn't have to be word for word. I want you to tell me in your own words how this all took place. It will have a bearing on your sentence."

The defendant stood silent as he tried to remember what he had told the authorities. Suddenly he spoke and was articulate in describing once again the details of the night he and Hezekiah killed Harmony Day. The Judge listened to Krueger's story and compared it to the written confession and the police reports he had lying in front of him. He had read and reread them several times and knew the contents well. "Your story doesn't tell us everything, Mr. Krueger. You've left out a few facts that are pertinent to your case. One thing in particular intrigues me, how did you drown her?"

"Your Honor, like I told the officers, I don't remember drowning her. Me and Hezekiah were so out of it cuz' we'd been doing drugs and drinking beer that I don't remember much else. Maybe

Hezekiah drowned her, I don't know, Your Honor. All I know is we killed her. I know that for sure."

"I'm uncomfortable that you don't remember some very important facts but I can't overlook the overwhelming amount of evidence against you. That you were her boyfriend is an important fact alone. Also, her relationship with Hezekiah Hadley intrigues me. The evidence in the car; the hair samples and the blood samples found in the car seem to confirm your story. The sword that was used to stab her was yours. Your fingerprints and one print from Hezekiah Hadley were on this shaolin sword. All in all this adds up to a lot of evidence. I have weighed this over and over in my mind and I feel that it would be in your best interest to plead not guilty to these charges but your attorney informs me that you are insistent that you killed her and want to be punished for it. So I am thereby sentencing you on a charge of second degree murder which carries a term of not less than fifteen years or more than twenty two years in the State Penitentiary at Stillwater. You are reprimanded to the custody of the County Sheriff until arrangements can be made for your transfer to Stillwater prison. Remember, Mr. Krueger, your conduct there will determine your length of sentence. You have a history of anger and fighting. If you carry that to the prison you will have a tough time of it."

Three days later Hezekiah Hadley appeared in front of Judge Armstrong to enter his plea of not guilty. With him was his attorney Bill Pierce. There would be no plea bargain. They were both standing when Hezekiah Hadley entered a plea of not guilty. He looked at his attorney not knowing what to do next. He glared at the Judge and decided to sit down. Bill Pierce remained standing and asked to confer privately at the bench with the assistant County Attorney Mitchell Slade. A court calendar was looked at by the Judge, the County Attorney and the defense attorney and a time and date was set for jury selection.

CHAPTER 40

Andy Taylor was about to toss the jury summons he had received a few days earlier into the kitchen garbage can when his eye caught the last paragraph of the letter. In bold print he was informed he would be compensated for his time and would receive free meals while serving on the jury. The part of the letter mentioning money caught Andy's attention and he reread the sentence again before folding the letter and placing it in a small wire basket on the kitchen counter. When another notice appeared one month later from the District Court he opened it more carefully this time, hoping for a trial. He was in luck, he was to show up for jury duty in ten days. He remembered the part in the first letter about free money and free food and thought to himself that he would make a very good juror. He called the Clerk of Court's office and told the lady that answered the phone that he had received the letter and he would be at the courthouse to do his civic duty.

More than two dozen prospective jurors showed up at the courthouse the morning of jury selection. The varied assortment of people were busy filling out a questionnaire they were given by the Court. They were sitting on several benches outside of the courtroom answering the typed questions when Andy Taylor entered the courthouse and checked in at the Clerk of Court's office. He received his clipboard and took a seat on one of the benches. He would have a harder time filling out the questionnaire than the other prospective jurors because he couldn't read very well; he would have to fake it as best he could and hope for the best. He didn't want to be disqualified because of his not being able to read. When he was through answering questions he returned the clipboard to the Clerk of Court's office and was told to wait until his name was called. At eleven fifteen, a bailiff opened the door to the court room and announced that Andy Taylor was next. He got up, not knowing what to expect, and walked into the courtroom. He was directed to one of the chairs in the jury box where he sat down and waited. In a few minutes the questioning began. He was questioned by the prosecuting attorney and the defense attorney. He was informed that the case would be State of Minnesota vs. Hezekiah Hadley and that the charge would be murder in the first degree. He secretly smiled.

"Have you heard about this case?" the prosecutor asked.

"Yes, everyone within fifty miles of Milrose has heard about the murder and the arrest of Hadley. Be pretty hard to find someone who hasn't."

"Did you know Mr. Hadley?"

"Only through my son, they were kinda' friends."

"Do you think Mr. Hadley's guilty?"

Andy Taylor wanted to be on the jury. He wanted Hezekiah Hadley found guilty but he couldn't say that. "Don't know, gotta' hear the evidence first."

When Mitchell Slade was finished with his questions, Bill Pierce stood up and addressed the prospective juror. "How do you feel about locking someone up for the rest of their life?"

"Hey, if you can't do the time, don't do the crime."

"Do you think that knowing Mr. Hadley on a personal basis will affect your judgment in this case?"

"Nope."

The questions went on for more than twenty minutes and then Andy Taylor was excused. He was told to wait in the hallway and he would be notified shortly if he was would be serving on the jury. It was after one o'clock when a clerk entered the hallway from a side door and informed Andy Taylor that he would be serving as an alternate juror. The clerk explained to him that his position as alternate juror would be requiring him to serve in the same capacity as the other jurors. He would have to attend the trial like the other jurors so that he would be familiar with the testimonies. If for some unknown reason he was needed to fill a vacancy on the regular jury, they wanted him prepared. The same clerk cautioned him that as an alternative juror he was not to discuss the case with any other person until the jury completes its deliberation or is discharged. If one of the jury members is unable to fill their duties as a jury member one of the two alternates would replace them. He told the clerk that he understood what she was telling him and he was told to report to the courtroom on Monday morning at nine-thirty. He walked out of the front door of the courthouse and took the steps leading to the courthouse lawn two at a time. He couldn't believe the luck he was having.

Mitchell Slade handed the jury list to Detective Carpenter who studied it and made a few mental notes and handed the list to his partner. "How did Andy Taylor get on the list? I know he's only an alternate but if something would happen to one of the regular jurors and he was impaneled, I shudder to think what things would be like in the jury room. Do you know this character?"

"I don't," the assistant County Attorney answered.

"He's probably the biggest jerk in the county. He's married and no one has seen his wife for years, his kids were pulled out of school when they were sixteen so they could help run the farm, he's drunk most of the time and he is not a man to be trusted. He's cantankerous, slovenly and every other word out of his word is a cuss word. He is the last person in the County I would have picked for jury duty."

"It's too late now. If I'd have known that before I would have done a peremptory challenge on him based on his past history and his alcoholism. Between Mr. Pierce and me we had done three peremptory challenges. All three of them were vocally biased against Mr. Hadley and we had no choice but to exclude them. Taylor didn't seem to be any threat. His actions when we interviewed him led both of us to believe he would make a good juror. He might have conned us. Based on what you say, let's hope that the regular jury stays healthy."

Sally's partner handed her the list. She didn't recognize the names of any of the jurors except Angus Sullivan, Parker Hill and Andy Taylor. "I know Angus. He's a good man, owns a lot of land and works hard. I am glad to see Parker Hill's name on the list. There isn't a man I would trust more in this town than him. He was the janitor at the high school when I was a student. All the kids liked him. It hits me as kind of ironic that Parker Hill and Andy Taylor will be sitting on the same jury. They're two total opposites."

The jury had been selected and in five days the trial would begin. Sally was prepared. Bob was prepared. The burglaries had been solved, the death of Florence Hadley had been solved and it looked as if Harmony Day's killers were found. For the next few days they would concentrate their efforts on finding Helen DuPont. They still had a key to Helen's apartment given to them by the manager. The forensic guys were done and they were waiting for the report. Josh would let them know as soon as it was ready. Her car was still parked in the same spot that it was when they searched the apartment. That bothered them but they remained upbeat that she would still be found alive. Both detectives were certain she had been kidnapped from her apartment and Nathan Brown was involved somehow but there was no proof as of yet.

CHAPTER 41

April 5th

  Easter passed and the arrival of spring was being anticipated. Seven inches of fresh new fallen snow greeted the citizens of Milrose in the early morning. The temperature had cooled off over night and wasn't expected to get above the mid twenties all day. It looked like the snow would remain for a few days more. The town was anxious for green lawns, budding trees and bright yellow daffodils, but the white ground let them know it wasn't time yet.

  The murder trial of Hezekiah Hadley was nearing and the town was anxious for the trial to start and finish as soon as possible. They wanted this part of their history over and forgotten. The court docket for the trial was set for ten a.m. and no one had any idea how long the trial would last. There were a lot of witnesses to be called and a lot of evidence to be presented. The two opposing attorneys figured the trial would last one or two weeks tops - no longer. At eight o'clock the court room was beginning to slowly fill up with a myriad of spectators along with the press. Those that wanted good seats were willing to wait a couple of hours to get them. This was the biggest event of the year in Milrose. Bigger even than Pioneer days.

  An aisle divided the courtroom in half. To the right of the aisle were sixteen rows of pews and in front of the first row was a balustrade that extended to the wall. In front of the balustrade was a wooden table with four comfortable looking brown leather chairs. The defense team would occupy these seats. To the side of this table was the jury box which contained fourteen chairs, all upholstered in a heavy cloth, dark maroon in color. There were twelve chairs for the regular jury members and two chairs for the alternates. The other side of the aisle contained another sixteen rows of pews with a balustrade also running to the wall. In front of this balustrade was another table with four chairs. This is where the prosecution would try their hardest to obtain a conviction. They wanted Hezekiah in prison for a long time - not only as a punishment for his crimes but also to protect society.

At ten o'clock the courtroom was full, the attorneys had taken their places, the jury was seated, and the court reporter was in position. The bailiff said "All Rise" and Judge Armstrong entered the courtroom from a rear side door that led from his office. He walked to his bench, his black robe loosely flowing and studied the courtroom. He sat down and said "good morning" to the jury and the court.

Mitchell Slade thought the Judge looked dignified in his courtroom garb. His thick black wavy hair was combed back and small patches of white were beginning to make their appearance around his temples. He was tall and stocky with thick black eyebrows that accented his hair. His black robe seemed out of character for him. He looked different when he was working in his office wearing his flannel shirt - his bare feet exposed to all; his shoes and socks hidden somewhere under his desk. He was clean shaven and Mitchell Slade didn't ever remember him with a beard or a mustache or even a five o'clock shadow. He was meticulous in his physical appearance but careless in his wardrobe selections. His eyes were dark and piercing and could cut through you like a knife if he thought you were out of line or had said something foolish. He was a no nonsense type of man but you couldn't ask for a judge who was any fairer than the man sitting at the bench ready to preside over this trial.

Bill Pierce and Amy Brown were standing like everybody else when the judge entered and sat down. Bill had known the Judge much longer than his associate and he remembered the good old days when they used to play golf together every Wednesday at the Country Club. That was before he bought his forty acre farm and became an agronomist, horticulturist and botanist. The Judge knew as much about those subjects as he did about the law. The Judge excelled at everything he pursued.

Judge Armstrong read the charges against the defendant. He faced the jury, addressing them and thanking them for the time they were sacrificing from their jobs and their families to do their civic duty. He explained how the court and a trial worked and what was expected of the jury during the trial. He asked if the prosecution was ready and Mitchell Slade rose from his chair as did his boss, County Attorney Mark Hutchinson. "Yes, Your Honor."

The Judge asked the defense table if they were ready. Bill Pierce and Amy Brown were the first to stand up. Their client was seated between them and had to be nudged to rise up to his feet. He did so unwillingly and defiantly and the judge noted it and wrote something on his legal pad while looking at the defendant. He was going to lecture him, but hesitated and decided not to. Hezekiah Hadley was wearing a new dark suit, carefully tailored and wrinkle free. Underneath the suit was a white shirt with a wide gold necktie. When they were all three standing Bill Pierce replied. "Yes, Your Honor."

"Then let us begin."

The prosecution began by calling Jerry Ringgold. He told of how he was out for a bicycle ride the morning of October sixth and that he was practicing for a bicycle marathon in St. Paul in which he came in fourth by the way. He was on his fourth or fifth round of circling the town when he had to stop and go to the bathroom. He pulled into Cedar Park and stopped at the bathrooms but they were all locked so he walked around to the back of the pavilion and that is when he saw this girl hanging on the wall. She was wearing a faded purple bathrobe and there were some leaves or something wrapped around her head. He told the court and the jury that he thought he fainted and that when he woke up he went to his bike and got his cell phone and dialed 911. He went on to say that he talked to Detective Fairfield later. He had gone to her office to look at photographs of the dead girl and he had recognized her. He had told Sally that he had seen the defendant and the dead girl walking together in Cedar Park. He noticed them because the man with her had his hair dyed lime green. Jerry looked at the defendant as he was telling the court this and noticed that Hezekiah was clean shaven and had his reddish blond hair cut short and military style. The prosecution showed a mug shot of the defendant to Jerry Ringgold and asked him if this was the man he seen in the park with Harmony Ann Day. Jerry answered that it was the person and that he was positive. The prosecution offered the mug shot of the defendant as Exhibit "A." The color picture depicted the defendant dressed in wrinkled, dirty clothes with long, greasy lime colored hair. An earring dangled from his left ear and a tattoo could be easily distinguishable on his neck. Mitchell Slade wanted the jury to see what the defendant really looked like and that his chameleon appearance in court was an attempt by Hezekiah and his attorney to appear to the jury as a clean cut young man.

Detective Sergeant Sally Fairfield was called to the stand next. She related her story from the time she first arrived on the scene to the gathering of evidence, the visit with Pamela Rosewood, going to Wolf Point, Montana to find Peter Krueger and the arrest of Hezekiah Hadley for burglary based on the information given to them by Peter Krueger.

"How long have you been in law enforcement, Sergeant?" Bill Pierce asked. He looked determined in his quest to have his client found not guilty.

"A little under five years. Four years as a patrolman and the last nine months as Detective Sergeant."

"This your first murder investigation?"

"Yes."

"What kind of training have you had in homicide investigation?" The defense attorney asked as he paced back and forth asking his questions. As he paced and neared the jury he would stop in front of the jurists, stop and study them. He wanted to make sure he had their full attention at all times.

"When I was promoted to this position I was sent to a two week homicide investigation school taught by a lieutenant on the Minneapolis Police Department."

"Wonderful, Sergeant. Two weeks to learn how to solve a murder. A two week crash course in finding a killer. I'm impressed. What did you learn there that helped catch this dangerous man sitting over there?" Bill Pierce asked, pointing to his client.

Sally was calm in the witness box as she watched the defense attorney's antics. "We have never had a murder in Milrose so none of us on the department or the Sheriff's Department for that matter had ever investigated a murder. We didn't have any experience in this kind of thing and that is why we called in Josh Trimble from the Bureau of Criminal Apprehension. He's had plenty of experience in solving homicides and he's from Milrose."

The defense attorney continued his pacing. "You were at the scene where Harmony Day's purse was found?"

"Yes, both myself and Lieutenant Carpenter were there."

"Were there any shoe prints left around the area where the purse was found?"

"Yes, several and we took pictures of those prints."

"Do you know what kind of shoes left those prints?"

Mitchell Slade stood up from his table. "Objection, Your Honor. Calls for speculation by the witness."

"Sustained," the Judge ordered. There had been very few objections at the trial so far and he was pleased how the trial was moving along.

"I withdraw the question and will save it for the specialist from the BCA lab." Bill Pierce was through with the witness for now but he requested that the court allow him to call her at a later time.

The Judge limited his trials to four or five hours a day. He had great respect for those serving on the jury and he didn't want them tired or bored. He also did not want to put a burden on them and their family life. Court started promptly at ten a.m. and around noon he recessed one hour for lunch. This would give the bailiff the time to order meals for the jury. He had to drive to a local restaurant, pick them up and bring them back to the jury room. The Horn Inn prepared the dinners for the jurors most of the time. The Horn Inn was the only restaurant in town that still made their meals from scratch and the jurors favored the food there. The judge glanced at the courtroom clock. It was eleven fifty. Sally's testimony was done and there was not enough time to call another witness. He adjourned the court until one o'clock. Some of the spectators left but a few of them stayed glued to their seats for fear of losing them if they left for lunch.

Sally, Josh and Bob were eating lunch at the Horn Inn when the bailiff came into the restaurant and walked to the counter. He was handed a medium sized cardboard box full of fourteen meals in styrofoam containers and left.

"The Judge runs a good court doesn't he?" Sally commented more as a statement than a question.

"He's strict on court procedure and starts court right at ten o'clock. If you are not there he'll start without you." Her partner answered. He had been in front of the Judge many times and had witnessed a few red faced attorneys trying to explain to their client why they had to go back to the county jail until another hearing could be set.

The detectives returned to the court at ten minutes to one and were escorted to their reserved seats by one of the bailiffs. The next witness called was Detective Lieutenant Bob Carpenter who was asked to substantiate what his partner had testified to. His testimony was short and to the point and he was not on the stand as long as his partner. Josh Trimble was called next. Mitchell Slade asked him to tell the jury about his background and experience as an investigator with the Bureau of Criminal Apprehension. He began by discussing his training at Quantico, Virginia at the Federal Bureau of Investigation Training Center and talked about his years as an investigator both with the Milrose Police Department and the Minnesota Bureau of Criminal Apprehension.

"I've worked on thirty four homicide cases and brought thirty three of them to a successful conclusion with an arrest and conviction in each of those thirty three cases."

"I'm impressed Agent Trimble," the assistant County Attorney added as he looked at the jury. He could see that they were satisfied with Agent Trimble's credentials. "Tell us about the resources that the Bureau has in helping you solve these heinous crimes."

The line of questioning by the prosecutor was routine and designed to give the jury an idea of how the whole process worked. Agent Trimble talked about the three portable crime labs that the bureau used and how they worked. He briefly touched on the main lab and how it was used to analyze and categorize evidence found at the scene of a crime. He suggested to the prosecutor that a member of the crime lab could do a better job in describing to the jury how the lab worked. The prosecutor agreed and changed his line of questioning.

Mitchell Slade handed a picture of the shaolin sword that Harmony Ann Day had been stabbed with to the witness. "Can you identify this picture Agent Trimble?"

"Yes. This is the sword that was embedded into the left side of Harmony Ann day. The tip of the blade was sticking through the body and exited on the right side."

"Were there any prints on the sword?"

"Yes, the lab found several prints from Peter Krueger and one right index finger print of the defendant."

"Who was the owner of the sword?"

"Peter Krueger, a friend of the defendant."

Agent Trimble went on to talk about the other evidence found at the scene. The nails that had been driven into the hands, the rose thorns that had been sloppily laid on top of the head, her unusual clothing, the excessive amount of bruising on the body, and the water in the lungs and stomach.

"Was there evidence that the victim was sexually assaulted?" Slade asked.

"None, and no semen was found on or in her body."

Slade offered fifteen pictures of the crime scene to the Agent Trimble and asked the witness to identify each one. Once they were identified they were marked as exhibits twenty three through thirty seven and handed to the jury. The fifteen pictures of the murder scene and the victim still impaled against the wall had an effect on the jury and Slade knew it. His case was going better than he ever expected. The knowledge and professionalism of the witnesses he had summoned had impressed him. If he was astonished, he was sure that the jury was also. The assistant County Attorney was through with Agent Trimble and yielded him over to the defense. His testimony had made an impact on the jury as he knew it would.

Bill Pierce slowly and carefully stood up. He straightened his tie and walked to the front of the witness box. "Did you find a sheath? The sheath that belonged to this sword, Agent Trimble?"

"Yes, the sheath to the sword used in this murder was recovered from the back seat of Peter Krueger's vehicle."

"Tell me, Agent Trimble, were there any fingerprints or footprints left at the scene - something that would connect my client to being there?"

"Nope, only the one fingerprint on the sword."

"Which really doesn't put him at the scene. My client freely admits that he was fascinated with that sword and had looked at it and held it a number of times. So you have no other physical evidence at all linking my client to the murder?"

"We have a confession from his friend Peter Krueger that he and Hezekiah were the ones that killed her. He told us in detail how they killed her. His story is consistent with the bruising we found on Harmony Ann Day. We found hair samples and we found blood samples of the victim in the middle front seat of his car."

The defense attorney was wearing a set of reading glasses as he was cross-examining Agent Trimble. He stood in front of the jury box and took off his glasses; he wiped them with a brown handkerchief and returned them to his head. He shook his head in disbelief suggesting to the jury that his client was being framed. "This Peter Krueger fella', is he wanted for anything?"

"Yes, he is being charged by the FBI for a bank robbery in Kingman, Arizona and is a suspect in a bank robbery in Kansas City, Kansas. He is also wanted for aggravated assault in Wolf Point, Montana. He is presently incarcerated in our jail. He has already pled guilty to killing Harmony Ann Day and has been sentenced and is awaiting transportation to Stillwater Prison."

"This Krueger is kind of a dangerous fellow, wouldn't you say, Agent Trimble?"

"Yes I would. I have been in on a couple of interviews with him and he is an angry young man."

"Were any deals made with him? It strikes me as kind of funny that with all these charges in other places that he is here in Minnesota already."

"We made no deals with him regarding his testimony. He implicated Hezekiah Hadley without any coercion from us. In his confession he freely admitted that they did the murder together. He had provided other information about the defendant that proved to be correct so we felt he was telling the truth in the confession. We did make a deal with him that if he admitted his guilt in the Harmony Ann Day murder we would extradite him to Minnesota and he could spend his prison time here in Minnesota rather than Montana or a federal prison. For some reason he opted to cop to the murder; he wanted nothing to do with being in prison out of state. He said he had a lot of friends at Stillwater and he wanted to serve his time there."

Bill Pierce took off his glasses and wiped them again with the same handkerchief. After he inspected the lenses he replaced the handkerchief and looked at the jury and turned toward the man in the witness box. He was silent, mimicking a deep thought, possibly waiting for a revelation and the courtroom was hushed waiting for his next words. Then the words came. "Do you think Hezekiah Hadley, the young man sitting at my table, killed Harmony Ann Day?"

Josh had never been asked to give an opinion as to the guilt or innocent of a person. He waited for the abstract question to be challenged by the prosecution and when it wasn't he answered that his job was to investigate the crime and provide enough probable cause to make an arrest. The rest of the work was up to the attorneys and the courts. "As to my opinion on whether Hezekiah is guilty or innocence I'm going to let the jury decide that."

The defense attorney advised the Judge that he had nothing more at this time. The courtroom clock had passed the three o'clock mark. The Judge announced to the jury that today's court session was finished and that court would reconvene tomorrow morning at ten o'clock.

Sally's work day was over and she was free to do what she wanted for the remainder of it. It hit her like a ton of bricks; she hadn't been off duty at three o'clock in the afternoon since her early days as a patrolman. Better yet, she didn't have to be back to work until ten o'clock tomorrow morning. When the Chief asked her to attend the trial every day she was disappointed - thought it would be boring. Now she was happy for the assignment and wouldn't mind if the trial went longer than anticipated.

There were two messages on her phone when she returned to her office before going home. One message was from Lois, her friend from the college. The other was from Josh Trimble. She called Lois first. One of the members of the bowling team had called in sick and they needed a substitute and could Sally be it. She agreed. She called Josh and he asked her if she wanted to go out for a few drinks and supper tonight. She told him that she was bowling and suggested that he come out to the bowling alley and watch their team kick butt. He agreed and told her that he would meet her at the bowling alley.

He took a sip of his beer and watched Sally roll her first ball down the alley. She was wearing a loose fitting blue bowling shirt with her name stitched above the pocket. The name of her team was embroidered on the back of the shirt in large white letters. The buttons on her shirt were sculptured to resemble little white bowling pins. Josh thought she looked provocative wearing the bowling shirt and a pair of tight fitting black cotton slacks. It was the red shoes that really caught his interest and he would be sure to mention how sexy she looked in them.

He watched as she picked up her ball from the return and prepared to throw her second ball trying to knock down the three pins that were remaining for a spare. The ball hit the alley in perfect alignment with the three pins. She easily knocked them over and did a slight jump and a twist before walking over to the booth where her team was sitting at and sat down. She was smiling and happy. Josh was thinking that she looked attractive without the bullet proof vest pushing in her chest and the nine millimeter hanging from her belt with a pair of handcuffs dangling from the other side of her belt. She had a petite figure but she wasn't skinny. The outline of her body made most women envious. Josh watched the team win three of the four games. When the last game was over she walked over to Josh, sat down next to him and ordered a beer. "The girls are going out to *Couplings* for a few brewski's and I was thinking I would join them. I don't have to be to work until ten. You want to come along?"

Eleven o'clock was closing time at *Couplings* on week days. Neither Josh nor Sally was ready to go home yet so they drove to the new Applebee's that had opened near the freeway exit into Milrose. They each ordered a hamburger, french fries and a beer. When they were through eating they decided to call it a night.

Dr. Goodland was the first witness of the morning. He had been on the witness stand many times as an assistant pathologist in St. Paul and he was familiar with court procedures and felt comfortable on the stand. He stood a good six foot-three and his dark skin had a youthful glow to it and his hair was beginning to gray. His voice was deep and easily heard by the jury. He testified of the autopsy and his findings. He talked about the water found in the victim's lungs. He mentioned the bruising and the small puncture wounds around the top of the head caused by the rose thorns. As he was describing the details of the autopsy Mitchell Slade was performing a slide presentation showing close-ups of the hair line and the small puncture wounds. When Dr. Goodland talked about the wound in the side of the victim the pictures taken at the autopsy of those wounds would be shown on the slide. The effect on the jury was dramatic as the profound voice of the pathologist described every detail to the jury. Dr. Goodland's testimony was damaging to the defense. The jury was clearly touched by the photographs.

When Mitchell Slade was finished with the witness the Judge turned and looked at the defense table. Bill Pierce stood up and said that the defense had no questions. Dr. Goodland was free to go.

The next witness was Nathan Brown. When Sally watched him saunter to the witness box she straightened up in her chair. Her feelings hadn't changed toward him and it made her sick to see him get the attention he was receiving in the courtroom and wondered what he had done with Helen DuPont; she had been missing for ten days and Sally was getting worried that her body may never be found. He leisurely entered the witness stand and slumped down in the wooden chair. He raised one arm and rested it on the back of the chair and yawned. He kept his other arm in front of him resting it on his knee and twiddling his fingers. The Judge noticed his actions and looked at him disapprovingly. He was on the stand to testify he was the one that tagged the body when it arrived at the morgue and that the body autopsied was that of Harmony Ann Day who had been referred to as Jane Doe at that time. That was it. He was done and Sally watched him leave the witness stand. She watched him as he walked toward the back of the courtroom to the double wide doors that were the entrance to the proceedings. A bailiff held one of the doors open and he walked out and disappeared. Sally got up and hurried toward the same doors, hoping to catch Nathan Brown and talk to him. The bailiff once again opened the door for her as she walked out of the courtroom and into the hallway but did not see Nathan Brown. She turned to the bailiff. "Did you see where that man went that just walked out the door?"

"He walked to the front of the courthouse but I didn't see where he went from there, sorry."

Sally ran to the front of the courthouse and looked out the front doors and onto the lawn and the surrounding area. She didn't see him anywhere. She searched all three floors of the courthouse with no luck. He had disappeared for now but she couldn't wait for the day she would be arresting him for something.

Pamela Rosewood was called next and she told the jury about her friend and the effect her death had on the Day family. She talked about how she and Harmony had been friends since they were little girls. She discussed Harmony's deep faith and how she planned on being a social worker so she could help people. Mitchell Slade asked her about Peter Krueger. "He was Harmony's boyfriend. I didn't like him and she knew it. I told the officers that I don't even know why Harmony went out with him. They were totally opposites. He was a creep, he had tattoos all over his body and he was into kung fu or some oriental stuff. He was weird. He smoked, he drank, he did drugs so I don't understand it. She would be alive today if it wasn't for Peter Krueger and Hezekiah Hadley."

After the last statement by Pamela Rosewood the defense attorney stood up and spoke. "Objection, pure speculation on the part of the witness."

The judge agreed and asked the jury to disregard that last statement made by the witness. He looked at Mitchell Slade. "You may proceed."

The assistant County Attorney walked over to the witness stand, looked at the jury before looking at the witness. "Is it true that Harmony Day did not smoke, did not drink, did not do drugs and she hated tattoos?"

"That's correct. Like I said I don't know what got over her. The only thing I can think of is that deep down she thought there was some hope for this guy. I know she liked him a lot but I also don't think there was any real love there. If you know what I mean."

When the assistant County Attorney was certain that he had instilled into the minds of the jury that the victim was a decent, moral and clean living young woman he sat down. If the defense attorney tried to portray Harmony Day as something other than that he would risk antagonizing the jury.

Bill Pierce arose, looked at Mitchell Slade and walked over to the witness and began his questioning.

"You didn't like Peter Krueger very much, did you?"

"No I didn't."

"You'd say just about anything to get my client convicted, wouldn't you?" Bill Pierce asked, looking directly into her eyes.

"Objection." Slade immediately stood up and yelled.

Bill Pierce knew that the question would be objected to but the jury had heard it and they would wonder if Pamela Rosewood might be prejudiced against his client. "How about my client Hezekiah Hadley?"

"I didn't know him."

"Had you ever seen him with Harmony?"

"Once, me and Harmony drove down to the college one Sunday. She wanted to show me the campus. It was a beautiful day for a drive and I thought it would be fun. After she showed me the college we drove out to Cedar Park. She showed me around the park and we ended up parking in the blacktop lot by the lake. We sat at a picnic table and kinda' looked at the lake. We were both lost in our thoughts when this guy with green hair appears out of nowhere and walks up to Harmony and says that he needs to talk to her. She doesn't look too happy about this guy showing up, but she gets up and they go for a short walk. Maybe twenty minutes or so. When she returns she tells me his name."

"When you were interviewed by three detectives at your home you told them that you thought they should focus their attention on Peter Krueger as the one who killed Harmony. Why do you think he killed Harmony?"

Mitchell Slade objected on the grounds that it called for speculation on the part of the witness.

The question was rephrased. "Is there something about Peter Krueger that would make you think of him when you heard about your roommate's death?"

"Just that he was an angry man and he knew all these karate moves."

"So, Miss Rosewood, he was capable of killing someone all by himself. He didn't need help from someone like Hezekiah Hadley to do the job?"

"I don't know about that."

Bill Pierce was through with the witness. He needed to plant a small seed in the minds of the jurors that it was possible, probable in fact, that Peter Krueger killed Harmony Ann Day by himself. He had implicated his client only because he was angry with him.

CHAPTER 42

The *Milrose Sentinel* lay open on the kitchen table in front of her. On the third page was the continuation of a front page story that had intrigued the reader. A young woman had been found murdered in Cedar Park; her identity was unknown and there were no suspects in the case. The reader hadn't finished the article when she decided to get up from the table and pour herself a cup of green tea. She filled it to the brim and was careful not to spill any as she walked back to the table and sat down to finish reading the article. She had lived in Milrose all her life and there had never been a murder in the town. It was disheartening to her. She had a daughter herself, and could only imagine what the parents would be going through when they found out. She wondered what the world was coming to. She knew there were a lot of bad things out in the world but also a lot of good things too. They seem to balance each other out.

Ann Garner finished the paper and called her daughter to see how things were going with her and the family. When she was through talking to her daughter, she walked into the living room and gazed at the portrait of her husband proudly wearing his army uniform. The framed picture was sitting on his writing table that faced the bay window overlooking Elm Street. He had been gone a month now, the cancer had finally won. She missed him. They would have been married forty three years in October. When they both retired last year, they felt as if they were starting life all over again. They wanted to travel and see the country. They were getting ready to buy an RV when he was diagnosed with colon cancer. Four months later she was a widow. She was fortunate that the marriage produced four wonderful children who helped her through the difficult times and the readjustments of life.

They lived in other parts of the country and each of her children invited her to live with them but she had thoughtfully declined, wanting to stay in Milrose. She couldn't abandon her church and her friends or her neighbors. They were all precious to her. She would visit her children as often as possible but she needed to stay in Milrose.

Wherever she happened to be, whether it was at church or having coffee at the Horn Inn with her friends or shopping at the grocery store, the topic of conversation, lately, was the horrible murder of Harmony Day. When Florence Hadley was found murdered and stuffed in her freezer the townspeople became more guarded and suspicious. Homes that had never been locked were now dead bolted. Shot guns were cleaned and loaded and easily accessible if needed. The few men in town that owned handguns had them sitting on the nightstand next to them. They were loaded and ready to shoot.

When Hezekiah Hadley was arrested for the murders of his mother and Harmony Ann Day, the town breathed a sigh of relief. Ann Garner was just as relieved as anyone. She had been to the Horn Inn with two of her girl friends for morning coffee when she heard the news. The next hour was spent dissecting the character of Hezekiah. An hour was about as long as she could sit in a restaurant so she excused herself, left the restaurant and drove home.

When Ann pulled into the driveway she noticed that the mailman had dropped off her mail and was walking toward her neighbor's house. He was punctual as usual and when he left her yard she noticed that her mailbox was stuffed with mail. She removed the mail and skimmed through it as she walked to her house. One letter in particular caught her attention. It was from the Clerk of District Court. She opened it as she walked. She read the summons carefully as it informed her that she was to report to the courthouse on Monday morning for jury selection. She wondered what case she would be hearing. It had been several weeks since the Hadley boy was arrested. Could his trial be coming up so soon? She would just have to wait and see.

The sixty-five year old Ann Garner, who had recently lost her husband and had time on her hands, hoped that someday she would be called to serve on a jury. She had never been inside a courtroom and was curious what it was like 'in there'. A friend of hers from church had been called and they sat together on the wooden bench outside the courtroom and talked about church affairs. Ann was the first one called for examination and before the day was over she was a juror.

Juror number ten carefully digested every word uttered by the attorneys, the witnesses and Judge Armstrong. She was passionate about doing the best job she could as a juror. She was impressed by Pamela Rosewood and her love for her friend. To her, Harmony Day was the person that Pamela Rosewood portrayed her to be. After the testimony of Pamela Rosewood the Judge adjourned court. The jury was free to go and was to be back in the courtroom tomorrow at nine-thirty. As Ann Garner was walking out of the courtroom she bumped into an old friend of hers from a nearby town. The friend hadn't heard about the death of Ann's husband. Eager to talk about her husband and to talk to her friend, Ann suggested they walk downstairs to the courthouse cafeteria and discuss it over a piece of pie and a cup of coffee. Time passed quickly for them and before they knew it the courthouse was closing. It was five o'clock and time for both of them to leave. "Do you need a ride home?" her friend asked.

"Thanks anyway, I've got my own car."

Her friend had left her car in the courthouse parking lot and all she had to do was walk out the ground floor exit door and she was immediately at her car. Ann had parked in the front of the courthouse in the designated parking area for jurors. She needed to take the elevator up to the first floor, walk out the front door and down several concrete steps to the courthouse lawn. When she approached the front door she stopped, fidgeted in her purse for her car keys and finding them she opened the front courthouse door. She was about to step onto the first step when she felt something take hold of her shoulder and push her forward. The pressure from behind caused her to miss the first step and tumble down twenty-seven unforgiving steps where she ended up sprawled across the bottom step and the sidewalk. She was conscious but in a lot of pain. People quickly gathered around her asking if she was all right. She wasn't and she knew it. "You better call an ambulance," she whispered.

She woke up in a hospital room - her leg was in a cast and her wrist was in a sling and she ached all over. A nurse entered the room to take her vitals and noticed that the patient was awake. "You're awake. You had a nasty fall."

"How am I, nurse?"

"You've got a broken leg, a broken wrist and three broken ribs. You're going to be sore for a while, but you are going to be as good as new in a couple of months."

Ann thought she remembered someone pushing her but she couldn't be sure, she decided to say nothing about her suspicions to anyone. She knew she was not going to be able to finish her term as a juror and was thankful that one of the two alternates would be able to step in and fill her spot.

Early the next morning the Judge was told about Ann Garner. Andy Taylor was picked as the new juror number ten.

CHAPTER 43

The entire day was like reading a bad book; you wanted to know how it ended before the monotony of it put you to sleep. Three members of the forensic team from the Bureau of Criminal Apprehension were scheduled to testify. The jury would listen attentively at first and then their minds would begin to go in other directions - unfinished chores at home, plans for the weekend, thinking of family, the economy or anything else that a bored mind could think of.

The credentials of these experts were introduced by the prosecution with no objections coming from the defense. In great detail the witnesses explained to the jury how crime scene investigation works, from the gathering of evidence to its analysis and preservation. The jury learned about DNA and the testing of blood and hair samples. It was explained how rigor mortis and post mortem lividity played a roll in determining time of death. The wall clock hung in back of the jury and they didn't want to embarrass themselves by turning around to look at it. By late morning the clock had become a popular fixture to the spectators. The jurors had to settle for looking at their watches every five minutes.

Mitchell Slade felt he had successfully introduced to the jury the vital evidence of the case. He was aware that a day and a half of wearisome testimony played its toll on the jury but he was confident that they had retained the information and it would be reviewed over again in the jury room during deliberations.

The last BCA witness worked full time in the lab and had never been to a crime scene. He was kept busy with DNA testing, categorizing blood samples, classifying hair samples, matching fingerprints and analyzing most evidence that came into his laboratory.

He had a crew of twenty forensic people and chemists assisting him. It was his testimony that supported the findings of Dr. Goodland that the victim had been drowned prior to being hung on the wall. He testified that the contents of the water in her lungs and stomach contained small amounts of animal fecal matter and urine, straw particles and animal DNA from saliva found in the water. The water was agriculture water and unfit for human consumption.

Bill Pierce arose and walked over to the last BCA witness and asked him the same questions he asked the other two. "Did any of the evidence found at the scene and analyzed by your department implicate my client?"

"No sir," was the polite reply by the experienced lab specialist.

"So, of all the DNA evidence you gathered and all the blood samples and all the hair samples you took none of them linked my client to the murder scene. Is that right?"

"Yes, sir."

"You studied the photographs of the footprints taken at the scene where the purse was found. Is that correct?" Pierce asked.

"Yes."

"What was your finding?"

"The prints were made by a work boot, size ten and a half."

This was a piece of evidence that Bill Pierce was sure would put doubt in the minds of the jurors as to the guilt of his client. "What if I told you that my client, the defendant sitting next to me, wears a size eight and a half shoe? That would pretty much eliminate him as being at the scene where Harmony Day's purse was found, wouldn't it?"

The lab specialist was not on the stand to speculate; he dealt in facts, not speculation. "I can't say, I can only tell the court my findings as to the shoe size."

Bill Pierce paused; he wanted the jury to digest the findings of the forensic specialist. The inconsistencies in the shoe size found at the area where the purse was buried and the shoe size of Hezekiah Hadley was an important piece of evidence. It could put doubt into the minds of the jury about his client's guilt. "You gathered a lot of evidence at the scene, right? Isn't it unusual that out of all the evidence that not one shred of evidence links my client to this crime?"

"We did have one fingerprint of the defendant on the sword that was impaled into the victim's side and several of Peter Krueger's prints on the same sword."

"My client insists that his fingerprint got on that sword because he had looked at it at a prior time. Is there a way of telling us how old a fingerprint is?"

"Not really."

"But, if that fingerprint was eliminated from your investigation there would be no other evidence that you found at Cedar Park that morning that would link my client to the crime."

"No sir. Not at the crime scene."

Bill Pierce was done with the witness. He needed to build a 'shadow of a doubt' to the jury and they needed to remember that there was no evidence linking Hezekiah Hadley to the crime scene. The jury had not heard from Peter Krueger or his confession. He would have to tear that confession apart and needed to prove to the jury that Peter Krueger was the lone killer and that he held a grudge against his client and wanted to take him down with him.

Judge Armstrong wanted to get the testimony of the last BCA witness in before lunch. His testimony went longer than anticipated; when the lab specialist got out of the witness box it was after one o'clock. The Judge decided to adjourn court for the day. The jury looked tired and bored and he was sympathetic toward them. Tomorrow everyone would be refreshed to hear the testimony of the psychiatrists.

****

Two cameras on opposite walls scanned the twenty foot by twenty foot cell of Peter Krueger. The only place he had any privacy at all was when he was using the stainless steel toilet. It was in this area that he was carefully honing his hard plastic toothbrush into a three inch weapon. Using the tile floor as a makeshift grinder he worked and shaped the toothbrush handle until he was certain it would easily puncture human skin. Once the weapon penetrated the body the kill would be easy. He wasn't done with the weapon yet, he had to be careful not to draw attention from the eyes that were always watching him. He used the toilet a couple of times a day and worked frantically sharpening his tool. He wanted it done before he was taken to court to testify against Hezekiah. If he survived the weekend and did not have to testify until Monday, he would be able to set his plans in motion.

He had been in jail enough times to know he could deceive the deputies and the jailers and lull them into complacency. It was easy; all he had to do was be nice to them, always call them sir, thank them whenever possible and treat them with respect. That combination would get you almost anything you wanted as long as it was legal. It was difficult for him to be nice to anyone, especially a guard or a cop, but he begrudgingly did it and it worked. The jailors needed to feel comfortable around him for his plan to work. Once they were comfortable they would also be complacent. If they felt at ease with him they probably would not shackle his legs and that's all he wanted. He needed to convince them that he was not a flight risk and that he was resigned to his fate.

CHAPTER 44

The jurors would be as bored today as they had been the last two days. Two psychiatrists were to be called to the witness stand, each having an opposing view on the mental competence of Hezekiah Hadley. In an unusual step for the defense, their witness was called to the stand while the prosecution was still calling it own witnesses. The stray from courtroom procedure was made to accommodate the psychiatrist for the defense who was scheduled to speak at a convention in Chicago and needed to catch a late afternoon flight out of Minneapolis. Bill Pierce needed the jury to hear his testimony before he left for Chicago and the prosecution agreed to the change. The witness for the defense would testify that the defendant was not capable of knowing right from wrong. Bill Pierce was not asking the jury for a verdict of mental incompetency, he wanted a straight out not guilty verdict and needed the testimony of the psychiatrist to play on the sympathies of the jurors.

"Could you explain to the court how you reached this opinion?" Bill Pierce asked.

The doctor was young, sharply dressed and wore thick glasses. His tousled hair was long and hung over his ears. He faced the jury as he had been prompted to do by the defense team. "I interviewed Mr. Hadley for over two hours and I have not seen a more mixed up individual, it all goes back to his early childhood. His father deserted the family when Hezekiah was less than a year old so he never even knew who his father was. His mother was an alcoholic and a chain smoker who paid little or no attention to her son. She changed his diapers or fed him only when she was sober enough to do so. Hezekiah basically grew up without love. By the time he was eight years old he was wandering the streets alone at night and getting into trouble. He had no friends, no father and a mother who he thought hated him. He was confused and had not developed any social skills. He yearned to have friends but was never able to find even one. By the time he was twelve years old he drifted into himself more and more, resigned to the fact that he was in this world alone and he would have to make do with what he had. He needed some recognition from somebody, and when Harmony Day came along and befriended him, he was about as happy as he had ever been. He was devastated by her death and thinking that Peter Krueger had killed his only friend he wanted revenge. He wasn't sure what he was going to do to Krueger but he was going to do something." The defense psychiatrist occupied the witness stand for most of the morning; his analysis being that Hezekiah Hadley suffered from bipolar disorder, manic depression, and mild schizophrenia and antisocial behavior. The jury had a lot to digest when the first psychiatrist left the witness chair.

The second psychiatrist took the stand after the noon recess. His analysis differed from the earlier testimony of the defense psychiatrist. The afternoon witness was much older than his colleague. He wore an outdated brown suit, wrinkled yellow dress shirt with a brown clip-on tie. A large, thick handlebar mustache jutted from each side of his face and moved up and down with each word that he spoke. His long hair and mustache were white but he spoke with a mind that seemed as sharp now as it was twenty five years ago. He explained to the jury what it meant to not be able to tell right from wrong. All the disorders that the previous witness talked about were not illnesses that affected that ability except maybe schizophrenia and Hezekiah Hadley had a mild form which would not alter his concept of right and wrong.

Mitchell Slade was done with the state's witness and the defense had no questions. It was common for both sides to have their own psychiatrist take the stand and it was up to the jury to decide which psychiatric analysis was the most believable.

The day had gone by fast and the jurors weren't bored. Both witnesses had captured the attention of the spectators and the jury. Their knowledge of psychiatry was evident and everyone in the courtroom learned a little bit more about Hezekiah Hadley and who he really was. As the trial progressed it seemed like the jury was going to have a difficult time in reaching a verdict. The afternoon court session was over by three. A few witnesses were called by the prosecution to testify of the character of the defendant. Mitchell Slade wanted the jury to know that Hezekiah Hadley was capable of just about anything.

CHAPTER 45

Prisoner number 3424 was lying on his back on his bunk with an open Black Belt magazine sprawled upside down across his stomach. Peter Krueger stared at the bottom of the bunk that was above him when two deputies and a jailer entered his cell. "Time for court, Pete," the jailer said. "They need you there at ten o'clock."

"Can I dress up or do I have to wear these jail skivvies? I would prefer looking half way decent in court."

One of the deputies nodded to the jailer that it would be okay for the prisoner to dress for court. Peter Krueger was escorted to the small locker room where he slipped into his street clothes. When he was ready for court the jailer introduced the handcuffs and leg irons.

"Aw come on fellas. I can see the handcuffs, but not the leg irons, please. I promise I ain't goin' anywhere. I just want to get this done and get to prison. Have some compassion."

The jailer held the leg irons in his hand and hesitated; he looked at the deputy who shook his head in a sideways motion indicating to the jailer that the leg irons wouldn't be necessary. He was escorted to the sally port where he was placed in the rear seat. One of the deputies slid in the back seat next to him while the jailer took the passenger seat and the other deputy got behind the wheel. The metal sally port door opened and they backed out of the garage and began driving the short distance to the courthouse. They entered the courthouse and the prisoner was taken to a small room where the four of them waited. Fifteen minutes later Peter Krueger was sitting in the witness box.

"How do you know the defendant?" Mitchell Slade asked.

"We were friends. I'd known Hezzy for years. We've had some beers together over the years."

Slade handed Peter Krueger's confession to him and asked him to read it word for word. The witness took the two sheets of paper and carefully read them to the jury. The confession was detailed and graphic and had the jury's full attention. When he was through he handed the confession back to Slade.

"Why did you and Hezekiah Hadley kill her?"

"I don't really know, man. It all got out of hand. Hezzy started hitting her and hitting her hard. There was no reason, you know. And he was yelling names at her and we were both doing drugs and I kind of got into the whole thing too and I started hitting her. Then she went limp and we figured she was dead. I mean we were really pouncing on her."

"Do you remember anything else?"

"Just what's in the confession, like I said we were both out of it and none of us really remembered much."

"How did the water get into her lungs and stomach? The coroner, Dr. Goodland, told us that when he performed the autopsy there was water in the stomach and in the lungs. One of the lab experts tells us that a sample of the water revealed its contents which would indicate that Harmony Ann Day was drowned in an animal trough or a body of water that was frequented by animals - cows or horses in particular"

"I don't know, man. I don't remember nothing after she went limp and we figured we killed her. Maybe I passed out or something. Maybe Hezzy drowned her in Cedar Park Lake to make sure she was dead. We were kinda messed up that night."

"What did you know about the relationship between Hezekiah Hadley and Harmony Ann Day?"

"He was obsessed with her. All she wanted to do was try and get him straightened out and headed in the right direction. He never seen it that way, he figured she was nice to him because she liked him. She told me that she figured it was a waste of time working with Hezekiah and she was going to stop seeing him. She said she was starting to be afraid of him."

"You told the court and the jury that you and Hezekiah were friends but yet you shot him in the leg and you robbed him and then you implicated him in the murder of Harmony Ann Day. Is that how friends treat each other?"

The witness was feeling good. The jury and the spectators were focused on his testimony; they were quiet and all eyes were on Peter Krueger. He was the center of attention and he was glad he was allowed to wear street clothes. If he had on his orange skivvies the effect would not have been as good. What no one knew was that before the day was out he would be a free man. "I shot Hezzy cuz he was making passes at my girlfriend right in front of me. I didn't trust him. If he thought he had any kind of a chance with Lin Su he would have shot me first. He says I robbed him? I didn't rob him, I just took back the money he owed me and the reason I ratted on him wasn't because I really wanted to but when I heard he killed his mother I was mad. How can anyone kill their own mother? I decided I was going to take him down with me. Really, if it wasn't for Hezzy getting me all riled up I think Harmony would be alive today."

Mitchell Slade exhausted another hour with the witness going over his confession and his relationship with the murder victim. When he was satisfied that the jury had heard enough and was convinced that the two acted together to kill Harmony Day, he walked to his table and sat down.

It was Bill Pierce's turn and he was anxious and prepared. "You hated Hezekiah didn't you? He was weak and he was chubby - things you despised in a man - and that green hair, you hated that too, didn't you? You were never friends, you were enemies and when Harmony Day came along you got a little jealous. You couldn't see what she saw in him - this green haired freak. You had your girlfriend Lin Su shoot him and later on you framed him for a murder he had nothing to do with, didn't you?"

Krueger sat up straight for the first time during his testimony. He wanted to slash out at the defense attorney but that would put a halt to his plans. He smiled innocently and looked at the jury. When he looked back at Bill Pierce he was calmer. "You have it all wrong. How could I have made up something like that? I'm going down for her murder, but so is the guy that helped me do it."

Bill Pierce walked over to his table and retrieved a photograph from his briefcase and walked back to the witness and showed him the black and white picture. "Can you identify this photo Mr. Krueger?"

Pete Krueger looked at the picture briefly and handed it back to Pierce. "Yea, it's my car."

The photograph was introduced as an exhibit before Bill Pierce continued his questioning. "Tell us about the dent in the left fender. Looks fairly new."

"I had an accident with it, so what."

"Was anyone with you, Mr. Krueger, when you had your 'so called' accident?"

"Nope," he lied.

Pierce again walked to his table and was handed a document by his assistant. He walked back to the bench, handed it to the Judge to look at and introduced it as another exhibit. He turned to the witness and showed him the document. "I have in my hand a medical report of a doctor who treated Harmony Ann Day shortly after your accident. She had injuries to her head that required six stitches. Could that explain why traces of her blood and hair were found in your car?"

"I don't know nothing about that and I was alone when I had the accident."

"The doctor says she was with a young man who matched your description. I believe that she was with you in the car when you had the accident and that is why there was her blood and her hair were found in your car."

"I was alone in the car, I already told you that," he lied again.

"I must remind you that you are under oath Mr. Krueger."

"OH, I'm trembling in my boots. I might have to go to jail for lying," he answered before realizing he was letting his temper control his emotions and he couldn't let that happen. "I'm sorry, you're right. I would never lie under oath," he answered the attorney in a remorseful tone.

Pierce dropped the line of questioning. He wanted the jury to know about the accident and the possibility that the blood and the hair found in the front seat may have been from that of Harmony Day. He needed to convince the jury that Krueger was a liar and that he lied on his confession. Krueger may have killed Harmony Ann Day but his client wasn't along when he did it.

"What if I was to tell you that Hezekiah Hadley had an alibi for that night? What if I was to tell you that he was seen by Milrose police officers in downtown Milrose at the same time you say he was with you?"

"Object, Your Honor," Mitchell Slade arose and faced the defense attorney and the Judge. "We were not aware of this new evidence - sidebar please, Your Honor."

Both attorneys approached the bench. Bill Pierce explained that his office had just received this piece of information and that it had not been substantiated. The defense was going to subpoena the police officers to corroborate the story. Mitchell Slade told the judge that considerable damage had been done already. If this story is not substantiated, the jury could still be led to believe that the defendant was in downtown Milrose on the night of the murder, regardless of the outcome of the officer's testimony. Slade asked the Judge to instruct the jury to disregard the alibi story, which the Judge did.

Krueger had been on the stand for most of the morning. The prosecution needed to convince the jury that the defendant was involved in Harmony Ann Day's murder. The defense wanted to convince the jury that Peter Krueger acted alone in killing Harmony Ann Day and that he had a vendetta against his client and implicated him out of spite. It was simply a matter of who would the jury believe.

The Judge recessed the court when Peter Krueger's testimony was over. The prisoner extended his tattooed arms so the deputy could put the handcuffs on. He felt the sharpened edge of the toothbrush poke into his thigh, but he didn't flinch. It would be over soon and he would be a free man; he hoped the honed toothbrush had not poked his skin causing him to bleed. He didn't need for the officers to see blood dripping on his shoes. He was escorted to the Sheriff's car in the courthouse parking lot. The unmarked squad car would make it easier for his plan to work. No caged wall separated the front seat from the back seat. This car was not used for transporting prisoners. What a stroke of luck, everything was going his way so far. He slid into the back seat behind the front passenger's side; an armed deputy slid into the back seat behind the driver and studied him before looking forward. The prisoner eyed the 9mm sitting snugly in the holster on the deputy's right side. It would be easy to grab - there were no safeguards on the holster. He would be able to pull it out smoothly and quickly. The jailer opened the front passenger door, slid in and buckled his seat belt. He turned toward the deputy in the back seat and told him to hook the seat belt around the prisoner. The deputy responded and buckled his prisoner. Another deputy got in the drivers side of the squad car, turned the ignition and announced to the dispatch center that he was 10-15 - transporting a prisoner to the jail. It was going as Krueger planned it would but he had to work fast. He groped for the toothbrush and found it. He had practiced the moves over and over in his jail cell until he had it down to perfection. Being handcuffed and belted to the seat made the maneuvering a little more difficult but once his fingers touched the toothbrush he was able to produce it in an instant. He kept his left hand wrapped around it until the squad car left the parking lot. With lightning speed he lifted his handcuffed hands and jammed the homemade shiv into the throat of the complacent deputy. Blood immediately squirted from the deputy's throat as the prisoner yanked the nine millimeter from his gun belt holster. He pointed the automatic pistol at the driver and ordered him to keep both hands on the wheel and look straight ahead and drive where he told him to. The final destination would be a large wooded area three quarters of a mile from the Hadley residence. A narrow dirt road led into the center of the woods and Krueger told the driver to pull the squad car off of the gravel road and onto the dirt road. The deputy was reluctant but did as he was told. Krueger reached over and grabbed the dead deputy's keys from his belt. Holding the keys in his hand, he fumbled for the small silver handcuff key. When he found it he unlocked the cuffs and slid them into his pocket. With the handcuffs off he was in a better position to proceed with his plan. The squad car would be nearing the end of the road soon. He ordered the driver to undo his gun belt and toss it into the back seat. The jailer was unarmed but was ordered to unlatch the twelve gauge shotgun from the floor rack and toss it in the back seat also. He was now the only one with weapons and was clearly in control of the situation. When the squad reached the end of the road the driver stopped; both men in the front seat feared for their lives, silently cursing themselves for not following protocol when transporting a prisoner. Krueger ordered the jailer out of the squad car while aiming his weapon at the deputy who was sitting behind the wheel. He ordered the jailer to open the back door of the squad. His gun was poised at the head of the deputy, and the jailer did not want to take any chances that the prisoner would shoot either one of them. He had already killed the deputy in the back seat and they knew he would not hesitate in killing again. The jailer, not wanting to excite the prisoner, did as he was told and waited outside the rear car door for Krueger to exit. The nervous jailer was looking for an opportunity to jump the prisoner but Krueger was smarter than the jailer gave him credit for and he never let the jailer have that opportunity. Once outside the vehicle and with his gun pointed at the jailer he ordered the deputy out of the car. He marched them into the woods and when they had walked several hundred feet he ordered them to stop and take off all of their clothes. Krueger had found the tree he was looking for, a small oak, two feet in diameter and far enough into the woods that no one could hear them. He ordered the two men to each hug the tree facing each other and to extend their arms out and hold the others hand. The two officers were still not sure if their prisoner was going to execute them or let them live. They did as they were told and Krueger handcuffed the two men together. Once they were handcuffed he took their underwear and forced it into their mouths. Everything had gone well for Peter Krueger so far.

He gathered what he needed from the squad car and walked the short distance to Hezekiah's house. He needed to borrow Florence's Oldsmobile for his trip to Mexico. The cops would never guess what he was driving and he would be safe all the way to the border. This time he would go to Mexico and he would be safe.

CHAPTER 46

Mitchell Slade sat in his courtroom chair twirling a pencil between his teeth. He was about to get up and walk over to the jury to begin his summation. He had practiced his closing remarks over and over again and was confident he was ready. He needed to run it through his mind one more time. The courtroom waited and watched in silence as he slowly rose from his seat and made his way to the jurors.

He studied the jury before beginning his closing. They were hard to read and he had no idea of what kind of verdict they would issue. He hoped his closing would convince them of the defendant's guilt. "Hezekiah and Krueger were good friends up until recently. Something happened that turned that relationship sour, and it was that failed association that finally convinced Peter Krueger to tell the truth about what happened that night. If they had still been friends, I don't think he would have done so. His description of that night is consistent with the facts of the case and the evidence found. Peter Krueger and Hezekiah Hadley both had eyes for Harmony Ann Day and both wanted a relationship with her that went past friendship. It wasn't going to happen and they both knew it. The culmination of drug and alcohol use that night and their desire to get her into the back seat set off a chain reaction that resulted in her death. Remember - Hezekiah had committed nine burglaries and admitted to his friend Peter Krueger that he was burglarizing these places to get items he needed to commit a murder. I believe the defendant was planning on killing Harmony Ann Day anyway and the night in question just hurried things along. Remember -- Krueger tells us in his confession that Hezekiah Hadley began punching her first and that he later joined in. One thing led to another and Harmony Ann Day was dead. I don't know why they hung her up on the wall like the crucified Christ. I think it was because they wanted to mock her and her beliefs." He wanted to keep his summation less than thirty minutes, anything more than that and he might lose the jurors attention. He looked at the wall clock; he had used up more time than he had realized so he quickly touched on the evidence and the crime scene and finished. "I believe with all my heart that Hezekiah Hadley was a willing accomplice in this atrocious murder and hope that you would render a verdict of guilty. Thank you."

Mitchell Slade thought that his summation went well as he walked back to his table. It was now time for the defense to give their summation and he was interested in what they were going to say, although he had a pretty good idea.

Bill Pierce cleaned his glasses as he walked toward the jury. He stopped and studied them, as his adversary had previously done. He too was having a difficult time reading them. He had no idea of what they were thinking, but he wanted to convince them to think 'not guilty'. "Reasonable doubt - what is it? That which would lead an ordinary person to come to a rational decision based on fact. In other words if you have any doubts, any whatsoever, that my client committed this crime you must find him not guilty. I am going to give you some reasonable doubt and I hope you digest it and talk about it and come to an honorable conclusion. First of all. The BCA lab reports tell us that the victim was drowned before she was hung up on the wall. Yet, Krueger doesn't remember that part. He says they were too strung out on drugs to know what they were doing. The water in her stomach and lungs was from an animal trough or something similar. If my client and Krueger did this, why would they beat her to death and then find an animal trough full of water and put her in it. If she was already dead, why would they have to do that? And how about the shoe prints found at the scene where Harmony Day's purse was found? The BCA lab tells us that the shoe prints were made by work boots size ten and a half. Yet, my client and Mr. Krueger both wear a size eight and a half and neither one of them own a pair of work boots. So who buried that purse? I introduced a sworn affidavit by a Milrose police officer that attested he had seen Hezekiah Hadley hanging around downtown Milrose on the night that Peter Krueger says he and Hezekiah were together and killed Harmony Day. There are just too many inconsistencies. Krueger killed

Harmony Day all right, but my client was not with him when he did it. He is trying to frame my client and I know that you, as a jury, will weigh those inconsistencies and find him 'not guilty'."

Like Mitchell Slade before him, Bill Pierce was satisfied with his closing to the jury. He walked to his table and sat next to his assistant Amy Brown. He leaned back in this chair and looked at the Judge. The attorneys were through and it was time for the Judge to give the jury its directions.

The Judge ordered a fifteen minute recess, pounded his gavel for effect, arose and walked to the side door that led to his office. He wanted to give the jury a few minutes to absorb what the defense and the prosecution had left them with before he gave them their final instructions.

The jury waited for the Judge to leave the courtroom before rising and going to the jury room. The spectators, reporters, attorneys and court personnel remained where they were and waited the fifteen minutes.

The jury returned, then the Judge. He was silent for a moment as he looked at the jury. He was contemplating the directions he would give them. It would of course be the same directions he had always given juries but this jury was special. This jury would decide the innocence or guilt of a man and possibly send him to prison for the rest of his life.

He started. "The burden of proof is the government's responsibility - it rests wholly upon the government. It is your responsibility to determine if the government has done that. You will be asked to determine if there is reasonable doubt that the defendant did indeed commit this crime. What is the definition of reasonable doubt? The State of Minnesota determines it to be a doubt based upon reason and common sense after careful and impartial consideration of all the evidence received in this trial. Proof beyond a reasonable doubt therefore must be proof of such a convincing character that a reasonable person would not hesitate and act upon it. In deciding the facts you must decide what evidence you believe and what evidence you do not believe. You can believe all, none, or part of a testimony. Your responsibility is heavy and this court now adjourns you to the jury room. Thank you, ladies and gentlemen of the jury."

CHAPTER 47

The jury room wasn't much larger than a medium sized bedroom. Two over sized windows adorned the one wall that overlooked the parking lot. The other three walls were barren except for a clock on the wall opposite the windows. A large table designed and built by a local craftsman rested in the center of the room. The oblong table was made from a sugar maple tree and given several coats of lacquer to give it luster and to protect the wood. The table had been in the jury room since the courthouse was built. Twelve chairs sat around it, five on each side and one each of the ends. Angus Sullivan sat at the end chair with his back facing the window.

Parker Hill sat in one of the middle chairs on one side of the table and looked at Angus. He couldn't decide if Angus was chosen as the jury foreman because of his wisdom, because of his age or because of his wealth. Maybe all three. It didn't matter, Angus Sullivan was a good choice.

The jury foreman waited for everyone to take their seats and be quiet. That being accomplished he got up and introduced himself in more detail now that he was the foreman. He asked the other jurors to introduce themselves again, which they did. "I think the first order of business is to take a vote to see if we are all in agreement on the verdict. I am going to pass around paper and pencils to each juror and if you would please mark your ballot guilty or not guilty, fold it and pass it back to me. I will read each vote and then we will have a place to start. If the vote is unanimous, we'll have a short day."

Parker Hill wrote not guilty on his sheet of paper, folded it and handed it to the jury foreman. The other jury members did the same. Parker was surprised at how fast the verdicts were written down and passed along. What could it mean? Did everyone agree with him and it would be a short day or had every juror already made up their mind before the first vote.

Angus opened each one and read the verdict and wrote it down on a tablet next to him. The final count was nine 'not guilty' and three 'guilty'. The short day was not to be. "It is time for discussion and I hope each juror is forthright and honest in what he tells us. We need to know your thoughts if we are ever going to reach a unanimous agreement. I'll start with Parker. What are your thoughts?"

"The Judge explained reasonable doubt to us." Parker thoughtfully answered. "One thing that bothers me is size of the shoeprints left at the scene where the purse was buried. The prints were size ten and a half and both Hadley and Krueger wear a size eight and a half shoe so it could not have been them that buried that purse. If it wasn't them, the real killer might be still running loose and we have the wrong guys."

Andy Taylor could not control himself; he stood up and started yelling at Parker Hill. "That's nonsense. Maybe they had on larger shoes when they hid the purse. You know people always wear snow boots that are larger than the shoes they are wearing. That's stupid, what you just said."

The laconic Parker Hill remained sitting, stunned at the outburst. "What shoe size do you wear Mr. Taylor?" Parker asked accusingly.

"Ten and a half, but that's a pretty common shoe size. Anybody could have that shoe size," he replied and sat down.

Angus watched juror Taylor sit down. He hadn't expected the outburst of anger and was surprised. He would have to tighten the reins on juror Taylor if another flare up occurred. "I take it, Mr. Taylor, that you voted guilty - can you tell us why?"

"I sure can. I know Hezekiah Hadley and I know Peter Krueger and let me tell you, they are both more than capable of killing that girl. I believe Krueger's story."

One of the jurors sitting next to Andy Taylor agreed with him. "Me too. It is just too much of a coincidence that they both knew her. One was her boyfriend, one wanted to be her boyfriend and they both had it up to here (she brought her open hand up to her throat) and they had been doing drugs and alcohol. The circumstances were perfect for what happened to that poor girl. These guys are both criminals, we know their past history and we know they are capable of doing this. I agree with Mr. Taylor."

Another juror spoke up. "I voted not guilty for a couple of reasons. The autopsy revealed that Harmony Day was drowned, yet neither one of these men remembered drowning her. How can that be? Krueger remembered everything else perfectly but had a memory lapse when confronted about her being drowned? I don't think so. I think he made the whole story up. I think the real killer wore a size ten and a half shoe. I don't think either one of these boys had anything to do with the murder."

Another juror, a young woman in her early twenties nervously spoke. "I think Mr. Krueger's story is too good. He knew that his girlfriend had injured her head and that there would be blood and hair samples in his car to back up his story. I really think he had nothing to lose by concocting this story. He was going to spend the rest of his life in prison anyway so why not take Hezekiah Hadley down with him. Somebody, I don't remember who, testified that Krueger made the comment that he hated Hezekiah because Hezekiah killed his mother. The Judge told us about reasonable doubt and I don't want to send Hezekiah to prison if he had nothing to do with killing Harmony Day."

Andy Taylor was noticeably quivering he was so mad. "But what if he did do it? Do you want to let this man go to kill again?"

The young woman who had just spoken replied. "I would rather let a guilty man go than put an innocent man in prison."

Parker carefully listened to the jurors talk before he said anything. "I can see both sides of this. One thing that really puzzles me is why they hung her up on the side of that wall. She was already dead, why didn't they just bury her or throw her in the lake or something. I think if we knew the reason that the killer hung her up on the wall like he did, then we would know who our killer was. I have been trying to get a handle on the religious beliefs of Hezekiah or Krueger. That might help me in making my decision. Not much about their personal religious beliefs was brought up in trial. I wish they had."

"You people are so stupid." Andy Taylor said as he looked at Parker Hill. "I know both these men and neither one of them is religious. Hezekiah's a devil worshipper so that is why he hung her up on the wall. He wanted to make a statement cuz he hated Christians and thought they were weak."

Parker Hill felt that Andy Taylor was directing his little tirade toward him and he was angry. He returned the stare and questioned juror Taylor. "You know them both and you say neither one of them was religious and that Hezekiah was a devil worshipper. I believe that evidence would have been brought out in trial. It wasn't, so I am not sure about what you have just alluded to. What are your beliefs Mr. Taylor?" Parker asked, not knowing why, but his anger took over and he wasn't going to let Andy Taylor get to him.

"I don't believe in nothin'," he answered, still looking at Parker Hill with his dark, empty eyes.

Angus Sullivan was getting annoyed with Andy Taylor. He knew him to be unpredictable and violent and he knew he had to watch him carefully. The last thing he wanted was an old fashioned fist fight in the jury room. "We have all had a chance to discuss some of our feelings in the case and our reasons for voting the way we did. I would like to pass around another piece of paper and see if the vote is the same." The paper ballots were passed around and returned and the results were the same as the first round of voting.

Andy Taylor was getting disgusted and he got up and walked toward the jury door to leave. A bailiff met him at the door and forbid him to leave. He turned around, stomped to his chair, sat down and threateningly eyed each juror. He would intimidate them into a guilty verdict.

Eight females and four males comprised the jury. One of the men was a meat cutter for Clayton Barnes. He listened and watched with serenity as the drama unfolded in the jury room. Being a juror was not what he imagined. He needed to speak and give his perspective. "One of the reasons I voted not guilty was the fact that no one was able to find Harmony Day's car. Krueger says they picked her up at the parking lot of the college. If that was the case, she would have driven her car to the parking lot to meet them and left it there. Why wasn't her car ever found? It leads me to believe that she might have been killed by someone else who then stole her car and left Milrose."

Andy Taylor stood up again and pointed his finger at the meat cutter. "You're stupid, you're all stupid. You'll do anything and say anything to get this guy off. I know he killed her. Who knows what happened to her car, it doesn't matter. Who says she drove her car to the parking lot. You people are making an awful lot out of something that is very simple. You must vote him guilty. He did it. I know it."

Angus Sullivan had enough. "Mr. Taylor, I will not allow any more of your outbursts. We are trying to get to the truth here and you seem to be blocking that every chance you get. I think the juror who just spoke made a very valid point. If you insist on these outbursts I will have no choice but to ask the bailiff to come in here and quiet you down. Do you understand?"

Andy Taylor glared at the jury foreman but said nothing and sat down. It was quiet in the jury room. Angus decided to call it a day and dismissed the jury and ordered them back tomorrow at nine o'clock.

CHAPTER 48

Sally returned to normal work hours and was pleased. The extra leisure hours were nice at first but she needed to be busy, it was who she was. There was still plenty of work to do. The everyday smaller crimes found their way to her desk and she was still trying to find Helen DuPont. Helen had been missing far too long and it worried her, but she had hopes. They brought in Nathan Brown for questioning but he clammed up and wouldn't talk; he asked for an attorney and they had to stop the interview. They had no real reason to interrogate him but they kept an eye on his movements expecting him to lead them to Helen DuPont. He hadn't so far, but they were not going to give up on him. They knew he was involved with her disappearance and he knew they knew. He was extra cautious, staying in his apartment most of the time except for work. He walked most everywhere he went, afraid that if he drove his van he would get pulled over for some minor traffic offense and then the cops could search his car. He didn't want that.

Josh Trimble left Milrose after the jury was given its instructions. A double murder in a nearby town was now occupying his time but he checked in with Sally every day. He called for updates on the jury but was also anxious to hear her voice. They had been on a few dates and he wanted to see more of her; she felt the same way.

Bob Carpenter was told by the Chief that he needed to take some time off. He had built his vacation up so that if he didn't use it, he would lose it. He took three days off and flew to Utah to see his sister and his mother. He hadn't seen or talked to his family much since the murders and it was time to visit them. Family was important to him and he was anxious to see them once again. He wasn't worried about leaving Sally alone. After what they had gone through in the past few months he was certain she could handle anything that came up. He hoped that while he was gone she would find Helen DuPont alive and well and arrest whoever was involved in her disappearance.

The second day of jury deliberations were about to begin and Sally was inwardly apprehensive but struggled not to show it. She wanted to remain calm, await the decision and accept it. She was not convinced that Hezekiah was the killer or that Peter Krueger was the killer. She had a gut feeling that there was a third party, someone they had overlooked, someone who was more capable of murder than either one of them and someone who lived in Milrose. Her uncertainty bothered her; she wished the County Attorney hadn't been so insistent on prosecuting Hezekiah so quickly. She knew that the public demanded an arrest; they were getting anxious and angry at the County Attorney's office for dragging their heels. The public was aware that arrests had been made in the murder case and they wanted action and they wanted it now.

The green LCD light on her car radio showed seven fifty nine when she pulled into the law enforcement center parking lot. She didn't punch a time clock and her hours were hers to decide on, but she liked coming in at eight o'clock, reading the reports from the night before and having several cups of coffee before starting her day. She got out of the squad and walked to the front door of the law enforcement center. She pulled open one of the huge bullet proof glass doors and opened it. A wooden bench sat in the entryway for people to sit on while they waited to see the Sheriff or the Police Chief or one of the detectives. It was almost always empty when she walked in the door but this morning there were two people sitting on the bench and she recognized them both.

Faith Taylor had been crying; her eyes were red and swollen and she was leaning against her brother. Sam had his arm around her shoulder, comforting her. When Sally walked in the front door he turned to her and attempted a smile. "Detective Fairfield, could we speak to you?"

"Sure, follow me." She had a soft heart for young girls crying and she wanted to help Faith in any way she could. She opened the hallway door and they followed behind her without talking. She led them to her office and when she was inside she directed them each to a chair and then she closed the office door.

Sam looked at Sally and then at his sister. "Detective Fairfield, we've come here about our father."

CHAPTER 49

Angus Sullivan walked down his driveway to retrieve the morning paper from his mailbox. He noticed a difference in the morning's weather. The cold damp morning chill had disappeared and was replaced by warmth and a cloudless sapphire sky. This could be the signal that spring was finally here he thought to himself. He grabbed his paper and walked back to the house. He would read the newspaper, down two cups of coffee and leave for the courthouse. The jury was in its fourth day of deliberations and the vote was still nine to three. Angus, in frustration, wondered if he should let the judge know the jury was in a hopeless deadlock. Today he would try again to get the jury to reach a verdict. He would push for it, even insist on it and maybe keep the jury in the jury room until one was arrived at, even if he had to keep them there all night. The County had spent a lot of time and money on this case and he wouldn't allow the jury to take the easy way out.

Parker Hill felt the tension in the jury room. Something was going to happen today, he was sure of it. The jury was frustrated with their inability to reach an agreement and tired of Andy Taylor's outbursts. They wanted to get back to their lives but they took their responsibilities as jury members seriously and wanted to render the right verdict. Parker looked around the room when his eyes stopped at Andy Taylor. He was certain that Andy Taylor was drunk this morning or had a bad hangover. He got up from his chair and walked over to a jury member sitting next to Taylor and made some small talk. He wanted to smell Andy Taylor's breath. He couldn't detect an odor of alcohol but his actions were strange and his eyes were red, probably bloodshot from the previous night.

Angus Sullivan was the last member of the jury to enter the room. He was five minutes late and offered no apologies; he said "good morning" and took his seat at the head of the table. He noticed Andy Taylor staring at him and that the table was brightened by the sun shining through the undraped windows in the room. He was about to speak when juror number three stood up. She was a large bulbous woman and the enormity of her size cast a shadow like an ominous cloud over the table. She had remained quiet up until now and Angus was interested in what she had to say. "We've been here too long already. The state has not proved its case beyond a reasonable doubt. We know that just by listening to the arguments in this room. The judge told us about probable cause and anybody with half a brain would know that there isn't enough probable cause to convict. Why don't we just get this over with, vote not guilty and get out of here." She sat down but could feel the furious eyes of Andy Taylor staring at her. She looked fearlessly at him, knowing he was about to say something. "You say one more thing Andy Taylor and I am going to come over there and sit my ass down on top of you until you shut up. You're getting on my nerves and you're the reason we're still here."

"Juror number three is right. We've been here too long already. I am going to pass ballots around again and if we're still deadlocked I am going to keep us here until we reach a decision, I don't care if takes us all day and all night and all the next day, we're going to reach a verdict," Angus declared, speaking louder than normal.

Small square sheets of paper were passed around to the jury and a vote was taken; the ballots were marked, folded and returned to the jury foreman. Angus counted them and announced that some progress was being made. The vote was eleven not guilty and one guilty. After the vote was announced, the eyes of the jury members focused on Andy Taylor.

Parker Hill may have been the only jury member who suspected Andy Taylor was drunk and he was going to take advantage of it. "Mr. Taylor, you keep telling us that your kids knew Hezekiah and Peter Krueger. You must have known them also; so what was it about them that convinced you they killed Harmony Day?"

He glared at Parker Hill and tried to think of an answer. "Look at the way they looked, green hair, tattoos and earrings. Something wrong with people that look like that. My kids both said they were weird."

"Doesn't make them killers. What other reasons you got?" Parker asked.

"They hung her up on the wall just like that Christ person was killed. They both hated religion and were tired of Harmony preaching to them. When they killed her they wanted everybody to know that she was killed because she was a Christian. Good riddance too. Them Christians think they are so high and mighty with them not drinking and not smoking and going to church. They think they're better than everybody else. Makes me sick."

"Did you say that Harmony stopped out to your place a couple of times? What did you think of her?"

"I don't remember saying that but yea, she did stop out a couple of times but her and my kids they talked in the barn and no wheres around me. They knew I didn't want anything to do with Christians."

"So you don't like Christians either?" Parker asked.

"Nope, religion is for suckers." Andy Taylor replied, folded his arms and leaned back in his chair.

"What did your kids think of Harmony?"

Parker struck a nerve. Andy Taylor sat up in his chair and glared again at Parker before standing up. He almost fell over as he was getting up and had to steady himself by grabbing the edge of the table for support. The other jury members were now aware of his condition and felt uncomfortable with an intoxicated person in the room making important decisions. "My kids forgot everything they learnt from me when they talked to that slut. She filled their heads with stupid religious stuff and I was getting tired of it. If I ever got Harmony alone I was going to make it clear to her that I didn't want her around no more. She should've kept her nose out of our family business. She got what she deserved. That's all what I got to say."

The jury room was quiet, the rantings of Andy Taylor had taken them by surprise. Parker wouldn't give up, there was more to the story and he was beginning to think that Taylor may know something about Harmony's death - something that no one else knew.

"When was the last time she was out to your place?"

"Just before she got herself killed."

"Were your kids home?" Parker asked.

"Nope, they were both working."

"If you never talked to her, how did you know she was at your house?"

"Cuz I seen her truck pull into the driveway and then turn around and leave."

"If she took the trouble to come out and see your kids, why wouldn't she have parked the truck and come to the front door and ask for either Faith or Sam?" Parker was confident that Andy Taylor knew more about Harmony's death than he was letting on. Maybe he had seen who'd murdered her and that is why he was insistent on Hezekiah Hadley and Peter Krueger being found guilty.

Andy Taylor sat down; he was tired and angry and he wanted this over with so he could go home and get drunk. He needed a drink and a cigarette. "Maybe she did come to the door, I don't remember, I wasn't feeling very good."

"Is that because you were drunk, Andy?" Parker asked.

Andy's temper was ignited and he wanted to get up and punch Parker Hill in the nose but he was too tired and too weak to do so. "I might have been, I don't remember."

"You talked to her that night didn't you?"

"So what if I did."

"What'd she say?"

"She asked if Faith or Sam was home. I said no and she left."

"She came in the house, didn't she, Andy Taylor. You invited her in, didn't you, and she came in."

"Listen you son of a…," he caught himself in mid sentence and stopped, not wanting the jury to align themselves with his adversary.

"She came in, I didn't invite her, she just walked in like she owned the house, like she was holier than thou and could just walk in my house anytime she wanted and she was wearing this tight dress like she was showing off."

There was silence in the room as the jury members tried to rationalize what Andy Taylor was saying. He seemed confused and appeared to be losing control of his thoughts and emotions. What they didn't know was that he needed a drink and a cigarette badly and was losing control because of it. He needed out of the jury room and he needed a drink and he needed a smoke.

"What did you think when you saw this pretty young girl in front of you, in your house and all alone with you. It was only you and her, your kids were gone; and it was a good opportunity to get to know her better, wasn't it."

Andy's hands were shaking as he looked at the juror that was questioning him. He hated him and he wanted to kill him. "I tried to kiss her a little but she shoved me off, she wouldn't have nothing to do with me."

"That must have made you angry."

"Who did she think she was anyway? One of those goody two shoes Christians, I hate 'em. The world would be better off if they were all dead."

Parker was surprised, he was now certain that Andy Taylor killed Harmony Ann Day. He had not expected this, he thought that Andy knew something about the murder but he never thought that he might be the one that actually killed her. "Did you kill her?"

Andy Taylor got up from his chair and bolted toward the door; he opened it and collided into an unsuspecting bailiff who was guarding the door. Both men were knocked to the floor and briefly dazed. Andy was the first one up and grabbed the bailiff's sidearm and ran for the stairway that would lead him to the basement and out the first floor doors.

CHAPTER 50

"Have a seat." Sally offered as she pointed to two dated chairs in her office. "What's this about your father?"

Faith sat down first and her brother waited until she was seated before he sat down. He put his arm around her as he had in the front foyer of the Law Enforcement Center. Satisfied that his sister was comfortable he cleared his throat and began his story. "We think our father killed Harmony Day."

Sally was taciturn, unable to speak as she stared wide eyed at the two young people sitting in front of her. She had her doubts about Hezekiah being the one that killed Harmony Day but neither she nor her partner had been able to come up with any other suspect. She took a small tape recorder out of her upper desk drawer and placed it on the corner of her desk near Faith and Sam Taylor. "I would like to tape this conversation, is that all right with the both of you?"

They both nodded in the affirmative and Sam grabbed Faith's hand, holding it tight. "This morning I was in the barn and I noticed a bale of hay had fallen off the top of the hay pile. See, we have a huge stack of hay in the barn and it is all in bales. We got one horse and two cows so we feed the hay to them. There is enough bales in the barn to feed our animals for a year. The bales are stacked about twenty or twenty five feet high and this one fell off the top and was laying in the middle of the barn floor. I picked it up and was going to put it back where it had fallen from. I was climbing up the hay bales when another one came loose and fell to the floor. When I looked at the hole it made I seen some metal so I removed some other bales and it was then that I discovered Harmony's pick-up. I pulled all the bales of hay away from the car and backed it out of the barn cuz the keys were still in it. I think my father killed her one time when she come out to see us and we weren't home."

"Did your father know Harmony?"

Faith remained silent and watched her brother talk. "Yea, he knew her and he hated her. For some reason he hated Christians, I think it was cuz my mom was a Christian and that caused some problems between 'em but I don't really know. He's got this picture of Christ hanging on the living room wall where Jesus is hanging from a cross and there is a large red circle painted on the picture and a black line is running through it. One night we told him that we were gonna' be Christians. He really got mad when we told him that we were both thinking of getting baptized and that Harmony was going to take us to her church so we could get baptized cuz we were gonna' be Christians. He went wild and his eyes got really big and he glared at us. Pretty soon he was swearing and throwing furniture around in the house and yelling at us saying that he would kill us first before we got baptized and that he would kill our friend if she ever came out here again."

Sally listened to Sam Taylor's story, amazed and curious. She didn't want to interrupt him but she needed a question answered before he went any further. "Do you have a water trough on your farm?"

He answered immediately. "Yea, there is one just outside the back of the barn. We use it to water our horse and our cows."

"Is it always full?" Sally asked.

Sam couldn't understand why Detective Fairfield needed to know this but he answered that it was and then he continued. "I got this room fixed up in the back of the barn and I use it a lot, it is where Harmony and Faith and me talked a lot. We talked mostly about religion and Christ and we felt good when we talked to her about these things." He turned to his sister. "Right, Faith?" he asked. Faith nodded yes and Sam continued. "When my dad got mad that night, me and Faith we went to the barn and stayed there until he got drunk and passed out. He got drunk every night so we knew he would do it again that night. We talked that night about leaving but we had no place to go and we didn't know what we were going to do. We couldn't live with our father but we couldn't go anyplace else either, we didn't know what to do."

"You know, your father's on jury duty right now and I feel very uncomfortable approaching him about this until the jury is done for the day. I want you two to go home. I'll get in touch with you as soon as I talk to your father."

Two Milrose police squads roared out of the Law Enforcement Center with their overheads flashing and their sirens yelling. Sally noticed the cars speeding toward the courthouse and contacted the dispatch center and asked where the squads were headed

"*They were called to the courthouse. One of the jury members overpowered a bailiff and stole his gun and ran out of the courthouse. We're trying to find him.*"

Sally knew which jury member the dispatcher was talking about and so did Faith and Sam Taylor. "I want you kids to stay right here in my office. I am going to go and help find your father. We don't want anybody getting hurt. I'll get back as soon as I can." Sally examined her belt, making sure she had her 380 and her handcuffs securely fastened before putting her belt on. She grabbed a light winter jacket and hustled out of the building and into her car. She turned on the siren and the flashing red grille lights and sped to the courthouse.

A police squad car was already parked in front of the courthouse, its red lights flashing while another was parked in the rear parking lot. A half dozen patrolmen were exploring the grounds and more were inside conducting a room by room search. They had not found Andy Taylor and were convinced he was no longer in the courthouse or on the courthouse grounds.

The officer in charge had interviewed the jurors who quickly identified Andy Taylor as the juror who bolted out of the jury room, overpowered the bailiff, took his gun and ran down the hall way and disappeared. They had no idea where he went. Parker Hill had gotten up from his chair and ran after Taylor but by the time he stopped to check on the bailiff Andy Taylor had disappeared. The bailiff told the officer in charge that Taylor got away with his nickel plated .357 magnum. The revolver was fully loaded with six live one hundred and fifty grain rounds. "That'll do a lot of damage, one of them bullets could go right through a man," he said, worried that his personal handgun might be the cause of somebody's death.

Andy's twenty year old pick-up was nowhere to be seen. A couple of courthouse workers claimed to have seen the pick-up parked in the lot this morning when they came to work. The stall in the parking lot that Andy's pick-up was parked in was vacant and no one saw him leave.

Sally stood in the middle of the parking lot and studied the area. There were two exits from the parking lot and both led to Main Street which led out of Milrose in two directions. One of the directions would take Andy Taylor to his farm and Sally was confident that is where he went. Parker Hill said that he appeared drunk this morning and as the day wore on he seemed to be going into DT's. His quavering got worse after lunch and he made less and less sense in what he was saying. Parker told Sally that Andy Taylor ran out of the jury room when he asked him if he killed Harmony Day. *So he was drunk and he was going into DT's, a bad combination for a man armed with a .357. She needed to find him and find him fast.*

Sally called the Law Enforcement Center and talked to Sam Taylor and told him she thought his father might be at the farmhouse. She said she was going there with some other police officers and that he and Faith should remain in the office.

"Check the barn first and be careful," Sam cautioned her.

Andy Taylor had to be found before he hurt himself or someone else. Sam Taylor knew his father better than anybody else except his sister. He had good reason for telling them to search the barn first because that is where he kept his liquor and cigarettes and he hoped she would follow his advice.

Detective Fairfield was the first squad to pull into the farmyard. She was followed by two marked squad cars. The three cars stopped in front of the barn. Andy Taylor's pick-up was parked next to the machine shed and was empty. Sally was about to order him out of the barn when they heard a shot fired. She opened the car door, slid out of the seat and hid behind the opened car door. She had the outside speakers on. She held the microphone to her mouth and ordered Andy Taylor to come out of the garage with his hands up.

There was silence and then two more shots echoed from the barn. The officers remained crouched behind their car doors, not sure what to do next. Three shots had been fired, there were three shots left. Did he shoot himself? If not, where were those shots aimed? Another shot went off; he was alive and had two shots left. She turned up the volume on the speakers and spoke into the microphone again. She ordered him to throw out his gun and come out of the barn with his hands up. Two more shots were fired and this time one of them came through the side of the barn and lodged in a maple tree near Sally.

His bullets were gone and it was time for a decision. She was certain he had no more fire power. Two more squad cars pulled into the yard. They were aware of the situation and the officers got out of their cars and remained crouched near the ground awaiting orders from Sally. She decided it was time to enter the barn and find Andy Taylor. The two officers that had just pulled into the driveway were ordered to the rear of the barn and she and two officers would go in the front of the barn. The remaining officers would stay by their squads and wait. Sally entered the barn with her gun drawn. She wished she had worn her nine millimeter instead of the small .380 she held in her hands now, but it was too late for hindsight. She yelled for Andy Taylor to come out from wherever he was. She heard nothing, then the sound of straw being pushed or kicked. She looked in the direction of the cow stallions. Two cows occupied the stallions and were standing and chewing cud. She could make out movement behind one of the cows and she slowly walked over to the cow with her gun aimed in the direction of the movement. As she neared the Holstein she could see Andy Taylor aiming the .357 at the barn windows and dry shooting. He either didn't realize the gun was empty or he was shooting out of frustration. She ordered him to put down the gun. He looked at her, stunned and confused as he raised the gun and pointed it at her. One of the officers had slipped behind him while he was looking at Sally. The young and agile officer tackled Andy Taylor and cuffed him.

Sally called the Law Enforcement Center and talked to Sam. She told him that they had his father in custody and she would be arriving shortly.

CHAPTER 51

The Sioux County Sheriff asked Detective Fairfield into his office for a very good reason. One of his deputies had spotted an older model mini-van parked in the driveway of an abandoned farm house southeast of town. The van was encrusted in mud making it difficult to tell if it was black or dark brown. The deputy remembered that Detective Fairfield had asked the Sheriff's Department and the Police Department to keep their eyes open for an older model black van with Minnesota license number MSX 361 and to let her know immediately if it was spotted. She had given out the description of the vehicle and the license number a week ago but nothing had come up. The deputy thought the van he had seen from the road matched the description of the one Detective Fairfield had given out so he drove into the farmyard to get a closer look. The license number matched and he called his boss immediately.

Detective Fairfield was thrilled to hear the news and knew what had to be done. She thanked the Sheriff for the information and left his office to find her partner. As she was walking down the hallway the Sheriff yelled to her from his desk to come back. She returned to his office and he informed her that he was sending another deputy to go with them to the farmhouse in case they needed back-up. She thanked the Sheriff again and found her partner, who had just returned from his short vacation, at his desk. She told him about Nathan Brown's van being located at an abandoned farmhouse. He quietly got up from his chair and grabbed his jacket. "Let's go," he said as he joined his partner in hurrying out of the Law Enforcement Center and into her squad car. She toggled the red flashing grille lights as she left the parking lot but kept the siren silent.

Sally was trying to keep the Sheriff's car in sight; she was in unfamiliar territory and travelling at eighty five miles an hour on gravel roads. She was doing a good job keeping up with the Sheriff's car but was uncomfortable driving on rough, unpaved county roads. She was glad the Sheriff insisted that a deputy go along and lead them to the place. She had no idea where she was or where the farmhouse was. The squad in front of her began slowing down and she noticed another squad car parked in a grove of trees to her right. "That must be the deputy that called it in, we must be getting close," she informed her partner. The squad in front of her pulled into a dirt driveway and she followed. The long driveway led to an abandoned farmhouse and Brown's van was parked next to a dilapidated grain bin. Sally looked into her rear view mirror and the squad that was parked in the grove of trees was now behind her as she pulled to the front of the old farmhouse.

Detective Carpenter got out of the squad car, unholstered his gun, ran to the open front door and entered the house. Sally waited for her partner to enter before she ran toward the rear of the house. As she was running, she passed a window that had been entirely broken out. Through the corner of her eye she glanced into what appeared to be a small bedroom and noticed someone sitting on the floor. She stopped, backed tracked and looked inside. Helen DuPont was sitting motionless on the floor with her hands behind her back and her legs outstretched. Her ankles were tied with clothes-line rope and chain was visible leading from her ankles to a hook in the ceiling. Sally noticed her eyes were unfocused and distant. Sally guessed that she was drugged. Nathan Brown entered the room and walked to his victim. Sally couldn't believe that Brown hadn't heard the cars drive in or heard her partner enter the house. But when she studied Nathan Brown closer she realized that he was stoned. In his left hand he was carrying a filet knife and was walking behind Helen and bending down. Sally yelled through the window, ordering Nathan to drop the knife. He looked at her with glassy and confused eyes. He started to lower the knife, pointing it toward Helen. Detective Carpenter entered the room and noticed what was happening. He immediately pulled his service revolver, aimed it at Nathan and ordered him to drop the knife. Nathan tried to focus on Carpenter and then he looked at Detective Fairfield. His glazed eyes stared at her as she once again told him to put down the knife. He looked back at Detective Carpenter and then lowered the knife toward Helen's throat. Detective Carpenter and Detective Fairfield both cocked their weapons and aimed at Brown. He looked at them both again, hesitated for a second and dropped the knife onto the hardwood floor. Detective Carpenter walked over to Nathan Brown, forced him to face the wall with his legs extended and apart. He cuffed him, led him out of the room, walked him outside and loaded him into one of the waiting squad cars.

Sally climbed through the bedroom window and untied Helen. She was dazed and emotionless. Sally called for an ambulance and sat on the floor next to Helen. She held her until the EMT's arrived. She would call Helen's parents after she was safely in the ambulance and on her way to the hospital.

Nathan Brown was booked and put into the same cell as Hezekiah. They didn't speak to each other for two days. Hezekiah was annoyed that his space was being invaded and Nathan was angry that he had allowed himself to get caught, although he knew it was his fault. If he had stayed off the drugs until after he killed Helen DuPont he would have never gotten caught.

"Whatcha' in for?" he asked Hezekiah while they were having breakfast.

Hezekiah finished his Fruit Loops and annoyingly answered his new cell mate. "Murder," he calmly answered as he took the last bite of his toast.

Hezekiah had Nathan's attention. "Tell me about it."

"I killed my mom. I hit her over the head with a frying pan and then I stuck her in the freezer. Cops found her when they were doing a search warrant on the house. I was going to hang her up on the back of the pavilion at Cedar Park so the cops would think she was killed by the same person that killed Harmony Ann Day but I never got the chance for that. The cops found her before I got that far. I also done a bunch of burglaries so I guess I am going to prison for a while. Cops tried to pin another murder on me but it didn't work."

Nathan was starting to be impressed by his new roommate. "I killed someone once." He didn't want to tell Hezekiah that his victim was a little girl. He was a little ashamed that he had killed someone so young. His troubles in juvenile detention were not because of his attitude or his dress; it was because he killed an innocent little girl. His life had been threatened many times because of it, so he never mentioned her age to anyone. "Spent six years in juvenile detention for it."

"I killed someone else too," Hezekiah proudly announced. He was starting to like Nathan Brown and he needed to prove to him that he was more dangerous than the man he was sharing his cell with. He waited for Nathan to ask him about it.

"So how'd you do it?" Nathan asked.

"There was this old man sitting at the end of the dock at Cedar Lake. He was fishing and sitting on an old chair with his back to me. It was almost dark and I thought I would have some fun with him so I pushed him off of his chair and into the lake. I didn't know he was ninety four years old and couldn't swim. They found his body the next morning but it was ruled an accidental drowning. I was lucky; I got away with that one."

Nathan lifted his index finger to his lips and looked at Hezekiah. "The guard's coming. Must be lunch time." Nathan wondered where the morning went. It was fun talking about murder, he thought to himself.

Hezekiah was also surprised that the time had gone by so fast. Conversations of murder intrigued both of them and the morning slipped by. He got up and walked to the cell door as the guard was about to pass two styrofoam containers through a small opening in the solid metal door. Hezekiah knew what each container held, a meat sandwich, an apple, some potato chips and a brownie. Except for the meat, everything else was the same each day. He grabbed the containers and put them on the metal table. Nathan Brown sat across from him and lifted up the lid of his styrofoam container. Not bad, he thought to himself. "This is better than what I got in juvenile detention. Everyday, a peanut butter sandwich and a banana. No dessert - I hated that place."

Hezekiah took a large bite of his roast beef sandwich and set it down inside the container and looked at Nathan. "So did you kill anybody else?"

Nathan noticed that Hezekiah's eyes sparkled every time either one of them talked about murder. He may have found a kindred spirit in Hezekiah Hadley. Nathan had never talked about his other murder to anyone. He had gotten away with it and didn't want to take any unnecessary risks. He was sure he could trust Hezekiah and knew that Hezekiah would be impressed with his last murder. "Yea, a co-ed in Ames Iowa. There's this junk yard in Ames called Mel's Junk. Mel doesn't know it but in one of his refrigerators way in the back there is a body. I figure that refrigerator is long gone and crushed into scrap metal. Killing her was my best one so far. I figure I committed the perfect murder."

Hezekiah finished his brownie, closed the food container, got up and walked over to the garbage can by his small sink and dropped it in. He came back to the table and sat down. He was in awe of the man sitting across from him. "How'd you do it?"

"I killed her because I wanted to commit the perfect murder, simple as that. I was at this bar one night and this chick walks in, she's alone and sits at the bar a few stools down from me. There is no one between me and her and I am trying to get her attention but she pays no attention to me. Well, I buy her a beer hoping that she notices me. The bartender tells her that I bought her this beer but she still ignores me so I start to get pissed at her. I figure she's the one. I find out who she is and I start following her around. She doesn't know I'm tailing her, and I'm waiting for the right time. Then one Saturday night I'm in this bar again and she walks in and sits a couple of stools down from me and pulls the same crap. I decided right then and there that tonight was going to be her last night on earth. She left the bar alone and I followed her to her car, and as she was fumbling for her car keys I throw a rope around her neck and strangled her to death. I opened the car door and toss her in and then I push her over and drive her car away from the parking lot. I drive around for awhile not knowing what to with her. I come across this junk yard and ended up stuffing her in an old refrigerator. After I got rid of her, I drove her car into a lake somewhere around Des Moines and then I hitchhiked back to Ames. It must have been a deep lake cuz I drove up there a couple of times to see if I could find the car and I couldn't. I figure I committed the perfect murder."

"I seen somebody get killed once, long time ago. I got the skull locked up in a box under my bed."

"Neato," Nathan replied. "I never seen a real skull."

Hezekiah got up and walked to his bunk, sat down and faced Nathan who was still sitting at the table. He fidgeted for a cigarette and cursed the Sheriff for not allowing the inmates to smoke. He needed a cigarette badly and so did his cell mate.

Hezekiah wanted to finish his story about the skull and waited until he had Nathan's attention. "I wasn't very old, maybe five or six. Me and Sam Taylor, that's my friend, were hunting squirrels out at his farm. When we were done hunting and were coming back to his house we heard a lot of screaming and hollerin' going on in the barn. We both walked over and looked in one of the barn windows and saw Mr. Taylor hitting his wife. He was hitting her a lot and she fell to the floor. Sam was watching too and he got scared and ran to the house but I stayed and watched. Mr. Taylor bent down and put his arms around her throat and squeezed hard. Then he threw her in the animal trough and held her head under water for a long time, I guess he wanted to make sure she was dead. Then he went and got a shovel and dug a big hole in back of the barn. When he was finished digging the hole he pulled his wife out of the trough and carried her out of the barn and dumped her in the hole and covered it up. I told Sam about it and he cried, but we never talked about it again. Anyway, when I got older, I remembered what happened, so one night I went out to the farm. It was after midnight and there was a full moon so I could see what I was doing and I dug where I thought he buried her. She wasn't buried very deep so after I found the skeleton I decided to keep the skull for a souvenir. I took the skull home and covered the body back up. Like I said, I still got the skull."

"That skull is your ticket out of here, Hezekiah."

"How do you mean?"

"It's simple, man. You seen a murder that the cops don't know nothing about. You tell them that you know about someone gettin' killed in the county. You tell them that only you and the murderer know about it. You tell them that you want to bargain the information. You tell them you want the burglary charges dropped and you want the murder charge dropped. If they won't do that you tell them that you want a reduced sentence. I guarantee you they will jump at the chance to solve a murder."

"You think so?" Hezekiah excitedly got up from his bunk and began pacing the floor.

"I know so."

"Tomorrow I'll talk to Detective Fairfield."

****

The dispatcher was seated at her desk and watching the television camera that monitored cell four. Behind her stood Lieutenant Carpenter and Sergeant Fairfield. They had been watching and listening to Hezekiah Hadley and Nathan Brown for almost five hours.

"You got this all on tape?" Lieutenant Carpenter asked the dispatcher.

"Yes, every word," she answered.

"What a couple of idiots. Don't they know they are being watched and that we can hear everything they say?" Lieutenant Carpenter added.

When it was determined that the conversation between the two prisoners was over with the two detectives left the control room and went to Lieutenant Carpenter's office. They were both quiet as they sat down and reflected on the surprising events of the day.

By three o'clock in the afternoon the Ames, Iowa Police Department had been contacted and told about Mel's junkyard. Judge Armstrong had signed a search warrant for digging up the ground around the farmhouse, the barn and the silo at Andy Taylor's farm. Hezekiah Hadley was charged with the murder of a ninety four year old man who had been found last year drowned in Cedar Park Lake. Nathan Brown was charged with attempted murder and kidnapping.

The two detectives were sitting in the squad room alone. They were contemplating and discussing the events of the last few months when Josh Trimble walked into the room. "Got some news for you. Our friend Peter Krueger is in Juarez, Mexico and he doesn't plan on leaving anytime in the near future."

"That's interesting," Detective Carpenter answered. "We heard he made some rumblings about going to Mexico but we thought it was just talk."

Sally wasn't surprised to learn that Krueger had fled the country. "He'll screw up. He'll cross the border someday, get himself in trouble and be back in jail where he belongs."

"I agree Sally." Josh answered as he looked at the gold watch on his wrist. "I'd love to stay and talk to you guys but I gotta' be in St. Paul in an hour." Josh hesitated before leaving. "I had a short interview with Andy Taylor at the detox center. The reason he put Harmony in the animal trough was because he had murdered his wife and drowned her in the same animal trough. Says he was drunk and remembered how he killed his wife and decided to do the same with Harmony."

"Amazing," Sally thought out loud. "Did he say why he hung her up on the wall and why his footprints weren't at the scene?"

"He was vague about it. He was coming down from DT's and he was hard to understand. I don't think he remembered much from that night but he mentioned to me that Hezekiah had once told him that if was going to commit a crime he should be sure and wear only stockings on his feet so as not to leave shoe prints. I think he hung her on the wall because in his own little twisted way he thought he was mocking Christians. I am not sure if we will ever know the real answer. One thing we know, he is going to be locked up for a long time." Josh answered their questions as best he could before leaving.

Lieutenant Carpenter was silent as he watched Agent Trimble leave the squad room. He turned his attention to Sally and asked something he hadn't had the courage to do during the investigation. "Would you like to go out tonight for a nice meal?"

Sally shockingly looked at her partner. "Are you asking me out on a date?"

"Yes I am," he answered.